THE INVISIBLE CORD

THE INVISIBLE CORD

Catherine Cookson

E. P. DUTTON & CO., INC.
NEW YORK
1975

Contents

Part One

THE WHITE WEDDING

1

'Who said I shouldn't wear white?'

'Nobody, Annie, nobody.'

'Don't tell me nobody. You wouldn't have the bare-face to come out with that on your own, Mona Broadbent, so don't tell me that nobody put you up to it.'

'Nobody put me up to it, it was just something that I . . . Aw you, Annie; you're like a ferret.'

'Then there was something said then? Who said it?'

Mona Broadbent sucked in her thin lips, pushed her thin fair hair first over one ear then over the other, and wagged her long melancholy face at Annie Cooper, her best friend, as she would tell you again and again if you had a mind to listen, her only real friend. More like sisters they were, she would say, having started school together at St Peter and Paul's, Tyne Dock, having changed schools together when both their parents shifted to High Shields, and having left school together in 1940 and got their first job together in Culbert's biscuit factory. Then, a year later, again they made a move together; this time into the munitions works, where they got almost twice the money and enjoyed a bit more carry on. They were still in the munition works, but separated for the first time because they had been put on different shifts.

It was three weeks ago now when Mona, as she would have told you, got the shock of her life on Annie informing her, out of the blue, that she was going to be married. And who do you think to? *Georgie McCabe.* Georgie McCabe, that big galoot they had known all their lives . . . well, anyway since they had moved to 114 Weldon Street.

Mona couldn't get over it. Annie and Georgie McCabe! Him a cook in the R.A.F. stationed in some god-forsaken place called

3

Madley. A cook mind you, and he could burn water! Lorry driving was his trade and they'd made him a cook. As her da said, he was Hitler's best friend, a fifth columnist working through the guts. Fry the blokes' eggs in axle grease, that's what he would do. Her ma, too, said Annie must be mad or gone soft in the head, for if anybody in their street could pick and choose it was Annie. Her ma was very fond of Annie; they were all very fond of Annie; because Annie was good-hearted and jolly. You couldn't be dull for long where Annie was. And now she was going to marry the dimmest bloke in the street.

What was up with her? That was the question she had asked Annie three weeks ago. 'What's up with you, Annie Cooper?' she had said. 'There's Peter Riley, and him first mate. Cock-eyed he's been when he's come home these last two trips squintin' at you. And then there's John McIntyre; he's not to be sneezed at, neither on the parade ground nor off it. He's a sergeant already and they say he won't stay there.'

It was at this point that Annie had turned on her like she had never done before, telling her to shut her mouth, she was marrying Georgie McCabe because she wanted to marry Georgie McCabe, and if she, Mona, didn't like it she knew what she could do. Then she had banged the door in her face.

Now here she was demanding to know why she shouldn't be dressed in white when she knew flaming well why she shouldn't be dressed in white; and she said exactly that to her.

'You know flamin' well, Annie, what Katie Newton was sayin' an' I was just tryin' to break it to you gentle like. But I see you're in one of your moods again so I won't beat about the bush. I heard her sayin' to Florrie Turnbull that it was no use using a white oven cloth to take a burnt loaf out of the oven.'

'Burnt loaf! Just wait till I see her, I'll smack her cheeky face for her. I'll go right up to her, I will, and I'll take my hand right across her. . . .'

Annie's voice stopped abruptly, her hand dropped from its demonstrating position, her chin drooped on to her chest; she sat down on the bedroom chair with a plop and there was silence in the room until she raised her head and looked with pleading eyes at Mona and asked, 'Does it show?'

'No, no, Annie, it doesn't at all, you're still as flat as a pancake.' Mona's voice was soft.

Annie screwed up her eyes tight and got abruptly to her feet,

4

then walked towards the window, saying, 'You were never a good liar.'

As she stood looking out of the narrow aperture of the black-out curtains she heard the bed springs creak as Mona sat down. Only once before had she been made conscious that the bed springs creaked, that was the night when Georgie McCabe had eased himself down beside her. She had tried to push him off but not too much; no, she had to be fair, not too much.

They had sneaked away from Hilda Tressell's wedding. Every-one from their part of the street had been to Hilda Tressell's wedding. Her da was paralytic, and her ma had had a drop an' all. It was her da who had made her drink the whisky, and that on top of the sherry had made her go daft. They had cleared the floor and she had done the Highland fling by herself until Georgie had joined her, and then everybody had laughed fit to burst.

Georgie had given her another whisky, and she'd had more sherry, and when she felt a bit sick he took her outside. She couldn't remember why they had made for home or who sug-gested it. But she could remember them stealing up the street and the creaking of the bed as he lay down beside her.

It was the first time it had happened to her and she had cried, and then she had really been sick. The next morning, even while she felt terrible, she had knelt by the bed and prayed to Our Lady not to let anything happen to her. She had gone to late Mass, and Georgie was there. He had looked a little shamefaced but what he said to her was, 'You'd think I'd get out of bloody church parade on leave, wouldn't you?'

She remembered thinking, him just coming out of Mass and swearing; but then Georgie's swearing was like God bless you! he punctured everything with bloody. His mother and father did too. Yet she wasn't unused to swearing; her da could hold his own at it, at least when he was upset about something. But he never swore like the McCabes, and her mother never swore at all. Her mother was a bit prim, except when she had drink on her and then she let her hair down. She herself took after her mother in a way, not that she was prim, far from it, but once she had taken drink her hair came down too.

When she had told her mother she was going to marry Georgie she just stared at her, stared and stared at her, but she didn't open her mouth to ask why, yet her eyes had held the question . . . and

5

the answer. It was a full five minutes later when she asked, 'When is it to be?' and she had answered, 'Soon. He's getting a forty-eight.' And that had been that.

Her mother wasn't natural. She should have probed and gone for her. But her father was natural. His probing had gone deep, and when it was finished there had been tears in his eyes. But all he had said to her was, 'My God lass! to wreck your life like that.' Then he had added, 'Well, it's done and can't be undone; and for what part I have in it I'll see it's done properly, you'll have a weddin'.'

Annie looked down on to the street. The houses on the opposite side, not more than thirty feet away, were misted, not only with the November dullness but with the Sunday dullness. Even in wartime Annie thought, Sunday had the power to blot out life; except the service canteens and the churches, the town died on a Sunday. It was fear that filled the churches, her da said. Perhaps he was right there, for she herself was always praying that she wouldn't be hit by a bomb, and if she was, that she would be killed outright and not made blind. She had a fear of going blind because once she'd had her eyes bandaged for a fortnight after getting an infection in them.

Her gaze became focused on three children playing on a doorstep. They were the Ratcliffes. Sunday made no difference to them, they were let out at any time. The two older ones belonged to Betty Ratcliffe, and she was married, but the three-year-old was Jane's. She'd had him the first year of the war when she was sixteen and she had fought her mother to keep him. Her da had said that it was very commendable of Jane; her ma, as usual when faced with such matters, had just tightened her lips, neither condemning nor sympathizing. But Jane had had to pay for her mistake for her name became mud in the street. They said she'd had two miscarriages since and that she was making a pile out of the army, navy and air force, she wasn't choosey. Well, no matter what they said about her, she seemed to enjoy herself and was always well dressed in spite of clothing coupons. Nevertheless, she always wore a defiant look on her face and never spoke to any of the neighbours.

When she knew she herself had fallen she wondered whether she, too, should brave it out like Jane, but she knew she couldn't, she wouldn't be able to stand the shame of it.

Mona was saying now, 'How you goin' on for coupons?'

6

She turned and leant her back against the window-sill, saying flatly, 'Me ma and da are givin' me theirs.'

'Are you going to make it yourself?'

'No; I'd only make a hash of it. I'm going to ask Mrs Tyler to run it up.'

There was silence between them now while they looked at each other across the small room; then Mona said, 'Is there any chance of him being sent abroad?'

'What do you mean, chance?' Annie had left the support of the window-sill; her back stiff, she repeated, 'What do you mean, chance? You suggestin' that he should be sent over so that he can be knocked off?'

'No, no, I'm not. You know I'm not.'

There was no conviction in the answer, but Annie's attitude now gave the assumption that she had received an apology – for, her body slumping, she sat down in the wicker chair by the side of the bed. . . . Any chance of him being sent overseas? That very question had been in her mind for days, filling her with guilt and remorse. Not that she would want him dead, but she wished he'd be taken out of the way until, as she put it, she could pull herself together.

It wasn't that she disliked Georgie, she didn't, you couldn't dislike him. On the other hand she was only too well aware that he was no cop, and she felt she deserved somebody better than him, somebody with a little more up top. She had always imagined marrying someone better off than herself, and decidedly she had never intended to marry anyone from these parts.

After she left school she had lain in bed at nights and thought how wonderful it would be if she could click a lad who lived in Westoe, or somebody who worked in the town hall. But since the Americans had come her aspirations had grown, even beyond Westoe and the town hall. What if an American officer fell for her? or a sergeant? or even a corporal, because all Americans . . . well most of them, were rich.

But here it was 1943 and she had never spoken to an American, not even a G.I., and she hadn't caught the eye of even one English officer in the army, navy, or air force; nor yet that of a sergeant; what she had caught was a bellyful from a cook in the R.A.F.

Her head moved in slight admonition at the vulgarity of the thought, for such everyday thinking that pervaded her environment had, until recently, been condemned by her as vulgar. She

7

had ideas of bettering herself, if not by marriage, then by getting herself a better job as soon as this war was over. She had in mind to take up shorthand and typing and of becoming a secretary, the kind of secretary that a boss relied on, like you read about in the magazines, and the kind of boss who eventually married his secretary. But now all that nonsense was over and the sooner she faced up to facts the better. She was pregnant, she was going to marry Georgie McCabe, she would have one bairn after another until she finally put a stop to him. She'd live in a three-upstairs or two-downer and eventually consider herself lucky if she had two up and two down like this one. Eventually she'd lose her figure and people would forget that she had ever been bonny, and she herself would forget that she had ever wanted anything better. . . .

No by God! I won't. She was standing on her feet, her head wagging at Mona, who moved her position on the bed and, staring up at her, inquired softly, 'You're not goin' to marry him then?'

'Aw you, Mona Broadbent!' Annie was bending forward, her two hands flat in the middle of the bed. 'Some friend you are, sneering about me being married in white, then wanting him dead, and now wishing that I'll not marry him and leave the bairn like Jane Ratcliffe's. Aye, some friend you are. Well, I am going to marry him, and the bairn will have a name, and what's more I'll make something out of him, Georgie, I mean. And I'll not stay in Weldon Street; you can take that from me.'

'All right I'll take it, but don't ram it down me throat.'

'You don't like him, do you?'

'I liked him all right until he . . . well, got you into trouble. I used to think he was harmless, all right for a giggle. But he wasn't so harmless, was he?'

'Don't keep on.'

'You started it.'

Annie straightened her back, walked to the box-seat set opposite a chest of drawers on which stood a little swing mirror, and leaning forward, she stretched her top lip downwards and pushed her nose to one side in search of elusive blackheads; then nodding at her friend through the mirror she said, 'I'll surprise you one of these days, you'll see; I'll make something of him if it kills me.'

'It might that an' all.'

Slowly Annie turned on the seat and looked over the bed rail, along which Mona now had her forearms folded with her chin resting on them, and she said, 'You rub it in, don't you?'

Shading her eyes Mona now looked down towards the floor as she answered, 'It's 'cos I'm concerned; and if the truth was told I'm a bit jealous.' She raised her eyelids and grinned at Annie, and Annie asked softly, 'You're not, are you?'

'Aye. Well, it'll be different when you're married.'

'There'll be nothing different; it'll just be the same, we'll always be friends.' She felt better now since Mona had said she was a bit jealous. 'Come on.' She rose and pulled at Mona's arm. 'The tea'll be ready, let's go downstairs.' But as she went to open the door she stopped and, turning and facing Mona, said quietly, 'If you hear Katie Newton saying anything more will you deny it for me?'

'Aye, of course.'

'Ta . . . and when it comes I can say it was premature.'

'Aye, you could.'

''Cos they do come afore time, don't they?'

'Oh, aye, they do.'

They smiled at each other; then Annie said again, softly, 'Ta, Mona.'

Mona did not ask why she was being thanked again but when Annie opened the door she drooped her head and went out.

As Annie followed her friend down the stairs she thought, Don't let's kid meself. Jealous? She's no more jealous of me than she is of Lottie Collins. And no one in their right mind would be jealous of Lottie Collins, and her the street idiot who had to be taken everywhere by the hand.

2

To say it rained was putting it mildly, bucketing was the expression that was being generally used. It had bucketed from the Friday morning all through the Friday night, and Dennis Cooper had assured his daughter that this was a good thing because there couldn't be much more left up there, and it would dry up first thing. But at eleven o'clock on the Saturday morning he was forced to remark that it was a pity there was no rationing up there. He had seen rain of all kinds in his time, from smut-laden to sleet-laden but this lot he termed spite-laden. He kept up his tirade against the weather for so long that Annie was forced to cry at him, 'Oh, Da, give over! it's not helpin' any you keepin' on. Nobody can stop it, so give over, do.'

Annie knew that her da was going on as he was doing for her sake because he thought the rain would spoil her wedding, her white wedding. Well, although she couldn't stop the rain she could take its effect away by stopping the wedding. She had the power to do that, hadn't she? There were three hours to go yet. She could get into her outdoor things, pack a bag, take the money she had saved, leaving the little Georgie had added in an envelope with a letter to him, then take a single ticket to somewhere. Where? Yes, that was the question, where?

She had asked herself the same question last night as she had lain awake peering into the future, not into the years, but to the coming twenty-four hours when Georgie would be lying beside her in this bed.

It was funny them spending their first night in this house; and funnier still that it was on her mother's suggestion that they were doing it. No use spending money on hotels, she had said, when he was due to get the train at twelve o'clock on the Sunday. She herself had thought there was some slight indecency about the suggestion. Her da, too, might have been of the same mind for he had said neither yes nor nay to it.

Her mother was a puzzle to her, she just couldn't understand her; yet during the past few weeks she had come to realize that her ma didn't want to lose her. 'As long as the war's on,' she had said, 'you can make this your home, 'cos he'll be away most of the time and you'll need someone to see to you.' She hadn't added, 'When the bairn comes.'

At times she wished her mother would put her arms around her and hug her and say, 'There, there, hinny, don't worry; you've got me and your da, we'll see that you're all right.' In a way, she had said the words, but without the actions, and it was the actions, the actions of tenderness that she had needed very badly these past days.

And now, here she was thinking again of taking a single ticket to somewhere. But you had to have somebody waiting for you in that somewhere, and the fact was she hadn't a relative outside the town. Her mother and father were only children, and her mother's parents were dead, while her grandma and granda Cooper lived just a mile away. You couldn't get a single ticket to Laygate.

She turned from her father who was peering out through the lace curtains into the backyard, and she hesitated a moment in the middle of the kitchen while looking towards the scullery, where her mother was wrapping a stack of sandwiches in a dampened tea-towel, and going slowly towards her, she stood in the doorway and looked for a moment at the stubby hands folding over the points of the cloth before she said, 'The table looks lovely, Ma.'

'Well, I've done me best.'

'I know you have.'

'A body can't do more.'

'No . . . Ma.'

It seemed as if it would take an effort for Mary Cooper to raise her hands from the packed sandwiches and look at her daughter, and when she did all she said was, 'Aye.'

Annie gulped on a mouthful of spittle, bit on her lip, then hung her head before she said, 'I just want to say, th . . . thanks for all you've done, Ma.'

She didn't know which way to jump when Mary, flinging out her short arm, pulled the door closed, shutting them in the small well of the scullery, and now, looking into her daughter's face, she said tersely, 'I'm your mother, aren't I, what did you expect from me? To throw you out on the street?'

'No, Ma, no, I didn't. But . . . but you've been kind.'

'Haven't I always been kind to you?'

Annie's eyes flickered to the side for a moment; then she was nodding her head. 'Aye . . . aye, yes, you have; you've brought me up well. I'm not sayin', but . . . but what I mean to say is that, well, under the circumstances you've been –' her head drooped on to her breast and as her voice broke and she said, 'Oh Ma!' her body swayed forward and it seemed a long second before Mary's arms came out and held her, held her tightly, even crushed her. They were both crying now, both muttering, Annie saying, 'Oh Ma! Oh Ma!' and Mary saying, 'Lass,why had you to do it? Why? Why?'

The sound of the front-door knocker being rapped hard and Dennis's voice calling, 'Mary! somebody here,' brought them apart. Their heads turned from each other, their hands rubbing at their faces, and Mary, taking up the corner of her apron, blew her nose then pressed both hands down from the centre parting of her hair which, unlike Annie's, was jet black. Then quickly turning, she pushed at her daughter, saying, 'Get yourself upstairs and get ready.' And on this Annie opened the door and went into the kitchen, to see her father coming in from the passage with Mrs McCabe behind him, and behind her the fourteen-year-old McCabe twins, Archie and Mike, one carrying a large bundle, the other an old kit-bag.

'Hello, hinny.' Mollie McCabe edged her way past the sofa and the table and, her big slack-lipped mouth wide, she laughed towards Annie, saying, 'I've brought some of his toggery along. He's still dead to the world; the bugger was sodden last night but I'll see he doesn't get any till he leaves the church. Don't you worry, lass.' She thrust out her arm, her fist doubled, and punched Annie playfully in the chest as she went on, 'Did you ever see a mornin' like it? Aw well, we'll all be as wet inside as we are out come this time the night. What do you say, Dennis?' She turned now and poked her finger towards Dennis. Then swinging her big flabby body around she exclaimed, 'Where's your mother? Oh, there you are, Mary.' She looked towards the scullery door, and Mary, walking slowly into the kitchen, said, 'Hello, Mrs McCabe.'

'Aw!' Mollie shook her head from side to side. 'How many

12

times have I had to ask you not to call me Mrs McCabe. Mollie's me name. Everybody calls me Mollie, even them that hates me guts.' She turned round now and nodded at Dennis. 'Aye, an' there's a few of them I can tell you. Fetch them here, you two.' She now waved at her sons, and they came from the doorway, each humping his bundle forward with one hand and a knee. Then pointing from the kit-bag to the bundle, Mollie cried, 'His odds and sods. I thought I'd bring them along an' you can settle them in afore the dirty deed's done, and at the same time say hello, and ta very much for seein' to things.' She turned now and nodded towards Mary.

She waited for some response, and when none was forthcoming she grabbed the bundle and kit-bag from her sons and, looking at Annie, said, 'Come on, lass, I'll take them up to your room.' And no one saying her nay, she went out into the passage towards the stairs, and Annie, after dividing a startled look between her mother and father, followed her.

In the bedroom, Mollie McCabe dumped her son's belongings into the corner between the chest of drawers and the wall, then she turned and looked at Annie. Her face, now without its wide splitting grin, looked flabby and old, and momentarily Annie contrasted her with her mother. Her mother looked like a young woman compared with her future mother-in-law. But then her mother wasn't all that old, only thirty-six, whereas Mrs McCabe must be all of fifty. Anyway, she looked it.

'Well, it's nearly time, lass.'

Annie blinked, then said, 'Yes, Mrs McCabe.'

'Now, now, lass, you at least'll have to get used to callin' me Mollie, no matter how stiff necked your ma remains. That's if you don't want to call me ma, or mam, or mother, or go the whole hog and call me mater, like they do on the pictures.' Her face went into a grin again, but only for a second; and then she said, 'There's just one thing I want to say, an' it'll be different from what every-body else is sayin', 'cos I know how the yappin's gone. You've let yourself down a mile, they're sayin', taking' up with our Georgie. He's got nothin' up top, they're sayin'; like all the McCabes', they're sayin'. Well, let me say one thing in our Georgie's favour, lass. He's kind; he'd give his shirt-tail away in the winter, he would that. And another thing. You could get a better lad, I won't say you couldn't with the looks of you, but there's some-thin' that I don't think you know, 'cos he's short of words like.

But it isn't only the day or yesterda' that he started caring for you, he's watched you since you were a bit of a bairn. On his twenty-first birthday when we had a bit of a do he said to me on the side, "I wish that Cooper lass was a bit older, I would have asked her round." An' I remember laughin' me head off and sayin' to him, "What! you'd be brought up for baby snatchin' and learnin' her to drink." But I understood how he felt, 'cos you looked over fourteen. You look much older than seventeen now, lass; you could be taken for twenty and that's no offence, just the opposite. But what I want to get over to you is, he cares for you, and that bein' so you'll be able to handle him like putty. You mightn't think it, me being like I am, likin' me drop an' all that, you mightn't think that I worry about the bairns, but I do, and our Georgie most of all. I've wondered what kind of lass he'd finally end up with. Some dirty slut, I thought, who couldn't keep her snotty-nosed bairns clean. Bad as I am they could never say that about me, that me bairns weren't kept clean, and their bellies full. Well –' she now hitched up her bust with her forearm – 'what I really want to say, lass, is, I'm kind of grateful to you for havin' him. Mind –' Her forearm, now depriving her bust of its support, shot out and, pointing her finger at Annie, she said, 'Not that I don't know that you were forced into it. Oh aye; you don't jump over a cliff unless there's a bull behind you. But as I said to his da last night, if anybody can thatch a roof with rotten straw it's that lass. Mind –' her finger was stabbing now – 'I'm not sayin' that there's anything rotten about our Georgie, but you get me meanin', which is, if anybody can make anything of him it'll be you. Well –' she took one step backwards now – 'I've had me say, lass, so I'll get meself downstairs, open me big mouth an' laugh me bloomin' head off, and your ma'll say, polite like, "Good-bye, Mrs McCabe" while thinkin, That woman! common as clarts she is! . . . Ta-rah, lass.'

'Ta-rah . . . Mollie.'

Mollie now gave her a nod and a knowing smile, then went out quietly. But a minute later her high laugh came to Annie where she was standing staring at her reflection in the mirror, her hand over her mouth but her lips moving as she repeated, 'Thatch a roof with rotten straw.'

The reflection moved its head wildly at her. She watched the tears run down the cheeks in the mirror. Thatch a roof with rotten straw. She was only seventeen, it wasn't fair. Through the mirror she saw the white satin wedding dress lying over the foot of the bed. . . . Oh God! what a farce. Life was a farce.

The word farce brought back to her a tale that Georgie had told her about the twins. When they were seven years old they were in a class where, on a Friday afternoon, the teacher let the pupils recite or sing a verse of a favourite song, and Archie had put his hand up and said he would like to sing 'All By Yourself In The Moonlight'. Having been granted permission, Archie walked to the front of the class and sang the recognized words, until he came to those in the chorus:

> There ain't no sense
> Sitting on the fence
> All by yourself
> In the moonlight,

for which he substituted:

> Life's a farce
> Sitting on your arse
> All by yourself
> In the moonlight

She had thought it rude, but nevertheless she had laughed, primly at first, then loudly; but that was the night she'd had the sherry followed by the whisky.

But life was a farce, everything about today was a farce. The only good thing, she felt, she would remember about it was that her ma had held her in her arms for the first time in years.

3

It was done.

Two umbrellas had been held over them as they ran from the church doorway across the pavement to the waiting car. There were no sightseers, and for this she was grateful. She had told herself she should be thankful for the rain for she would have died if Katie Newton, and Florrie Turnbull, and the rest of that crowd had been waiting outside the church. And they would have been if it hadn't been the kind of day it was.

Father Carey had married them in a sort of word-gabbling rush; he had seemed in a hurry to get it over. There she had stood in her white dress with her veil held in place by a wreath of Virgin Mary blue forget-me-nots; Mona had made the wreath for her. She had even gone to the trouble of bringing it to the church yesterday and sprinkling it with holy water in a kind of blessing. Mona was nice. She glanced through the rain-filled window of the car before it started and saw Mona standing inside the church door with the best man, Arthur Bailey. He seemed a nice fellow, this Arthur Bailey, superior like. She had met him last night for the first time. Georgie had brought him back from Madley with him. His home was in Hereford; he seemed a different type of fellow from Georgie. She wondered at them being friends; perhaps it was because they both worked in the kitchen.

'Well, love.' She was pulled back on to the seat within the tight circle of Georgie's arm, and now she was looking into his face. It wasn't a bad-looking face, sort of homely; he had his mother's wide slack laughing mouth and his eyes were dark brown, much darker than her own. His eyes were his best feature; the kindliness his mother had talked about was in his eyes. He wasn't very tall, not much taller than her, and she thought that she was still growing. Five-foot eight, she supposed he was, but he appeared taller because of his bulk, he was heavily made.

'Well, it's done.'

It was as if he were repeating her words, and she echoed them, saying, 'Yes, it's done.'

'Happy?'

'I . . . I don't know yet.' Oh dear God! she hadn't meant to say that. She should have just answered a plain yes, it would have satisfied him. Fancy telling a man on his wedding day that she didn't know if she was happy or not. She saw that his face had clouded.

He said soberly, 'Well, I'll have to try to make you know, won't I? It's up to me then, isn't it?'

She didn't answer, she just stared at him. Then they both swung to the side as the car veered round the corner and his arms tightened about her and he looked down into her face, muttering, 'I love you, Annie. I can't put it like I should, I'm not much use with words, the bloody things won't come for me, never would somehow.' His mouth spread into a quick grin, reminiscent of his mother's ever-ready defence, before he went on, 'But one thing I'll tell you. I'll do me best for you. I'll try to go steady, I mean with the drink an' that, and we'll get a home together for the bairn. . . . You know what me ma said just afore I came out?'

He was grinning widely now, and she shook her head. 'No.'

'She said she'd break me bloody neck if I didn't do the right thing by you. What do you think about that for a mother-in-law? I asked her whose side she was on. She said Hitler's. That's me ma; she's a case but . . . but she's all right me ma. We would have known some pretty tough times if it hadn't been for her 'cos me da's no bloody good, never has been. Him and work never agreed; he used to get the smit if he went near it, but she wouldn't have it that he was lazy, bawl you down if you said he was. . . .Hie! Hie! you're not cryin', are you?'

'No, no. Well, I don't know what I'm doing, laughing or crying. . . . You're funny, Georgie.'

'You think I'm funny?'

'Well, not funny that way, amusin'.'

'Aw well, amusin' am I? Well that's one thing I've got in me favour anyroad, an' that's not bad for a start, is it?'

'Georgie.'

'Aye?'

'Promise me something?'

'Anything, anything in the world.'

'Don't . . . don't get drunk the day.'

He stared at her, then smiled, a quiet smile, and bending his head he kissed her on the lips, then said, 'That's a promise.'

As the car came to a stop opposite 114 she asked herself why she had made him promise such a thing, because once he started to drink he'd soon become paralytic, and such being the case she might have warded off a repeat of the incident following Hilda Tressell's wedding.

There were twenty-one at the reception in the front room. Annie and Georgie were wedged in at the top of the table, while five of those seated down the left side and five down the right were also wedged in. The rest had room to move their chairs back. Mary and Mollie McCabe and Mrs Rankin from next door, the only neighbour, together with her husband, who had been invited to the wedding, saw to the filling of teapots and the replenishing of plates.

There had been general acclaim at the sight of the well laden table. How had Mary done it? Cold brisket, a leg of pork, and half a ham, besides salmon sandwiches! Where on earth had she got the salmon! Some of them hadn't seen a tin of salmon for years.

The answers with regard to the food were given by Dennis with nods and winks in the direction of the top of the table, and the guests looked at Georgie and said, 'Ah! ah!' Georgie was a cook, and cooks were no fools.

Annie hadn't looked at Georgie but at her mother who, although she didn't like Georgie, hadn't apparently been above taking the tins of stuff that he had brought on his last few leaves. Then she chided herself. She mustn't think anything against her mother; she must remember what happened in the scullery this morning. Her mother had feelings that she didn't show.

Her da was on his feet, speaking now, her da knew how to do things properly.

Dennis looked up the table towards his daughter and new son-in-law and the action brought a cessation of the gabble and the room became quiet. 'It has fallen to me,' he began, 'to say a few words on this auspicious occasion. For it is an auspicious occasion.' He nodded his head twice. 'My daughter this day has not only changed her name from Cooper to McCabe, she has written that name at the head of a page to a new life.' Again he nodded his head twice. 'It's a clean page and it's up to her what she writes on it.' He turned his gaze now from Annie and brought it to rest on Mary, where she was sitting at the bottom of the table, her hands in her lap, her eyes cast down towards them. And she didn't raise them when, speaking to her pointedly, he said, 'There's her mother. She was only a year older than Annie the day I married her, and from the day Annie was born she has looked after her like a mother should. What credit goes to Annie today is due to her mother.' There was a long pause here while he stared at the bent head. Then turning his eyes once more towards the top of the table, he went on, 'I'm goin' to cut this short, lass, I'm only goin' to say this, that if you look after Georgie as your mother has looked after me and our home, then you won't go far wrong. Now –' his eyes swept the faces all turned towards him, and he commanded, 'Get on your feet, lift up your glasses and drink. . . . To Annie and Georgie.'

'*Annie and Georgie. Annie and Georgie. Annie and Georgie.*'

When the company was again seated there followed a babble of voices, everyone talking at once, until the stranger, the best man, rose to his feet; then everyone gave him their attention. Even the twins stopped stuffing food into their mouths and looked at the foreigner, the fellow who talked different. And Arthur Bailey's voice was definitely different from that of anyone in the room. He began to speak with a slow softness, and he kept his eyes on Annie and Georgie as he spoke, saying, 'If there's anyone wishes Georgie and his bride health and happiness it's me. Georgie and I have been pals for the past eighteen months, and I want to state here and now that I'll never find a better. As good fellows go he's one of the best, and I know that Annie will have a happy life ahead of her as long as she has him by her side. Here's wishing you both happiness and contentment.'

The best man's speech was greeted with more applause than Dennis's had received, and Georgie, red in the face, looked at Annie and asked, 'Well now, what do you think of that for a reference, eh?' He leaned over her and punched his pal in the shoulder. Then his attention was drawn towards his mother, whose voice, well above the rest, was exclaiming, 'Now, that's for you. Wasn't that nice? Talk about a pal.'

Nodding in the direction of Arthur Bailey, Mollie now called,

'Thanks lad. Good for you; you'll always be welcome in our house.' Then turning to her husband she shouted at him as if he were at the far end of the street, 'Did you get an earful of that?' and when he replied, 'Aye, aye, I heard. Couldn't help but, could I?' she pushed him almost off his seat as she cried, 'Well, let it sink in then, let it sink into your puddle head.' And at this the twins and her married daughter, Daisy, and Daisy's husband, Frank Stewart, and Winnie, her sixteen-year-old daughter, who was but a younger replica of herself, all howled with laughter as if at some great joke, while Mary and Mrs Rankin exchanged looks, then rose from the table, each picking up a teapot, and went into the kitchen.

'That woman!' Mrs Rankin pursed her lips. 'She's as common as muck. It's just as well you'll have Annie here under your wing.'

Mary made no reply to this but she filled her teapot from the spluttering kettle, then placed them both side by side on the hob and, looking to the deepening twilight of the rain-drenched day, she said, 'I think we'd better do the black-outs and put the lights on.' She glanced at the clock as she spoke, and the clock said quarter to four.

The air-raid siren went at a quarter to nine.

The table had been cleared, the two end additions, boards on trestles, had been taken out and stacked at the bottom of the bunks in the air-raid shelter in the yard. Most of the chairs had been brought into the kitchen, but the centre table had been up-ended and placed in front of the little china cabinet. The radiogram had been put in the passageway, allowing for one person only to pass at a time towards the front door, and then this could only be achieved with indrawn breath.

In the front room, interpreting a quick step in their several ways, were Mona and Arthur Bailey, Daisy and Frank Stewart, while Winnie and her mother, shaking with gales of laughter, were trying to get Dennis to do Knees-up-Mother-Brown.

Arrayed around the kitchen were Annie's grandparents and Mona's mother and father, and in between them sat Georgie, talking quite amiably as he was apt to do when nicely warmed, which stage he usually reached with a couple of drops of hard and four pints. This intake in no way suggested that he had broken his promise to Annie, for as he maintained, he always knew where he was until he'd had half a dozen doubles, or failing that, a mixture of anything he could come by from port wine to cider.

He glanced now to where he could see Annie in the scullery drying the glasses that her mother was washing up, and he paused in his talking, until Mrs Broadbent said, 'You're spinnin' them, Georgie, aren't you? Anybody getting bacon and eggs any time they like!'

He turned his attention to the little fat woman again, saying, 'No, no, it's a fact, Mrs Broadbent, true as I'm sittin' here. You get on a bike and go into the country outside Hereford an' stop at one of them cottages or little farms, an' you'll get a feed fit for a king. It's a fact. An' butter and eggs away with you an' all. Lots of our blokes do it, especially the ones living out in Hereford. Cor! you want to see what they bring back. I once refused to give a fellow on guard duty extra butter, 'cos I didn't like his bloody guts, big head he was, and the next week when he was off he comes back and pushes a bloody great slab of country butter under me nose. Even the colour of it made our stuff look like lint. "There, McCabe," he said, "you know what you can do with your butter."' He now closed his eyes and raised his hand, palm outwards, saying, 'Ladies present, ladies present; better not say what he told me what to do with that butter.'

It was when the laughter was at its highest that the siren went.

For a split second there was a startled calmness in the house as they listened to the wailing sound. Then like a fusillade of bullets they were scattering for the doors, that is all except Georgie, Arthur Bailey and Dennis. It was Dennis who yelled, 'Don't go mad. Don't go mad,' and the answer he got from all quarters was, 'Fancy it happening the night of all nights.'

'Get in!' Mary was pushing Annie towards the steps of the airraid shelter in the backyard when Annie suddenly stopped and, turning to her mother, whose hand was still on her arm, said, 'I'm not going in yet, Ma. Anyway it isn't right, we should see them off home . . . everybody.'

'They can see themselves off home, you get in.'

As Mary went to force her down the steps Annie evaded her mother's hands, saying harshly, 'Have a bit sense, Ma; the siren's just gone, they could be ages.'

'They weren't ages last week, were they?'

Before Annie could answer a voice came out of the darkness,

21

saying, 'You get down, Annie. I'm away to see me ma and them inside, I won't be long. Arthur's comin' along of me.'

'Get somebody to see Mona and her ma home, will you, Georgie?'

'Don't be silly girl –' Mary was pulling at her – 'Isn't Mr Broadbent there!'

'Aw, Ma, you know he's got bad sight. He can hardly see in the daylight never mind the dark. . . . See to it, Georgie, will you?'

'Aye, aye, I'll see to it. Get yoursel' in, don't worry. But my God, it would happen the night, wouldn't it. . . . That bloody man! All this through one bloody man. He's a bastard. . . .'

When Mary reached the bottom of the steps and went into the air-raid shelter she could still hear Georgie's voice coming from the direction of the scullery describing what he would do to that bastard if he only had him within arm's length.

'It's a pity he can't open his mouth without swearing.'

'Who better should he swear at than Hitler, Ma?'

The silence told Annie of her mother's set lips and tight face, and when she had lit the old-fashioned lamp that hung from a nail on the brick wall between the bunks it showed Mary's face as she had visualized it, and she said softly, 'I'm . . . I'm sorry, Ma.'

Mary made no answer, and after a moment Annie said, 'Where's me da got to?'

'Where would he be but at the A.R.P. post.'

'It isn't his night on.'

'No, it isn't, but he's got an urge like other people I could mention to get themselves killed.'

'Oh, Ma!'

They sat on the bunks, one on each side of the shelter, opposite to each other, their knees almost touching, their postures almost identical, heads bent, hands gripped on their laps. After a time Annie said, 'We didn't bring the flask, will I go and get it?'

'No, you'll do no such thing.' Mary's head jerked upwards. 'I've . . . I've got a feeling on me. I don't know why, but I feel it's goin' to be a night of it.'

Annie restrained herself from saying, 'You've had those feelings before, Ma, you have them every time you come down here.

A second later her mother's prophecy brought them hurtling together, their arms about each other. Then they were on the floor, their heads bent towards their knees and making identical sounds as the trembling of the earth passed through them.

When the earth settled they heard the distant pop-popping of the anti-aircraft guns. They didn't speak; their arms still about each other, they waited, and there came the second earth shudder, not so strong this time, further away. Still they waited, not moving. Then came the third, distant this time, just like an echo.

Into the stillness now Mary's voice crept like that of a doddering old woman, saying, 'Hail Mary, full of grace, the Lord is with thee. B . . . blessed art thou amongst women and b . . . blessed is the fruit of thy wo . . . womb Jesus. Holy Mary, Mo . . . Mother of God, pray for us sinners now and at the hour of our death, Amen.'

'Hail . . . hail Mary, full of Grace, the L . . . Lord is with thee. . . .' Again the prayer was repeated. And again . . . and yet again.

When Annie went to straighten up, her fingers caught in the beads dangling from her mother's hand and she interrupted the rosary, saying, 'Ma! Ma! come on get up, it's over.' She had to shake Mary twice before she could get her from her knees.

When they were sitting side by side on the bunk Annie whispered, 'I wonder who got it; I hope they're all inside. I . . . I hope they reached home. I . . . I think I'll just have a look outside. . . .'

'You w . . . won't.' It was as if Mary had just woken up. 'You'll do no such thing, you'll st . . . stay where you are till your da comes.'

'But, Ma! if there are places flat he'll be at it to the middle of the night. Look . . . look, Ma.' She pulled herself away from the clinging hands and stood up. 'They've gone. There's no sound, and the guns have stopped. I'll just go in and look out of the front door. . . .'

'No! No! you'll not. You'll . . .'

'Stop it, Ma; I'm going.' When she slapped at her mother's hands Mary stared up at her and her face quivered in a conflict of fear and anger.

Annie quickly mounted the steps to the yard, then stopped. Fancy slapping at her ma like that. Eeh! they were all in a state. She should have said she was sorry. But her ma wouldn't let her forget it; oh no, she could be sure of that.

Everything was quiet. She looked upwards. The stars were shining, the rain had stopped, it was a clear night.

Who had got it? It had been very near, that first one. She went through the house and opened the front door and, standing on the pavement, she looked up and down the street. There were no

23

fires, no busy to-and-froing of people. Everybody here was all right. But beyond the end of the street, more towards the main road, there was a glow in the sky. When she heard footsteps approaching on the opposite side of the road she called out 'Where is it? Who got it?'

And the voice answered her from the dark, 'Armada Street, Primrose Street, and around there.'

She put her hand to her mouth. Armada Street. That, that was where Georgie lived, Armada Street. Had . . . had they reached home and managed to get into the shelter before it dropped? Her breath stuck in her throat. They could all be dead, all of them. Georgie . . . Georgie could be dead!

The wave of relief that this possibility brought to her also swung her round and caused her to bury her head in the crook of her arm against the stanchion of the door. Oh dear God! how could she? But apparently she could, for her thoughts went on. If he was dead it would solve everything. The child would have a name; she'd still be a married woman and she would get a pension. . . . Oh my God! she was wicked. That's what she was, wicked. She'd have to go to confession, and she wouldn't have to skip it, she'd have to tell Father Carey exactly what she had thought. Fancy . . . fancy wishing Georgie dead.

After a moment she went into the house again, being careful to bolt the front door after her. The whole place looked chaotic. In the scullery she made a fresh pot of tea and put it on a tray with the crockery and carried it down into the shelter.

Her mother was sitting exactly where she had left her. She looked up at her and said, 'Well?'

'Armada Street and Primrose Street and around there.'

'Armada Street?'

The hopeful tone of the voice brought Annie's head down and she felt sick enough to vomit. 'Don't wish him dead, Ma!' She was shouting at the top of her voice.

'Wish him dead? What's the matter with you, girl? Wish who dead?'

'You know, you know . . . Armada Street. You know all right.'

'You're out of your senses, girl. Everything's been too much for you.' Mary sounded now as if she had completely regained her composure.

'Yes, yes, it has.' The tears were spurting from her eyes, her voice was spiralling upwards as if aiming to force its way through the stones and soil above the shelter. 'I know, I know. Happy release it would be, wouldn't it? Happy release.'

'Take a pull at yourself, girl –' Mary was shaking her by the shoulders – 'and stop that screeching. Sit down there.' She pushed her on to the bunk, then busied herself with pouring out the tea. When she handed Annie the cup she said, 'Get that down you. You've had too much to drink, that's your trouble.'

'I haven't, I haven't.' She was shouting again. 'I've only had a port, only one.'

'Drink that tea. And you want to remember, girl, before you indulge yourself in hysterics, that your carry-on is going to affect what you're carrying.'

Her head moving with each sobbing intake of breath, Annie stared up at her mother. It was the first time she had referred to the child. She turned her gaze away, then raised the cup to her lips and slowly began to sip the tea.

It was just as Mary had seated herself on the bunk again that the heavy footsteps sounded on the steps; then the door was slowly pushed open, and Dennis stood there. He looked like a man who had been loading cement, for from the top of his tin helmet to his boots he was covered in a grey dust. His face was all grey, the only spots of colour being the small round dark globes of his eyes and the red gap that appeared and disappeared as he opened his mouth a number of times to speak.

'What is it? Oh my God, look at you! What's happened, man?' Mary was pushing him down on to the bunk.

Staring into her face, he muttered, 'Gi' us a drink of tea. . . . Have . . . have you any hard down here?'

'Hard? No, no, we haven't.' The words were jerked out. Mary put her hand back towards the tray and lifted her own cup from it, saying as she did so, 'Tell us what happened, man.'

When he took the cup from her it wobbled in the saucer and she put out her hands to steady it. He brought the cup to his mouth and swallowed the whole of the contents; then he said, 'Billy . . . Billy's dead.'

'Billy? You mean Mr McCabe?'

'Aye, Billy McCabe.' He nodded his head twice. 'Him who was laughing fit to bust an hour or so ago, he'll laugh no more.' He turned his eyes to Annie who was standing close by his side now, her teeth pressed down tight on her fingernails, and he went on, 'They were nearly home, just passing the corner of Primrose

25

Street so they tell me, when the whole side of a house fell flat on him. He was the last one. He said he wasn't goin' to bloody well run for Hitler or nobody else. Georgie and his mother and the bairns were all knocked flat, must have been knocked yards but they weren't scratched, only shaken. But –' he now put his hands up and gripped Annie's arm as he said, 'that's not all, lass. Mona, she got it an' all. An' the young fellow, Arthur. They . . . they had branched off and gone round the bottom of Armada Street, it . . it caught them both.'

'Oh no, Da, no! no! not . . . not Mona.'

'It's all right, lass, at least it isn't as bad as it could be. They're . . . they're in hospital. But it's the finish for him poor lad as far as the forces go, 'cos one of his legs was crushed to pulp. And . . . and Mona, poor Mona, she got it in the face.'

She thought she was going to faint. She screwed up her face and covered it with both hands. After a moment she brought them to her throat and stood gripping it as she asked, 'Where . . . where are they? Where've they taken them?'

'Ingham. Look, lass.' He put out his hand and grabbed her. 'It's no use you goin' down there, the place is like a shambles. Wait till the morrow. But where you can go, and where you should go now is along to see how Georgie's gettin' on. He had his hands full when I left him.'

'No! No! The all-clear hasn't gone yet.' Mary thrust her hand out to stop Annie turning around, and Dennis's voice, sharp for the first time since he had come into the shelter, snapped, 'One of us has to go along there, and it's her place. Get it into your head, lass, it's her place. . . . Go on.' He pushed Annie and again said, 'Go on!'

She went scurrying up the steps and into the black backyard. In the kitchen she paused for a second and groaned aloud, 'Oh God!' Mr McCabe was dead. She felt as if she had picked up a gun and fired and hit the wrong one. When her stomach heaved and she went to turn towards the sink she checked herself, saying, 'Give over. Pull yourself together.' Then she ran upstairs and dragged on her coat.

There was a lot of movement in the streets, people hurrying backwards and forwards, voices calling. It took her five minutes to reach the McCabes' house. She had only been in it twice before and hadn't been enamoured of what she saw. The furniture was a mixture of dilapidated and modern, with the modern additions more kicked about and knife-scarred than the older pieces.

She knocked on the door. It was opened by Winnie. Winnie was crying; she was still wearing her bridesmaid's dress which had been chosen with an eye to utility rather than to prettiness. Earlier in the day it had been a dark blue colour, now it was grey and black in parts.

The door led immediately into the kitchen and there, seated round the table, were Daisy and her husband and the twins. Mollie was standing by the open fire pushing a pan from the hob into the glowing coals. She turned about and looked at Annie, and Annie walked towards her, then stopped as she almost fell over the end of the oxidized kerb.

'I'm . . . I'm sorry. Ever so sorry.'

'Aye . . . aye, we're all sorry, lass.' Mollie straightened her back. Her mouth was no longer slack and her face looked as if it had never smiled. Annie noticed with surprise that she wasn't crying and that her eyes showed no sign of recent tears; her voice was level when she spoke, and her manner, in fact everything about her, was quite different from what she had expected. She watched her turn towards the table and sit down opposite a plastic tray decorated with cabbage roses, on which stood a brown earthenware teapot and a tin of condensed milk, and, reaching out to the nearest cup, she ladled a running spoonful of the milk into it, then filled it with the black steaming tea and handed it to her.

Annie didn't want any more tea, she felt she never wanted to eat or drink again. Her throat was so full that nothing would pass down it, but nevertheless, she took the cup from the proffered hand and said, 'Ta. Ta, Mrs . . . Mollie.'

'Sit down, sit down, lass. . . . Move yourself over, our Archie, along the form there.'

When Archie had shuffled along the form and pushed against Mike, Annie sat down in the place he had vacated, and Mollie, looking at her, said, 'He had his faults but I ask you, and God, who hasn't? But he wasn't lazy. No, he hadn't a lazy bone in his body. He drank. Aye, more than his share, but I'm tellin' you this, he sweated his guts out to work for it. But afore anything else he saw that we were all fed.' She looked around the table. 'Aye, he did that. An' clothed an' all, for as he used to say, if their bellies were full they wouldn't need so many clothes on their backs. He was one for a joke when he could think of it. He was like Georgie.'

She now stared into Annie's face and, as if she were qualifying the statement she had just made, she added, 'He hadn't much up top either, but there were worse. Aye by God! there were worse. He never looked at another biddy, I'll say that for him.'

Annie had been shivering with the cold when she entered the house, now her body was hot all over. She wished, oh she wished Mollie, in fact everybody, would stop referring to Georgie as a nitwit. Where was he anyway? Where was Georgie? She asked the question.

'Where is Georgie now?' she said.

'At the hospital, lass. Aye, I suppose you heard, your da would tell you about . . . about Arthur. Aye, our Georgie's proper cut up with one thing and another, an' he feels responsible like for bringin' Arthur all this way. It's his leg. He said it was in a mess when they got him out. An' your pal, Mona; hit her in the face it did. My God! this has been a night. Marriage an' death; only the middle has been missed out, we only wanted a birth, that's all. . . . Pity –' her head nodded now – 'pity you're not on your time, lass; you could have completed the sayin' the night; ·from the church to the birth, from the birth to the burial, from the burial to hell in the mornin'. You know, it goes to the tune of John Peel.'

Annie was gazing at Mollie with a stupefied stare. She wasn't meaning to be funny, yet there she was sitting, sullen looking, dry-eyed, saying a thing like that, and telling you it went to the tune of John Peel. She felt she wanted to laugh, high screaming laughter. Was she going to go off her head? She looked around at the others. Nobody had spoken, not a word; they all looked half-asleep, dazed. Was she dreaming?

The front door opening abruptly proved to her that she wasn't dreaming. She turned with them all to watch Georgie coming in. He looked at her as he walked to the table, and when he reached her side, he said, 'Hello,' and she was forced to answer, 'Hello.'

'You shouldn't've come out,' he said.

'I'm all right,' she answered.

'How . . . how did you find them?' asked Mollie, looking up at him.

He turned to her, saying, 'Wouldn't let me in; they're not lettin' anybody in.'

'Do you want a cup of tea?' she said.

'No.'

'Have somethin' to eat then?'

'No, no, I want nowt to eat. What time is it, me watch has stopped?' He looked at his wrist-watch, and Mollie turned towards the mantelpiece and, after gazing at the clock for a second, she said, 'That says ten to eleven, but it's either fast or slow, you can never go by it.'

There followed a silence, during which he placed his hand on Annie's shoulder; then after a while, he said, 'Come on, I'll see you back home.'

When Annie had risen to her feet he looked down at his mother and added, 'I'll be back shortly.'

'No need, lad.' She, too, had risen to her feet. 'No need.'

'I'll be back all the same.'

Annie made no farewells but walked towards the door, with Georgie behind her, and Mollie behind him, saying again, 'I tell you, lad, there's no need.' And on this he turned on her, crying, 'Well I'm bloody well comin' back whether you like it or not.'

The three were standing on the step now. Mollie pulled the door behind her to shut out the light and she asked quietly, 'Where did they put your da?'

'The mortuary.'

'Think they'll let me see him?'

There was a pause in the darkness before he said, 'It wouldn't be much good.'

There was another pause before she answered, 'Like that, is it?'

'Like that.'

Annie heard Mollie smacking her lips as if she had just eaten something tasty; then she said, 'Look, lad, I mean this. Frank'n Daisy are stayin' an' there'll be no place for you to sleep. It's like that, you see, so go on with Annie an' sleep where you intended the night. Come round first thing in the mornin' an' we'll talk things over. Perhaps you could ask for a bit of compassionate leave or somethin'.'

'Aye, I'll try for that. . . . But you're sure you'll be all right if I . . .?'

'I'll be all right, lad. Though it doesn't matter much at the moment one way or t'other.'

There was another silence before Georgie said, 'Ta-rah then, Ma.'

'Ta-rah, lad. Ta-rah, lass. I'm sorry for all this, hinny.'

Annie couldn't speak for a moment; it was as if his mother was blaming herself for the raid, for the upheaval of the wedding, for the spoiling of their first night together. She said softly, 'Ta-rah, Mollie,' then turned away.

They had walked the length of three streets before Georgie spoke, and then he said, 'I'll never forgive meself.'

'What?'

'Arthur catchin' it. Comin' this way just to do me a good turn and then bloody well catching it. He's a nice bloke.' His head was turned towards her and she peered at him through the darkness; she wouldn't have been surprised to know that he was crying for his voice had a cracked sound. 'Best pal I've ever known, never made a pal like him. And he's class. He is, you know, he's class.' His voice had risen. 'Not like us, me, scum. His people've got a fine house in Hereford, ten great rooms and a bloody big garden. Near as big as a park it is, two acres. He's got a sister married to a solicitor, and two brothers. One's an accountant. He's the black sheep himself he says. Hasn't got any brains, he says, but he has more brains than the whole bloody establishment at Madley. But he plays them down. He has a kink that way makin' on he knows nowt. His people are swell. They are, they are, Annie, swell. When he first took me to his place I was like a cat on hot bricks; you never saw such a house. And after what I come from there was all the difference atween Buckingham Palace an' the netty. And another thing, his mother made me as welcome the second time an' the third as she did the first. I was just meself, I'd be hard put to try an' be anything else, an' she nor his dad didn't think, Aw, here's Georgie, the bloody numskull, comin'. . . . You know somethin', Annie, you know somethin'?' He was shouting now. 'You're just as good as you make folks think you are. That's somethin' I've learned, you're just as good as folks think you are. Tell them you're a numskull an' you are a numskull. By God! I've learned somethin' since I've been away. I could buy the lot around here at one end of the street an' sell them at t'other, I could that. And you know somethin' else? Arthur stayed as an A.C.1. 'cos he wanted to be along of me, along of me mind. He could've been L.A.C. Bloody fool, I said he was, bloody fool, 'cos there he was, helpin' the other bods with their papers to get through. He's got a kink; I keep tellin' him, he's got a kink. He was nearly a conchie, an' he said he would be if he was moved out of the kitchen. Ask him to kill a bloke he said an' that's what he would be, a conchie. And I believe him. By God, there's not many like him. And to bring him all this bloody way to give him a packet. He was as safe as houses in Hereford. Hereford, they don't know there's a war on there. I've been there eighteen months, an' they've had one bloody raid, one bloody little raid and the bastards thought it was the end of the world. The only ones that get their packets are the poor bloody goons coming down in the Black Mountains. But Arthur . . . but Arthur –' his voice had dropped now to a thick murmur – 'without a leg, maybe both. And he loved to walk. Tramp the countryside he would whenever he got the chance. . . . God Almighty! I'll never forgive meself to me dyin' day.'

'Don't! don't! Georgie. 'Tisn't your fault.' She gripped his arm. 'Don't look at it like that. Perhaps it was for the best; if . . . if he didn't want to fight. . . .'

She slipped into the gutter as he pulled his arm from her, crying, 'Christ! he wouldn't want to lose his legs to save himself from fightin'. He could have been classed as a conchie and had it easy on some farm or other. Christ! to lose his legs.'

'I'm sorry, Georgie, I didn't mean. . . .'

After a while he said, 'It's all right; I know you didn't mean anythin' like that.' He took her arm again, and his voice almost indistinct now, he said, 'Aw, Annie, the night of all nights. I was goin' to show you what a decent fellow I could be, I wasn't goin' to get drunk. Well, I didn't get drunk, but I was goin' to treat you as I know you would like to be treated 'cos . . . 'cos like Arthur you're different. And I know you're different. I'm bloody lucky. I've thought all day, when I was in the church, an' especially as I was sitting at the table, I thought, Georgie McCabe you're a bloody lucky bloke. You've got a pal like Arthur, an' a wife like Annie. . . . And now, now this. . . . I'm sorry.'

She wanted to say, 'I'm sorry an' all, Georgie,' for she'd come near to loving him at this moment; but they had reached the door of the house and she opened it and as they went in the thought occurred to her that he hadn't once mentioned his father.

Her mother was in the kitchen busily putting things to rights. She stopped what she was doing and looked at them; and then her eyes focused on Georgie. His clothes were begrimed, his face was dirty, but besides being dirty it had a sad heavy look about it and in spite of her feelings towards him she said kindly, 'Sit down, lad. How's your mother taking it?'

'Pretty well, thanks, Mrs Cooper. Pretty well, considerin'.'

'Have you found out how your friend is?'

31

'Pretty bad, Mrs Cooper, pretty bad. Mona an' all. But we won't know the details until the morrow, things are pretty hectic down there at the hospital.'

'Yes, yes, they would be. Can I get you a drink of anything?'

'I'll . . . I'll have a drop of hard if there's any left, Mrs Cooper. Thank you all the same.'

'Yes, yes, of course, Georgie. What . . . what about you, Annie, do you want anything?'

'No, Ma, nothing. I'll go up and take me coat and things off.'

'Yes, do that, do that.'

As she made to go towards the passage doorway leading to the stairs she was stopped, as also was Mary about to go into the scullery, by Georgie saying, 'You go on to bed, I'll be up later.'

It was as if they had been married for years. She glanced over his head towards her mother before swinging her gaze sharply away; then, with her back turned towards him, she said, 'Yes, I'll do that, I'm tired.' And to this she added, 'Will . . . will you look in, Ma?'

There was a pause before Mary said, 'Yes, yes, I'll be up in a minute.'

In her bedroom under the muted light given off by the green crinkled paper over the pink lampshade, she undressed rapidly, not pausing as she sometimes did to examine her figure through the foot square of mirror, or hold it at an angle as she peered for a blemish on the skin of her shoulders or thighs. She did not even stop to take the powder off her face with a thin layer of Pond's night cream, before adding a thicker layer which promised beauty in the morning. Scrambling, she got into her nightdress, not a new one, but her best one, which she had made herself and adorned with a herring-bone yoke; then bundling her under-clothes into a drawer, for there seemed to be something indecent in the casual way she had draped them over the back of a chair, she got into bed.

Her bed wasn't a single bed, nor yet a full-sized bed, it was of the size her mother had once described as, doing at a pinch. It was covered with an artificial pink silk bedspread under which was a matching feather-stuffed eiderdown. Even in her present state she had been careful to turn the bedspread well back – her mother couldn't stand the top being crumpled.

Stretching her length out, not in the middle, as she was wont to do, but towards the edge, she pulled the sheets up under her chin and lay waiting. And within five minutes her mother opened the door.

Mary had always come in and bidden her daughter goodnight. She would walk to the bed, straighten the turned-down bedspread, pulling the corners into points, sometimes even folding it once more to ensure it was not rumpled. At one time she had taken it off altogether, until Annie had complained that the eiderdown slipped off in the night when the bedspread wasn't there to hold it in place. Then she would pat the bed two or three times, saying, 'Well now, settle down; you're all right, aren't you?' and Annie invariably answered, 'Yes, Ma.'

'Very well then,' would be Mary's response; 'goodnight. Don't keep that light on, mind. Goodnight.'

But tonight she did not enter the room, she was beginning a new pattern. The door half-open, she stood with her hand gripping the knob and, looking towards her daughter, she said, 'All right?' and when Annie, after a moment, answered, 'Yes, Ma,' she said, 'Goodnight then.'

'Goodnight, Ma.'

When the door closed Annie bit tight on her lip to stop herself from crying. She could have come in, she could have done what she always did, turn the bedspread, pat the bed, stand near her. She never kissed her, she didn't expect to be kissed, but she could have come in; tonight of all nights she could have come in. After she had held her tightly in the scullery she thought things would be different. Oh, her ma! her ma was a funny 'un.

She heard her da's voice now coming up from the kitchen talking to Georgie. She was glad he was back. Georgie wouldn't feel so bad having him to talk to.

As she lay listening to the deep rumbling of the voices her body relaxed somewhat. Then after some time she heard her mother come upstairs and the door across the little landing open and close, and she knew her da would soon follow.

But her da didn't soon follow. The voices downstairs went on, and on, and on, and their low drawl turned into a lullaby so that in spite of herself she dropped asleep. . . .

She didn't know what had wakened her. It wasn't Georgie entering the room or getting out of his clothes, for when she opened her eyes she saw him sitting in the wicker armchair to the side of the bed dressed in pyjamas. His back was bent, he had his elbows on his knees and his face was buried in his hands. She lay

33

staring at him for some time. He was making a smothered sound and aiming to compress it with his hands.

Slowly she hitched herself over to the other side of the bed and, throwing the clothes back, she brought her feet to the ground. Then tentatively she put out her hand and touched the side of his head, whispering, 'Georgie! Georgie!'

His head jerked and sank lower, and she moved nearer to him and said again, 'Georgie!'

Like a child now he turned towards her. Her arms instinctively went about him, and as his head pressed into her shoulder and she felt his wet face against her warm flesh she stared, slightly open-mouthed, at the wall in front of her.

She had imagined all kinds of things happening on this night but the last thing on God's earth, she told herself she could have imagined, would be holding him while he cried. It was odd but she had never heard a man cry, she had never seen a man cry; women at funerals, yes, howling their eyes out, but men, no. Yet in this moment, Georgie, who was crying like a child, appeared more of a man to her than he had done before.

She did not question her actions when she eased him up from the chair and sat him on the side of the bed; then, having thrust the bedclothes well back, pressed him gently downwards and pulled the covers over him; after which she put out the light.

Getting into the bed from her side, she now drew him towards her, muttering softly, 'There now, Georgie. There now. It's all right.' But instead of her gentleness easing his grief it seemed but to increase it, and she had to pull the bedclothes up over their heads in case the sound of his sobbing should penetrate across the landing.

When his spasm of grief eventually subsided he muttered thickly, 'I'm sorry, Annie, I'm sorry.'

'Nothing to be sorry for, Georgie.'

He lay inert against her, spent; then after a time he said, 'Me da wasn't such a bad bloke, you know.'

'No, Georgie, no, he wasn't.'

'I'll never be able to look Arthur in the face again.'

'That's silly, Georgie; you're not to blame.'

'I am. I begged him to be me best man.'

'He wanted to be.'

'Aye, aye, he said he did, but . . . but he had an awful lot of trouble to get off. He'd had two forty-eight's recently, an' what's more he's been on a charge. He's against church parades.' There was another pause before he said, 'I'll . . . I'll have to stand by me ma, Annie. She'll need help; she's still got three of them to see to; there'll be no pension, him being casual like in the docks.'

'That's all right, Georgie. We'll sort that out after, don't worry about that.'

'There's nobody like you, Annie.'

She was silent.

'Me da said that, he said it only yesterday mornin', and he was solid and sober. He said "You're lucky, chum, she's another like your ma, she'll stand by you." Me da was all right; he was what he was 'cos things made him that way. Bloody governments, Conservative or Labour or National, all alike; no work, no bloody chance for a man with brains, never mind without. It's like Arthur says, you're what your en-environ makes you, Annie.'

'Yes, Georgie.'

'I'm, I'm sorry I'm no good the night, Annie.'

'Oh, Georgie! be quiet, be quiet. Go to sleep.'

'Thanks, Annie. There's nobody like you, Annie. . . .'

He was no good the night. . . . It was funny how your prayers were answered; but what a price to pay for such an answer.

Part Two

———◆———

DEMOB

1

—◆—

'Ma, don't give him any more taffy; his first teeth won't be in five minutes afore they'll be ruined. You're spoiling him.'

'Spoiling him! Look who's talking. If I'm spoiling him you've already ruined him, lifting him up every time he whimpers. If he's able to walk by the time he's five he'll be lucky. Spoiling him indeed!'

'Will you two stop it!' Dennis's voice was low and tired-sounding. 'If that bairn ever survives it'll be a miracle to me. Torn in two he'll be between you. An' she's right.' He was nodding towards Mary now. 'He won't have any teeth by the time you've finished stuffin' bullets into him.'

'They're less harmful than sips of beer.'

'Sips of beer won't do him any harm, woman.'

'No? Between you and Mollie McCabe he'll be well on the bottle afore he can walk, and then by the way you're going on he'll never walk straight. Next time I see her at it I'll tell her about it, no matter what you say.'

'You'll do no such thing, d'you hear?' Dennis's voice was grim. 'Twice you've seen her give the child a sip, and that's all, and the way you manoeuvre things she doesn't get much chance to get near him. If you had your way you'd put a notice up: No McCabes allowed. Not even the father. So there you have it.'

Dennis had risen to his feet, thrown down his paper, and was stamping out of the kitchen when Mary's 'Well!' checked him, and he turned to her and repeated, 'Aye, well, now you've had it.'

'Perhaps you'll think of moving your lodgings.'

Dennis had reached the passage, but he seemed to spring back to the doorway and, poking his head in, he cried, 'I might at that, you never know,' before disappearing again.

39

Mary turned and looked at Annie, but Annie had her head bowed over the child. When, however, Annie did look at her mother, the expression on Mary's face made her say, 'Don't take any notice, Ma; you know he's only kiddin'.'

'It's come to something.' Mary's lips were trembling. 'That family, that woman.'

'She means no harm, Ma.'

'That's right, you take her part an' all.'

'Well, she doesn't. What harm has she ever done you? She's got an awful life of it really. Having to go out to work and still see to the others when she gets home, and Winnie being such a handful, and the twins not much better. That's one thing I'll be glad about anyway when Georgie is demobbed, he'll see to them.'

They now looked at each other. Then, her gaze dropping away, Annie turned about, hitched the child farther up into her arms, and went into the scullery, where she took a wet flannel from a peg by the sink and wiped the child's mouth, saying, 'Keep still now, keep still.'

The child had been named Terence which had quickly been shortened to Rance. He had fair curls, a round face and dark eyes. To match the face the eye sockets too should have been round, but they were oval-shaped and gave to the eyes an oriental quality. He was apt to go into deep sulks; deprived of his own way, he didn't scream or kick as might have been natural but, pressing his lips together, he would hold his breath until he nearly choked, then when thumped on the back and forced to take in air he would assume a grieved silence which in one so young made the adults say, 'Now would you believe it! He knows what he wants that one and means to get it. By! he's a marler.'

In his small world young Rance captivated all adults, with the exception of Dennis, who was wont to say more often as time went on, 'That young fellow wants his backside smacked, an' if I had anything to do with it he would get it afore and after meals.'

When Mary came into the scullery Annie went on wiping the child's face as she said, 'Ma, I . . . I think I'd better tell you, I'm after a house.'

'. . . What!' The word had a startled sound; it gave the impression of utter incredulity. 'What!' she said again, then added, 'After a house? Since when?'

'Oh. Oh, I've been on the lookout for some time.'

Well, of all the underhand. . . .'

'Now, Ma.' Annie turned round, throwing the flannel into the sink as she did so, then said bitterly, 'Georgie will be out next week, he'll be out for good, and what life do you think we're going to have here? You still can't stand the sight of him; nothing he does is right.'

'Is it right for you? Let me ask you that. Truthfully, answer me truthfully, girl. Is it right for you? The things he does!'

'Not all, Ma, not all. But I'll have a chance to correct them if we're on our own.'

'He can't open his mouth but oaths come out . . . obscenities.'

'Don't dare say that, Ma. You know I wouldn't stand that. He doesn't use bad language, it's just swearing, just ordinary swearing. And you'd think you'd never heard swearing. Believe me, me da can hold his own when he gets going. Bloody and bugger are nothing to it.'

'Don't you foul your mouth, girl. Huh! this is forthcoming events casting their shadows before; you'll be as bad as his mother before you finish up.'

'I won't be as bad as his mother.' Annie's voice was low now. 'And if I was like her I wouldn't be bad. Mollie isn't bad, she's rough, but not bad. She's better than some I could put a name to.'

'How dare you! How dare you, girl! My own daughter saying. . . .'

'I'm not meaning you, Ma.'

'Oh no!'

'Look, Ma. We're fighting, we're fighting now and Georgie isn't here. If Georgie was here he wouldn't sit by and let you get away with it. He mightn't, as you infer every time you can, have much up top, but he's got that much up top he wouldn't stand by an' see you going for me. That's just one of the things I want to avoid, so we'll be moving. Just after Christmas we'll be moving.'

Annie turned away as she saw her mother's face crumple, saying softly now, 'It won't be far, just down below Thornton Avenue.'

'My God! Thornton Avenue, near the Arab quarter. You've taken it? You haven't, have you? You haven't taken it?' Her voice was a thin squeak and Annie answered, still quietly, 'Yes, Ma, I've taken it; and it's not in the Arab quarter.'

'It's the dock quarter. If it's round the dock quarter it's round. . . .'

'Yes it's the dock quarter. It used to be Hanlin's coal depot. The house is in the yard. It's not bad at all, and I'm lucky to get it.

It's got two up and two down like this, but it's bigger. I mean the rooms are bigger. And the scullery, why, why I'm tellin' you, Ma, it's nearly as big as the kitchen, it is.' She went on talking as her mother slowly turned from her and walked away. And when the child put its hands on each of her cheeks and pressed her mouth outwards she leant her face towards him and whispered, 'Oh Rance. Rance.'

The atmosphere in the house was not much lighter when at six o'clock that evening Mona came in unexpectedly.

'Why, hello! I didn't think to see you till the week-end. When did you get back? . . . Ma!' Annie turned her head and called upstairs. 'Here's Mona. . . . Sit down. Sit down. By! you're looking fine. Well tell us. Why did you come back so soon?'

Mona, an entirely different Mona from the bridesmaid of that February day in '43, smiled broadly and turned her head fully round to look towards Dennis as she said, 'Tell us, she says, Mr Cooper, and she doesn't let us get a word in, does she?'

'Well, you should know her by now, Mona,' laughed Dennis. 'But as she says, sit yourself down. Have you had any tea?'

'Yes, yes, I went straight home from the train and had a meal.'

'You're looking bonny, Mona.'

The smile did not slide from Mona's face as it sometimes did when any reference was made to her appearance. At first she had found it hard to adjust to a glass eye and a zig-zag scar that started at the lobe of her left ear and traced its way across her neck to disappear between her breast bones. Yet the fight to adjust to the new condition had given her a self-assurance and an animation that hadn't been hers before. Before the raid she had been a plain girl, a dull girl some would have said, mousy. She was still plain but it was a different plainness; her nervous animation had, in a way, released her personality.

She swung round now in her chair and looked to where Mary was entering the room, saying, 'Hello, Mrs Cooper.'

'Oh hello, Mona. You're back soon. I thought you were staying until the week-end?'

'I was, but something happened.'

'I knew it.' Annie nodded at her father. 'I knew something had happened to her. I could tell as soon as she came in.' Annie now pulled her chair up close to Mona, adding, 'Well, come on, don't keep us in agony. And anyway, if you don't open your mouth and tell us, I'll tell you, and I'll only have one guess out of three.'

'Aw you!' Mona pushed at her, and they laughed at each other knowingly. Then whipping off her glove, Mona held out her hand.

'My! My!' Dennis's exclamation was deep and sincere. 'By lass! isn't that lovely. A half-hoop of diamonds. Aye, it's bonny, grand.'

'Oh, it is, Mona. Oh, it's beautiful, lovely.' Annie's response was utterly genuine, without a trace of jealousy in it, but when at last Mary spoke, looking down at the extended hand she said, 'Very nice. Yes, very nice. You're very fortunate. I suppose you know that, Mona, very fortunate.'

'Yes, Mrs Cooper; nobody knows it better than me.'

Annie looked at her mother as she turned away and it was on the tip of her tongue to exclaim, 'You're a bitter pill, Ma. That's what you are, a bitter pill. Yes, she's fortunate, but trust you to rub it in.' She said now, quickly, 'What are they like, his people? I'm sick to death of hearing Georgie on about them. Royalty, that's what he thinks they are, royalty.'

Mona dropped her hands back into her lap. Then with her head on one side and her face straight, she looked directly at Annie as she said, 'They were a surprise, Annie. Perhaps it was me, but somehow I don't see them like Georgie sees them.'

'Snotty?'

'Snotty!' Mona turned and looked at Dennis and, a smile breaking her lips now, she nodded at him, saying, 'Yes, Mr Cooper, that's what I would say, snotty. Nice you know, nice, but snotty. And, and Arthur, well, he doesn't seem to belong among them. He's not a bit like them, except perhaps his sister, Olive. She's just a year older than him. She's nice enough. I like her. We didn't have much to say to each other but . . . but I liked her. Though I couldn't say the same for her husband. Oh now –' she again nodded towards Dennis – 'if he lived around here do you know what they'd call him, Mr Cooper?' She gave a little giggle. 'A b . . . nowt.'

'Oh, one of them, eh?'

'Yes, Mr Cooper, one of them. But Annie –' she turned fully round again – 'you'll see them all for yourself at Christmas.' She hunched her shoulders up. 'You've been invited, you and Georgie, for the Christmas holidays.'

43

'What! Us?'

'Aye. . . . Eeh! there I go sayin' aye. . . . Yes, Mrs McCabe.' She now assumed a high-faluting tone. 'Your husband will be bringing you the invitation come Wednesday week as ever was.' She now burst out laughing, then looked towards the scullery door where Mary was standing. They all looked towards the scullery door, and Mary said, 'What's that I was hearing?'

'I was saying that Annie and Georgie have been invited to go to Hereford for Christmas, Mrs Cooper.'

'That's what I thought you said.'

'Well –' Annie was now on her feet – 'if that's what you thought she said, Ma, you're not looking very pleased about it.'

'Well, should I be, leaving us here on our own, at Christmas an' all?'

'Oh my God! Ma.' Annie put her hand to her head, and Mary said quickly, 'That's it. Start to shout and wake him. . . . And mentioning him, what about him?'

'He'll come with us, of course.'

'You're not traipsing the countryside with that child in the depth of winter and bringing him back here with pneumonia. Oh, no. Oh, no, me girl.'

'Ma!' Annie's voice was ominously quiet. 'Let me ask you a question. Whose child does he happen to be?'

'Aye, that's a good question.' Dennis rose from his chair and gave his wife one long look before leaving the kitchen and going into the passage. There was a pause that gave him time to put on his coat and cap, then the front door banged.

Annie now looked towards her mother, and Mary, through tight lips, muttered, 'You're determined to spite me, aren't you, girl? Not only jumping at the chance to spend Christmas with strangers but depriving me of the child at the same time.'

'Ma!' Annie's voice was still quiet. 'It surprises me, an' it has done since he was born, that you should take such an interest in him. Hating the father of him as you do, I wonder you look at him, 'cos don't forget, he's Georgie McCabe's child. And it's Georgie McCabe will let you know that once he's back for good. As for this Christmas business, I'll see what he says, and if he's willin' that I should leave the child with you I will, otherwise he'll come along of us.'

Her face red now, she turned to Mona, saying, 'He'll be asleep but would you like to come up and see him?' and without waiting

44

for an answer she stalked from the room and Mona followed her.

Quietly Annie turned the handle of the bedroom door and they went in, and when they stood by the side of the cot that was placed near the bed Mona whispered, 'He gets bonnier.'

Annie made no comment on this but, staring down at the child, she said, 'Life's hell here, Mona; I'm getting out. I've got a house. It's not in a very good quarter, it's not far from the Mill Dam docks. It used to be Hanlon's coal depot, near Bunton's Corner.' She lifted her eyes and looked at Mona, then nodded and said, 'I know what you'll say, sailors, Arabs, the lot. But to tell you the truth, Mona, I wouldn't mind if there were Arabs upstairs and downstairs and left and right of me, anything will be better than living here when Georgie's back.'

'Yes, I can see that, Annie.' They moved from the cot to the farthest corner of the room, and there Annie asked in a low murmur, 'Do they really want us to go for Christmas?'

'Arthur does.'

'You say Arthur does, what about the rest?'

'Oh, it's a kind of open house, there's always people dropping in, all kinds of people. They're a bit arty-crafty. You know the type. You remember the Miss Burgess that used to teach standards four and five at school, well, they're something of that type, only more so if you know what I mean. During the war I understand they entertained all kinds.'

'That's why they accepted Georgie I suppose.' Annie's voice was flat.

Mona forced herself to say, 'No, no; they like Georgie. And Arthur thinks the world of him, he does really.'

'Oh, I know Arthur likes him, but I think that's just because Georgie likes him so much. Georgie's always been grateful because Arthur took notice of him.'

'I don't think it's like that.'

'Oh, I know what I know, Mona, and we two don't need to cover up things. Anyway –' she turned towards the door – 'they must have liked him for himself in some way else he wouldn't have kept going back. He's not so thick-skinned that he wouldn't have noticed how they felt, I mean if they were just tolerating him for Arthur's sake. Anyway –' she turned her head and looked at Mona and whispered, 'I'll see for meself if I go, won't I? And tell me, how did Arthur come on about the job?'

45

Mona smiled wryly and jerked her head. 'He got it and turned it down. He said he didn't fancy sitting on an office stool for the rest of his days. You know what he's after now? A little pub out in the wilds. It's sort of two stone houses stuck together, miles from anywhere. And the views are beautiful. But I said to him, "Nobody'll come here for beer", and he said I'd be surprised 'cos in the summer the hills are thick with hikers. It's costing four hundred and fifty pounds, but he says when he's finished with it it'll be worth one thousand four hundred and fifty. I think his father's glad about it, if only that it's a good distance away. Arthur gets in his hair. They're an odd family, a mixture. Anyway, as you say, you'll see for yourself. And we'll get a giggle, if nothing else, eh?'

'Aye, Mona.' Annie nodded at her. 'I could do with a giggle. My God! yes, I could do with a giggle.'

2

'So you have left your baby at home?'

Annie stopped herself from exchanging a glance with Mona who was sitting to the side of her; instead, keeping her eyes on the woman opposite, she answered briefly, 'Yes.'

'Nice to get away from babies at times, isn't it?'

'Yes.'

'It was at your wedding that Arthur caught it, wasn't it?'

'. . . Yes.' She knew fine well that Arthur had caught it at her wedding. She was his mother, wasn't she, yet anyone more unlike a mother she had yet to see. She was sixty-five if she was a day but she acted like a skittish lass. Arthur was the youngest and she must have had him late. His brother, Peter, the one sitting on the couch near the fire, looked older than her da, and he was at that. From what she had gathered from Mona he was thirty-nine and the brother, David, sitting near him, was thirty-eight. There was over ten years, Mona said, between those two and Arthur and his sister Olive.

Having bairns late must have knocked her back into her second childhood, Annie thought. Talk about being mutton dressed up as lamb; she jumped about like a spring lamb, she was never still. And if she had remarked on her leaving the child once, since she had come into the house, she must have done it half a dozen times. She didn't seem to pay attention to what anyone was saying to her except when she was talking to the men. Oh, she paid attention then all right.

The house seemed full of men. There was the father, whom everybody called Gerald and who in his way was as skittish as his wife. Then there were the brothers, David and Peter, and the snotty one, Olive's husband, James Partridge they called him. He

47

was standing now in the far corner of the drawing-room talking to another man named Ron. Ron had a tiny moustache and he looked like one of those fellows in that funny book Georgie had brought home, called *Plonk's Party*. It was all about the air force and the types in it. Then there were Arthur and Georgie; they were at the moment in the billiard room knocking the balls about. She hoped they stayed there, at least that Georgie did. The way he had greeted everybody when they came in made her feel embarrassed, he had acted as if he were back home. He had called the mother Gwen, and she had called him Georgie boy.

Mona was right. She had hinted pretty broadly that they would all take some sorting out, and they would that. She had been right about Olive, too. Olive was nice, she was what you would call a natural kind of girl – or woman. She looked thirty-five but she could be only twenty-eight, as she was just a year older than Arthur. And she had a nice child too, cute; he had spoken to her a short while ago. He had taken her hand and said, 'Hello. Do you know what I am going to get from Father Christmas?' He spoke beautifully. She would love Rance to speak like that one day, but there was little chance with Georgie about.

She had replied no, that she had no idea; and then he had made her laugh by saying sadly, 'Nobody seems to know what I am going to get from Father Christmas.'

'David.' The mother was calling across the room while screwing round on the couch and drawing her legs up under her like some loose-limbed carefree girl. 'Let's have a drink before dinner.'

Annie looked towards the son, David, who had his slippered feet well on to the big open hearth, and he yawned before he answered, 'If you have it now, sweetie, there'll be nothing for after. And don't forget it's Christmas Eve in the morning.'

'Christmas will be taken care of, darling. Richie has promised to drop in.'

'Oh! Oh!'

Annie's eyes followed David as he pulled himself up languidly from the second sofa and walked across the room to where a miniature bar had been erected in the corner. It had a counter stretching between the walls, and the shelves arranged against the walls supported bottles, all empty, and hanging from a wrought-iron bracket, that had once graced the front of an inn, was a sign on which was painted in red letters THE NAUGHTY BULL.

Annie turned her head slowly and looked at Mona. They were exchanging glances when the mother let out a high girlish shriek and, unwinding herself from the couch, stood straight with her face clasped between her hands while looking towards her eldest son and exclaiming, 'Oh Peter! you'll never forgive me. I forgot to tell you, Liz phoned when you were out. She wanted you to ring her back. Oh darling, I'm so. . . .'

The man with the balding head almost sprang from the couch now, crying, 'My God, Mother! that's hours ago. And she'll have been waiting all this time. She'll blow her top.'

As he hurried towards the door he looked towards his brother-in-law, James Partridge, and exclaimed, 'She's the limit. I tell you, she's the limit.'

Mrs Bailey now dropped petulantly down on to the couch again and, addressing Annie and Mona in a plaintive voice, she said, 'Well, there's so much to be thought of. And it was just as Olive arrived, and I wanted to see the child. He's sweet, isn't he, I mean Alan. Wonderful for five; so advanced, don't you think? . . I must go and see about dinner or we'll never eat.'

She again bounced to her feet and turning her attention from the girls to her son, who was standing behind the bar filling glasses, she called to him, 'Bring mine into the kitchen, David, that's a dear boy.'

'Will do.'

Annie leant her head against the back of the couch. It wasn't real; all this wasn't real. Did they live like this all the time? Had the war made them like this? No, no; you could see similar set-ups on the pictures. Yes, that's what it was like, like looking at a film where all the people were larger than life, and funnier than life, and odder than life. Oh aye, odder than life.

But that woman, the mother of three grown men and a daughter, and a grandmother into the bargain, she wasn't real. Yet there was one thing real about her, and she knew what that was all right. She was man-mad; she was the kind of woman that would still be man-mad when she was seventy. That type never gave up. In a way she was like that Miss Swillwell back home, who even went after the young priest. There had been quite a do about that. She used to come to Mass dressed up to the eyes in the most startling colours. Way out she was. They said the gas man wouldn't go to her house alone, he always took a pal with him. . . . But then there was an excuse for her; you could be sorry for her for she had never been married. But this one here was well married. Why hadn't her husband put a stop to her gallop years ago? But he seemed like all the rest, treating her as if she were a young scatter-brained girl.

Of a sudden she had a great desire to be home. Over the distance 114 Weldon Street glowed with comfort and sanity. But they were to be here till the day after Boxing Day, and it wasn't Christmas Eve yet.

To save the last minute rush they had travelled down today, for tomorrow the trains would be crammed full. As it was, they had been bad enough; they'd had to stand for five of the eight hours in the freezing corridors. During the whole journey Georgie had aimed at cheering them up with details of this place and the reception they would get, and what Arthur and his mother and the rest of them would say when they saw him in civvies.

Their arrival was in a way the beginning of the end for her. She hadn't believed her ears when Mrs Bailey had taken Georgie in her arms and hugged him as she cried. 'Oh Georgie boy! you look wonderful,' for in her opinion nobody with two eyes in their head could say that Georgie looked wonderful in civvies. His suit, besides being a workhouse grey, was as ill-fitting as any she had seen on the old fellows who came out on a Sunday from Harton Workhouse. As her da said, it fitted where it touched; and he had said it openly to Georgie, but Georgie's answer was, he didn't care a bloody damn; he'd wear anything, even a shift, as long as it wasn't air force blue.

As she looked down the long drawing-room that was over furnished with couches and chairs, she had the crazy idea of saying she was going for a walk, then phoning Mr Wilson's shop on the corner and asking him to bring her mother to the phone. And when her mother came she would say to her, 'Phone the house and tell them me da's bad and I must come back.'

Eeh! the things that came into her head. She pulled herself up from the couch, saying softly to Mona, 'I'm going upstairs a minute,' and Mona said quickly under her breath, 'I'll come with you,' and they left the room without anyone commenting.

The drawing-room led into a large hall. This, too, was over furnished and had a musty smell. The whole house, Annie thought, had a musty smell, and it could do with a good spring clean, especially their bedroom. She had already remarked on the condition of the house to Georgie, but he had laughed and said,

'They're not like us back home, lass; they don't lay stock by the same kind of things. You'll see, you'll see.' He had appeared very knowledgeable, and she had thought how odd it was that Georgie, of all people, should be mixing with folks such as these, for in spite of their odd ways they were what you would call educated. Oh yes, she granted them that, for their accents hit you.

In the bedroom, she went straight to the wardrobe, took out her coat and, putting it round her, said softly to Mona, 'I'm freezin'; the whole place is like ice.'

'I know, I should have warned you. I've got two vests on under this and some fleecy knickers.' Mona plucked her dress away from herself at different points.

'Mona.'

'Yes.'

They stared at each other. 'I don't like it here.'

There was a pause before Mona answered, 'You'll get used to it; you'll get used to them; but I'll tell you something. I don't take much to it meself, 'cos I know they think Arthur's let himself down a mile in takin' up with me. Yet at the same time I sense it was sort of expected of him. You know what I mean? He's not one of them, he's the odd man out.'

'Good thing too. That's something in his favour. Oh my goodness! Mona, we'll get our death here. Are all the rooms like this?'

'Yes, except Gwen's.' Mona pulled a long face as she added, 'Arthur says that's the only thing his mother concedes to age, the need of a fire in her bedroom. And she has them all choppin' down trees in the wood. When I was here last she said to me, 'Ooh! I wouldn't dream about using the co-al; that's needed for every-one's comfort; but a lettle bit of wood now. . . .'

Mona's imitation of their hostess was so true to life that they had to smother their laughter against each other.

'Put another cardigan on,' said Mona now, 'and let's go down to the billiard room. . . .'

Just before they left the room Annie asked, 'Are there any other women coming, the place seems full of men?'

'David's wife is due tomorrow; the Peter one, he's parted from his.'

'Then who's this Liz who's going to blow her top?'

'Oh, his fancy piece.'

'Coo! they have them here an' all?'

They pushed at each other and again they laughed. . . .

In the billiard room, Georgie hailed them loudly, crying, 'Wondered when you'd turn up. Come and stand by me, love; you always bring me luck. This bugger's going to fleece me.' He nodded and grinned towards Arthur who was chalking his cue. 'Lost five bob to him already; we won't have enough for the groceries when we get back.'

Annie did not go to Georgie's side but stood with her back to the low fire in the deep grate and, lifting her skirt slightly at the back to catch the warmth, she said, 'Serve you right for throwing your money about.'

'I'll stand by you, Georgie.' As Mona went round the table Arthur turned towards Annie and, after looking at her for a moment, said, 'Cold?'

'A little; it's freezing outside.'

'It's freezing in here too. I'm sorry about that.'

'Oh no, it's me, I always feel the cold.'

Arthur now came towards her with his jerky gait, which spoke only slightly of his artificial leg, and still chalking the cue, he said, 'I want you to enjoy yourself, Annie.'

'What?'

He now raised his eyes to hers and added softly, 'You must find my people rather strange, their ways I mean. I do myself at times. And not just at times, most of the time. But there, we are as God made us.' He stopped speaking and stared at her, and she knew he wasn't referring to the whole family but to his mother.

She answered quietly, 'Don't worry about me, Arthur, I'll enjoy meself. It's Christmas, the war's over, it's marvellous, everybody startin' a new life.'

She glanced towards Georgie, who was standing beside Mona and explaining the game to her, talking of in-offs, off the red, and potting, and in the seconds she listened to him he used two bloodies. She brought her gaze back to Arthur's and, her eyes blinking now and her head drooping slightly, she said, 'Georgie and his swearin', don't they object?'

'Object! . . . To bloody? No, of course not. And it's just like God bless you! coming from Georgie. Is that what's been worrying you?' His long pale face widened into a smile. 'Don't be silly, Annie.'

'I can't help it; it isn't everybody that would take it as God bless you! And he gets a bit much at times.'

'Georgie's all right – nobody better.'

She looked straight into the face before her, and for the countless time she asked herself what this man saw in Georgie, because in every way they were as opposite as poles. His face had a tender refined look, and she could only class his manner as, learned. In this moment she was puzzled too that he should choose Mona for a wife, because Mona was ordinary. Well, by that she meant just like herself; and let her face it, they were both like fish out of water in this house. Georgie alone was unaffected by the atmosphere. If he was out of water, he wasn't aware of it.

'Come on –' Arthur took her hand – 'we'll take them on and show them how to play, eh?'

She was protesting that she didn't know the first thing about it when the sound of a bell echoed through the house.

'Ah, now we can eat.' Arthur smiled at her, adding, 'We'll show-em after dinner eh?' Then lifting his arm, he bent it at the elbow and looking across the table at Mona said, 'Miss Broadbent, allow me,' and Mona, laughing, put her arm through his. Then Georgie, in an absurd imitation of Arthur's voice, said, 'Mrs McCabe, aa-low me. Aa-low me.'

As they marched out of the billiard room, across the hall under the gaze of James Partridge who was descending the stairs, Annie thought, We must look daft, ridiculous; no wonder he looks down his nose.

The following morning they were forced to rise early in an attempt to get warm for the room was like an ice-box and the bedclothes were inadequate. As Georgie exclaimed under his breath while laughing indulgently, it was bloody well worse than a Nissen hut, for there you did have the old stove going.

It was only eight o'clock when they went downstairs but Arthur already had the breakfast going, and in the muddled, none-too-clean kitchen, Annie sat close to the stove and made her way through two large rashers of bacon, two sausages and an egg while Georgie disposed of twice as much.

The next to arrive for breakfast was Mona, looking as frozen as she felt. The two brothers, Peter and David, followed, but they took their meal into the dining-room. Then Olive brought the child down. 'Isn't it terrible?' she said. 'How did you sleep?' She looked from Annie to Mona, and they both said together, 'Oh, very well, thank you.' Then they laughed.

53

After Olive had given the child his breakfast and was eating her own she looked at her brother and asked, 'What's the programme for this morning?'

'Well,' Arthur smiled, 'if I can gather anything from the sight of your faces I think it's warmth we want both inside and out, so if we don't want to freeze for the next few days I propose we go wood cutting. What do you say, Georgie?'

'Suits me. And I'll make these two work for their grub.' Georgie nodded from Annie to Mona.

'Would you take him with you?' Olive made a slight motion with her head towards the child while looking at her brother. 'He'd love that. I've got to go into town; there's one or two things I need for the X...m...a...s tree.'

'Of course, of course.' Arthur rumpled the small dark head of his nephew. 'We couldn't go wood cutting without Alan. Fancy you suggesting such a thing.' He now bent down to the boy. 'We wouldn't dream about chop-chopping without you, would we?'

The round, dark, merry eyes looked up into the long face, and the child said, 'You're funny, Uncle, funny ... funny ... funny peck ... Daddy says you're funny peck.'

'Get on with breakfast, Alan, and stop chattering.' His mother's voice was sharp. She turned from putting the finishing touches to a breakfast tray and pushed her son none too gently on the shoulder, saying now, 'Behave yourself and stop your chattering.' Then glancing at Arthur with an apologetic look she said, 'I'll take Mother's up,' and left the kitchen.

As if he were just answering the boy's remark, Arthur now muttered under his breath, 'There are some of us funny peck-culiar and some funny ha-ha.'

There was deep bitterness in the words and Annie looked sharply from him to Mona, who was staring at him as was the child; only Georgie wasn't giving him any attention, he was busy lighting a cigarette. . . .

The frosty air was bracing, and the men were sawing with more energy than skill, while Mona, endeavouring to keep a small log upright in an attempt to split it had them all laughing at her efforts.

It was as Annie and the child were gathering frozen chips from a previous chopping that the boy, suddenly dancing from one foot to the other said, 'I want to go to the jig.'

'Jig? Oh, I get you.' She laughed out loud. 'Come on then.'

She took his hand and ran him behind some low bushes. But there he continued his dance and, looking up at her, said, 'I mustn't do it outside; Mummy said I mustn't do it outside.'

'You mustn't? Oh well, then we'll go inside.' She took him by the hand again, and shouted to the others, 'I won't be a minute, just taking him to the . . .' She poked her head forward and in a loud whisper called, 'The jig.'

'The what?' It was Mona's voice following her, but she didn't stop to explain.

The road through the wood was rough in parts and she drew the boy from a run to a walk, saying, 'We'd better go careful or we'll be sliding on to our . . . bottoms, won't we?'

For answer the child said, 'I want to go to the upstairs jig.'

'All right, you'll go to the upstairs jig. . . . Why do you call it the jig?'

'"Cos.'

'"Cos what?'

'Well, 'cos Mammy calls it the jig, thing-me-jig.'

'Oh.' Her laugh was high. 'Thing-amy-jig.'

'Daddy says water closet, Grandma says parlour, but I say jig. . . . What do you say?'

She was laughing inside as she thought, I'd better not tell him netty. 'Oh, I say jig an' all.'

'You do? How old are you?'

'Oh, very old, nineteen.'

'Nineteen? I'm nearly five. My birthday is on the first day of the year.'

'New Year's Day.'

'Yes; I'll be five on that day.'

'My! My! Here we are then.' They were going through the side door. 'You go upstairs; I'll wait in the sitting . . . drawing-room for you.'

'You won't go away?' He gazed up at her.

'No. Go on –' she pushed him and stopped herself from adding, 'before you do it in your pants.'

She watched him run to the bottom of the stairs, but there he turned to her and, crossing his legs, he did a little dance while he said, 'I like you.'

As she watched him now scampering and laughing up the stairs she thought, And I like you; you're about the only natural thing in this house.

There was no one in the drawing-room. She went towards the fire that had only recently been lit and stood with her back to it and lifted up her dress and exposed her legs to the flame. The communicating doors leading into the dining-room were partly open and after a moment she was aware of someone entering and a voice saying, 'We'd better get this while it's hot.' She recognized the speaker as that Partridge man, Olive's husband, and the voice that answered, 'Where is everybody?' she attached to the man Ron.

'Oh, about. I saw from my window that Arthur has taken the Geordie aborigines down to do some wood cutting. There's a gang, don't you think?'

'Odd types.'

'Odd! that's putting it mildly. Just been dug up, I should say. What do you make of Beauti-bloody-ful McCabe? Did you ever hear anything like it last night? Talk about an ignoramus.'

The answer came on a laugh 'He's a bit much.'

'A bit much! The man makes my hackles rise.'

Annie had left the fireplace. She was standing within a foot of the communicating door. She could see them both sitting at the table, and she wondered that they weren't aware of her presence, or aware of the anger that was oozing from her in sweat now. Geordie aborigines! She wasn't sure what an aborigine was but it was something nasty. . . . Ignoramuses!

'How did Arthur come to take up with him?'

There was a short silence now before James Partridge answered in a quiet tone, 'Well, you know. Politics red, and tastes masculine, if you know what I mean.'

'No . . . really!'

'Well, I can't see any other explanation, can you? McCabe's impossible, in every sense of the word. Now why should Arthur. Well, I ask you!'

'I see what you mean. But it's a bit of a nerve bringing him home, isn't it?'

'Oh, not when you work it out. He became one of Gwen's suppliers when Arthur got his packet at the fellow's wedding. Her source of bacon, butter, cheese, etc., etc., etc., would have dried up if she hadn't cultivated dear Georgie. Of course the supply had been double when Arthur was there to carry home his share; but the Georgies of this world are very versatile. The swill cart from the camp used to pass the bottom of the road here.

Georgie and the driver had an understanding. A special swill can for him if he dropped a swill can off in the corner of the wood. . . . Oh, Mother Gwen's an organizer in more ways than one. Richie, he's good for the drinks; Arthur Tollett, he's the beef, mutton and pork end; then there's Sam Rawley from near Breinton Springs, he supplies the poultry, eggs and cream; the only thing she hasn't been able to organize is a coal man. It was stooping a bit too low even for her, yet I think she scraped the barrel when she co-opted dear Georgie. But if dear Georgie only knew, this is his farewell party. She has no more use for him now that he's de-mobbed; it was only on Arthur's insistence that he was invited. There was a sort of family conference and to say the least, it was embarrassing. . . . I'm no snob, but I considered it a bit much. Apart from everything else there's still the officer and men part of it. You know what I mean?'

'Yes, yes, indeed, I do. It's a pretty awkward situation, es-pecially with Taggart coming this afternoon. He's not the one to suffer fools gladly.'

'I'd thought of that and I'll have to put him in the picture. God, I've met some fellows in my time. There were a mixture in my company, real prize types, but that McCabe beats them all. The fellow gets up my nose like no one else has. . . .'

'*Does he now? Does he? Does he?*'

As the doors were flung back the two men jumped to their feet, their faces turning scarlet as they looked at the infuriated girl facing them.

'Well, let me tell you something, Mister Upstart. He might get up your nose, but no matter how far he went he wouldn't be able to stop you smelling your own stink, because you're rotten, putrid, that's what you are. Your mind and everything about you. When I tell my Georgie what you've suggested about him, he'll knock your –' she paused, then she said it; she didn't only say it, she bawled it, 'bloody brains in. That's what he'll do to you. You! Who do you think you are anyway? They tell me your father keeps a draper's shop; well, let me tell you that my grannie kept a draper's shop an' all.' There was no need to explain that her grannie's shop had been in a house window and was run on the shilling club basis. 'So we're both from the same social standard, aren't we?'

They continued to stare at her as she glared at them while some part of her mind was telling her that standard wasn't the word she should have used. But what the hell! she wasn't looking for right words the day. This fellow! She wanted to swear at him, really swear. She wanted to cry at him, 'You snotty nosed bugger-a-hell!' which expression was a favourite one of Mollie's. It was odd, but at this moment she felt like Mollie. And she might have said it had not the far door opened and Gwen Bailey, entering hurriedly, said, 'What's the matter? What's all the shouting about?'

Annie stormed down the room towards her now and, pushing her face close to that of the astonished woman, cried, 'Ask them. And I've got something to tell you, an' all. You won't have to put up with our obnoxious presence over the holidays because we're goin', we're goin' now. You've got no more use for Georgie; he's served his turn. An' let me tell you something. I haven't known you twenty-four hours but it didn't take me a quarter of that time to realize that I've got no use for you.' And on this she stormed past the startled Gwen, across the hall and to where the child was standing at the bottom of the stairs watching her approach, and she spoke to him as if she were speaking to her own child as she said, 'Go into the wood this minute an' tell Georgie to come in at once. I want him. Do you hear?'

Looking up at her, his mouth gaping, the boy said, 'Yes.' Then, 'Yes, I'll tell Georgie,' and at this he ran out of the house, and she ran upstairs.

Once in her room, she almost staggered towards the bed and leaned over the bottom rail gasping. That lot! that rotten, snotty lot! Geordie aborigines are we? And him saying that about Georgie. Georgie'll kill him, if Arthur doesn't. Oh, I'll be glad to get out of here. On this she straightened up, rushed to the wardrobe, pulled out her clothes, then opening her case, she bundled them in, swept the few toilet accessories off the dressing table, grabbed up the two pairs of shoes standing under the side of the bed, and was dragging on her coat when Georgie burst into the room.

'What the hell's up? What's happened? What you say to Gwen? She looked at me daggers, she did. Look! I'm asking you, what the bloody hell's up?'

She snapped his hands away from her coat and stood staring at him. She had meant to blurt out everything that she had heard, but in this mood he might go downstairs and knock that fellow's brains out. She had seen him in a fight once when he was drunk; he had not only used his hands but, like a wild bull, had rammed the fellow with his head. And were she to tell him now what that Partridge had suggested it would likely have a worse effect on him than drink. She gulped in her throat and said, 'They've, they've been using you; we're only here on sufferance. We're . . . we're going home. We're going home this minute.'

'Now look here, you hold your hand.' He took her by the shoulders. 'You just can't walk out like this. Who was it anyway? What was it you heard?'

'That Mr Partridge and his pal, he, he . . .'

'Aw them! Gob skites, bloody gob skites, that's all they are. Aw, I know them. I've got their measure, they don't frighten me. Look. . . .'

'No . . . you look, Georgie.' She pulled herself away from him. 'We're going home, at least I am. You can please yourself, but I'm leavin' this house this minute.'

'You're bloody well not! You're not gona bloody well show me up.'

'I'm leavin' this house, and now.' Her voice was quiet, the tone coldly decisive.

He stared at her. Then grasping his hair, he swung away from her, then back to her again before he said, 'But what they bloody well gona think?'

'They've thought already. In any case let me tell you something. This was the last time you were going to be invited here. She's got no more use for you; you've got no more to carry from Madley. Get it?'

'Yes, I get it, and I'm not such a bloody numskull as you take me for. I know that half me welcome's because I've kept them supplied, I know that. You're not tellin' me anything.'

'And what do you think the other half of your welcome was made up of, eh? Go on, tell me. Not because they liked you.'

'And why not? Why shouldn't they bloody well like me? Look, I haven't got the mange or anything.'

'Oh!' She bowed her head. 'Oh, for God's sake! Georgie, shut up. Are you comin', or are you not?'

'I'm not bloody well gona walk out of the house just like that because you found they haven't fallen on me neck just 'cos of me personality.'

'Georgie!' Her tone was quiet again. 'There's more to it than that, but I'm not telling you the rest of it until we get out of this house . . . until we're home.'

59

His brows contracted, his cheeks moved upwards, pushing his eyes back deep into their sockets and through narrowed lids he said, 'More to it? What do you mean?'

'I'm saying no more until we're out of here. Now are you coming?'

'Look, I want to know. More to it, you say?'

'You won't get another word out of me until we're out of here. An' I've told you. Look, our things are in the case; you only need to put your hat and coat on. It's up to you.'

'Just give me an inkling of what you mean.' ..

'I'm doing no such thing, not now, and that's final . . . final.'

His eyes on her, his mouth slowly dropped open while his tongue moved over his lower lip; then turning suddenly, he grabbed up his coat and cap from a chair, grinding out between his teeth, 'Talk about a bloody kettle of fish! Nice state of affairs. An' what you gona tell your mother, eh? What you gona tell her? That we've been thrown out?'

'I'll think of something.'

'You bet your bottom dollar you'll think of something. I'm not having her lookin' down her bloody nose at me and saying "Ah! Ah! Georgie's friends. There's friends for you, turfed them out. . . ."'

'Shut up! an' come on.'

There came a knock on the door and when Annie opened it Mona was standing there, her face white and her one good eye wide and staring. Sidling past Annie and into the room she looked from one to the other and asked in a whisper, 'What's it all about?'

Annie shook her head and looked down as she said, 'I can't go into it now, Mona, I'll just say I overheard enough to realize that we're only here on sufferance, and to them downstairs we're just a lot of . . . Geordie aborigines. That's what they think we are, Geordie aborigines.'

'What!'

She turned and looked at Georgie. 'That's what he said we were. Geordie aborigines!'

'Who the hell said that?'

'Him, Partridge.'

'I'll Geordie aborigine him. By God! let me. . . .'

'You'll do nothing of the sort.' She pushed at him, then turned quickly to Mona, saying, 'I'm sorry, Mona, but it'll make no difference to you. . . . Where's Arthur?'

'He's . . . he's in the dining-room raisin' Cain.'

Annie turned to Georgie now. 'Have you got everything?'

'No, I haven't got everything; I've lost me bloody senses. If I hadn't I'd slap your blasted mouth for you and put you in your place.'

It was with a sense of weariness that she turned from him, saying, 'That'll be the day.'

The trite expression seemed to deflate him and after staring at her for a moment he picked up the case and followed her on to the landing. There, he turned to Mona and said quietly, 'Go and tell Arthur I want a word with him, will you?'

A few minutes later they were standing in the conservatory with their faces turned from each other, looking out through the glass partition on to the overrun garden and weedy drive.

A wave of high voices came to them as a door opened and closed; then Arthur hurried towards them, pulling on his coat. His usual pale complexion was almost scarlet, his eyes were blazing with a temper she would have never thought him capable of. He was looking at Georgie and it was a full minute before he spoke. 'I'm sorry,' he said; and it seemed just as an afterthought that he turned to her and repeated, 'I'm . . . I'm sorry, Annie.'

She did not speak but made a movement with her head and closed her eyes, and when she opened them again he was once more looking at Georgie.

Georgie had his head to the side, looking down towards the floor. He hadn't spoken to Arthur. His silence on the matter appeared odd to her, his manner appeared odd. She stared at him.

It was Arthur who spoke again, saying, 'Olive will drive you to the station; I won't come along, Georgie, I'm packing up.'

Georgie's head jerked upwards at this and he began now, 'There's no need for you to. . . .'

'It was bound to come sooner or later.'

'Where will you go?'

'To the Crawfords.'

'Oh!' Georgie was nodding his head slowly now as he repeated, 'The Crawfords,' but it didn't appear that he was very enamoured of the Crawfords.

'What about Mona?'

Arthur turned his glance towards Annie, saying, 'She'll come with me of course. This will only mean we'll settle into the other place sooner than I thought.' He now pointed through the conservatory window, saying, 'There's Olive going to the garage. I'll keep in touch.' Again he was looking at Georgie, and Georgie said briefly, 'Aye, aye,' then turned away, opened the door and went out on to the drive.

'I'm sorry, Annie.' Arthur was looking into her face now. She didn't answer him but stared back into his eyes. They were nice eyes, kind eyes. He was a nice fellow, seeming in no way connected with any of them back in the house. He turned hastily from her and, running out, caught up with Georgie. She watched him speaking earnestly for a moment before she moved, and before she reached them they had parted.

Olive was standing by the car. She made no remark, she just looked at them, then opened the door and they got in. Nor did she speak during the three-mile journey to the station; not until they were again standing outside the car did she open her mouth, and then she almost repeated the words that Arthur had said, 'This was bound to come sooner or later, you know. I mean, with Arthur. I'm sorry, I'm very sorry you've been involved in it. It . . . it isn't fair.'

There was a short silence, during which neither Annie nor Georgie made any comment. Then, her eyes cast down, Olive said, 'Further, I . . . I must apologize for my husband, his attitude is unforgivable.'

It was now impossible for either of them to make a comment.

She raised her eyes and held out her hand, and when Annie took it Olive said, 'I wish I could have got to know you better. And . . . and Alan will miss you; he quite took to you.'

There seemed a slight hesitation before Olive held out her hand to Georgie, and to him she merely said, 'Good-bye,' while he replied as briefly, 'Good-bye.' Then they turned from her and went into the station.

Nobody but a fool would travel on a Christmas Eve. If she had heard that once from fellow passengers during the journey she had heard it a hundred times. When they did manage to get a seat they were packed like sardines, but for most of the time she had sat on the case in the corridor, that was when she wasn't standing up to let people pass. The only time Georgie had made any comment on the situation was when they were changing trains at

Birmingham. Standing on the platform he had muttered, 'Bloody nice state of affairs . . . Merry Christmas!'

She had made up her mind that what she had to tell him must be said before she entered the house, but she didn't know how she was going to put the thing over, because as soon as they got out at High Shields he would most surely start questioning her, and he'd raise the street when he heard what she had to say.

But when they left the station at High Shields and walked down the dismal and almost empty road leading into King Street he didn't open his mouth. His head was down, his shoulders were hunched against the cold and he carried the case as if it were filled with lead. They walked up towards the market and crossed over it; it was no use taking the tram, it was quicker going up the side streets.

When they were almost half-way home and he hadn't spoken she suddenly bawled at him, 'Well! you been struck dumb?'

Still walking on and looking ahead, he answered her, 'Do you want me to start in the street?'

'Well, that would be better than starting when you get indoors.'

'There's no need to start at all.'

'What!' She paused in her walking, astonished at his attitude.

'Well, put the onus on me if you like. Tell her I opened me mouth as usual an' had a row with one of them. Tell her what you bloody well like. We'll soon be out of it, so it makes no matter.'

She was walking one pace behind him now, peering at him through the weak lamp light. Suddenly her hand shot out and, grabbing his arm, she pulled him to a stop and half towards her, and thrusting her face forward she hissed at him, 'Do you know what he was saying about you? Do you? I didn't tell you afore in case you would do something, like murder, but do you know what he was saying?'

'Look, that fellow would swear that Jesus Christ was on the fiddle.'

'It wasn't anything to do with fiddles.'

'Look, there's folks passing, stop your bawling.'

She drew her head back from him, and her eyes narrowed still further. Him checking her for raising her voice in the street! *Him!* There was something odd here. She felt a sickness in the pit of her stomach, and as if the nausea had suddenly erupted and burst from her mouth she spewed at him in a hiss, 'He hinted as much as you . . . you and Arthur . . . were queers . . . pansies.'

63

His face, which was usually fresh coloured, was tinged blue with the cold, but as she stared at him she watched the hue change into a dark red. She heard him rather than saw him gulping. She was about to endeavour to calm him by saying, 'Now, Georgie. Georgie, look,' when his voice came at her, not bawling, in fact when he spoke he scarcely opened his lips. His wide mouth looked frozen into a thin line, and his words sounded thin and his indignation forced as he said, 'Why, why didn't you tell me this back there?'

It was a second before she answered, 'Because I was afraid of what you might do.'

'If you had told me I would have knocked his bloody head off, the dirty minded bugger. . . . You didn't believe him, did you?'

'Believe him? Believe him? . . . No!'

'By God! if I had him here I know what I would do to him.' He turned from her and walked on, the case seeming to pull his shoulder down more than ever now, and he had gone four full paces before she moved and then with each step she took she protested loudly in her head, 'No, no! you're crazy.'

Anyway, it couldn't be, could it, not with a fellow like Georgie, big, tough, strong? And he had given her a bairn! And he was full of it still, couldn't satisfy him. And Arthur? Well, Arthur wasn't big, or tough, but he was refined, educated, and he was going to marry Mona. . . . Yet there was something, *Something*. She felt it inside of her, and it was making her sick. She wanted to vomit, really vomit.

She had adjusted herself to his swearing, his uncouthness, giving herself compensation by thinking about his generosity and the certain kind of honesty he possessed, but there were some things you couldn't give yourself compensation for.

There was something between him and Arthur Bailey. What was it? It couldn't be that, could it? Just look at him. She looked at him, and the very fact that he was walking on ahead and hadn't turned and said, 'What's up with you? What you doddering behind there for?' increased the sickness in her.

She wished she could explain things to herself. She knew she was very ignorant about most things relating to sex at any rate. She would have said she knew enough to get by. A normal man took you, you became pregnant, you had a baby, and that was that. On the reverse side of the coin there were pansies and queers, yet what the name actually implied she didn't know, only that it was something nasty. With a sudden movement she turned towards the end wall of a house, put her hand out, bent over and vomited.

He was by her side now holding her head, saying, 'God! what's up with you?'

When it was over and he had wiped her mouth on his handkerchief she leant against the wall and, her head down, she muttered, 'I'm sick.' And he gave an answer that made him normal to her again. 'It wouldn't take a bloody blind dog long to sniff that out. Come on,' he said; 'come on and get home.' Picking up the case in one hand, he put the other arm around her shoulders, and thus they returned home.

She was sick on Christmas morning; she was sick the following morning, and the following morning after that. She was pregnant again.

Part Three

THE GARAGE

1

'Hold that bag up straight, Rance.'

'Oh! Ma, I'm all mucky.'

'You'll be more mucky if you don't do what I tell you. Hold it up straight.'

Annie stooped down, thrust a shovel into a heap of coal and went to scoop it into the bag, but when Rance took one hand away from the top of the canvas sack and half the coal sprayed on to the ground, in one movement she threw down the shovel and thrusting out her other hand boxed his ears.

When she saw the tears spurting from his eyes and his hand holding the side of his face, she had to stop herself from throwing her arms around him and hugging him to her, crying as she sometimes did, 'Aw I'm sorry, I'm sorry. Your ma's sorry.' But tonight she felt worn out and irritated to the point of screaming, besides which she was filthy dirty with coal dust.

As Rance ran across the yard towards the house door Anastasia, whose name had hardly been repeated from the moment the priest had spoken it, came towards her and said solemnly, 'Will I hold it, Ma?'

Annie sighed as she answered, 'All right, Tishy, get a hold of it. But it'll mean you'll have to have a bath afterwards mind.'

'Aye, Ma . . . I don't mind havin' a bath.'

'Hold it steady.'

Annie shovelled up more coal, and because her five-year-old daughter could not be expected to hold the sack as firmly as Rance, she did not throw the coal into the sack but tipped it gently forward, thinking to herself as she did so, I'll get a long way in a long time like this, an' it getting dark an' all. By! I'll have something to say to him when he gets in. Where does he think he is till this time? If he's stopped at The Red Lion again I'll eat him wholesale, I will. By God! I will. She had to stop herself from throwing the next shovelful into the bag, and this irritated her further and she said to the child, 'Leave it down. Go indoors and wash your hands. I tell you what. Put the kettle on, and when it boils give me a shout and I'll come and make a cup of tea. Go on, that's a good lass.'

'All right, Ma.' As the child ran across the yard Annie paused for a moment to look at her. Of her four children Anastasia had the kindest nature. Sometimes she thought, and without vanity, that she was the only one who took after herself; yet at the same time she wished that it wasn't only her nature that she had given to the child, but one or two of her presentable features as well; or that, if she had only inherited Georgie's eyes, which were his one good feature. But Tishy was like nobody on either side of the family.

From the moment she was born she was 'as plain as a pikestaff. For the first three years of the child's life Annie comforted herself by thinking, They say it's the ugly ducklings who turn into swans; but here she was now, five years old and there was no trace of the swan to be seen; nor did she think there ever would be. The child's hair was a mousy brown and was as straight as a die, not a kink in it. Her brows too were straight, as was her mouth. Her nose was snub, so snub that, as Georgie said, you would think somebody had wiped it along the flags. Then her eyes, although quite large, indeed seemingly too large for her face, appeared colourless at times, while at others they looked merely a light grey.

And so Annie would comfort herself with the thought, Well, there's plenty of time, while telling herself that even time couldn't alter her child's nose or put a bow to her mouth. Her final thought always with regard to her daughter was, that apart from her temper, she had a nice nature, and that was something.

Bill had arrived the year after Anastasia. Bill took after his father in looks, but already at four he seemed much brighter than Georgie, for he could read and count rapidly, and when he once started talking nobody could shut him up until he himself decided he had no more to say. His silences at times were as forceful as his conversations. Bill, Annie thought, was a case. Then her latest acquisition to the family was Kathy. Kathy was two years old, as pretty as a picture and the star in Georgie's sky, as Rance was in hers.

Rance. She felt guilty at times about her feelings for Rance. Perhaps she had poured her love out on him because she found no outlet with Georgie. Perhaps it was because he was her first child, or perhaps it was because he had inherited her own looks. Whatever it was she knew she loved him more than all the others put together; and she knew this wasn't right, because whereas Bill was a case, Rance was a handful, for he was always getting into scrapes, and she had a devil of a job at times to stop Georgie from lathering him.

It wasn't so strange that the boy didn't like his father for from an early age he had felt Georgie's hand across his bare rump. Then again, Georgie never spoke to him but he swore. It was odd, she thought, that Rance hadn't picked up Georgie's swearing, but Bill had. Bill at four often came out with bloody, or bugger, and protested with hands, feet and voice when he was chastised for it. Yes, Bill was a case, but it was Rance, she knew instinctively, who needed her more than the others.

Even Kathy at two had an independence about her that was lacking in Rance, yet the boy was as loud-voiced and bumptious as his father at times. Of course, the bairns he mixed with round about didn't help any, she was well aware of that, and if it rested with her, another year, two at the most, would see them out of it. She had thought at first there was a lot in coal, but the most that was in it, at least for her, was damned hard work. But it was paving the way to better things.

When they had first moved in here in the January of '46 she was living in a sort of dull despair. The Hereford business, as she had come to think of it, was still very much in her mind, yet lessened somewhat by the very fact that Georgie had made her pregnant again. How could a man be like that . . . odd, queer, if he could give you a bairn and want you at all odd times of the night or day? It didn't fit in, did it? She had wished there was someone she could talk to about it. The only person who would know about such things was Mollie, but she was the last one she could go to, being his mother.

When Mona and Arthur were married in the middle of January '47 and they weren't invited, she had been indignant. The excuse that they were being married in a registry office in Hereford didn't satisfy her as it seemed to Georgie. The fact that Georgie rarely spoke of Arthur kept her suspicions alive, yet his answer to her statement, 'You seem to have dropped Arthur, and he you,' seemed logical, for he said, 'Look, it was wartime. You strike up friendships in wartime an' they just last during wartime, the majority of them anyway. Left alone, they die a natural death. Some silly buggers like to keep things goin', so they have these get-togethers each year. Well, I met Arthur an' he met me. We were different types, as has been bloody well pointed out often enough. He was educated an' I was as ignorant as a pig, a come-easy-go-easy-God-send-Sunday type, but all right to have beside you when you had your back to the wall. Well, he had his back to the wall when he first joined up, an' I stood beside him. An' that's what it was all about.'

Georgie's summing up had given her a new aspect of the situation. A refined type like Arthur would undoubtedly have his back to the wall among some of the roughs who were in the forces, and he'd be grateful to have a big bouncer like Georgie for a friend to fend off the enemy so to speak.

So there she had left it, and got on with the business of carrying Anastasia – which name she had taken from a story in a weekly magazine – and furnishing the house, which necessitated travelling around the second-hand shops looking for bargains.

When Georgie had failed to get set-on with his old firm, or with any firm that required lorry drivers, for the town at that time seemed full of ex-lorry drivers, he took the job of helping to unload coal at a yard which supplied a number of coal merchants. It never struck Georgie that he had the facilities at hand to start up a business of his own, and even when she broached the subject he had laughed it to scorn. 'Where am I goin' to get the money for a lorry?' he said. 'Or are you thinkin' of me going round the streets with a bloody cart and horse?' To this she had answered that everybody was hiring things these days. Pentons, behind the station, had lots of second-hand cars and lorries in; she had seen them.

It took her three months to persuade him that there was some-thing in the suggestion. His last stand against it was, he'd be working eighteen hours a day and he couldn't last long at that rate humping coal.

He started with loose coal on a flat lorry, selling it by the bucketful. It took almost eighteen months before they graduated to sacks. The problem here was that he required another hand, but, as he said, if he had to pay a fellow to fill the sacks he might as well give up for they would never be able to save enough to buy a decent lorry and get started properly. And so she became the other fellow.

Each day she filled the sacks ready for the following day, that is when her stomach wasn't too big and prevented her stooping. She also attended to the barrows that came to the yard.

The barrows were usually soap boxes balanced on a pair of bicycle wheels, the shafts rough pieces of wood, and the usual order from a barrow-holder was, 'Bob's worth, Missis.'

Filling a bucket, she would measure out a bob's worth; then, no matter how pressing would be the call from indoors with one or the other screaming, she had to watch the barrows until they were well outside the gate. A couple of nice big 'roundies' whipped up every time a barrow came into the yard could deplete the profit considerably by the end of the week.

Her five years of drudgery in the house and the depot had caused anger to develop in her mother, and pity in Mollie. Mary considered it a disgrace that her daughter should shovel coal like any cinder heap picker, whereas Mollie was emphatic in saying that it was a bloody crying-out shame that a lass like Annie should have to work so and be blacked up to the eyes every day. But there, as she had said at the beginning, if anybody could make a roof out of rotten thatch it was Annie, and by damn! she was doing it.

Annie liked Mollie, more than liked her; she had a deep affection for her such as she had never had for her mother. Moreover Mollie was kind, and those first hard days she had never come to the house empty-handed; even now, she always brought something for the bairns; whereas the only thing her mother brought with her was disdain.

Her da, too, had been kind to her in the early days. When he came on his own he talked all the time, had a good crack, as he put it, but when he came along with her mother he just sat silent.

As the years went on Annie had become more and more sorry for her father, and she warned herself that no matter how Georgie turned out she must never treat him like her ma did her da. And yet the strange thing was she knew that her da loved her ma. She didn't think her mother loved anybody, not even herself; she seemed incapable of affection. . . .

Well, there they were. Annie looked at the sacks, ten of them. They would give him a start tomorrow. Now she was going to have a bath, but oh Lord, she wished she hadn't to heat the water and carry it into the shed. That place was like ice. If they were here for good she'd have had a bath put in before now, but they weren't here for good. No! Oh no!

For some time she'd been chewing on an idea. She hadn't said anything to Georgie about it because he would have bawled her out. 'What!' he would have said. 'Are you mad? Takin' on a bloody garage! What next?' Yet he could take an engine to bits and put it together again and not mislay a screw. He couldn't write a letter to save his life; his own name and address was about as much as he could manage. She had to do all the bills because he couldn't reckon up, but give him a piece of machinery and his mind seemed to work. It was very odd, she thought, but he never seemed to realize his own capabilities, perhaps because he had come to accept the general opinion of himself, he was dim.

She went through the back door and into a large stone-floored scullery, where a gas stove stood next to a shallow brown sink. Fixed in the corner of the wall opposite was a wash-house boiler with a wooden lid on top, and pressed against the front stonework of the boiler, his two hands holding a knife which was inserted in a piece of box wood, was Rance, and she cried at him, 'What you doing, boy! Be careful; you'll cut your hands off.' She grabbed the knife from him, saying, 'What's this?' as she tossed a pile of narrow laths to one side.

'Aw, Mam, give over, I've just cut them. I'm goin' to make a hutch.'

'You're going to make no such thing. Haven't you been told you can't keep a rabbit out there. Now we've had all this out afore. Your da's told you.' She pushed him to one side. 'Are you stupid, boy?' Even as she said it she knew that he wasn't stupid, only grimly determined to have his own way. This was an odd trait in the boy. You could tell him and tell him he mustn't do a thing, and he would go on doing it as if he had never heard you speaking.

He stood by the wall now, his hands behind him, staring at her grimly as he said, 'I want a rabbit.'

'When we move. If we move into a cleaner place where . . . where there's no coal dust, then you can have a rabbit. And . . . and a dog. I told you, I told you the other night.'

'I want a rabbit now.'

'Will you be quiet, Rance!'

'Peter Smedley's got a rabbit and he's only four doors down.'

74

'Well, he's four doors down, he's not in this yard, and we want all the space we've got. You know we do. We can hardly turn the lorry now, and the walls are taken up with the sacks.'

'I could keep it in the backyard here,' he jerked his head towards the door.

'You're not keeping it in the backyard here.' She now closed her eyes and bowed her head and said 'Rance! Rance! Don't let's start this all over again. Look, I promise you as soon as we leave here you'll have a rabbit, and anything else you want.'

'When's that?'

'I . . . I don't know yet but . . . it'll likely be soon.'

'I want it now.'

'Get in there!' She thrust out her arm towards the kitchen door and when he didn't move she pulled him from the wall and pushed him forward. 'And let me hear another word about that rabbit from you and I'll tell your da. Mind, I mean it, I mean it this time. Mention that rabbit again and I'll tell your da; and then you know what'll happen, and you needn't come to me to save you.' She thrust him into the kitchen where Kathy, Bill and Tishy were sitting on the mat before the high-grate open fire and she called to Tishy, saying, 'You were going to get yourself washed; then get yourself washed. And get Kathy's clothes off and wash her face and hands, an' Bill's an' all. Then get yourselves to bed. That goes for you an' all, Rance.'

Having banged the door on them she stood for a moment with her hands gripping the sink. When Rance went on like that he did something to her, churned her up inside. Oh, she was tired, dog, dog tired; she must put an end to this before it put an end to her. She knew she was strong and healthy, but the coal would break her heart before it broke her body.

When the outer door opened swiftly she turned her head and looked at Georgie standing there. 'I'm back,' he said.

'I didn't hear the lorry.'

'No, I made it take its boots off an' come in in its stocking feet.' She laughed wearily. He could be funny at times.

'You all right?'

'No, I'm not.'

'Thought you weren't. See you've got all the bags ready.'

'Me back's telling me that an' all.'

'I'm starvin'.'

'Well, you'll have to wait while I get this grime off me.'

75

'Oh aye; how long will that be?'

'The water's hot –' she nodded towards the boiler – 'Give me fifteen minutes.'

'Leave it for me if it isn't too much like glar, an' I'll get the thick off me an' all.'

'All right.' She nodded.

After he had closed the door again she remained standing and looking towards it. He had spoken to her for some minutes and he hadn't sworn once, not even a bloody.

She'd gone for him last week about his swearing, that was after Bill had come out with a mouthful in front of him. 'You see,' she had said, 'four years old and swearing like a trooper. Nice state of affairs, isn't it?'

'Aw,' he had laughed. 'You know me. I can't remember a time when I didn't swear.'

'Well you could try to curb it in front of them, couldn't you?'

'It comes out natural, lass,' he had said.

'Then try being unnatural for a change.'

'What! d'you want a bloody miracle?' he had laughed.

She was about to turn towards the boiler when the door was pushed open again and he thrust his head through and said, 'You know somethin'?'

'No, what is it?'

'I opened me mouth and I bloody well didn't swear. Didn't you notice?'

'Aw, Georgie!' She burst out laughing. 'Go on. Go on.' She flapped her hand at him.

'Is that all you're gona say, go on, go on? No praise? Why can't you be kind to me an' say, "Georgie, you're a bloody marvel, that's what you are, Georgie, a bloody marvel"?'

Swiftly she picked up a dish cloth from the bench and threw it at him, and he caught it in his hand and rubbed it round his black laughing face and closed the door again.

It was moments such as these that lightened the load and made living bearable.

2

'It's a crying-out shame. And I would put it stronger than that if these bairns weren't here.' Mollie glanced down to each side of her to where Tishy and Bill were hanging on to her hands. 'By! I would an' all. 'Cos look at you! What do you look like? A docker, that's what you look like, a female docker. Twenty-five you are and the way you look now you could give yourself another ten years. Carry on like this, me lass, an' your bonny looks'll be no more. I'm tellin' you. Just look at your hair. . . . Oh! our Georgie. I could bash his brains in for him, I could that.'

'Oh, be quiet, Mollie. Sit yourself down, and I'll wash me hands and make a cup of tea.'

'You'll do nowt of the sort. If anybody's goin' to sit down it's you. Get out of me road, you two.' She playfully pushed the children aside; then lifting the kettle from the hob she thrust it into the heart of the fire, and as quickly lifted it back on the hob again, saying, 'I'll put it on the gas, it'll be quicker. And don't say "Aw, but think of the gas."' She pulled a face at Annie as she went towards the scullery.

Annie, sitting back in an old leather chair, closed her eyes for a moment. It was good to have somebody to boss you nicely.

Mollie's voice came to her now, crying at the children, 'Don't do that, else I'll skelp your backside for you,' and they answering her with a laugh. They all liked their Grannie McCabe; except Rance. He preferred his Grannie Cooper, because she had always spoilt him.

After a moment she called out, 'How's things?'

'Oh, fine, lass. I've got a new lodger.'

'What! . . . Another?'

'Aye, another. Micky was gettin' a bit too hot, even for me.

77

Talked about marryin'. But you know what?' Her head came round the door and her voice, although tones lower, was still loud. 'I've got an idea he's got a wife in Liverpool.' She now took three quick steps into the room and, bending over Annie, said, 'More than a bloody idea. I found a letter in his pocket, an' the piece that wrote it wasn't just a very dear friend. God! the things she said.' She now put her head back and laughed, and as her whole body wobbled with her emotion she flapped her hand sharply against the mound of her stomach, crying as she did so, 'Lie down! your father's not workin'.'

At this Annie let out a roar of laughter, and she and Mollie pushed at each other until the children's voices came from the scullery, yelling, 'Kettle's boilin', Gran. Kettle's boilin'.'

As Mollie ran into the scullery with a lightness of foot that was surprising for her bulk, Annie sat back in the chair again. Aw, Mollie was a tonic. In some ways Georgie took after her. 'Lie down! your father's not workin'.' That was funny that was. Pregnant women were supposed to have said that during the days of the slump when the child inside them kicked. It was a favourite saying of Mollie's and never failed to elicit Annie's laughter.

When Mollie brought the tray of tea into the kitchen Annie said, 'I've got hopes we may be out of this soon, Mollie.'

'No! What's in your head now, lass?'

'A little garage. A lock-up. We could rent it for five pounds a week. It isn't very big but it's got pumps an' all that. The snag is he wants a hundred and fifty for the goodwill. And then he wants to sell the tools an' things. When we get in what's owing to us, it'll only come to just over a hundred; but I mean to borrow the rest from somewhere, even if I have to go to a money-lender.'

'By God! you'll go to no money-lender, lass. That's jumpin' into the jaws of the wolf all right. No money-lenders.' She came towards Annie now, and bending over her she wagged her finger in her face as she said slowly, 'Now promise me, no money-lenders. By! the ruinations I've seen caused by money-lenders. By God! I have that. Court, that's where the money-lender'll lead you to, court. Look, tell me what you want an' I'll lend it you. But no money-lenders, lass.'

'You!' Annie pulled herself up straight in the chair. 'But ... but how can . . .?'

'Never you mind. . . . I've been workin' behind the bar for years, haven't I? An' when they say, "Have one yourself, Mollie,"

78

what d'you think I do? I'd swim out of that bar if I took all that was offered me. What I do is chalk it up to meself. Trust Mollie. And then there's our Winnie and Archie and Mike, they've been workin' for years, an' they pool their bit. Not forgettin' the lodger.' She knocked Annie back into the chair, and again they were laughing, but only for a short time for Annie said, 'But . . . but I might need a hundred pounds, Mollie.'

'Well, you can have a hundred pounds, lass.'

'Aw, Mollie!'

'Now, now, don't take on. I'd give anythin', lass, to see you out of this place for you're killin' yourself. Aw, give over, stop it. What the hell are you cryin' for?'

'Aw, Mollie! Mollie!' Annie had turned her face into the corner of the chair, and when Tishy began to whimper Mollie shouted to her, 'Go on you! don't you start. Look, take Bill outside. . . . Here!' She pushed her hand into her bag and drew out sixpence. Go and get some bullets. Share them mind. Go on.' She pushed them towards the door.

When she came back to Annie she said, quietly now, 'Come on, give over, lass.' And she shook her gently by the shoulders, and Annie, reaching towards the rod that ran underneath the mantelpiece, pulled from it a tea towel and dried her face with it, then, looking at Mollie, muttered, 'What can I say? What can I say, Mollie?'

'Say nowt.'

'You're so good.'

'Me!' Mollie now drew herself up and, giving a good imitation of Mae West, said the famous words, 'Goodness had nothing to do with it, dearie.' Again they were laughing; only, Annie's laughter was still mingled with tears, and suddenly she stood up and, throwing her arms about Mollie, whispered, 'Aw, how I wish you were me mother, Mollie. Time and again, how I've wished that.'

'Well!' Mollie's voice was slightly thick now as she held Annie and patted her back. 'That's the nicest thing that's ever been said to me. An' I wish I was your mother, lass, I wish I was. Now look.' She pushed her away. 'Have this cup of tea, then go an' get yourself washed an' done up a bit. Make yourself as bonny as you really are, then take me along to see this place. . . . But wait, you say it's a lock-up, where are you gona live?'

'We'll have to stay here until I can find some place.'

'Well, the sooner the better. . . . Just a tick now.' She wrinkled her brow and, with her finger pointing, she said, 'Wait; there's a Mr Stanley comes in our place, the best end, saloon. He lives somewhere behind the town hall. He's movin'; going to Harrogate; opening a business there. His house is his own property an' he wants to rent it. I heard him, I heard him tellin' the boss. I don't know what kind of a place it is, but it'll be no hole in the corner if he had it, 'cos he's respectable. Look, I'll ask him the night. He's bound to be around the night.'

'Oh, Mollie. But behind the town hall . . . they're all big houses there.'

'Not all of them. And anyway, why shouldn't you go to a big house if the rent is reasonable. There's six of you, you need a big house. Look, lass, start the way you mean to go on. By God! if I had me time over again you wouldn't find me in Primrose Street. If I was your age and had your head, lass, by! I would go places even if I had to take our Georgie along of me.' She smiled derisively now, then said, 'God forgive me! I shouldn't always be at him; he's me own, and he's not bad, is he?'

'No, Mollie, he's not bad. He couldn't be, he's too like you.'

'Go on with you.' Mollie gave her a push towards the far door, saying, 'Now hurry yourself up and get that muck off you; I'm dying to see this garage. An' I tell you what, we'll go round about the town hall, an' have a look at the houses there. Why not, eh? why not? *Westoe, here we come!*'

3

They had rented the garage, they had rented the house near the town hall, and even bought some of the furniture in it, and were moving in two weeks' time, and today was Rance's seventh birthday and everybody was happy . . . except Rance.

'What's the matter with you, boy?' asked Annie.

'Nothin', Mam.'

'Well, stop sulking.'

The boy made no denial against sulking.

'You've had a lot of presents, haven't you?'

'Presents!' When he turned his eyes disdainfully up towards the ceiling she cried at him, 'You should consider yourself lucky, damned lucky. Just look at the other bairns around the doors; some of them don't get a decent meal never mind presents like you've got. A fountain pen, a school bag, a train set, and what else? Money, you've had over a pound in money. Boy, you don't know when you're well off. What do you want?'

She regretted asking the question as soon as it was out, and she expected him to say, 'You know what I want, I want a rabbit,' but he didn't open his mouth, he just turned away and went and sat in the corner of the room near the fireplace. And now she barked at him, 'You keep that face on when your granda and grandma Cooper come and just see what you'll get when they leave. Anyway, there was something I was going to ask you, where've you been all afternoon?'

'Out.'

'I know fine well you've been out 'cos you haven't been in, I haven't seen hilt nor hair of you. Where were you out? I sent Tishy looking for you. Where were you?'

'About.'

81

'Oh, my goodness boy, one of these days I'll lose my temper with you and knock you from here to Hull. Go on, go and get yourself cleaned up, you look like a muck heap. They should be here any minute. Go on.'

She watched him turn slowly about and with dragging step go into the scullery. She shook her head. That rabbit, it was coming between him and his wits. She had promised him he could have one when they got into the new place – there was a big backyard there – but no, no, he wanted one now for his birthday. Where did he get his stubbornness from? Not from her, and not from Georgie. Yet for all that he remained so lovable. And he was so bonny. Every time she looked at him she wanted to put her arms around him and hug him. . . . She knew what she would do. On Monday she would take him down to the pet shop and let him pick a rabbit. She'd pay for it to be kept there until they moved. Perhaps that would satisfy him.

She was about to call him and tell him what she intended to do when the back door opened and she heard Mollie's voice, saying, 'Who knows but you'll be goin' to work in a bowler and umbrella yet, lad,' and she knew that Georgie was with her.

They both came into the kitchen laughing, Mollie crying at the top of her voice, 'I'm tellin' this'n here, with a garage of his own, an a house not a kick in the backside from Westoe, he'll be goin' to work rigged out in an umbrella an' bowler.'

'On the bloody dole more like. If you want my opinion, we've bitten off more than we can chew.'

'Georgie!' Annie spoke his name with a heavy flatness, and he replied with equal flatness, 'Aye, Annie.' And Mollie burst in, 'You leave everything to Annie, lad. If anybody's got a head on their shoulders she has. Just you leave the reins in her hands and you can lay your bets on the race.'

'Bets on the race.' Georgie looked towards Annie where she was arranging plates of cakes down the centre of the table, and he laughed as he said, 'I've never taken long shots, always been against betting on bloody outsiders.'

'She's no outsider, she's a favourite, aren't you, lass?' Mollie leant over and gave Annie a whack on the buttocks, and after a startled exclamation Annie, laughing now, turned to them and said, 'Would you like me to do a gallop round the house to show you?'

There came the sound of the back door opening and Mary

Cooper's voice, saying, 'Happy Birthday, dear,' and the voice seemed to subdue Mollie's exuberance, for with an unconcealed sigh she sat down to the side of the fireplace. When Mary entered the room it was a moment before Mollie turned her head and looked at her, then they exchanged a cool greeting.

Mary gave no greeting to Georgie, but looking at her daughter, she said, 'You didn't get him a rabbit then?'

Annie nipped at her bottom lip before answering quietly, 'No, Ma. He's had to do without one all the time he's been here, and as we'll be gone in a fortnight I can't see the sense in fixing up a hutch now.'

'The yard's cleared of coal.'

'I'm well aware of that, but as I said. . . . Oh! –' she shook her head – 'for heaven's sake let's forget about that rabbit. He'll get one.' Now her voice was rising. 'He'll get one in the other place. I promised him . . . and I promise you, Ma.'

'There's no need to raise your voice.'

'It would make God raise his voice.'

There followed a short tense silence until Rance and Bill with Kathy toddling behind them came into the room, and Mollie, turning to Rance, said on her usual high note, 'Well now, boy, we only need your granda and Tishy here and then we can start on that tea. Just look at that cake, did you ever see anythin' like it? Seven candles on it an' all! . . . This'll be them now.' She screwed round in her chair and looked towards the scullery, and a minute later Dennis Cooper came into the room holding Tishy by the hand.

Dennis's face was unusually straight; his mouth had a grimness about it that caused Annie to say immediately, 'What's the matter? What's up?' Then she looked down at Tishy, whose face was white, and Dennis said, 'She's been sick.'

'Sick?' Annie went to her daughter and, dropping on to her hunkers, looked into her face and said, 'Been eating something, dear? What did you spend your pocket-money on?'

For answer Tishy put her hand into her coat pocket; then holding out her palm showed her mother the sixpence, and Annie said, 'Well, what's made you sick? You didn't have anything greasy for your dinner.'

'She'll be all right, just let her sit quiet.' Dennis drew the child away from Annie and placed her on a cracket near the fender, saying, 'Sit quiet, hinny; you'll be all right. Sit quiet.'

'And what's the matter with you?' Mary looked keenly at her husband and Dennis replied, 'There's nowt the matter with me, except perhaps I'd like a cup of tea.' His voice was lighter now but there was still no smile on his face.

Annie stared at her father for a moment. There was something wrong here. Her da had taken no notice of the other three, and he never entered the house but he ribbed and joked with one or the other of them. 'Well –' she answered him now – 'the tea's ready; if you'll all sit up I'll get you served. . . . No, don't you sit there, Rance, sit you opposite your cake.'

Smiling, she pulled her son to the chair opposite the cake, and amid chatter and laughter they all seated themselves round the table and she began to pour out the tea. It was as she placed the last cup in front of herself that there came a hammering on the back door.

As the heads turned in the direction of the scullery Georgie said, 'Somebody still thinks we're sellin' coal, an' he seems in a hurry. Perhaps his fire's gone out.' His wide mouth stretched into a laugh as he pushed back his chair. A minute later Annie, straining her ears above the renewed chattering of the children, heard him exclaiming loudly, 'I don't believe a bloody word of it. He wouldn't.'

There was another voice now, angry, high; then Georgie entered the room again, followed by Mr Peter Smedley from four doors down.

Their entry and the looks on their faces silenced all at the table. Georgie looked at his son and Rance stared wide-eyed back at him.

'Where you been this afternoon?'

There was a moment's pause before Rance answered, 'Just out, Da.'

'Out where?' Georgie slowly advanced towards the boy and Rance, his face draining of colour, his voice quivering now, said, 'J-j-just out.'

'You went along the river.'

'No . . . no, Da.'

'You're a bloody little liar.'

Annie was on her feet now staring at Mr Smedley. 'What's he done? What's the matter with you? What's he done?'

'Drowned wor young Peter's rabbit, that's what he's done.'

Annie's hand went to her mouth and pressed her lips tightly for a second; then she was protesting loudly, 'What! Don't you tell me that, he wouldn't do that. Rance . . . never! He loved that rabbit as well as young Peter did. You never did such a thing, did you, boy?' She was stretching across the table towards him now, and Rance, looking straight into her face, said, 'No, Mam, no.'

'There you are then, there you are.' She had rounded on Mr Smedley, and he, barking back at her now, cried, 'Well! he did.'

'Did you see him?'

'No, I didn't, but Tommy Blake did. He had threatened he would do it, an' not for the first time. My Peter came back home from the match an' he found the hutch empty. Tommy Blake said he had seen that one there –' the man's arm was thrust out towards Rance now – 'leaving the backyard with something under his coat. He said he was makin' for the river. You drowned her, didn't you? An' her full of young. You drowned her, you cruel young bugger you!'

Annie was staring not at Rance, and not at Peter Smedley, but at Georgie now. Peter Smedley had called his son a cruel young bugger and Georgie was doing nothing about it, only staring down at the boy.

When Georgie's two hands gripped Rance's shoulders and lifted him bodily from the chair she screamed at him. 'Leave him alone! He would never do such a thing, never!'

She thrust her way between the wall and the intervening chairs and went to grab the boy from Georgie's fierce grip; but, taking one hand from Rance's shoulder, Georgie thrust her roughly away, almost overbalancing her, and when she fell against her father Dennis held on to her arm while he shook his head sharply at her, warning her to remain quiet.

'Did you drown that rabbit?' Georgie's voice was unusually quiet, but when the boy gave no answer, just stared at him, he bawled in such a way that everyone in the room started. 'Do you hear me? Did you drown that rabbit?'

When he began to shake the boy like a dog would a rat Annie shouted, 'Stop it! Stop it,' and Mary, getting to her feet, went towards them crying, 'Leave the child alone! Do you hear me?'

At this, Dennis shouted in turn, 'An' you hear me, woman. Sit yourself down an' mind your own business.' Then looking at Annie, whom he still held firmly, he hissed at her, 'Keep out of it. Leave them alone.'

Annie turned an agonized glance on her father but the look in

85

his eyes stayed her further protests. She could see he was for Georgie. It was as if he believed what they were saying about the child.

'Did you drown that rabbit, yes or no?'

The boy's head was wobbling on his shoulders like a wired jack-in-the-box and at last he gabbled out, 'N . . . no, Da. N . . . no, Da.'

When Georgie released him the child fell to the floor with a thud and Georgie turned and looked at Peter Smedley, and Peter Smedley said, 'He can say no till he's black in the face, but I know he did.'

'He says he didn't.'

Georgie was advancing on Peter Smedley now and there was menace in each step he took. What would have happened next was prevented by Tishy, who during the altercation had left the table and had sat on the cracket, with one side of her pressed tight against the wall. But now she was on her feet, screaming at her father, 'He did! he did, Da. He did! he did! we saw him. Granda an' me, we saw him, an' I was sick. He did. He did.'

Georgie stopped and, turning, looked down at her. Then he moved his body slowly round until he was facing Dennis, and Dennis answered the question he was silently demanding, 'She's right,' he said dully; 'we saw him at it.'

Like a scurrying rabbit himself, Rance now dived under the table screaming hysterically, 'I didn't mean to, Da, I didn't mean to. It was 'cos he was braggin'. It was gona have little 'uns an' he said he'd have more than me. She was going to have little. . . .'

When Georgie hauled him out by the legs Annie dragged herself from Dennis and, rushing at Georgie, tried to pull the boy from him, at the same time screaming at him, 'Leave him be! I'll deal with this, leave him be.'

'You've dealt with him too bloody long.'

She was knocked flying by the flat of Georgie's hand; then with the other he picked the boy up bodily and made for the door.

It took Mollie and Dennis all their time to hold Annie now, and in the melée of her shouting and the children crying, Rance's screams came down to them from above.

Mary, standing with joined hands, gazed up at the ceiling and cried, 'He'll kill him! he'll kill him. He forgets what he's doing when he gets that belt in his hand. I've seen him at it afore,' and Dennis cried at her in turn, 'Well, if he does, you'll have something on your conscience, woman, 'cos you've helped to ruin him . . . an' you an' all, lass.' He glared into Annie's face, showing her an anger that was unusual for him. 'You've broken his neck one way and another; between you you've broken his neck. Vied with each other, you have, to give him what he's cried for. Well, listen to him now; he's getting what he's cried for an' rightly this time.'

The screams had faded into a muted sobbing. Mollie, who had shown Mr Smedley the door, now shooed the children out into the yard, and into the comparative silence that had fallen on the house Dennis, turning to Mary, said, 'Get your hat and coat on.'

'I'm not going, I'm not leaving this. . . .'

'Get your hat and coat on, woman, an' now. And see if you can mind your own business for once.' As his hand came out to push her she cried at him, 'You! Dennis Cooper, mind who you're talking to.' Nevertheless she put her hat and coat on and under his grim stare went out without a word of good-bye.

A few minutes later, when the sobbing became intermittent, Mollie said with unusual quietness, 'Well, I'll be off an' all. . . . But lass, don't hold it against Georgie for what he's done, 'cos you know, I agree with your da, that bairn's been spoilt as none of the others have. Sometimes it happens with the first one an' sometimes it's the last. With me it was our Winnie, still is; I always made Georgie carry the can for everythin' that the others did. What he's just done is what I should have done to our Winnie many a time, an' she'd be less trouble the day. So don't hold it against him, lass. Ta-rah; I'll be seein' you.'

'Ta-rah, Mollie.' The words came from Annie's mouth as if she hadn't used her lips for a long time.

Alone in the kitchen now, she sat away from the table. The plates were still full of sandwiches and fancy cakes, not a bite had been eaten; she had baked and iced for two solid days. But what did it matter about the food? What did matter was that Rance, her bairn, her beloved son, and he was her beloved son, had taken another lad's rabbit and drowned it, and she was to blame. Oh yes, she was to blame. She should have let him have a rabbit in the yard even if it had been choked to death with coal dust. She hadn't realized what the rabbit meant to him. But she should have, for he had told her often enough; she had become sick to death over the past year listening to his craving for a rabbit.

The door opened and Georgie entered. His face and thick neck were scarlet; the blue of his eyes was pale, like steel. He looked at her across the room and after a moment said, 'Nice thing we've bred, haven't we? Well, I've made sure of one bloody thing, it's the last rabbit he'll drown.'

She gave a gasp as she thought for a moment he had killed the child, but a distant snuffling brought from her a long-drawn-out breath.

She stared at the man opposite her, who in this moment was unrecognizable. Gone was the gauche good-tempered softie, and it looked as if he might never return.

Bringing up the children had lain with her and she hadn't believed in punishment, at least no lathering with a belt; a box across the ears or a hand across the buttocks was the most they ever received. If anyone had told her that Georgie would unmercifully thrash his son she would have laughed and said, 'I'll believe that when I see it.' And now she had to believe it, and although her heart was sore for her son there crept into her lukewarm affection for the burly man standing staring at her a modicum of respect.

4

The street was one of those that went off Erskine Road. It had the distinctive name of Bewlar Terrace. The house was No. 17 and its advantages were many; besides having six rooms, it also had the real luxury of a bathroom. There was a large backyard and an eighteen foot by twelve foot, iron-fringed front garden; moreover, it was within a few minutes' walk from the church and not much further from the Bents Park and recreation ground, and this latter solved the problem of the bairns having somewhere safe to play.

Annie's main joy in the house was the bathroom. For the first week she had taken a bath morning and night and saw to it that the children had at least one bath a day. The only one she couldn't get into the bath every day was Georgie. He'd had enough washing back there in Madley, he'd said, to last him a lifetime. Once a week would do him, twice if he was pushed, and nothing she could say would alter that.

She had warned him about his swearing. Although he had cut it down quite a bit he had only to get excited and his language coloured the air like blue smoke.

Apart from a polite nod, Mrs Tressel, her neighbour on the right, had studiously ignored them. She had an opinion of herself that one, Annie considered, all because she engaged a daily from nine till twelve. But Mrs Brooks on the left of her was all right, kindly she was. She had looked over the wall one day and given the bairns a bag of bullets; it was a kind of introduction. Although she had been nosy and wanted to know all about them she had seemed quite impressed when Annie had informed her that her husband was in the car business and had his own garage. She had ended by saying they had been in the coal contracting business

89

but had given it up as it was much too dirty; she had hoped that Mrs Brooks wasn't acquainted with Burton's Corner and Hanlon's coal depot.

Yet she didn't bother about her neighbours. Let them hang as they grow, she said to herself; you mind your business and they'll mind theirs. She was starting a new life in a respectable district, in a fine house. And a fine rent they had to pay for it an' all, seventeen and six a week. Still, she supposed they were lucky to have got it. And the pieces of furniture she had bought from the owner were, in her estimation, simply wonderful and dirt cheap. A three-piece chesterfield with covers on for seven pounds, and a big sideboard that filled one wall of the dining-room – he had only charged three for that, and it was made of beautiful wood that you could see your face in – furthermore, he had sold her a complete bedroom suite, a carpet and other odds and ends all for ten pounds.

She was set up, they were all set up. The main thing for her to do now was to see that Georgie made a go of that garage, and if hard work could do that he would certainly achieve something in a very short time, for during the past month he had been there from seven in the morning till nine at night.

On this particular afternoon Annie was about to get herself washed and dressed up to take the bairns for a walk to the garage, at the same time taking Georgie his tea. She liked going to the garage. When a customer came in for petrol she willed him to ask for six gallons, not one or two as was the rule, and on a day when there wasn't a car in for repair she felt depressed, even while telling Georgie that they must creep before they walked and it was early days yet, and a slow start augured a fast ending. She wasn't quite sure about the latter saying; she wanted trade to come fast but not to end.

She said to Bill, 'Come and get your face and hands washed, we're going to see your da,' and Bill replied as always with a question, 'Walkin' or on the bus?'

'Walking.'

'Aw.'

'Aw.' She ruffled his hair, and he now said to her, 'When can I go to school?'

She gave a little sigh as she replied, 'I've told you, not until next year when you're five.'

'Tishy goes.'

90

'Yes, but she's five.'

'I'm as big as Tishy.'

'I know you are but you're not five.'

'Why have I to be five?'

'Oh, Bill, come on.' As she went to grab his hand the door bell rang and, leaving him, she crossed the hall, thinking, 'Who's this now? Somebody else selling things? Honestly, they were worse round here than they were at Burton's Corner. . . Then she opened the door and gasped and exclaimed on a high note, 'Well! Mona!'

'Hello, Annie.'

'Hello, hello. Come in, come in.' She put out her hand and drew Mona over the threshold and led her into the front room, talking all the while. 'When did you come? You should have let me know; another ten minutes and I would have been out. Well! you're a sight for sore eyes. Sit down, sit down. Where's Arthur? My! this is a surprise. Look, don't let's sit here, come into the kitchen and I'll make a cup of tea; come on . . . Oh, it's good to see you.'

All the time she was talking she was warning herself not to lay it on too thick. She hadn't seen Mona more than half a dozen times since that memorable Christmas and the last time was two and a half years ago when she came home for her father's funeral; Arthur hadn't come with her. She had seemed different then but she had looked smart, so smart she had felt a little jealous of her. But now she looked anything but smart, she was as different again. In her perceptive way she knew that something had happened to Mona. It wasn't that she was suffering under the handicap of having only one eye, she had got over that; she had once said it was the price she paid for Arthur and it was cheap. But there was something not right. She looked low, bad.

Abruptly, she stopped her chattering and quietly asked, 'Anything wrong, Mona? You been bad or something?'

'No, no, Annie. No, I haven't been bad. How's the bairns?'

'Oh, look at them.' She pointed to where Bill and Kathy were standing silently gazing at the visitor, and she called to them 'Come and say hello to your Auntie Mona. Come on.' She reached out and pulled them towards Mona, and nudging Bill, she said, 'Say hello, Auntie Mona.'

'Hello.' Bill now cast a sharp glance up at her and Annie knew that his next question would be, 'How is she me Auntie Mona,

I haven't seen her afore?' and she put in quickly, 'Lost his tongue. He'll deafen you with his chatter in a minute. This is Kathy. You haven't seen her.'

'No, no, I haven't seen her. Hello, Kathy.' Mona bent towards the child and touched her fair curling hair, then moved her fingers gently around the pink cheeks as she said, 'She's bonny, beautiful.'

'Yes, the only one of them that's got any looks, except Rance isn't bad. But looks don't matter so much with a lad. Tishy though is still as plain as a pikestaff. Poor Tishy, she's going to feel it later on. Still, there's plenty of time, she might change, plain ones often do. . . . Oh, the kettle's boiling. Have you had anything to eat?'

'Yes, we had some lunch at my mother's.'

Annie noticed that Mona said lunch, not dinner. She had changed in more ways than one. After a moment she asked, 'Do you ever see Arthur's folks?'

'Very seldom; his mother's only been to see us once.'

'Only once?'

'Yes, but it suits us. I've seen Olive once or twice since James died. Oh, did you know he had died?'

Annie put the teapot on the tray then turned slowly towards Mona, saying, 'No.' Then, after a pause, she added, 'I suppose I should say I'm sorry, but then I'm not all that much of a hypocrite. How is Olive?'

'To tell you the truth she seems much more alive since she's been a widow. The boy's nice, Alan. He's ten now. Arthur is very fond of him. Olive let him stay with us for a holiday this year.'

'I wasn't wrong about Olive; she seemed nice then.'

'Yes, she's nice.'

When the tea was poured out and she had buttered some scones and placed a sandwich cake on the table she asked, 'How's Arthur getting on?'

It was a moment before Mona said, 'Oh, all right.' Then lowering her head, she gave it an impatient shake, a characteristic gesture that Annie remembered from the early days.

'What is it, Mona? Something is wrong.'

Mona still had her head bent and there was another pause before she said, 'Yes Annie; everything's wrong, everything's wrong.'

'I'm sorry, I thought. . . .'

'Yes, so did I. I thought it was going to be heaven. The little

92

pub out in the wilds, just us two until the family started.' Her head had sunk deeper on to her chest, and Annie asked quietly, 'No sign?'

'No; nor will there be.' Her head came up sharply now and showed the tears dropping slowly from her left eye. Then swallowing deeply, she muttered, 'He doesn't . . . he can't. What I mean is he's . . . he's incompetent.'

As Annie watched Mona's head swing down again thoughts began tearing along the by-roads in her mind, irrelevant facts, such as Mona was talking differently. A few years ago she would have explained Arthur's inadequacy with the term, he's no use. Another by-road was being swept with a remembered sickness, and along another the essence of fear was rising like a thick mist.

'He tries. Oh, he does, and he gets upset. But he's so nice. Oh, he's so nice, Annie. That's the worst part of it. I go through agony because of myself and how I feel, but at the same time I go through agony for him an' all. I don't think we can go on like this. You see he won't discuss it. Now he's talking about moving away from there because it's too lonely for me . . . and it is. Oh, it is lonely. It would be different if . . . if there were bairns about. You know what I mean, Annie . . . .'

Annie nodded slowly.

'But . . . but for most of the year just him and me together. He reads . . . reads and reads, all the time. I say all the time, that's wrong, he's very good about the house, and he keeps the garden lovely. And of course in the height of the holiday season there are people in the bar. But . . . but that only lasts for a few weeks. Other times we can go days and never see anyone, and in the winter. . . . Oh, Annie, the winter. He used to talk to me about books and music, and at first I thought it was marvellous, I was being educated. Now when I see him putting a record on, or sitting down with a book, I want to scream and throw things.'

They stared at each other in deep sorrow filled silence until Annie said quietly, 'Drink that cup of tea.'

Mona sipped at her tea, and Annie, words of comfort failing her because of the significance of Mona's confidence, sat staring down into her tea. . . . That Partridge fellow had been right then; he was right after all. And where did that leave Georgie?

As the sickness reared up in her she attacked it. Georgie's a normal man; if ever there was a normal man he's one. My God! doesn't he prove it enough. . . . But back there in those war years, had he been normal then? Yes, yes, of course he had. Aw, there was something she couldn't understand about this, something fishy.

She started visibly when Mona said, 'Arthur thinks he'd like to work around here; it would be better for us both, me being back among my own people.'

Now her mind was yelling at her, Oh no! not that! She made no comment, and Mona went on, 'But it's funny, I seem to have fallen between two stools, I don't feel a bit at home here now, at me mother's I mean. Her way of life seems different altogether from what I've been used to these last few years. You know what I mean?'

When Annie nodded but still made no reply, Mona looked about her and said, 'It's a lovely kitchen. It's a lovely house altogether. What a change from the depot. I bet you didn't know you were born when you moved in.'

'That's true enough.' Annie smiled weakly. 'We' were lucky to get it, and there's nobody knows it better than I do. . . . About Arthur getting work around here. There's, there's nothing for his type. Well, what I mean to say is, he couldn't do labouring and he wouldn't go into a shop or anything like that.'

'He wouldn't mind going into a bookshop; a good class bookshop, he's always fancied running a bookshop.'

Annie got to her feet and went to fill the teapot, saying, 'He'd die a slow death with a bookshop round here. Well, what I mean is, it would have to be something besides books, sweets and cigarettes and a paper round and such. A bookshop . . . well. . . . Of course that's only my opinion; but you know few people buy books except paperbacks, they go to the library for proper ones. By the way, where is Arthur?'

'Oh, he went down to see Georgie. We called in at your mother's as we had to pass the door before going to Burton's Corner and she told us of the change, so Arthur said you go and see Annie and I'll go and have a natter with Georgie.'

A natter with Georgie. A natter with Georgie. What was she getting all wound up about? Her life was secure, nothing but death could alter it. Or could it? Anyway, why was she getting in such a lather? It wasn't as if she had any real feeling for Georgie, was it? She knew that she hadn't been in love in her life, and there was very little chance now that she ever would be. What was she frightened of, apart from the other thing, and that in itself was ridiculous? Was she afraid that he would go off and leave her to fend for herself and the bairns? Now that was daft, because that was the last thing he would do. But even if he did she was quite capable of working and she would bring them up somehow. Other women had had to do it and she wasn't like some who married just to have a pay packet coming in without going out to graft for it. There was still a lot like that about. So what was she afraid of? What she should be doing at this moment was sympathizing with Mona because, my God! she must have had a life of it. You could, she knew from experience, get too much of a good thing, but taking all in all she considered that was the lesser of two evils, for to be married to a man who was 'no use' must be awful. Well, it had certainly told on Mona. It had put years on her. She said now, 'Has Arthur been to a doctor?'

'No.'

'Well, he should; you should tell him to get himself there.'

'Oh, I couldn't, Annie. We . . . we don't talk about it.'

'Don't talk about it! Then you should; it's about time.'

'Mam, are we gona see me da?' Bill was standing in the kitchen doorway.

'In a minute. Go and play. Where's Kathy?'

'Sittin' on the front room couch wettin' her knickers.'

This brief and telling reply brought Annie springing from her chair, apologizing to Mona as she rushed past her into the front room. She brought Kathy back into the kitchen, divesting her of her wet pants the while and chastising her with, 'You're a naughty girl. You know how to go to the lav now. Oh, I've a good mind to. . . .'

'She did it on purpose.'

'Be quiet! and don't be silly. She turned on Bill. How could she do it on purpose? Now, now! stop that snivellin'.' She shook her small daughter impatiently while Bill insisted, 'She did. She said she was gona an' she did.'

For the first time since coming into the house Mona laughed. She leant her elbow on the kitchen table and, supporting her head with her hand, she laughed while Annie, keeping her face straight, said under her breath, 'I mustn't let on . . . I don't know what he's going to be when he grows up, likely something in Parliament, 'cos he'll have the last word if it kills him.'

Of a sudden Mona rose to her feet, saying, 'I'll be going, Annie; I promised Mam I wouldn't be long. She wants me to go and see

95

Auntie Joyce, and I expect Arthur's back by now. We'll look in tomorrow night. Will that be all right?'

'Course. Course. Any time.' Annie did not protest at her going, nor did she say, 'Just wait a minute till I change her and get her coat and hat on and we'll walk down with you.' Instead, leaving Kathy and Bill in the kitchen, she accompanied Mona to the front door, and there they looked at each other in awkward silence for a moment before Mona said, 'Well, bye-bye, Annie. See you tomorrow night then.'

'Bye-bye, Mona. We'll be looking forward to it. Don't have too much tea for I'll have a meal ready.'

'Now don't put yourself out,' Mona answered from the front gate, and Annie replied jocularly, 'Would I ever now!' Then she watched Mona walk down the street before she closed the door.

She did not go immediately into the kitchen but went into the sitting-room and straight to the couch and felt the cover to see if it was wet. Yet she wasn't thinking of the cover but planning what she was going to do. She next went into the hall and looked at the clock. Rance and Tishy should be in from school any minute now.

As she entered the kitchen she heard the back gate open and Rance came racing up the yard and burst into the kitchen, crying, 'Mam! Miss Warrington said me drawin' was the best in the class, she said it looked like a real mota car an' I told her it was a real 'un, one of me dad's.'

'Oh, that's fine. I'm glad she was pleased with you.' She smiled down on him. 'Where's Tishy?'

'Comin'.'

'What do you mean comin'? I've told you to see to her from school, haven't I?'

'Aw, you know what she's like, Mam, she won't stay with me. I tried to grab her and she kicked me.'

She shook her head. It was strange but her two eldest children had never got on, not even when they were babies. Rance had resented the arrival of a second baby and his reactions to it had made the elders say, 'Oh, it's natural, he feels his nose has been put out.' And as she grew, Anastasia's reaction to her elder brother was even more aggressive than his, and it had deepened since the business of the rabbit.

'I'm goin' out to play. Can I have a slice, Mam?' Rance was on his way to the pantry when Annie checked him, saying, 'No, hold your hand a minute, I'm going to set your tea. Now listen. I'm . . .

96

I'm going down to the garage to see your dad, an' I want you to look after the house till I come back.'

'Aw, Mam, I want to go out to play.'

'You're going to stay here till I come back; I won't be more than half an hour, and then you can go out to play.'

'Has our Tishy got to stay in an' all?'

'You've all got to stay in.'

'She'll fight me.'

'I'll speak to Tishy.'

'She'll still fight me, an' if she does I'll kick her, I will, I will.'

'Now, Rance, behave yourself. If there's any trouble when I'm out that'll put paid to the puppy. Now mind, I'm warning you, there'll be no puppy for you.'

As she hurriedly laid the table for the four of them, the boy sat sulking. His chin resting on his folded arms on the kitchen window-sill, he stared down the backyard. Rance worried her at times, because the traits of his nature were so opposed. She knew that among boys of his own age he did quite a bit of bullying, yet he was afraid of Tishy, and his fear caused him to retaliate – she never used the word underhanded or sneaky when thinking of his reactions to his sister, but told herself that against the open hostility of Tishy he had to be on the defensive.

When he turned quickly from the window and seated himself at the table she knew Tishy had entered the yard, and when the child came into the kitchen she said to her, 'Hello there.'

'Hello, Mam. . . . Mam.'

'Yes, dear?'

'Guess what?'

'I don't know. Something nice happened?'

'A-hah. I think I'm gona be picked for the May pocession.'

'Procession, Tishy.'

'That's what I said, Mam, pocession. Miss Willard heard me singing, "O Mary, we crown thee with blossoms today, Queen of the Angels an' Queen of the May"; an' she said I sang good.'

'Oh, that's nice. Wash your hands now quickly an' sit up and get your tea.'

'Am I . . . am I not goin' out to play?'

'Not until I come back. I'm just going to slip down to the garage to see your dad and I want you to be a good girl.'

Tishy went to the sink and washed her hands. This done, the tap still running, she put her hands under it and scooped some

97

water into her mouth and started to rub her tongue with her fingers.

It was her choking that brought Annie's attention to her and she cried, 'What are you up to, child? Are you trying to choke yourself?'

Tishy spat into the sink, wiped her mouth on the roller towel, then walking to the table, took her seat before she said casually, 'Father Ryan says people who swear should have their mouths scrubbed out.'

'But you don't swear . . . do you?'

'No . . . but . . . but I think things, swear things.' The child stared up at Annie, her mouth set in a thin line, her eyes wide and serious.

Suppressing a smile, Annie put out her hand and touched her child's head, saying, 'Get on with your tea.' At times this daughter of hers was so honest she was embarrassing.

She now ran upstairs and put on her coat and hat, and glancing at herself quickly in the mirror she turned her face first to one side and then the other. Was she getting a double chin?. . . Aw, of all the things to ask herself at a time like this when her mind was full of the other business. She was barmy at times, stupid, daft.

In the kitchen again where they were all seated round the table, she addressed herself to Rance, saying, 'Now mind, remember what I told you.'

The boy didn't answer, but Tishy asked, 'What did you tell him, Mam?' and before she could speak Bill supplied the answer, saying, 'He'll not get his puppy if he wallops you.'

Annie sighed, then cried at them, 'Now I'm warning you, all of you. Any trouble an' you're all for it. Now mind . . . and see to Kathy. Do you hear, Rance? See to Kathy.'

'If Grandma Cooper comes she'll see to her, then can I go out?'

'No, Boy, you can't, an' that's final.' She stared at him hard before turning away.

Grandma Cooper! Her mother had not been near them since they moved. She'd made her mouth go about them living at the depot but since they had got some place decent, and better by a mile than what she had, she had ignored the fact. Her da had said, 'Leave her be, she'll come round, if it's only out of curiosity.' But she was a long time in coming round. Oh, her mother was a queer creature.

She caught a bus to the bottom of Fowler Street, from there she walked to the garage.

The front of the garage lay back from the main thoroughfare. It had two sets of double doors at the front and two petrol pumps. It also had a back entrance, and it was to this Annie made her way. Having passed through an alley, she came into a broad lane, bordered on both sides by six-foot stone walls. In the middle of the lane a large single door led into the back of the garage. It was partly open and she went through, past the car pit, above which a car was suspended, and round the corner into the main area. At the far end near the front doors was a make-shift erection that served as an office, and she came to a dead stop when she saw, standing in its doorway, Arthur Bailey, and facing him, Georgie.

When neither of them turned towards her she realized they hadn't seen her, and instead of going forward she stepped back into the shelter of the raised car and stood with her fingers against her lips. When she heard their footsteps approaching the middle of the garage she urged herself to move. She didn't want to be caught standing here as if she were listening. But she didn't move for the footsteps had stopped.

'It would be like a new life, Georgie.' That was Arthur Bailey's voice, and now Georgie answered, 'I cannot understand you, man; there's nowt but muck around here.'

'It isn't places that matter, you know that, Georgie, it's people.'

'Aye, aye, you're right there.'

'You could expand. As I said I'll put all I've got into it. I could do the buying and selling, and you could teach me a bit of the mechanics . . . Think about it, Georgie, will you? You've got no idea what it'll mean to me. As I said, it'll be like starting to live again. . . . Think about it, Georgie. . . . Please?'

The last words were a plea and they brought her fingers pressing tighter against her lips.

'I'll . . . I'll have to talk it over with Annie.'

There was a pause before Arthur Bailey's voice came again, saying, 'Yes, yes, of course. And . . . and you could point out to her that she'd have Mona with her again. She would like that, I'm sure, they used to be good friends. It could work out, Georgie, it could.'

'All right, Arthur, all right.'

When she saw them standing close together, Arthur Bailey's two hands gripping Georgie's, her body swayed forward, and she had no power to stop the protest rushing up from the depths of her and spurting from her lips almost in a scream, *'No! No!'*

The men started as if they had both been shot, then stood transfixed for a moment gazing at her before she turned and ran.

When she reached the entrance to the alleyway she heard Georgie's voice calling after her down the back lane, and as she came out of the other end of the alleyway and ran down the street, she could still hear him shouting, 'Annie! Annie! Do you hear me, Annie?'

A passer-by tried to stop her. 'What's up, lass?' he said. Frantically she thrust him off and went on running.

Because she knew she must look mad tearing along the main street she jumped on to a bus that was picking up passengers and she alighted at the next stop, boarded another and within ten minutes was back in the house. . . .

Preparing for what was to follow, she bundled the children out to play; then she waited. She knew he'd either close the garage up or leave it in care of the lad.

He stormed in the front way almost banging the door off its hinges. She heard him go into the kitchen, then the front room, then come up the stairs. She had chosen to wait for him in the bedroom, for here their voices would be less likely to carry to the neighbours on either side, at least they wouldn't be able to make out word for word unless they made a point of coming up into their own bedrooms and putting their ears to the wall.

She was standing with her arms folded looking out of the window when he entered the room.

'What the hell do you mean?'

She turned slowly towards him. Her lips trembling, but her voice low, she said, 'If you don't want the whole street to know what I mean stop your bawling.'

They glared at each other, their angers equal, Annie's depriving her face of all colour, Georgie's flooding his to a purple hue.

She said now, still low, 'You're not taking him on.'

She watched him gulp twice before he replied, 'That's up to me.'

'Oh no, it isn't. Let me tell you somethin', Georgie McCabe.' She took one step nearer to him and gripped the end of the bed rail. 'You bring him into the business and I walk out. Now think on what I'm saying. That fellow comes in, I go out.'

Again they were staring at each other in silence. Then taking his fist, he beat it against his head, and the sound made her wince. She watched him go round in a small circle, his body almost bent double, and when he stopped he was gripping his grease-streaked hair, and he cried at her, 'What the bloody hell's up with you, woman? Spit it out! Go on, spit it out!'

'All right, all right, I'll spit it out.' Her head was bobbing on her shoulders. 'That . . . that Partridge fellow. I told you what he suggested, I told you, and when I did you didn't fly off the handle, did you? One would have expected a fellow like you to go back there and wring his bloody neck but you didn't, did you? You didn't even put up a show of doing it.'

He was leaning towards her now, his hands flat on the middle of the bed. His lower jaw worked from one side to the other before he could get his words out, and then, the saliva spraying from his lips, he said, 'Do you know what you're saying? You're telling me I'm a bloody queer.'

She stared at him while the tears swelled her throat to bursting point. Yes, yes, that's what she was telling him, she was telling him he was a bloody queer, and she knew he wasn't. What was up with her? Was she mad? No, she wasn't mad because there was something fishy, something not quite right, and she said so.

'I'm . . . I'm not saying anything of the sort, but what I am saying is there's something not right with him. You know it yourself, you do, you do.'

She watched him droop his head slowly forward now and she cried at him, 'I'm right aren't I? I am, I know I am.'

As he twisted his body round and slumped on to the edge of the bed the sickness within her erupted, but it, too, stuck in her throat. She leant back against the dressing table, her two hands pressed tight into her breasts as if to check the heaving inside her.

Leaning forward now, Georgie put his elbows on his knees and dropping his joined hands between them he began to speak in a tone which seemed to be derived of all emotion. 'All right, he's queer,' he said, 'but I'm not . . . not that bloody way anyroad.' He cast an infuriated glance towards her. 'And what's more he's not, not really. He's the odd man out, an oddity if you like. God help him, he's neither one thing nor the other. I'll tell you something now.' He turned his head slowly and looked at her. 'I wish he was queer, real queer, for his own sake, then he'd have something. As it is he has nowt.'

He now rubbed his hand around his face, and there was a pause

101

before he went on, 'When we first met in the cookhouse I knew he was different in more ways than one 'cos we were bloody well poles apart. But you know somethin'? He was the only one up till then who hadn't treated me as a bloody numskull. I appeared as somebody real to him, so he said, an' I could understand what he meant after meetin' his folks. And that's another thing I'll press home to you, I was never taken in by them. Me brains might be scarce but what I lack in them I bloody well make up in cuteness. I can weigh people up. Oh aye, I can that. I'm like me mother there, and the more they take me for a bloody fool the more I learn about them. Oh, I took his folks' measure all right. I was good for a laugh, I suited their purpose. But at the same time they suited mine, an' . . . an' I was seein' a different way of life, a kind I'd never seen afore, a different way from our bloody hand-to-mouth kind. If you want to know something –' he turned his head and looked at her – 'I was grateful to him for noticin' me, just noticin' me. Do you understand that?' He thrust his head forward now. 'Not a bloody soul afore had given me credit for havin' a grain of gumption. I was Georgie, the easy-going gullible galoot, on a level with Barney Skillet and John Fowlcroft, the two blokes in our street who couldn't even keep their bloody noses clean. So there you have it. An' as for what you heard that stinking sod Partridge say, well whatever grounds he had for it I don't know, but it didn't apply to me, let me tell you that.'

He turned his head from her now and gazed down at his joined hands and said with unconscious humour, 'If you think I'm queer then I must have bloody well created a new species. Four bairns I've given you an' could do with it six times a day, that's not countin' overtime. An' then you think I'm queer. Bloody God!'

She rushed out of the room and across the landing and into the bathroom, and when she stood heaving over the sink he came and put his arm around her shoulders and held her head. Then he wiped her mouth, as he had done on the only other occasion when this subject had been mentioned between them.

The tears streaming from her eyes, she now gazed into his homely looking face, and there came to her in one great shock of surprise the fact that she loved him. She loved Georgie McCabe, the big loud-mouthed numskull, and that was the reason for her . . . carrying-on, as she had done. Whatever affection or love he had to give she wanted it directed towards her, and her alone.

Intuitively she knew it wasn't love he had for Arthur but compassion, but her intuition had warned her all along that compassion was a dangerous ingredient when combating love, and she was still afraid of it.

She said softly, 'Don't take him on, Georgie; please, please, don't take him on.'

He looked back into her eyes for a full minute before he answered. 'All right, lass. If that's how you feel about it, things'll stay as they are.'

When she fell against him and her crying mounted and her arms, for the first time that he could remember, held him tightly he stared over her shoulder while stroking her hair. A question slowly coming into his mind, he pressed her gently from him and looking into her streaming face, he asked her quietly, 'Tell me, Annie, do . . . do you like me? I mean . . . I mean more than just puttin' up with things . . . with me like?'

When she blinked and nodded her head twice he said, 'Honest?' and she muttered, 'Honest. Honest, Georgie.'

His lids blinked rapidly before he pulled her to him and held her tightly, and what he said thickly, and with a certain wonder, was, 'Bloody strange thing, life.'

Part Four

ALAN

1

Georgie McCabe had got on like a house on fire. Everyone said so; even Mary grudgingly admitted as much, but she never failed to qualify it with, 'Our Annie's been behind it all. If it hadn't been for her he would still be shovelling coal in the yards.'

Mollie, of course, gave Annie full credit for her son's success. She would continually say, 'Well, lass, didn't I say if anyone could make a roof with rotten straw you could?' And she would add, 'But the straw wasn't so bad after all, was it, lass?' to which Annie invariably answered, 'It was you that said it was rotten, not me, Mollie.'

In the thirteen years that had elapsed since they had moved to 17 Bewlar Terrace, everything, from an outsider's view, had seemingly gone McCabe's way; not only had he been able to buy the garage but also to extend it by acquiring two shops to the right of it and a house to the left, the latter having since been converted into an office downstairs and a mechanic's flat above.

The McCabe family itself had also expanded in a truly surprising fashion. Take the daughter, Tishy. At eighteen she was about to leave home and go to a teachers' training college. She was a clever one was Tishy, relations and friends alike said this. They said it to her face; but, as some said behind her back, she had to have something to make up for her looks; it was a shame that she should be so awfully plain and it showed up more so because Kathy was so bonny. It didn't matter about Kathy not having any brains, you didn't need brains when you looked like her. A great future was prophesied for Kathy by both relations and friends. She could win a beauty contest, she could be a model, she could even be picked for a film star.

Then there was Bill. Bill was the brightest of the lot. Bill had passed his 'O' levels with flying colours and even the masters at school prophesied that his 'A' levels were a foregone conclusion. In another year's time, Bill would be heading for the university. . . . And Rance. Rance was his father's right-hand man in the garage. He was a marvel with cars; that's why he had left school at fifteen. If he liked he could have done as well as Bill. At least this is what Annie persistently said, and in his hearing.

Yes, the McCabes had got on. And now they were thinking seriously of another move, to a bigger house in Westoe. Although Tishy and Bill would soon be at college, Rance showed no sign of leaving home. He had girls in plenty but their acquaintance didn't last long. And then there was Kathy to consider. Annie decided that Kathy would have a better chance of meeting someone nice if they moved into Westoe, and she was anxious that Kathy should meet and marry someone nice, because she knew that Kathy, like Rance, needed to be taken care of.

And with regard to Annie herself; both family and friends all agreed that no one would believe that she was the mother of two strapping young men and two fine girls. Why! they assured her, she didn't look twenty-eight, let alone thirty-eight. But when she looked in the glass Annie knew that such reckoning was fulsome praise. Nevertheless she also saw that she didn't look her age. Surveying her unlined skin, clear eyes and abundant healthy hair, she would sometimes nod at herself and say, 'Thirty-two, Annie, perhaps thirty-three. Long may it last.'

She was standing in front of the mirror now trying on a new dress. Up till three or four years ago she hadn't bothered very much with her own appearance, her time had been taken up with running the house, seeing to the children and trying to control Georgie's increasing intake of liquor, besides keeping the accounts of the garage. But since she had passed the latter business over to Rance she had more time to give to herself and, what was equally important, money to buy decent clothes. She went to Binns now for her things, and her last two outfits had select name-tags attached to them.

She was very pleased with what the mirror showed her at this moment, and then, as she often did, she thought of Tishy, and was attacked by a spasm of guilt. As at other times she saw now imposed on her reflection in the mirror the face of her daughter. How was it, she asked herself yet again, that the others were all so presentable, Kathy beautiful, Rance good-looking even in spite of his sullenness, and Bill, although not promising to be Rance's height, was at seventeen very attractive, his stocky body and blunt features giving him something which, she grudgingly admitted, was lacking in Rance; while Tishy, poor soul, had nothing to recommend her but her voice. It was this, her only asset, that also emphasized the difference between her and her brothers and sister still further, because even from a child she had spoken differently from them; the northern inflexion was less noticeable in her voice than in theirs, and she always pronounced her g's. That was why, Annie supposed, she had come out top in English. It was strange, she thought, that her daughter should speak so well when all her life she had listened to her father reiterating bloody and bugger.

But what, after all, was a good voice when you looked like she did. Her face so thin, her mouth still made up of two straight lines, and her nose still as snubbed as it had been when a baby. . . . And her eyes. Well, her eyes could have been bonny. . . . No, that wasn't the word, not bonny . . . attractive? No, not that either. Compelling? No. No, she could never find a word with which to describe Tishy's eyes. But she remembered once when Tishy first went to the high school her rushing in one night saying her teacher had given her a book of poems to keep because she had read her poetry so well. And there and then she had sat down at the kitchen table and started to read, just like that. She hadn't known she could read aloud; she knew she read a lot but she had never heard her read aloud. And in amazement she had listened to her saying:

> Woman much missed, how you call to me, call to me,
> Saying that now you are not as you were
> When you had changed from the one who was all to me,
> But as at first, when our day was fair.

Tishy had looked up at her then and her eyes were full of tears when she said, 'It's called "The Voice". It's by Hardy, Thomas Hardy.'

It was at that moment that she thought, her eyes are beautiful, but she had never seen them beautiful since for she had never read aloud again.

And of the four of them, Tishy was the most stubborn. Whatever she thought was right out it would come, and no arguing would change her opinion. The things she said at times startled her. None of the others talked as Tishy did, not even Bill; although she had heard her and Bill discussing things which were beyond her. Only last week they had been on about ghettoes and protest marches and the rights of the individual, as if everybody they knew was in prison. That discussion had nearly ended up in a row for Rance had turned on them, saying, 'For God's sake! shut your traps, the both of you, you make me sick.' It was then that Tishy had come out with one of her irritating wisecracks. 'One day,' she said, 'you'll take ill and they'll find you've got an abscess on the brain and when they open it up it'll be so full of ignorance it'll be a record.'

On this particular occasion she had caught hold of Rance's uplifted arm even while she knew that he wouldn't dare strike Tishy, knowing she would have turned on him like a wild cat.

Annie had always been puzzled about Tishy's attitude towards her elder brother. She could have understood it if her frustration had been turned on Kathy for, since she was a baby, Kathy's looks had emphasized her own plainness. But she had never been nasty to Kathy, and she had always had an open affection for Bill.

Over the past weeks Annie's feeling of guilt with regards to Tishy had increased for she found she was looking forward to the late summer when Tishy would leave home and go to the training college.

Thinking of her now she said to herself as she tried to get a back view of her dress in the mirror, 'I must get her well rigged out, smart things, good cuts; her figure isn't bad, but it could be better.'

At this moment the door opened and she started slightly as Georgie came into the room.

'I didn't hear you come in.'

He looked at her for a moment, then walked to the bedside chair and, dropping on to it, stretched his legs out before saying, 'You know I wish I had a penny for every time you've said that to me over the years. I've got feet like a corporation horse –' he wagged them from side to side – 'I can hear them clop-clopping even in me stocking feet. The trouble with you is your mind's always on some damn thing or other.'

She looked back at him through the mirror and asked, 'Do you like it?'

'I've seen it afore, haven't I?'

'No, you haven't seen it afore.'

'Aye, it's all right.'

'Oo . . . h!' she groaned. Then, her eyes becoming fixed on his through the mirror, she asked, 'What is it, something up?' And she had turned to him before he answered, 'Aye, there's something up; it's our Rance.'

'Our Rance?'

'Aye, our Rance.' He brought bitterness into the name. 'Mr Phillips came into the garage this mornin' and after I'd filled him up I just put it to him nicely. "Do you want to settle up your bill?" I said.

'"Bill?" he said. "Why, you're gettin' a bit sticky, Georgie, aren't you? You've never asked for me bill afore. I settled up last month; I never let it run more than two months." Was my bloody face red! I didn't know what to say. I said there must've been a mistake. I'd take a look at the books again, perhaps it hadn't been entered. But that didn't pacify him very much 'cos he left, sayin', "Then you want a new book-keeper, don't you?" And away he went, an' it's my bet he won't be back again.'

'Did he have a receipt?'

'Aye, he says it's home and he's goin' to bring it along. By the tone of his voice he'll push it under me bloody nose. . . . Well, I looked at the books again and there it was, nothing down. Three months owing for petrol and twenty-five quid for repairs.'

'What did our Rance say?' Her voice was quiet.

'I'll tell you what our Rance said.' He got to his feet now. 'Our Rance said he couldn't understand it. Aye, he said, he had given Mr Phillips a receipt and he had put the money in the till. Why he hadn't taken it off the book he just didn't know.'

'Well then he's explained it. Don't you believe him?'

'Look woman, I may not be so bloody hot on figures but if he had put that money in the till wouldn't the balance have been a bit on the heavy side at the end of the week? Two months' petrol and twenty-five quid for repairs would have tilted the weekly check-up wouldn't it?'

'But you don't always check up at the end of the week.'

'No, I don't, I leave it to him most times, but once or twice lately I've had a check up on me own, 'cos now I'm goin' to tell you somethin', Annie. This isn't the first time I've suspected him.'

'What! Our Rance? Don't be silly. Don't be stupid, man. Our Rance! It would be like cutting off his nose to spite his . . .'

'Oh no, it wouldn't; he doesn't happen to own the bloody garage, does he?' His words were slow as were the movements of his head. 'And another thing I'm gona tell you, somethin' that you don't know, somethin' that I should've told you a while back but knowin' how you worry your guts out over one and another of them, him in particular, I kept it to meself. . . . He's at the gamblin' lark.'

'Our Rance!'

'Oh, bloody St Patrick! stop repeatin' our Rance. Aye, our Rance. Get it out of your head, lass. He was never meant for the priesthood or the monastery. He's got faults, and as I see them, bloody big 'un's. Of course, for you the sun shines out of him. You've wiped his backside for years.' He was walking up and down the room now. 'The others could go to hell, me included, as long as . . . our Rance was all right.'

'That's not fair, that's not fair. I've treated them all alike.'

'Like hell you have! I could flay the living daylights out of Bill, but let me lift me hand to Rance and all hell was let loose. Well now, face up to it, your wonderful Rance has been fiddlin' me books, our books, so he could sit in at nights at Connelly's. And what's more he's got in with the right bunch, Pete Cullender and Maurice Boulder an' that lot.'

'Pete Cullender!' Her voice was a mere whisper now. 'You mean the Cullender that was in the papers last week?'

'Aye, the one and the same Cullender who was in the papers last week.'

'He wouldn't, not our Rance.'

'Aw, for God's sake!' He was bawling now, and she hissed at him, 'Stop it! Keep your voice down; do you want the whole street to know?'

His voice lower, he leant towards her, saying, 'It won't be only the street that'll know, it'll be the town if he keeps this up. You'll have to speak to him. He won't listen to me, I'm only his bloody father; but you tell him from me that his bloody father knows what he's up to, an' let me find out one more thing and he's out. Do you hear? I mean that, he's out on his arse. Well now –' he tugged both sides of his coat together, pulled in his lips and ended, 'Having said that I'll have some tea,' and he walked out of the room leaving her standing staring at the door.

Rance. Rance. Rance fiddling the books. She couldn't believe it. Well, if she didn't believe it Georgie must be making it up. But she knew her husband well enough to know that it would be impossible for him to make up something like that against his own son. Yet the relationship between him and Rance had always been strained. Up till Rance was fifteen he had lathered him for his misdemeanours and she had to admit he had been justified. The last lathering he had given him was after the school-master had asked to see them both and told them that Rance was running a small gang of shop-lifters who operated on a Saturday morning between the market and King Street. They hadn't been able to believe their ears, at least she hadn't. Thankfully the matter hadn't got into the court, for which clemency they had to thank the fact that one of Rance's henchmen was the son of a man of some influence in the town. On that occasion she had thought that Georgie would kill him, and perhaps he might have if she hadn't thrust herself between them and taken some of the blows from the leather belt which were meant for the boy.

The idea of Rance going into the garage was not only to provide him with training towards a career but in order that Georgie could keep an eye on him. And apparently he had up till now, for there had been but one incident over the past few years, and this she had never got to the bottom of. She hadn't told Georgie of it, and when she had confronted Rance and demanded why a man called Bilby should come to the door and tell her that if he didn't keep away from his daughter he would do for him, he had answered, 'Aw, my God! would you believe it. It's her he should be doing for, not me; she's still at school an' I can't walk down the street for her.'

'Where does she live?'

'Sunderland Road.'

'But what do you have to do along Sunderland Road, you don't go that way?'

'I met her when I went to meet Alec comin' from the tech. He knew her, he said she was bloke barmy.'

'But why should her father pick on you?'

'Don't ask me. God! the things folk get up to, they would hang you!'

His indignation with regard to this incident had reassured her he wasn't in the wrong, but all the indignation he might show with regard to the present affair wouldn't prove his innocence to her for she had only to think back over the last few months. The fine gold wrist-watch he suddenly sported. Came by it second-hand, dirt cheap, he had said. The new suit that she knew now had never come from Burton's. And then there were the odds and ends in his room: that real leather brief-case, not plastic like Bill's and Tishy's; those two silk shirts that he had supposedly bought at a sale in Newcastle, again dirt cheap.

The old feeling of sickness began to churn in her stomach. She'd have to speak to him; more than speak to him, go for him, and she hated going for him. He had only to look at her in that particular way with that look he kept only for her, that look that always seemed to cry out for her love, and she was undone.

When she had discovered that she had a deeper feeling than mere toleration or affection for Georgie, it hadn't detracted one iota from the feeling she had for her elder son; in fact her feelings towards the boy had seemed to deepen as if to prove to him that her love for his father was in no way derived from that which she had for him.

'Mam.' The door suddenly opened and Kathy put her head round. 'Can I come in?'

'Yes, yes, dear.'

'What's the matter with dad? Somebody's going to get it if I can read the signs. He's got his billy-goat look on. You two been at it?'

'No, we haven't been at it, miss. What do you want?'

'Oh, nothing, nothing.' Kathy shook her pretty head and her pony tail swung from side to side. 'I was just going to give you details of my latest suitor, that's all, that's all.'

In spite of herself and the way she was feeling, Annie laughed and said, 'What! another one?'

'Oh, this one's different. This one will suit the house in Westoe. Oh yes, yes.' She now strutted up and down the bedroom while Annie took a comb from the dressing table and drew it through her hair.

'What's his name?'

'Mr Percy Rinkton.'

'Never-'eard-of-'im.'

'Well, from what I know you certainly will soon; he wants to come and see you . . . or dad.'

Annie swung round and they looked at each other, and Kathy made a deep obeisance with her head. 'Yes, yes, he's that kind of a fellow, everything aboveboard.'

'Well, that's a change.'

'What do you mean, that's a change? All my boys are above board.'

'You want your ears boxed.'

'I want a new dress.'

'You've got some hope; you've had three already this year.'

'I'm a growing girl.'

Looking through the mirror at her daughter's quickly developing bust, Annie nodded and said, 'And how!' And at this they both laughed. Then Annie, her tone serious, asked, 'Well, what about this fellow?'

'Ever heard of Doctor Rinkton?'

'Yes, yes, I've heard of Doctor Rinkton.'

'Well Percy Rinkton is Doctor Rinkton's son. No kiddin'. No kiddin', Mam.'

'We're flying high all of a sudden. How old is he?'

'Twenty-odd. What do you think of that, a man.'

Annie turned fully round now and looked at Kathy and said seriously, 'Yes, a man; and you want to be careful. Have you been seeing him?'

'I've spoken to him –' she pursed up her mouth and screwed up her eyes and counted on her fingers – 'one, two, three, four times. I first saw him at a dance, St Patrick's do. But be prepared to receive the first shock, he's not a Catholic. The second time I met him was when I got off a bus. I lurched into him. The third time was in Phillips's bookshop, you know, at the bottom of Fowler Street. He was buying books; he looks a bit bookie. And the fourth time was this very day. He was waiting for me coming out of school. Stopped me at the corner and very precisely asked when I was going to leave school, and I told him as soon as ever I possibly could 'cos I hated it.'

'Oh, Kathy, you didn't!'

'Honest I did. I did. And anyway, as I've told you before, it's no use keeping me there. I haven't any brains; I'm not like Tishy, I'm all bumf.' She gave a lift to her bust, and again they were laughing, leaning against each other now. But after a moment Annie chastised her, saying, 'You'll get your ears boxed one of these times, me girl, for the things you say. But go on.'

'Well then, he asked how old I was, and I told him knocking sixteen. "When?" he said – he's a stickler for details. "Next month," I said. Then you know what? He said would I ask my parents if he could come round and see them.'

They were standing apart now and Kathy, laughing at the expression on Annie's face, said, 'No kidding, he did. That's what he said, could he come round and see you? And I said, what for? and he said, well, he would like to get everything straightforward.'

'What did he mean, straightforward?'

'That's what I would like to know.'

'What did you say then?'

'I said ours was an open house, people were going in and out all the time, it was like jail, and I was sure you'd make him very welcome.'

'You didn't!'

'I did, Mam.' She pursed her lips again. Then he asked if tomorrow afternoon would be convenient, and I said, yes, tomorrow afternoon would be quite convenient, being Saturday and you having nothing to do and being very bored with life....'

Annie's hand came out quickly and slapped the side of her daughter's face, but gently.

'Well, what could I say? You have to meet him, he's a scream. He's ... he's ... well, I can't tell you what he's like, he's so, what's the word? aboveboard. Yes, that's the word, aboveboard. Aw my goodness!' She closed her eyes and shook her head widely from side to side now. 'And how aboveboard! He tickles me to death, Mam.'

'I don't know about being tickled to death –' Annie raised her eyebrows – 'it's a new approach, I'll say that. Does ... does he look very old-fashioned?'

'Old-fashioned! No. He's just precise, like his name, Percy. Awful name isn't it, Percy?'

As Annie was about to speak she heard Georgie's voice shouting from below, and she said, 'We'll talk about this later, there's your dad bawling for his tea.'

'Mam.' Kathy pulled Annie to a halt as they were going out on to the landing and whispered, 'I'll die the day I see me dad and Mr Percy Rinkton together. Aw, that'll be something.'

Annie now pushed her daughter none too gently towards the stairs, saying, 'And you've got something coming to you, you young monkey.' Then she added, 'I'll deal with Mr Percy Rinkton.'

They were both laughing as they went down the stairs, but before Annie reached the bottom she knew that she would have someone else to deal with before she met her youngest daughter's latest suitor, and in that confrontation there would be no laughter or amusement.

Georgie had gone out for his usual evening drink, and so, apart from Tishy who was upstairs studying, she was alone when Rance came in. Before he had taken off his coat in the hall she tackled him. 'Come on in here a minute,' she said, going towards the sitting-room.

He didn't immediately follow her but, straightening his tie, said, 'What is it? I want me tea, I'm going out.'

'You'll get your tea in a minute; I've got to have a word with you.'

He followed her into the room and closed the door but he didn't look at her as he walked towards the empty fireplace, and there, taking a cigarette packet from his pocket, he extracted a cigarette and lit it.

She let him do this and take the first whiff before she said, 'What's this I'm hearing from your dad?'

'Well, what is it you're hearin' from me dad?' He had his back to her, looking down on the ornamental glass screen that fronted the empty grate.

'Now, Rance, I want no hanky-panky.'

Glancing at her over his shoulder he said, 'Who's giving you hanky-panky? I don't know what you're on about.'

'You know fine well. What's this about Mr Phillips's bill that you forgot to enter up?'

'Well, that's all about it, I forgot to enter it up.'

'Twenty-five pounds for repairs and two months' petrol, that surplus would have stuck out like a sore thumb any week. We don't deal in thousands you know.'

'Look, Mam –' he turned, took a step towards her and held out his hands as if in supplication as he said, 'He checks up the till every night, doesn't he? He goes over the books every Friday. . . .'

'You know fine well he makes pretence of going over them, he hasn't got a head for figures; you've always known it.'

'Hasn't a head for figures? By lad! you try doing him out of sixpence and he'll let you know whether he's got a head for figures or not.'

'It's different when it's in writing.'

'Look, Mam –' his voice was soft, appealing – 'are you accusing me of pinching the money?'

117

She stared into his eyes and as always, like some young lass in love, she felt herself assailed by a weakness which now prompted her to say, 'No, of course I'm not.' But one of the level-headed chambers of her mind opened its door and out of it came the answer to his question. 'You're gambling,' she said.

His voice still quiet, he replied, 'All right, I'm gambling. And I've been winning. I've got proof of it upstairs, the things I've been buying. You've noticed them surely.'

'You said you had got them on the cheap.'

'Well, I had an' all, and that's gambling. Anyway, what's wrong with sittin' at the tables now and again? Our auspicious neighbour three doors down, she's there every bloomin' night.'

'Well, you must be an' all to see her.'

Of a sudden his quiet demeanour vanished and his teeth ground against each other for a moment before he burst out, 'What the hell! Christ Almighty! I'm not a boy any more, Mam, I'm a man. I'm bloody well doing a man's work and more.'

'Stop that swearing and cursing.'

'Oh my God!' The words came out on a rising, mirthless laugh. 'That's the funniest thing I've heard in years, you tellin' me to stop cussing, when you've lived it and breathed it for how many years? Twenty-one. Twenty-one years you've been married, and your husband's got the nickname of "Bloody McCabe" and you chastise me for swearing. God! that's a laugh. Look –' he bent towards her – 'don't you see the funny side of it?'

'Don't change the subject.' He was an expert in this line. She would start on one thing and before she knew where she was he was arguing about something entirely different. 'Stick to the point, Rance . . . for once,' she added; 'and the point isn't swearing, it's . . . it's stealing, thieving, and from your own. And there's your dad. Be he what he may he wouldn't do anybody out of a farthing. . . .'

'Aw, Dad! Dad wouldn't do anybody out of a farthing.' He was mimicking her now. 'Dad's a bloody saint and that's swearing to it again. Underneath that rough exterior of his an' his big ignorant mouth he's a bloody saint. . . .'

'Rance!'

'Never mind Rancing me, Mam, I'm gettin' tired of hearing about Dad's virtues. Hardly a week goes by but it's: "He has his drawbacks, he's rough and ready, but . . . but underneath. . . ." Well, let me tell you something. In my opinion you must have

118

been bloody well blind all these years not to see you've been married to a gormless nowt.'

Her hand was raised to come down on him when he barked at her, 'Don't! Don't do it, Mam, because if you do I'll walk out, and that's the last you'll see of me.'

As her hand slowly dropped to her side and she felt the blood draining, not only from her face but seemingly from her whole body, he said, his tone now as different again from what it had been a moment previously, for it was now like that of a young boy, 'I meant it, Mam, I meant it. I would, I would I tell you, I'd leave you. . . .'

The more he protested the more she knew that it was an empty threat. Rance would never leave her unless it was for a woman, and the woman would, unknowingly, have to be taking her place.

When her head bowed and the tears ran down her face his arms came about her and he held her, muttering all the while, 'Oh, Mam! Mam, give over. Come on, give over. Look, I swear to you I didn't take that money. Look at me.'

She looked at him through her misted eyes and she muttered, 'You're speaking the truth?'

'Honest. Honest to God.'

She said now, 'What about the lad, young Jimmy, could he have got at the till?'

He turned his head to the side as if thinking; then, looking at her again, said, 'Not that I know of. Look, Mam, as I see it the money was in the till and Dad picked it up on the Friday night. You know what he is, he stuffs everything into his pockets. He's got no method.'

'But . . . but he brings the money straight back home.'

'Not always. Remember that night he didn't get back here till half past ten and then he was paralytic?'

Yes, she remembered that night about a month ago. He had met two fellows he had known at Madley and had taken them to the club, and the three of them had staggered back here at closing time. She drew herself slowly from his arms and as she wiped her face she said to him, 'I'll put up with anything, Rance, as long as I know you don't fiddle, especially your own. You know what I mean?'

He put out his hand and touched her cheek. The touch was a caress such as none of the others ever gave her. Still, she never blamed them for that, because there wasn't the same feeling between them and herself. Although she loved each one of them the feeling she had for her eldest was akin to passion. The colour came flooding back into her face at the thought.

He was smiling at her now. 'Now can I have me tea?'

'It's all ready,' she said quietly turning from him. When she went to walk out of the room he put his arm around her shoulders and when in the hall he looked up and saw Tishy coming down the stairs he deliberately hugged her to him before taking his arm away.

At the sight of her daughter Annie lowered her head and hurried into the kitchen, but Rance didn't follow her; instead, he made for the stairs, saying, 'I'll have me wash first.'

He did not wait for Tishy to descend the last two stairs but pushed past her, and in the passing she said quietly, 'Dear Rance,' and he said in the same ironic tone, 'Dear Tishy,' and the exchange was like blows delivered straight into the other's face.

2

Tea on a Saturday was a haphazard event. It was usually a busy day at the garage and Rance might not get in before six, and Georgie nearer seven. If the school was playing football or cricket at home, depending on the season, Bill would come in demanding a meal any time between six and eight o'clock – the refreshments he'd had at the school tea never counted. When he was playing away she never knew what time to expect him back, but as she remarked, she always knew when he was in because he banged every door he came through.

Tishy usually attended some project or other on a Saturday afternoon. If not, she would take the train to Newcastle and wander around the old quarters, or spend hours in the museum, or the library; and she always took these trips alone.

The procedure for Kathy on a Saturday evening was to take the time between five and seven to get ready for the weekly dance, to which she never went unattended.

But on this particular Saturday the pattern had altered slightly. Kathy had been invited to spend the week-end with her best friend, Van Brignell, and an hour ago she had left the house to make the two-mile journey to Harton village with enough clothes in her case to last her a week. And Tishy, showing the first signs of a summer cold which, from experience, she knew would make her snub nose scarlet and keep her eyes watering for a week if not taken in time, had decided to forgo her Saturday jaunting and to nurse her cold while getting on with a bit more swotting.

So Annie, having the house practically to herself, decided she would wash her hair. She went to the hairdresser's only when she needed a trim for she had what she called good-tempered hair; it had a deep natural wave in it, and fell into place immediately after washing. Once her hair was dry she'd do her face and get into her new dress and be ready if Georgie managed to get home early; then perhaps they would go to the club for an hour. She felt she wanted to be taken out of herself. That scene with Rance last night had upset her, and then, later in bed, she hadn't been able to convince Georgie that Rance hadn't touched a penny of the money. His last words to her before he went to sleep were, 'You know summat; you still take me for a bloody numskull,' and she had been more disturbed than she cared to admit when he had turned his back on her. That had never happened before; she was always the one who did the turning away. . . .

She did not wash her hair in the bathroom but in the kitchen sink, because it was larger and if she splashed a bit it didn't matter. She hated to see the bathroom messed up.

She had just wound a towel around her head and was about to switch on her electric hair-drier when the front door bell rang.

'Oh no!' She said the words aloud. Who could this be on a Saturday afternoon? Everybody was accounted for; there was only Tishy in and nobody ever called for Tishy; and it wouldn't be anybody selling on a Saturday afternoon. Strange, but they didn't come round selling on a Saturday afternoon; the morning yes, but never in the afternoon. She had often thought that was strange. It was no use shouting for Tishy to go and answer the door because she hardly showed her face to the family when she had a cold on her. Oh Lord! She glanced in the mirror, doubled the lapels of her blue woollen housecoat further across her chest, tightened the belt, then went out of the kitchen, across the hall and opened the door.

'Oh.' She gaped at the strange man standing before her. He was tall, taller than any of her men, six-foot and more he must be, and he was big made with it. His face was long and his lips full and his eyes a dark brown, a very dark brown. Well! well! Kathy had hit it this time. Mr Percy Rinkton was indeed a man, every inch of him. This fellow was certainly nothing to laugh or joke about; if she didn't do any worse than this she'd be all right; in fact, she couldn't see her doing any better, at least where looks were concerned. His face wasn't exactly handsome but it had something about it that, in her estimation, was better than good looks. He had taken off his hat and he was staring at her, his mouth slowly widening into a smile, when she said, 'You're Mr Rinkton, aren't you? Oh, I am sorry.' She put her hand on to her head and patted the towel. 'Fancy seeing me like this! But they're all out, and I was washing my hair.' Again she patted the towel. 'Kathy's gone to stay with a friend; she'll be ever so sorry she missed you. . . .' That monkey. She hadn't believed her. Wait till she saw her. And her to go off for the week-end like that knowing this fellow meant what he had said.

'I . . . I think there's been a slight mistake.'

His voice was nice an' all, quite posh, and there wasn't the slightest trace of a northern accent in it. 'What's that you said?'

'I said I think there's been a slight mistake, I am not Mr . . . who did you say, Rinkton?'

'You're not?'

'No, I'm not.' His smile had widened even further. He looked very amused and she became slightly embarrassed. 'You're not Mr Rinkton?'

'No, as I said I'm not Mr Rinkton. But we've met before, you do know me.'

'We've met before?' She screwed up her face at him. 'Never, never.' Now she was shaking her head as she thought, He's a con man; that's what he is.

'But yes, yes. I might have changed somewhat, but you, you haven't at all. I would have known you anywhere in spite of your turban.' He nodded towards her head, and again her hands went up to the towel. Her face was straight as she said, 'Who are you then?'

'My name is Alan Partridge; we last met when I was five years old.'

She had to snap her lower jaw up to prevent it dropping any further, and then her mouth opened wide again before she brought out the name, 'Alan . . . little . . .?' She closed her eyes and shook her head, then said, 'No longer little. Oh please, please, come in. Come in.' She stood aside and let him enter the hall. 'Well! well! who would believe it. But . . . but you didn't recognize me, you can't.'

'Oh yes I did, and I do.'

'Look. Look.' Her hands were moving at random. Then closing her eyes tight again, she said, 'Oh, give me your hat and coat and let me get this thing off my head and then we can talk. My! my! is this a surprise! I . . . I thought you were the young man I was expecting to come and ask after my daughter, my youngest daughter. He was doing it in the old-fashioned way, he

123

was coming to ask if he could take her out. Look, would you mind coming in here and waiting a moment?'

'Not at all.'

He walked past her into the sitting-room, and she darted to the side of the fireplace and switched on the electric fire; then patting the cushions into place on the couch she said, 'Do . . . do make yourself at home. Give me five minutes, will you, five minutes?'

His smile was wide again. 'Ten if you wish it, fifteen.'

'Look, my eldest daughter's upstairs; I'll bring her down and she can talk to you.'

'No, please, don't bother. Go on, dry your hair; I'll sit here and wait, very, very patiently.'

They looked at each other, then both burst out laughing, and she turned from him and ran into the kitchen and, picking up the hair-drier, she flew up the stairs and plugged it into the bedroom socket.

Her hair was only partly dry when she switched off the machine. Quickly getting into her dress she applied a dab of powder to her nose and a lipstick to her lips. Then as she went to leave the room she stopped, drew in a deep breath and asked herself what all the excitement was about. And she gave herself the answer. He had remembered her. After all these years he had remembered her. As Kathy would say, it was enough to boost anybody's ego. What was your ego anyway? Oh polony! When her mind got going it asked the daftest questions. Get downstairs, she said to herself.

When she passed Tishy's door she paused and, an idea flashing into her mind, she thought, Oh that would be wonderful. But it would be too good to be true. And with that cold on her there wasn't a hope.

Get downstairs, she said to herself again.

When she entered the room he rose to his feet. Wasn't that nice. Nobody had ever done that for her since she had met Arthur Bailey. She had forgotten for a moment that he was connected with Arthur Bailey; he and Mona seemed to have dropped entirely out of existence. She had seen Mona only once since the day she confided in her, and that was when she had come to bury her mother. They had exchanged a few words at the graveside, nothing more, they had been like strangers. She had been very upset about it.

After saying, 'Do sit down . . . would you like a cup of tea?' he answered, 'Yes, but not yet. You come and sit down.'

124

She sat down on the edge of the settee and asked, 'How's your uncle, your Uncle Arthur?'

'Oh, he was very well the last time I saw him.'

'Have you come this way on holiday, though –' she shook her head and laughed now – 'I don't know why you would pick Durham after Herefordshire.'

'Well, I have picked Durham, at least Northumberland, but not for a holiday. I've . . . I've just been appointed to a post in Newcastle University.'

'No!'

'Yes.' He gave a chuckling laugh. 'I was on the short list and, three parts of the selection committee being out of their tiny minds, they chose me. I still haven't got over it yet.'

She knew that he was talking himself down and she shook her head as she said, 'What's . . . what's your subject?'

'Mathematics.'

'Oh! mathematics. Bill, that's my second son, he has nightmares about maths. He's pretty good at most other things but maths have always bedevilled him. He's going to be a teacher too.'

'He is?'

'And my daughter, Tishy – short for Anastasia – she's going to be one an' all.'

'Oh.'

'She's clever, Tishy is, cleverer than Bill.'

'How many family have you?'

'Four. Rance is the eldest, he's twenty; Tishy eighteen, Bill seventeen and Kathy just on sixteen. That's the one I thought you were after; the fellows are never off the door.' She put her head back and laughed.

'She sounds attractive.'

'Oh, she's that all right, and very well aware of it. But tell me, how did you know where to find us?'

'Oh, Uncle Arthur gave me your address. He said you might still be here. He said if I found you I had to give you his regards and also remember him to your husband.'

A chill passed over her causing her to shiver slightly.

'How's your Aunt Mona these days?' She felt she should have asked this before, but she was still peeved with Mona. She felt she had been snubbed by her, yet in her heart she knew the real reason for Mona's silence. Mona knew it was she who had squashed Arthur's proposal to join Georgie in the garage.

'Oh.' He uncrossed his legs, then recrossed them again before he said, 'I . . . I don't know, I haven't seen her these last five years. They . . . they separated you know.'

'Separated? . . . No, no, I didn't know. Where is she?'

'In London as far as I can gather.'

'I'm . . . I'm sorry. And . . . and your uncle?'

'Oh, he's still in the same place. It's rather a lonely life for him but he seems to prefer it that way.'

'Yes, yes.' She nodded her head; then on a lighter note, she said, 'And your mother? I remember your mother very well.'

She remarried about a year ago and is now living in America.'

'Really! and you're all on your own?'

'Yes, and I like it that way. I had to practically knock her unconscious before she would go. She still looked upon me as thirteen and not twenty-three.'

'But I suppose you miss her?'

'Oh yes, I miss her. Not so much now; I've had a year to get used to it. My life's very full, and besides I was away from home so much. I was at Oxford for four years.'

'Oxford!' There was a slight note of awe in her voice, then she added, 'Bill hopes that he might get into a university . . . it must be wonderful to go to a university.'

'Oh, I don't know. It's just like school, only you have a longer leash on you.'

When a silence fell between them and he sat staring at her, a half-smile bringing one side of his mouth upwards as if he were amused at something, she blinked and said, 'I can't get over it. Fancy you remembering me from all those years ago.'

'Well, I was five, and they tell me a very precocious five.'

'I can't remember anything from I was five, hardly from I was seven.'

'I can remember the conversation we had regarding an unmentionable place.'

'An unmentionable place?' She screwed up her face at him.

'The jig.'

'Aw, yes.' She was nodding and laughing now. 'The jig. Yes, yes, I remember.'

'And so did my mother. She said I repeated that conversation daily until I was nearly eight. She was for murdering me. And then I suddenly stopped and never mentioned it again until I was almost fourteen; then out of the blue it came into my mind and when I said to my mother "Do you remember how I used to go on about the jig?" she put her hands over her ears and said, "Oh, don't start that again." So you see what an impression you made upon me.'

'You mean the jig did.'

'No, you. But, you know, I still call it the jig.'

Again there was silence, and again he was staring at her. And then he burst out, 'You know, it's amazing, I can't get over it, I mean how little you've changed. It's as if I were five last week; you're so like the memory I've retained of you.'

'But . . . but it's such a long time ago, over eighteen years.'

'Yes, it is.' His face unsmiling now, he nodded; then after a moment he said, 'I suppose what helped to imprint you in my mind was that I remember that Christmas as one big holy row. My mother went for my father, my grandmother went for my father, then she went for my Uncle Arthur; if I remember rightly practically no one was speaking to one another on Christmas Day, and they practically threw my presents at me, so the only happy memory that remained of that particular Christmas was of a lady who ran with me through the woods and laughed with me and discussed – jigs. And I must tell you this, a lady who I thought had come from a strange land.'

Annie put her hand over her mouth as she laughed. 'My Geordie accent.'

'No.' He lifted his finger and wagged it at her now. 'I won't say it was your Geordie accent, not after listening to some of the townspeople this past week or so. But seriously –' he shook his head – 'I can't understand a word some of them say.'

She now cocked her chin upwards as she said, 'Well, all I can say is your education has been sadly neglected in one quarter, anyway.' Getting to her feet, she added, 'I'm going to make you a cup of tea whether you want it or not. When did you last eat?'

'Oh, at lunch-time, I had a good meal.'

'And you're not hungry?'

He smiled at her again with his lips closed, and she said, 'That's my answer. Would you like to come into the kitchen? We can talk while I get you something.'

As they went towards the kitchen the door opened and Tishy came out, and they all stopped for a moment and looked at each other.

'Oh, Tishy, there you are. You won't know who this is. Someone

I knew a long time ago, Mr Alan Partridge. Alan, this is my eldest daughter, Tishy.' Oh – Annie groaned to herself – didn't she look a sight; her little nose was like a red blob.

Alan smiled at the tall young girl standing before him, holding her handkerchief to her nose. She had an unusual face, he thought, and didn't look a bit like her mother. He held out his hand. 'How are you?'

'It's pretty evident,' she said, 'isn't it?' and Annie thought helplessly, That's Tishy all over, straight to the point.

Alan laughed and said, 'A double whisky, a whole lemon and a spoonful of ginger in boiling water. You'll be a new man – woman, in the morning.'

'I'm going to make a cup of tea –' Annie looked at Tishy – 'and something to eat. Come on back and talk; you're bound to have something in common as Alan is going to teach at the university, Newcastle. What do you think of that?'

Tishy turned a sidewards glance towards the tall man and after a moment she said, 'You are?'

'Yes.' Alan moved his head towards her. 'And I hear you're going in for the same racket.'

'Well –' Tishy was walking back into the kitchen – 'nothing so grand as the university; I'm going to a teachers' training college.'

'They informed me politely at headquarters that I would have been better equipped for the job if I'd had a year's training, too.'

'They did?'

'Yes.'

'Well –' Tishy sat herself down and crossed her legs – 'if I could trade, I know which one I'd take. What's your speciality?'

'Maths.'

'Oh! maths. . . .'

'Don't say it like that, Tishy, you are very good at maths.'

Tishy turned and looked at Annie, and in a patient tone she said, 'There are maths, Mam, and maths. What I was very good at was merely maths.'

As Annie watched her smile at Alan, her cold apparently forgotten for the moment, wild ideas again began darting through her mind. She drew in a quick breath and said, 'Well, you two can get on discussing maths – and maths, I have something better to do. Maths comes very low down the list of my subjects, food is my speciality.' She nodded towards Alan, and he, with a broad smile, said, 'Well, I'll attend your classes any day; food, too, is my speciality – the eating of it anyway.'

During the next twenty minutes Annie busied herself about the kitchen, but kept her ears cocked to the conversation which moved from maths to the present student attitude, then on to teachers' salaries, and from there to the writings of Tolkien – she had never heard of him – and from time to time she wanted to stop and look at them, particularly at Tishy. She had never heard Tishy talk like this. Then, of course, she didn't know how Tishy talked outside the house, she had never met any of her friends. Tishy didn't seem to make friends, she was a loner, that was the trouble. Yet here she was talking twenty to the dozen.

Now they were on about old books and the various places you could get them in Newcastle. Tishy was mentioning particular shops by name, and recommending them to him. Well, well! she was a deep one. But then, there was nothing deep about knowing the names of second-hand bookshops. But it wasn't that she was really meaning. For the first time she was seeing her daughter in a new light. She glanced again at her face. It hadn't altered . . . yet it had. Her mouth, when she was talking like this in an animated way, didn't look so thin; and there was a light in her eyes. Nothing could ever take away her plainness, but definitely her daughter had another face if she cared to show it. And now she was showing it as she said excitedly, 'I came across an old book the other day, not in a bookshop, in a junk shop. It was lying among the tuppennies, it's called *Elbert Hubbard's Scrap Book*. It's marvellous, the things it's got in it. Look, I'll get it.'

Annie stopped to watch her rush out of the room, then she looked at Alan. Alan was already looking at her and he said, 'You've got a highly intelligent daughter. How old did you say she is?'

'Eighteen.'

He moved his head to one side, then said, 'Well, if she's a sample of your family I'll have to keep up to the mark with the rest, won't I?'

'Oh, they're not all like Tishy. Well, I mean, Rance – he's the eldest – he had no head for learning, not Tishy's type of learning. Bill has; he's a year younger than Tishy. And Kathy, oh Kathy's like me, all tongue and no brains.'

'Nonsense!' It was like a schoolmaster speaking, and she laughed out aloud, but she immediately turned to her work again as Tishy came into the room holding a faded red-covered book in her hand.

Thrusting the book on the table before Alan, Tishy opened it and, showing the portrait of a dark-haired, intense and rather handsome-looking man, said, 'That's him, Elbert Hubbard. Isn't he nice?'

'Yes, very handsome. And an American I'd say.' Then he added, 'Oh, 'tisn't so old, it was printed in 1923.'

'Well, it's over forty years ago.'

Alan looked at her for a moment and laughed gently, then said, 'Yes, I suppose that's a long time.'

'Look,' she said, 'it's got everything, articles, quotations, the lot. Look at that one: "The religions of the world are the ejaculations of a few imaginative men." Emerson. What do you think of that?'

'Very good. But you must remember that Emerson himself was an imaginative man.'

Again Annie stopped and looked towards her daughter. Tishy was a Catholic, a firm Catholic because she never missed Mass, and there she was talking about the religions of the world as if she believed in them. She watched them turn the pages, then listened to Alan saying, 'Oh now, I'm with Darwin and what he says here: "If I had my life to live over again I would have made a rule to read some poetry and listen to some music at least once a week; for perhaps the parts of my brain now atrophied would thus have been kept active through use. The loss of these tastes is a loss of happiness and may possibly be injurious to the intellect, and more probably to the moral character, by enfeebling the emotional part of our nature."'

'Do you like music?' Alan was looking at Tishy, and she answered after a moment's pause, 'Yes, and no. I don't really know what I like yet, I haven't had time to sort it out. One thing I do know, I don't like heavy classical.'

'No?'

'No. And another thing I do know is I don't like pop. Oh, I loathe pop.'

Tishy now turned and glanced at Annie, and Annie stopped mixing a batter and, pursing her lips while she assumed an indignant pose, looked from Tishy to Alan and said, 'She's getting at me. That's who she's getting at; she's getting at me because I like pop. Well, light stuff you know, like they have on in the mornings.'

'Like they have on in the mornings,' repeated Tishy scornfully. Yet she smiled as she spoke. Then looking at Alan again she made, at least to Annie's knowledge, the first joke in her life for she said, 'You know she's not my mother, she's not the mother of any of us. I mean, how could she be, just look at her!' She thumbed over her shoulder and in sotto voce ended, 'She's gaga, but she might grow out of it when she's turned twenty.'

As Annie compressed her lips and knocked her floured hands against one another as if getting ready to do battle, Alan leant his head towards Tishy and said, 'I know what you mean, she was just like that when I was five years old. And her conversation, oh dear, dear! Do you know what she used to talk about? – jigs.'

As Annie said 'Oh! Alan,' it seemed to her that he had been in that kitchen all his life, at least since he was five, for he already seemed a part of it.

It was at this moment that she heard a key turn in the front door. Wiping her hands quickly on a towel, she went out of the kitchen and saw Rance making for the stairs, and she looked towards him, saying, 'Why, I didn't hear the car. What's the matter, you're all grease? Why didn't you come the back way? Come in the kitchen and get washed, and I want you to meet somebody.'

'Is there any hot water?'

'Plenty.'

'Well, I'm going to have a bath.'

'But you had a bath this morning. Where've you been? I thought you were going to the match. Your dad said Jimmy was staying on this afternoon with him.'

'I . . . I did go to the match.' He was partly up the stairs now. 'But I had a job to do after for a friend. I'm going to have a bath.'

She stared at him for a moment before she returned to the kitchen. There, Tishy was saying, 'I like this bit because I know heaps of people like this. Listen: "There are some faults in conversation, which none are so subject to as men of wit, nor even so much as when they are with each other. If they have opened their mouths without endeavouring to say a witty thing, they think it is so many words lost; it is a torment to the hearers, as much as to themselves, to see them upon the rack of invention and in perpetual restraint, with so little success. They must do something extraordinary in order to equip themselves and answer their character else the standers-by may be disappointed and be apt to think them only like the rest of mortals."

'Don't you know people like that? They've got to be clever or bust. I've taken an oath that when I get in front of a class I'll only tell them half of what I know and let them find the other half out for themselves. We've got a teacher at school; my hackles rise every time he opens his mouth. . . .'

'Are you forgetting something, Tishy? You're talking to a teacher now.'

'No, I wasn't forgetting anything, Mam.' Tishy turned and looked at Annie. 'What I'm doing in a roundabout way is to inform him that if he knows what's good for him, he'll not spread his brains out on the desk.'

As Annie, aghast, said, 'Tishy!' Alan began to laugh. It was a deep rollicking kind of laugh that didn't seem to match his refined-looking exterior. It was a laugh you might have expected from some burly sailor, it was an infectious laugh, and the next minute both she and Tishy were laughing with him. Yet all the while she kept her eyes on her daughter. Never, never, had she seen Tishy like this with anyone else, and with a cold on her an' all. Wouldn't it be marvellous, marvellous, if he and Tishy. . . . Oh! wonderful. And why not? Looking at her daughter now she seemed no longer plain. A few moments ago she had thought her animation could do nothing for her looks, but it had.

Annie moved her head slowly as she kept rubbing the tears of laughter from her face and she thought it was funny how life worked out. She had always regretted letting herself be persuaded to go to the Baileys that Christmas, yet if she hadn't gone this man, because he was a man, he wasn't just a youth he was a man, wouldn't be sitting at her kitchen table now laughing into her daughter's face, and she into his, the daughter for whom she'd had no hope. Oh, it was wonderful how things worked out.

Tishy, still laughing, was on the point of saying something when the clatter of a bucket rolling, followed immediately by a spate of cursing, came from the backyard. Putting her hand to her mouth, she looked at Alan and said, 'Now you'll see something I bet you've never seen before, and hear something too. That's Gran McCabe. What a pity Gran Cooper isn't here. Boy, you'd know what entertainment was then. Arsenic and old lace. . . !'

'Tishy, be quiet! That's enough now.' Annie spoke harshly as she pulled open the kitchen door and called, 'You all right, Mollie?'

132

'All right? Do you leave that bloody bucket and shovel stickin'
out there on purpose? The times I've split me shins against it.'

Mollie limped over the threshold. Then, her mouth half-open,
she gaped at the man standing at the opposite side of the table, and,
glancing quickly from him to Annie, she said, 'Oh, I'm sorry,
lass; I didn't know you had company.'

'Get yourself in.' Annie pushed her; then closed the door before
saying 'This is Arthur's nephew. You remember Arthur?'

"Course I remember Arthur, I'm not in me dotage. Hello, lad.'
Mollie extended her hand.

'Hello. How are you?'

'Almost bloody well legless if you ask me.' Mollie sat down
now and began to rub her shins. 'There hasn't been a time in the
last ten years when I've come in that yard but somebody's set a
trap for me. An' what you laughing at, miss?'

'At you being legless, Gran.'

Mollie stared at her granddaughter for a moment as if she, too,
were noticing some difference in her. But as usual she said what
came foremost to her mind, and this was, 'You've got a cold on
you again, I see.'

'Yes, Gran.' Tishy's voice was flat now. 'Don't let me forget it.'

'What you cooking at this time of night for?' Mollie now
turned to Annie, and Annie replied, 'I'm not cooking, I'm just
knocking up something for the supper. Bacon and egg pie and a
batter pudding. You going to stay for a bite?'

'Not just for bacon an' egg pie. Is that all you've got?'

'Well, there's cold meat, cold ham, or a leg of raw pork in the
fridge, help yourself.'

'Poor meat house.' Mollie leant across the table towards Alan
who was staring at her fixedly. 'Mingy on the grub.' She winked
as she finished, and he, falling in with her mood, nodded solemnly
and replied, 'I thought as much.'

He continued to stare at the old, fat, flamboyantly dressed
woman, who he guessed was Georgie's mother. She looked a
character. He watched Annie now put a hand on her shoulder and,
bending forward, say, 'Well, you'll stay for a cup of tea?' Annie
was nice to the old girl, not a bit ashamed of her, as many would
have been, for she not only sounded but also looked a type. He had
come across some different types in the few days he had spent in
this northern and foreign quarter of the country, and not only
among the working class, yet he found them all refreshing, it was

133

as if he had come into a new world. On reflexion, he didn't think he could be more interested in, or more amused, or entertained by people if he had gone as far as Australia. These people were different, a class on their own, although he had already learnt that they were sharply divided into top, middle and bottom, much more so than back home. There was a snobbery here that he hadn't met with before.

'What did you say your name was, lad?'

'Alan.'

'Oh, Alan. Well, Alan, what do you think of the north?'

'Not much.'

'You'd better watch it, miss.' Mollie was wagging her finger at Tishy. 'An' let him speak for himsel.' She now leant across the table towards Alan, saying, 'Best place on earth, lad. We're one big family in this neck-o'-the-woods. But mind, just like any family, there's good, bad an' indifferent in it, an' if I had me way I'd put half of them in sanitary confinement. . . . sanitary confinement.' Her laughter gushed out. 'But you know what I mean?'

They were all laughing as he said, 'Yes, yes, I know what you mean.'

'There's one or two saints, a few sinners, but the majority are buggers. Just like any family. You know some folk think there's only three good people in the world, themsels, the Pope, an' God, an' he's a bit of an also-ran these days; I'm sorry for the poor bugger.'

'Oh, Mollie! Mollie!'

As the laughter filled the house Mollie got to her feet, adding, 'And here's another bugger off home. Good night, lad.' She held out her hand and he, already on his feet, took it and shook it warmly. His mouth was wide and his eyes wet, and when he said, 'I hope we meet again,' Mollie turned to Tishy and, digging her in the shoulder with her finger, said, 'There, what do you think of that? He sounded as if he meant it an' all; I'm not past it yet.' And on this she went to go out of the back door, but Annie taking her by the arm, led her firmly round the table, saying, 'The bucket and shovel's still there and I don't know why on earth you've got to use the back door every time.'

"Cos I'm on me way to our Winnie's and it's a short cut.'

When they stood at the front door Annie said, 'Are you on your way to Winnie's?'

'Aye, I was goin' along there but I thought I'd drop in an' tell you I've just left our Georgie; he was in the bar of the Wheel-barrow shortly after opening time. I had just popped into the snug an' I caught sight of him, an' during the time it took me to down a gin he had knocked back two doubles, and likewise the fellow that was with him an' all, an' there was no standin' of turns, he paid for both lots. I thought if that's the pace he's goin' and early on in the evenin' he'll have to be carried back home the night, so I asked Phil to tip him the wink and tell him I wanted a word with him outside. And you know what?' She laughed now and pushed at Annie with the flat of her hand. 'When he came out he said straightaway, "What the hell do you want? You know, Ma, I left school last week." That's our Georgie. Well I just said I wanted a word with him, I hadn't seen him for the past two weeks or so, an' I asked him who his friend was as I hadn't seen him around either, an' he must have been of some importance to have two doubles stood him. He said it was business; he said he had the fellow interested in a car, a new one, and the bloke was going to trade his in. An' what do you think?' Again she pushed at Annie but, her look aggressive now, she said, 'The bloke had won a packet on the pools only last week, but there was our bloody daft Georgie doin' the payin'. Anyway –' her voice dropped – 'I told him to get himself around home while he could walk, but the answer I got, lass, made me think that you won't see him for some time. An' then you know what to expect when you do. So I just thought I'd drop in and warn you in case you were sittin' waiting to go out. You've had some of that afore.'

'Thanks, Mollie, it was good of you. And you're right, I was expecting to go out; I thought he'd be home early and we'd go to the club.'

Mollie walked carefully down the two steps on to the pathway and there she turned and said, 'As things are in the kitchen I hope he doesn't show up for a bit. An' I'd get rid of that nice young fellow afore he comes in if I was you.' Then, her voice rising, she ended on a laugh, 'I should think he's had enough of nature in the raw when he's seen me. What do you say, lass?'

What Annie said was, 'Oh! Mollie,' and her tone was full of deep affection. 'If he meets no worse than you through life he won't do so bad. By! he won't.'

'I wish everybody thought like you, lass. I shouldn't tell you this but I can't help it. I saw your mother in the market yesterday an' she cut me dead. She looked through me like a pane of glass.

Not that it bothered me mind, for if she had spoken to me every word would have been like a pin in me skin. But it made me think of what me own mam used to say. "Always treat women as snakes," she said, "until they open their mouths, and then you can hear if they've had their fangs removed." Good night, lass.' Then her voice quiet, she said, 'Did I ever tell you you were canny?'

When Annie closed the door she said again to herself, 'Oh, Mollie,' then, 'Oh, me mam! If it wasn't that her mother was under the weather these days she'd go along there and tell her something.'

She stood looking down the hall now towards the kitchen door while thinking, She's right, I'd better get rid of him and soon, within the next hour anyway.

A few minutes later she was saying, 'I hope you don't mind eating in the kitchen, it's warmer in here than the dining-room.'

'Aw, Mam –' Tishy made a face at Annie – 'stop putting it on.' Then she turned to Alan. 'Christmas Day, birthdays and funerals, that's when we use the dining-room.'

Annie swung the cloth over the table; then putting her two hands flat on it, she lowered her head and said, 'See what I'm up against.'

'Yes, yes.' Alan nodded, his smile broad. 'Handicapped on all sides; I'm terribly sorry for you.'

'You look it.'

As she set the table she thought it was odd she could banter with this stranger. She glanced at him now where he was sitting side by side with Tishy looking at the old book and laughing over the quotations. He was nice, so nice he could be one of the family. Wouldn't it be wonderful if he took up with Tishy, and at the same time made friends with Rance. Of course Rance was younger, but a man like this would have a steadying influence on him. And Rance hadn't a real friend, not that she knew of. What was that saying, 'God moves in a mysterious way His wonders to perform.' Yes, and every word of that was true. God did move in a mysterious way. She must get herself to Mass. She had been sliding of late, and sliding was putting it mildly. Her Easter duties, that's all she had gone to for some years now, but if God took in hand the destiny of her two children about whom she worried most, then there was nothing she wouldn't do for Him. She'd promise Him she'd be at his altar rails every Sunday morning, rain, hail or shine. . . .

'There, sit up, and I'm not going to apologize for it because if I do, that one –' she jerked her finger towards Tishy as she addressed herself to Alan – 'she'll say "Why! it's a banquet to what she usually gives us."'

Before sitting down she went into the hall and called up the stairs, 'Rance! are you coming? I've got your tea out,' and his muffled reply came back from the bathroom, 'I can't get down for a minute or so, put it in the oven.'

Ten minutes later when Alan had finished a second helping of the bacon and ham pie and pronounced it simply first-rate, she was saying, 'Our Rance must be giving himself a beauty treatment,' when the sound of a car door being slammed turned her eyes sharply in the direction of the hall and almost at the same time as Tishy exclaimed, 'That must be Dad,' the front door opened and banged with a resounding clash and Georgie's voice rang through the house, crying, 'Where is he? *Where are you, you bloody thieving snipe?*'

'Georgie! Georgie!' Annie had rushed into the hall and, catching at his arm, she gabbled, 'Be quiet! there's ... there's someone here. Look, listen.'

'Do you know what he's bloody well done, that weak-kneed golden boy of yours? Do you know what he's done? Now you'll have to believe this 'cos it's starin' you in the face, at least it bloody well stared me in the face when I opened the garage door. .... A stolen car and two bloody tykes working on it. The buggers were actually spraying it, new number plate, the lot, a Morris 1100; I tell you, they were in wor garage. ....'

'Georgie! Georgie! listen, be quiet!'

'No! You bloody well listen, for once in your life you listen to me, and not him. I had to choke it out of the buggers, but choke it I did. He's in this racket up to the neck, running it, running it, and underneath me bloody nose. You know what this could mean? The polis, jail.'

As he made for the stairs she held on to him, crying, 'Georgie! listen, listen.'

'I've listened to you long enough where he's concerned. Leave go of me!' When he thrust her from him she staggered back and fell against Tishy, and they both would have fallen if Alan hadn't thrust out his arm and steadied them. But once Annie had regained her balance she ran towards the stairs again. She didn't mount them however, for Georgie had stopped half-way up, and there above him on the landing was Rance. For some seconds they both stood looking at each other. Then Georgie spoke, and what terrified Annie now was the quietness of his tone as he said, 'You had it all planned, hadn't you? The old boy never goes back once he leaves the garage on a Saturday night. Had enough, he's always said, hasn't he? Everythin' would be clear until the Monday mornin'. But tonight I got a customer, bit of a bonus, and I go back to me garage, *my garage*, out of which I've kicked the arse of more than one whose asked me to join in a fiddle. Come to the wrong shop, mate, I've said. Out, at the double, if you know what's good for you. Honest Georgie, that's me.' Now his voice almost rose to a scream as he ended, '*And the fiddle was bein' played under me bloody nose an' by me own son!*'

When he leapt up the remaining stairs Annie screamed and as she went to run after him Alan gripped her firmly, saying, 'No, no, stay where you are.'

'Let me be! Let me be! Let me go!' She was twisting and turning in his hold; and now Tishy was crying, 'Stay out of it, Mam! Stay out of it!'

For a moment she stopped her struggling and gazed upwards, as they all did, towards Rance, whose crouched body had taken on the appearance of a wrestler looking for an opening, and his words came in a growl from his throat as he faced his father. 'Your garage. Your house. Your bloody this, an' your bloody that. Everything's yours, or so you'd make people think. But you own nowt. Do you hear? Nowt, because you haven't got an atom of brain in your thick skull; the only thing you've got is a big mouth. Everything you have right from the beginning you owe to me mam; if it wasn't for her you'd be scavengin'.'

It happened, seemingly, in the blink of an eyelid. One second Georgie was standing on the stairs, the next he was on the landing, his arm drawn back, his fist doubled. But the blow never reached its objective, for Rance's foot came up and caught him in the groin, and like a stick being snapped in two and with the sound of the crack escaping his lips, Georgie's body doubled and fell backwards.

Annie's and Tishy's screams did not die away even when Georgie lay in a twisted heap at the foot of the stairs; not until Annie dropped on her knees beside him and she tried to straighten him out did her yelling fade into a moan.

'Be careful, I wouldn't touch him. You'd best get a doctor.'

She took no heed to the low trembling voice at her side, but continued to tug at Georgie's legs. Yet when she felt herself being lifted from the floor she didn't struggle.

Alan now turned to Tishy, who was staring up at Rance, where he was leaning over the banister, his hands hanging slack and his eyes staring out of a chalk-white face. 'Here,' he said, 'take care of her for a moment.' He had to push Tishy on the shoulder before she turned to her mother; then he knelt on the floor by Georgie's side and slowly he laid his ear against his chest, and kept it there for a full minute.

When he stood up they were both looking at him and he made a small movement with his head, and on this Annie yelled, 'No! no!' and pulling herself from Tishy's hold she dropped to the floor again and, gripping the lapels of Georgie's coat, she looked down on to his still face, and again she cried, 'No! no!' Then 'Aw, Georgie! Georgie! don't go. Aw, don't go. . . . Oh my God! My God!' She now turned her head and looked up at Alan. 'He . . . he can't be. Say he can't be.'

'You'd better call the doctor.' Alan now wiped the sweat from around his mouth with his fingers.

'Oh God alive!' She put her hand out and tentatively stroked each side of Georgie's face; then her body jerked at the sound of Tishy's voice crying, 'You've done it! You've done it at last, haven't you? You always wanted to do it. You've murdered him. You dirty rotten, stinking swine you! you've murdered him. When they put you in jail for life I'll cheer. Do you hear? I'll cheer. I'll cheer.'

'Stop it! Stop it, Tishy!' Scrambling to her feet, Annie pulled Tishy from the foot of the stairs, and Tishy, staring at her through tear-blinded eyes, cried, 'You won't be able to save him this time, will you?'

'What are you saying, girl? Don't be silly.' Annie was shaking her.

'Don't, Mam, don't!' Tishy pulled herself away from Annie's grasp. 'I'm saying he murdered me dad, that's what I'm saying, and you can't get him out of that.'

Annie's lower jaw moved twice before she looked up to where Rance was still hanging over the banisters. Then returning her gaze to her daughter she said under her breath, 'It . . . it was an accident. You know it was an accident.'

'Accident? Oh no, you won't get him off with that, Mam. He lifted his foot, he kicked dad down.'

'They were fighting; it was. . . .'

'*No! No!*'

Annie turned to Alan and she moved her head from side to side in bewilderment for a moment before she muttered, 'Look . . . look, after her, will you? Take her into the front room.'

'Hadn't you better phone the doctor?'

'Yes, yes.' Annie now put her hand tightly over her mouth. 'I'll . . . I'll do it in a minute, but . . . but take Tishy away, will you?'

She watched him go towards Tishy and put his arm around her shoulder and forcibly lead her into the front room. Then holding her head in her hands, she stood looking down at Georgie and all her mind kept saying was, Oh my God!

It was a full minute later when she slowly mounted the stairs, and, lifting Rance from the banisters, she supported him as they went towards his room. Having pushed him down into a chair she slapped his cheek sharply with her hand, saying, 'Rance! Rance! look at me. Listen.'

When he brought his gaze to hers and spoke his voice sounded quite ordinary as he asked, 'Is he dead, really dead?'

She moved her head once and they stared at each other, her eyes looking deep into his, and the significance of what he had done getting through to him, his shoulders hunched up round his neck, he covered the sides of his head with his hands and groaned, 'Oh Christ Almighty! Christ Almighty!' After a moment he looked at her again and said, 'I . . . I didn't mean it, Mam. You know I didn't mean that.'

She didn't say, 'Yes, yes, I know.' What she said was, 'Listen. Listen, Rance.' She bent close to him now. 'You've got to convince Tishy.' In this moment she didn't think of the stranger, the man who had witnessed the whole thing, the outsider, she was only concerned with her daughter's reaction. 'Stay quiet now,' she said; 'just stay quiet. I've got to phone the doctor. I'll . . . I'll be back. Stay quiet.' She went out and closed the door but didn't go immediately across the landing; instead, she stood with her back to the wall asking herself how this had come about. Half an hour ago she had been in the kitchen laughing and happy, and now Georgie was dead, and Rance would go to prison.

Her mind went completely blank for a moment and when the blankness passed the first question she asked herself was, Why . . . why am I not crying? What's the matter with me? The pain in her heart was so great as to be almost unendurable: she had lost Georgie, Georgie who was a good man at heart. In spite of his rough ways and not having much up top, he had been a good man. He had known his limitations, nobody better; his blustering had just been a cover up. And to have his son throw his ignorance in his face, and to die at that moment. Oh, Georgie. Georgie. And Rance. Rance would die an' all. If they put him in prison he'd wither and die. She couldn't bear it, not to be parted from both of them at one stroke.

She went slowly down the stairs her eyes all the while on the still figure at the bottom. But she couldn't believe what she was seeing. Her world had gone mad. She stooped and touched his face again, saying, 'Oh my dear, my dear.' Her body was full of tears but her eyes were dry. Why wasn't she crying? Why couldn't she cry? She looked towards the table where the phone was, and as she went towards it Tishy's voice came from the room, saying brokenly, 'He's no good, he's bad, bad right through and she can't see it.'

She didn't pick up the phone but went into the room and they both turned towards her. She didn't speak until she had sat down on the chair opposite the couch where they were sitting; then looking at Tishy, she said, 'There's not much time; I'm going to ask you something. But first of all I'm going to remind you, lass, that I've given to you all your life.'

Like a flash Tishy's voice came back at her, filled with bitterness, saying, 'Given to me? You've given me nothing, Mam. Nor Bill, nor Kathy. What you've had to give you've given to him, and we all know it.'

'You're wrong, quite wrong, I love you all.'

'You like us all, but you only love him.'

'You're wrong, girl. Anyway, it's going to be up to you whether he goes to prison or not.'

'Me?'

'Yes you. . . . It was an accident; your dad slipped and fell downstairs. . . .'

'With a boot in his stomach.'

Annie closed her eyes tight and bowed her head, and remained like this for some seconds. Then looking at her daughter again, she said, 'You . . . you needn't have been there, you . . . you could have been in the kitchen with Alan.' She now looked at Alan, and he was staring at her through narrowed lids, a look of utter

141

perplexity on his face, and she said to him, 'You . . . you'll stand by us in this, won't you?'

His eyes widened now, his lips parted; then he turned his head to one side and looked towards the floor, and when she put out her hand and caught his and, gripping it, said, 'It . . . it means nothing to you,' he could make no answer. What could he say? Could he bring up principles, ethics? Could he say he had no intention of condoning a murder, because in a way that is what it had been? When that fellow's foot had come out and caught his father in the groin he himself had winced aloud. But she was repeating, 'It is nothing to you, is it?'

He was saved from making any comment at the moment by crying, 'Involve him. Go on, Mam, involve him. He's a stranger, he hasn't been in the house a couple of hours and you would involve him? I tell you –' she turned and looked at Alan now while she swept the tears from each side of her chin with the back of her hand – 'she would take the blame herself rather than let him suffer. It's always been that way.'

'Stop it, Tishy. Stop it this minute. I'm in trouble, bad, bad trouble.' There were tears in her voice now although her eyes were still dry. 'I've lost your dad, I don't want to lose my son too. I wouldn't mind so much if he had died an' all but if he goes to prison that'll be the finish of me. I couldn't bear it.'

Tishy lay back against the couch and put her forearm across her eyes, and Annie, getting to her feet, said quietly, 'I'll phone the doctor. . . .'

From the moment she phoned the doctor her mind began to work in a way that surprised her. In any one else she would have called it cunning. After she had put a blanket over Georgie she went into the back garden and towards the bottom end of the right-hand side, and there, peering over the railings, she looked up at the Tressels' house. It was in darkness, which meant they were out. And there was no light in the house beyond either. Thank God for that. The Brookses on the left; they were all right, they were away for the week-end. There was someone in the Lauries' beyond but they wouldn't have heard anything. And anyway, their youngsters always had the television or a record player blaring.

This done, she crossed the hall again, keeping her head turned from Georgie now, and went upstairs to Rance. He was lying on the bed but still had his shoes on. He sat up when she entered the room and looked towards her with the same look in his eyes that used to be there when, as a child, he would appeal to her for protection against his father's thrashings.

She sat on the bed beside him. She did not take his hands as she would have done when he was in trouble, but she said to him, 'Now listen to me. You were in your room, in here –' she now dug her finger towards the floor – 'changing to go out when . . . when you heard your father shout. You guessed he must have slipped at the top of the stairs, caught . . . caught his foot in that piece of carpet that overlaps. There's . . . there's a nail out, it's been out for some time. I . . . you'll remember –' she nodded her head now – 'I kept on at him to have it tacked. I could have done it meself if I'd only thought, a simple job like that . . . Did you hear me? Did you hear what I said?'

'Aye, Mam. Aw, Mam.' His hands came out and clutched at hers but she made no response to them as she asked, 'That's all you've got to say.'

He gulped before he said, 'Our Tishy, and that fellow?'

'The fellow, he's Arthur Bailey's nephew, Mona's husband you know. He'll . . . he'll be all right. It's our Tishy you've got to worry about. Now I want you to come downstairs and in your own words tell her, tell her you never meant to do it.'

'To our Tishy?'

'Yes, to our Tishy.'

'Aw, I couldn't, Mam.'

'What do you mean you couldn't?' Her voice was harsh now. 'It's either that, or prison.' She spat the word out at him, and when she saw his stomach contract as if he were going to vomit she said, 'Facts are facts.'

'She hates me.'

'Aye, she might, but you've got to convince her that you never meant to do this. And you didn't, did you?'

It was a second before he looked at her and said, 'No, Mam.'

She had not thought that the pain in her breast, the pain that was tearing her body apart, could become worse, but his answer had given it a new depth. There was a bitterness in her voice as she said, 'You'll have to be more convincing than that to her. Come on. . . .'

Annie had to help him down the stairs and pull him away from the support of the banister as he stood gazing down at the covered body lying at his feet. When he entered the sitting-room he staggered like someone drunk, then stood some distance from Tishy and stared at her where she was sitting alone on the couch. The man was now standing at the head of it and was staring at him; but he took no notice of him, he kept his gaze fixed on Tishy. He couldn't remember a time in their lives when she hadn't hated him, or he her. He swallowed twice, rubbed his hand up and down his thigh, glanced towards his mother before looking at Tishy again and saying, 'I . . . I didn't mean it, I didn't.'

She glared at him. Her eyes were red and swollen but she was no longer crying and she said slowly, 'You could go on saying that from now until eternity and I wouldn't believe you.'

His teeth clamped together but without force; he had no energy left in him, no feeling of anything but fear, and it was the fear that overcame his pride and propelled him to the couch to sit beside her and mutter in desperation, 'It's true, it's true Tishy. He was going to belt me. I wouldn't have stood a chance against him, I never have. He would have busted my face up, I could see it in his eyes. I . . . I only did what I did in self-defence. But I never meant him to . . . Honest. Honest. Oh my God!' His whole body heaved. He put his hand tight across his mouth, swung himself up from the couch and dashed out of the room. But he didn't reach the kitchen sink; it was with his head against the kitchen door and within sight of the prone figure at the foot of the stairs that he vomited and retched as if he would bring his heart up, while Annie held his head, as Georgie had so often held hers.

Perhaps it was the sound that softened Tishy somewhat, for, looking up at Alan, she said, 'And what will you say? She's taken it for granted you'll go along with her.'

For answer he said, 'She's in great distress, if I can help I will.'

'Distress about whom? Me dad or him?'

'I . . . I wouldn't know.'

'No, you wouldn't know, but I do. Me dad's dead and she hasn't shed a tear; her whole concern is for her darling Rance.'

He stared at her for a full minute before he said, 'I'm not meaning to minimize your emotions at the moment, I'm sure you were very fond of your father, but . . . but I think it's a known fact that when a person cannot cry their inward pain may be very intense, and if this state continues it can be very detrimental to their health. Crying is a safety valve; it's not to say that you feel less emotion, only it's shown in a different way.'

She looked at him for some time before saying, 'You've got

nothing to do with all this really, and now you're in the thick of it. Why don't you go before the doctor comes . . . and the police?'

'Well, as I see it the very fact that I'm here may help matters. . . . It's very odd –' he looked around the room then shook his head – 'I've been wanting to come for years. I knew I would some day.'

Breaking the silence that followed, she asked, 'Why?'

He looked into her face as he said, 'I wanted to see her again, your . . .'

'Mam?'

'Yes.'

'But you were only a child, a baby, when you last saw her.'

'It doesn't matter. I remembered her vividly, and I knew that sometime I'd have to see her.'

Tishy kept her penetrating gaze tight on him for some time, then slowly she took in a long deep breath and drooped her head on to her chest.

3

'If you insist on doing the books then that means you don't trust me.'

She couldn't say outright that she didn't trust him, what she said was, 'It isn't a case of trust. I'm concerned for the garage; it's my livelihood as much as it is yours.' She did not say, 'It's my garage.'

'Mam, look.' He leant towards her. 'I'll work me fingers to the bone if you'll leave things to me, but if you're going to be trotting around after me every minute. . . .'

She rose to her feet as she said, 'Whether you like me trotting around after you every minute or not, Rance, I'm coming to the garage, and I'm going to see to the books.'

He was facing her now. 'It's no place for a woman, it's a man's job, the garage.'

'No!' Her voice rose. 'Neither was Hanlon's coal depot any place for a woman, but I had to run that. And we wouldn't be where we are today if I hadn't.'

'I know, I know, Mam. And that's part of it. I want you to sit back and have it easy; you're getting on, you'll soon be forty.'

'My God! getting on. Soon be forty. But if I was sixty it would be the same. . . . And look.' She closed her eyes and sat down with a thud on the chair again. 'I'm tired, Rance; I'm not feeling too well. . . .'

'Isn't that what I'm getting at? I know you're not, and I just want to relieve you of . . .'

'You can relieve me of a lot of things, Rance, and worry is one of them. You can relieve me by going along steadily and remembering what we've just experienced.'

He turned away from her, his head hanging as he said, 'Aw God, Mam, don't bring that up again.'

'Don't say it like that –' her voice was low and bitter – 'as if it was everybody's fault but yours.'

He turned his head and looked at her over his shoulder. 'You're turning against me.'

'No, I'm not. I wish I was. Do you hear that? I wish I was. I wish I could; it would only be fair to turn against you. And another thing while I'm on. There's going to be no more gambling.'

'Look, Mam, don't tie me up altogether.' His thin, pale face was twitching. 'What's done's done, I'll never forget it, but you can't tie me up, you can't tie me hand and foot because of it.'

'I say there's no more gambling.'

'Mam, there's worse things than gambling.'

'Yes, there might be, but to me it's quite bad enough when it drives you into the stolen car racket.'

He had been about to speak; now he gaped at her while she stared at him. Then slowly he said, 'You believed that . . .?'

'I'm no fool, Rance. Neither was your dad, although you took him for one. And I'm going to tell you this, and it's taking me a lot to say it, but if I ever find you out in any jiggery-pokery like that again it would be the finish for you, at least with me. I've . . . I've stood by you in all things and my latest stand would be condemned by everybody if it ever came to light.'

'But Mam!' He was appealing to her with both hands. 'I tell you that car was on the level. The blokes were just sort of havin' garage space an' the use of the sprayer. . . .'

'Quiet, Rance!'

As she gazed at him she marvelled that he could protest his innocence so vehemently on this point. As she had said, Georgie was no fool, and if he had been blind drunk and his mind befuddled when he had accused him she would have still believed him. Let her face it: there was a weakness in her son, an underhandedness, a cunning, the awareness of which made her sick when she thought about it, for he was the same now as when a small child, he thought he had only to look her in the face and repeat a thing over and over again to convince her it was true.

Why did she love this son more than the others? Tishy was right, she liked the others but she loved Rance. Only once had she felt any hate for him; that was the moment when she stood by the grave and watched them lowering Georgie down into it. In that moment it was as if Tishy were inside her crying out, 'He's no good. He's no good. No man is any good who could lift his foot and kick his father down the stairs.'

There had been a coroner's inquest and they had brought in the verdict of 'Accidental Death'. There had been no queries; it was well-known that Georgie McCabe drank heavily. The only place there had been any talk was in the Wheelbarrow. Georgie, they said, had had a few doubles, yes, but what was a few doubles compared to what he could carry? He had been all right when he left there. It was a pity Pat Reynolds hadn't gone with him to the garage. He was to come to his house with the car, Reynolds said, but he hadn't turned up and it was just over an hour later when he had fallen downstairs. Funny, wasn't it? He'd be missed, would Georgie. Good sort Georgie; always open-handed, if you were broke you were always sure of a set-in if you met Georgie. Such was the public verdict on Georgie.

Annie rose again from the chair now, saying, 'Why don't you get yourself married and settled down?'

'What! married! Why should I? I don't want to marry, not . . . not yet anyway. And if I married I'd have to leave you. What about that?'

'Don't worry about me.' She shook her head slowly.

He came towards her, stood close to her and looked into her face as he said, 'But I do worry about you, Mam.'

She stared back into his eyes for a moment before turning away. She wished she could believe it, she wished to God she could believe that. She wished she could believe anything that he said.

Tishy was in her room sitting before the mirror. She looked first at one profile, then at the other. If she put colour on it might make her face look plumper, not so scraggy. She tried colour; then rubbed it off again. She'd wear a brownish lipstick, not a red. And what about her hair? Should she take it straight back or part it in the middle? She parted it in the middle. Her face looked softer now. If only her nose weren't so short and her lips were fuller. She pursed her lips and said, 'Prunes. Prunes. Prunes.' Then, with a swift movement turning her head to the side, she muttered aloud, 'Oh, what does it matter! He's seen me as I am, and he likes me as I am.' She looked in the mirror again and her smile softened her face still further, and she nodded at herself now, saying, 'He does like me; he wouldn't have taken me to Newcastle if he hadn't, would he?'

She thought she would remember last Saturday for the rest of her life. She had felt so proud to be seen with him for he was no boy, or lad, he was a man. He looked like a man, he talked like a man, and he acted like a man, not like the sixth-formers who used to follow them home from school. Well, they hadn't followed her. She wondered now why she had been so silly as to pray that one of them would. But last Saturday she had been out with a man. They had browsed around the bookshops, they had gone through the museum, then they'd had tea. He hadn't suggested taking her to a show, but she felt sure he would have if it hadn't been so soon after her dad's death.

She felt guilty about being happy and it being only a month since the funeral, but she couldn't help it. It was strange, but, in a way, it was because her dad had died that Alan and she had become so close. And they were close, weren't they? She asked the question of herself in the mirror, and it was some time before she answered, saying, 'Yes, because we think alike about so many things, and we get on well together.' He laughed at the things she said. He thought she was very witty, and she could be witty when she was with him. Her mind worked overtime when they were together; he stimulated her. When she was with him she forgot that she was utterly plain for in his company she took on a personality, a vivacity that made her bubble and brought her alive.

She knew that her mother was all for the association. For one thing, if she married Alan it would get her out of the house and away from Rance, and that is what her mother wanted more than anything. The fact that she'd be out of the house for months on end when she went to training college wasn't the same thing; this would still be her home, she'd still come back.

Oh, to be married, to be married to Alan; to have a man of your own, someone who belonged to you, loved you. She had never thought anybody would love her, not the way she looked. Why was it, when her mam was so good looking she should be so plain? . . . Why? And their Kathy beautiful, and Bill good looking an' all. It wasn't natural, to say the least. And what was more, it was unfair. And then there was their Rance, looking like a plaster saint, whereas he was a devil. But Alan didn't care how she looked; he liked her for what she was. Oh she wished he were coming today. He had been two week-ends in the last month. She wondered if her mother would suggest him living here when he came to take up his new post; he could always travel up to Newcastle. She would put it to her.

She went to the wardrobe and took out a dress. Although she wasn't in black all her clothes seemed dark and dingy. She'd like something bright, gay; but it was too early she supposed. Yet why not? Her dad would have said, 'Go ahead and don't be a bloody hypocrite.'

She went downstairs and found Annie lying on the couch in the front room. Going to her, she said, 'You all right, Mam?'

'Yes, yes, Tishy, only I'm so tired. I suppose it's not being able to sleep.'

'Are you taking the pills the doctor gave you?'

'Yes, I'm taking them.'

'What about the sleeping pills?'

'I'm not taking those; they make me feel terrible the next day. I don't want to get used to sleeping pills.'

'Mam.'

'Yes, dear.'

'Would . . . would it seem awful if I went out and bought a new frock?'

'Bought a new frock? No, lass, no. Why should it? Your dad used to say buy something cheery, bright, you remember? But you never did. Get yourself away, lass, and buy something cheery.'

'It . . . it won't seem disrespectful?'

'Who to?' She lifted her hand heavily and touched Tishy's arm; then patting it, she said, 'Go on, make yourself bonny.'

A cynical expression swept over Tishy's face as she said, 'Aw, Mam, don't ask the impossible.'

'Now, now, stop that. You've never looked better than you have these past few weeks. Get something warm looking, with a pink tinge in it, eh? Have you enough cash?'

'Yes, yes; I've never spent anything for months.'

'Go on then.'

'You're sure you'll be all right?'

'Yes, I'm all right, lass.'

They smiled at each other; then Tishy went out, and Annie, letting her head sink back into the cushions, thought, All right? I don't think I'll ever feel all right in my life again.

The feeling that was weighing on her wasn't, she considered, natural. Sorrow was one thing but she felt she was carrying a load that was becoming unbearable, and if it didn't soon drop from her then she would die. She had thought, quite often during the past few weeks, that she could quite easily die. The feeling wasn't only sorrow at Georgie's going, or at the crime her son had committed, it was more of a weakness, the sapping of her strength caused not a little by the stratagems she'd had to use when dealing with the doctor, and the police, and not forgetting Tishy. In the days between that dreadful night and the funeral she had marshalled and manoeuvred people like a general with an army. Looking back, she didn't know how she had accomplished it. The only one to whom she hadn't to lie to convince or coerce had been Alan.

Strange, she thought now, how he had to come into their lives on that particular night. It was, as she had said before, God moves in a mysterious way His wonders to perform, and although Georgie's death hadn't brought him to the house, the circumstances around it had certainly brought him and Tishy close together.

Tishy put her head round the door, saying, 'I'm off then, Mam. Sure you're all right?'

'Yes, lass, I'm all right. Don't forget, a nice colour, something warm looking.'

'All right, Mam. Bye-bye.'

'Bye-bye, dear.'

She had the house to herself. At one time it had been nice to have the house to herself, but now it was as if there were never anyone in it; even when the four of them were sleeping upstairs it was still empty. Although she had come to love Georgie in a peculiar sort of way she hadn't realized just how he had filled her life until he had gone from it. Seeing him off in the morning and waiting for him coming in at night had been but a habit, part of a pattern, but in bed, lying by his side and being loved by him, and being told in his own rough way that she was a wonderful lass and that he'd be nothing without her, that hadn't been a habit, or part of a pattern, that had been something special which made her realize that it was only she who knew the real Georgie, the man beneath the bluster, the man alive to his own inadequacies, the man who knew that his only defence was to bellow and curse. Oh, she missed him. Oh, how she missed him.

Her eyes closed, then opened slowly again as she heard a car draw up outside. It wasn't their car, she knew the sound of their car. Somebody after Kathy she supposed. She waited for the front door bell to ring, but it didn't. She imagined she heard footsteps going up the side path towards the back door. As she heard the back door open she thought it must be Rance. But it hadn't sounded like their car. When the voice from the hall said, 'Anybody at home?' she pulled herself up on to her elbow, saying, 'Oh, in here, Alan, in here.'

She was lifting her feet slowly from the couch when he entered the room.

'You're not well?'

'Just tired, Alan. I didn't expect you. Tishy's just gone out shopping. Sit yourself down; I'll get you a cup of . . .'

'You'll do nothing of the sort. You were resting, so go on resting.' He bent down swiftly and with one hand lifted her feet on to the couch again while with the other he pressed her back into the cushions.

'I'll make the tea; I can manage that, I think.' He smiled at her. 'Take your things off.'

'I will in a minute.' He pulled up a chair towards the couch and sat down, saying, 'Have you seen the doctor?'

'Yes, yes; I was there on Wednesday. He just said to rest.'

'You don't feel well, do you?'

'No, Alan, I don't feel well, but strangely I couldn't describe just how I feel, it's as if there were a gathering in here, you know –' she patted her breast – 'like an enormous boil coming to a head. But . . . but enough about me. How's things with you?'

'Oh, moving.' His voice sounded flat, and when he stopped and stared at her, she said, 'We didn't expect you.'

'I know, but . . . but I thought I'd better come. . . . There was something. . . .'

'Oh.' She waited, and after a moment he said, 'It's rather difficult. . . . It's been a strange month, hasn't it?'

'Very strange, Alan.'

'I . . . I feel I've known you for years, never stopped knowing you.'

'It's the same with me, Alan; there seems to have been no break.'

'That's it, no break. I . . . I was saying something similar to Uncle Arthur. I went over the other day and told him; he . . . he didn't know about Georgie.'

'No, of course not.'

'He ... he was very upset.'

'You ... you didn't tell him the facts?'

'Oh God no. You didn't expect me to, did you?'

'No, no.'

'He ... he was very fond of Georgie, you know that.'

'Yes.' She lowered her eyes and looked to where her hands were lying limply one on top of the other on her stomach.

'He cried.'

'Arthur?'

'Yes, he cried like a child. It upset me.'

'Yes, yes, I suppose it would.'

'I'm very sorry for Uncle. He's been cast out by some of the family, and to the others he's just a joke.'

'Why?' She wished she hadn't asked that, it was asking the road she knew. She saw him hesitate about giving her the answer; he was looking away from her as he said, 'Perhaps you didn't know, but that's why his marriage failed, he's a homosexual.'

There, that was the word, the word that had been buried for all these years. She was going to be sick. You could say odd, funny, pansy, you could say they wore drag, painted their faces, used scent, and went to bed in nighties, it didn't seem to matter until you put that word to them. . . . And what had he said just a minute ago, that Arthur had cried because he'd heard Georgie had died. He must think that Georgie. . . . She was sitting up straight now, her voice cracking as she cried, 'Georgie wasn't like that. He wasn't, he wasn't.'

'No, I know.'

'Then why did you say Arthur cried; that's inferring that . . .'

'No, no, Annie, no, no. Listen –' he caught hold of her hands – 'listen to me. He was telling me that Georgie was the only real friend he'd had. From what I can gather Georgie became friendly with him before he knew anything about that, but when he found out it made no difference to him. But it made a lot of difference to Uncle because at last he had found someone who didn't treat him as an oddity. He knew from the beginning that Georgie would have no hanky-panky, but as I see it he used Georgie as a sort of alibi, a sane clean alibi, if you know what I mean, to hold up to his folks, and others. If people saw he had a friend like Georgie, well they wouldn't think there was any hanky-panky. That's how I see it.'

The lump was moving from her breast up into her throat and

when she tried to get words out it halted them. 'Georgie . . . Georgie, he was . . . he was a . . . good man; there was nothing like that . . . about him.' The lump was choking her, she couldn't bear it. She put her spread hands over her face and when his voice came to her, murmuring softly, 'Oh, Annie, Annie, I'm sorry. Oh, Annie,' and his arms came about her, the lump burst. The tears spurted from her eyes and her nose, the saliva ran out of her mouth as if an explosion had taken place inside her. Her crying rose like wailing notes on a scale, and when they reached a crescendo she thrust her face into his breast and, as if he were talking to a child, he whispered softly, 'There now, there now. It's all right, it's all right. That's it, cry it out. This is what you need. Cry it out.'

When she had cried it out and her sobs were subsiding she raised her head and looked at him. She was still lying on the couch but he was sitting at the head of it and the upper half of her was in his arms. When she felt his fingers stroke her wet hair away from her brow she shivered.

'Feel better now?' he said, his voice still a whisper, and she made a slight movement with her head before saying, 'I'm sorry.'

'Oh my dear, what is there to be sorry for? You should have done this that first night, you would have felt much better by now. You've been storing it up.'

'Yes, I suppose so.' She had a strange feeling, as if her body had been drained of all its blood. She felt weak and empty, but at peace now. He was right, it would have been much better if she could have cried at the beginning. She knew she should get up, she shouldn't lie here, it wasn't right lying like this in this young fellow's arms. What was she thinking about?

She was on the point of putting her hand out to make a move when the door opened and Tishy entered, and as she looked into her daughter's face across the distance she wanted to die, really die.

As she struggled upwards away from Alan's slackening hold, she muttered, 'I . . . I collapsed. I've . . . I've had a good cry, and Alan . . . he came unexpected.'

She was on her feet now. Alan, too, was standing. 'Did you get your dress, lass?'

Tishy didn't speak. She looked from her mother to Alan and waited.

And Alan looked back at her for a moment before stretching his neck up from his collar. Then he began on a slightly hesitant note, saying, 'I . . . I know I wasn't expected, but I have something to tell you, to tell you both.' He turned his gaze to Annie for a moment. 'I thought, well I'd put it off long enough, but . . . but under the circumstances over these past weeks I didn't think you'd be interested in my business. But . . . but I think the time has come when I'd better tell you. You see, I'm . . . I'm going to be married.'

Tishy hadn't moved, nor had the expression on her face altered, but Annie sat down in a chair and stared up at him, her face still wet and her mouth agape. She stared at him as he went on in an apologetic tone, 'I . . . I would have told you that first evening if it hadn't been, well, for what happened. And then . . . well, you were so distressed. Following that I . . .'

His voice was cut off by Tishy holding up a paper bag and saying on a high note, 'I got the dress, Mam. It's pink. Get it bright you said, it's all pink.' She wagged the bag at arm's length before her, then turned round and went out.

Annie rose slowly to her feet and looked at Alan, and, her voice low and trembling, she said, 'You shouldn't have done this, Alan; it . . . it was cruel. You . . . you could see how things were going with her.'

'No, no, Annie, I didn't, not really. And she's so young, still at school. . . .'

'She's in love with you.'

'Oh no! No. She hasn't had time, it's only a month.'

'Don't be silly. What time does it take for a young lass to fall in love?'

'Not long, I suppose.' His voice was grim now. 'Nor that long to fall out of it again. I tell you it didn't strike me.'

'Oh, Alan.'

They stood staring at each other. His face was red and his Adam's apple jerked violently before he said, under his breath, 'If I were to fall in love with anyone here it certainly wouldn't be with Tishy, Annie. Don't you understand it wouldn't be with Tishy?'

She didn't move but she dropped her head backwards on her shoulders as if to see him better.

'I've been engaged for three years and the longer it goes on the less I want it. But everything's arranged. She's the grand-daughter of Grandma's friend. Friends of the family.' His tone was bitter again. 'Annie.' He leant swiftly forward and gripped her hands. 'It may seem mad to you, but not to me. If you would say the word, tell me that, if I waited a year, any time, then you would . . .'

'Shut up!' She jerked her hands from his and, putting one to her throat, she stroked her finger and thumb down each side of her neck as if to slacken the muscles. Then she muttered under her breath, 'You'd better go, Alan, and now.'

'Annie.'

'Please, that's enough. I'm fourteen years older than you, I'm nearing forty. Even the suggestion is indecent, not forgetting that my husband is hardly cold in his grave yet. Now go on, get yourself out, and I'm . . . I'm sorry to have to say this, Alan, but, but don't come back. . . .'

Not until she heard his car start up did she move. Slowly she sat down on the couch. Her hand outstretched gripping the rounded side of it, she stared before her, not thinking of Tishy upstairs, likely crying her heart out, nor yet of Georgie, whom an hour ago she had been missing so much, but she thought of the young girl she had once been and the dreams she'd had then, and she imagined that if such a man as Alan had come into her life at that time she wouldn't have had to bury her dreams. But they had been buried when she married Georgie and were now in the grave with him.

Alan had been born much too late.

Part Five

TISHY

1

'Stand still, will you, Kathy.'

'Oh, Mam, I told her it was too long; I said I didn't want it covering my toes.'

'It's not covering your toes. Don't forget you had high heels on when she measured you, and also when she fitted you. Why didn't you tell her that you intended to wear flat? But stand still, it only needs a little tacking up into the ruche, it'll never be noticed.'

'It'll make the hem uneven.'

'Oh, don't be silly, Kathy. It's supposed to be uneven, isn't it, scalloped.'

'Yes, but it'll hang down more on one side than the other.'

Annie got up from her knees and surveyed her daughter standing in her wedding dress. 'Well then,' she said, 'pull it up the other side and you'll create a new fashion.'

'Mam! Mam, don't joke.'

'What do you expect me to do, girl, cry? Aw, come on.' Annie put out her hand and tapped her daughter's cheek. 'You look as if you were preparing for your funeral instead of your wedding.'

Kathy sat down on the side of the bed, then jumped up immediately, saying, 'Oh, help me off with it.' And when the white gown was laid across the foot of the bed, Kathy, shrugging her long shapely body into her dressing gown, turned to her mother and said in a flat voice, 'Mam, I'm beginning to get nervous, sort of frightened.'

'And you'll be worse before you're better.'

'You're some help.'

'Come and sit here.' Annie pulled her down beside her at the head of the bed, and, looking at her with her head on one side, said, 'Everybody goes through this you know; although the things they're frightened of might be different. I'm not going to go into the birds and the bees with you.' She now pushed her daughter in the shoulder while bending forward and laughing as she continued, 'Do you mind the time I tried to give you a bit of advice on that subject? Do you mind what you said?'

Kathy, laughing now, said, 'Buck up and be a rabbit, Mam.'

'Aye, buck up and be a rabbit. I didn't know whether to laugh or box your ears, but I'll tell you something I remember feeling at the time.'

'What?'

'I felt you were much older than me.'

'I still feel I'm much older than you, Mam, because in some ways you haven't got a clue. Tishy says it's because you shut your eyes to things, but I think it's just you.'

'Well, thank you very much, both of you.' Annie turned her head away in mock indignation, and Kathy said, 'Well I like you like that. I always thought you were different from other mothers; Mrs Bates, for instance. When Jane first asked Linda round there to tea, Linda said that Ma Bates looked as if she was fighting off age with a hatchet and it had slipped and caught her in the face.'

As they both pushed at each other and laughed, Annie said, 'That was a cruel thing to say.'

'Well, you know Linda; she has a tongue like a rapier. But she's right, she's right most of the time. The other day in the shop when we had that beauty expert down from Newcastle and she kept yarping on about the indefinable something, charm you know, allure, she said people couldn't put a name to it, or lay a finger on it, and all the while she was putting over to us how much of it she had. Of course, Linda twigged this immediately and she nearly made me choke by whispering, "Poor soul she must have lost her something in the monkey puzzle".'

As Annie looked at her daughter's animated, beautiful face she recalled to mind a vivid picture of the times when she and Mona had sat on the bed talking like this. She herself had been to Mona what Linda was to Kathy, yet at the same time the positions were partly reversed for Kathy had the looks and charm yet idolized Linda whereas Mona had idolized herself; but her daughter's friendship, she felt, would fade away just as her own had with Mona once the marriage got under way.

The marriage! She would never cease to wonder what this beautiful girl saw in Mr Percy Rinkton. She could have had her pick of any fellow in the town; they had swarmed round her like bees for years; yet she was going to marry that stiff-necked, pedantic know-all. What was it about him that attracted her? His persistence? for God knew he had been persistent enough, and so formal about his courtship that at times she had wanted to scream at him.

He had allowed six weeks to elapse after Georgie's death before coming to the house to ask formally for her permission to take Kathy out.

Although Kathy had predicted his visit she had laughed her head off when she knew he had been; she had doubled her legs under her on the couch and rocked herself with her mirth. 'I wouldn't be found dead with him,' she had said. Yet when he called again and saw her personally and asked her to go out she hadn't laughed at him, she had been coy and said she was so very sorry but she had a previous engagement.

The name of Percy Rinkton became a household joke, bringing flashes of humour into the dull atmosphere.

During that year Kathy's suitors came and went, only Percy Rinkton remained faithful inasmuch as periodically he would knock on the door and ask if it was convenient to see Miss McCabe ... Miss Kathy McCabe.

It was during a slack period of suitors that Kathy first went out with Percy Rinkton and from then on she stopped laughing at him. He was no longer a joke, he was someone to hold up to the family, especially to Bill, as an example of manners and interesting conversation.

But it was Rance who said to her, 'You're not serious about that little runt, are you?' and when she had turned on him they'd had their first quarrel, because whereas Rance hated Tishy with a deep intensity, his liking for Kathy went just as far the other way. From then on Rance made it his business to pick an argument with Kathy's suitor whenever an opportunity afforded; that he repeatedly got the worst of it didn't seem to get through to him. Percy Rinkton's clinical logical reasoning was thrown aside as claptrap by Rance.

Bill, too, laughed at Percy. While conceding that the fellow had plenty up top he nevertheless pointed out at every opportunity in the beginning that the fellow was an inch, if not more, shorter than she was, and she was still growing. 'By the time you're twenty,' he joked, 'he'll need a step-ladder to reach you.'

But the more opposition there was to Percy Rinkton as a suitor the more Kathy became determined to keep him in that category; and now, three years later, she was about to marry him, and Annie still couldn't understand it.

It was, she supposed, a very good match for her youngest daughter. Percy came from one of the best families in the town. His father was a leading doctor, he himself was an accountant, a fully fledged one at that. She had nothing to complain of at his people's reception of them. His mother wasn't uppish at all, she was really a canny body. Mrs Rinkton was forty-six years old, only four years older than herself but she always looked upon her as an elderly woman. Percy himself was twenty-six and that was a nice age for a man to marry. Everything about Percy and his family was correct. Perhaps that was the trouble, it was too correct, it was irritatingly correct; it was all right being good mannered but when somebody popped up from his seat every time you entered the room it got a bit too much.

Last night she had tried to make a breakthrough when he had said to her, 'What am I to call you in future? I can't go on calling you Mrs McCabe,' and to this she had answered, 'You shouldn't have gone on calling me Mrs McCabe all this time, Percy.'

'Then what shall it be? . . . Mother?'

He had been startled when she said, 'Oh good God! no, make it Annie.'

The look of shock on his face had caused her to laugh, and when he said, 'Oh, I . . . I really couldn't,' she demanded, 'Why not? Anyway, call me what you like but not Mother.'

Mother to Percy, that would be too much. She smiled inwardly as she now said to Kathy, 'We were supposed to be talking about you, not me,' and, her voice losing all its banter, she added, 'Are you quite sure in your mind, lass, you know what you're up to?'

'You mean with regard to how I feel towards Percy?'

'Just that.' . .

'Yes, Mam. I love Percy. I know you think that's strange, but you see I . . . I know him like none of you do. When . . . when we're alone together he's not so starchy.'

Annie only just prevented herself from saying, 'Thank God for that.'

162

'It's ... it's sort of nerves with him, he's ... he's got an inferiority complex.'

'*Percy!* with an inferiority complex?'

'All right, Mam, you can say it like that, but that's what it is;
he's naturally good mannered and this shyness makes him force
it home more.'

Again Annie only just stopped herself from exclaiming, 'Shyness!' Percy Rinkton shy; a fellow who had persisted in knocking
on her front door for a full year, knowing that the object of his
attraction was likely to turn him down for some other fellow.
Percy Rinkton shy? Well, perhaps she hadn't a clue about people,
perhaps this daughter had a deeper insight into human nature than
herself, for all her experience; but then her daughter was the
product of this new generation. The young people of today
frightened her with their perception and knowledge; things that
were hidden in her young days were now stripped bare and flaun-
ted on posters, papers and books, not only laying bare the body,
but the mind. The latter was more frightening still. There were
things in the mind that should be kept hidden; everybody had
things in their mind that should be kept hidden.

'Mam, do you think our Rance will play up?'

'No, don't you worry about Rance; I'll see to him.'

'Tishy always says when he's quiet he's up to something. He's
been quiet for the past week or so.'

Yes, Rance had been quiet for the past week or so. She didn't
need that to be brought to her notice. He was up to something
all right; only one thing she was sure of, it wasn't connected with
the garage. The garage was clean, figure-wise with regard to the
books, and materially as to the place itself, for never a working day had passed since Georgie had died but she had visited the
garage. This remained the bone of contention between her and
Rance but she ignored it.

But Rance, she felt, had other irons in the fire. He wasn't
gambling, it wasn't that, he didn't stay out late enough. He'd
been at her this past while to move to Westoe. Only last week
he had tried to induce her to take a house that had been turned
into two large flats. 'Why two flats?' she had asked, and he had
answered that he'd like a flat of his own. 'Well, you go and take
a flat,' she had said, and he had looked at her a long while before
saying, 'You know I couldn't leave you.'

When he spoke like that to her she forgot her fears concerning him; she forgot that there was that cell in her mind in which was stored his real worth; such words blotted out his lifted foot and the kick in the groin. Rance would never leave her because he needed her. It was as if the umbilical cord had never been cut between them. When he spoke to her in that way it caused some part of her stomach to jerk as if he were tugging at the cord, reminding her that they could never be separated.

Sometimes in her anger against him she thought that nature, in siphoning off nearly all her affections into her first-born and leaving little for the rest, had played a dirty trick on her. Tishy was right, Tishy was nearly always right, she liked the others but she loved Rance. Yet of late a strange element had entered into her love and it disturbed her. It couldn't be said it was dislike. Or could it? Or hate, when she thought of his lifted foot? Oh no! No.

'Our Rance is drinking.'

'Rance drinking?'

'Oh, you didn't see it but he came in the other night late and almost staggered up to bed; he was all bright-eyed and sloppy, he even spoke civilly to Percy. Well, I wouldn't mind him getting drunk on my wedding day if it keeps him civil.'

Annie repeated, 'Our Rance drunk? He hardly ever touches the stuff.'

'He's sly, he does it on the sly.'

Annie rose from the bed and went towards the door, thinking, It might not be such a bad thing if he did drink, it would loosen some of the tensions in him, for a time at any rate. The door knob in her hand, she turned and smiled at Kathy, saying, 'Well, I'll get him bottled up on the day, eh?' She had ignored the remark that he was sly.

'Aw, Mam.'

Kathy looked at her and shook her head, and in the action and the words there was an impatience underlying a kindly tolerance, and it made Annie feel for the moment that indeed she was younger than her daughter; or was it that she was just gullible?

2

———

They were all in the front room, Kathy and Percy, Rance, Tishy, Bill and Annie. There was no talk of the wedding that was to take place in two days' time. Bill was talking about his future as a teacher. When he went back to the university after the Christmas vac it would be for the last time. He wished, he said, he was staying on now and trying for his Ph.D., for by the sound of things they were lining up for teachers' jobs.

To Tishy, who was in her first year as a teacher at the secondary modern, the solution was to move away, get out of the north-east. 'The trouble with us in this corner of the globe,' she said, 'is that we are too insular. Metaphorically speaking, everybody in the north-east has the chummy back lane, back-to-back mentality. People won't move. If they do it has to be within easy reach of the town in which they were born. If they go farther afield they develop symptomatic phobias.'

'I'm with you there,' said Bill.

'Don't talk rot.'

They all looked at Rance, but he didn't lift his eyes from the evening paper.

After a moment Percy Rinkton spoke. 'I should say that the regional feeling remains more marked in the north-east than anywhere else in the country,' he said, stressing as usual the last consonant of each word. 'Yet one cannot but say that things have changed. The two wars in this century have acted as catharses on society. For instance, in the First World War you needed money and education to die as an officer, whereas in the last war any Geordie could get some sort of commission in the army, or the navy for that matter, be he an insurance agent, a lorry driver, a car mechanic or a . . .'

'Or a bloody cheapskate accountant.' Rance had thrown the paper down and was glaring at Percy. 'Car mechanic!' His lip curled. 'Any apprentice car mechanic in this town could buy and sell you, mate. And let me tell you something. You wouldn't be where you are the day if it wasn't for your bloody . . . papa.'

'Rance! stop it!'

Percy's face had drained white in the last few seconds, but looking steadily across at Rance he said, 'You are bent on asking for trouble, aren't you? But I'm not going to argue with you.'

Rance had risen to his feet and was glaring at Percy where he was sitting, his back tight against a straight-backed chair, and he said, 'You know what you can do, mate, you can take a single ticket to hell.' And on this he went out, and Annie, after closing her eyes tight for a moment, followed him.

Tishy was the first to move. She got up, went to the fireplace and, grabbing a piece of coal with the tongs, flung it on the fire, saying, 'He's a pig, an utter pig.' Then turning to Percy she said, 'I'm sorry, Percy. Take no notice.'

'Oh, I don't, I don't.' Percy gave her a weak smile. Then looking at Kathy as she sat with her head bowed and her hands tight under her oxters as if protecting herself against the cold, he said, 'It's all right, dear, don't be worried for me. I . . . I understand Rance. Yes, yes, I understand him. He doesn't understand me but I understand him.'

Bill, leaning his head back in the corner of the couch, now exclaimed, 'Well, if you do, Percy, you're about the only one who does; even Mam can't understand him and she's worked on him long enough.'

'And for him.'

Bill nodded at Tishy as he repeated, 'Yes, and for him, and she'll likely go on doing it until the end of her days. . . .'

In the kitchen Annie was giving the lie to this. 'Look,' she was saying, 'we've had about enough of this, and we've all had about enough of you. You're not merely rude, you're ignorant, raw ignorant.'

'He makes me sick.'

'Because he's different from you.'

'Yes, he's different from me, and thank God for that. Who'd want to be like that pip-squeak? I ask you!'

'That pip-squeak, as you call him, has something, Rance, that you'll never have, and that's brains. And he uses them.'

'Aw, now we know whose side you're on. We know where we stand, don't we?'

'I'm on nobody's side, I'm only trying to point out to you that you can't go on like this. You've been like a bear with a sore skull for months.'

'And if you had any sense you would be acting in the same way and putting a stop to our Kathy making a bloody fool of herself letting her marry him. Do you want to get rid of her? With her looks she could have picked and chosen, but you let her take a neuter like him.'

'What do you mean, a neuter?'

'Just what I say. He's not half a man; you've just got to look at him.'

She stared at him grimly before she said, 'That's got to be proved, hasn't it?' Then she went on, 'Now look here, Rance, I'm warning you. You cause any trouble on Saturday and you and I are finished, finally. She's the first one to leave home and she's going to leave it peaceably if I have anything to do with it. You create the slightest bit of trouble and you're out. Do you hear me?' She placed her hands flat on the table and leant over it towards him. 'I've shielded you for years; I've got their backs up 'cos I put you first in everything. . . .' She stopped abruptly as the kitchen door opened suddenly and Tishy came in.

Tishy, the door closing behind her, stood with her back to it and stared at them, and they at her. Tishy at twenty-two looked tall, even taller than her five foot seven because of her extreme thinness. Her face had hardly altered at all in the last four years but she looked much older. This was due mostly to the way she dressed her hair, which was drawn tightly back from her forehead and kept in place by a band on the back of her head. Her thin lips scarcely moved as she said caustically, 'Having a job to get through to him?' She did not immediately take her eyes from her mother when Rance took a step towards her, his teeth gritting audibly, but when she did look at him she held his gaze for some seconds before she said, 'You do anything to upset Saturday, just anything mind, one little thing, and it'll give me great pleasure to go down to the police station and tell them that I've been withholding information, vital information, with regard to a murder.'

She made no movement when she saw Annie's body slump further over the table, but kept her eyes tight on those of Rance and watched them darken to a blackness in which his hate smouldered.

It was the sound of the doorbell ringing that snapped the tension. Turning away she went out of the kitchen, but was back within a minute and, looking to where Annie was now sitting by the side of the table, she said, 'It's . . . it's Mr Wilkins from down below, he wants to have a word with you.'

'Mr Wilkins?' Annie rose slowly to her feet.

'I've put him in the dining-room.'

Annie stood for a moment holding the back of the chair, then her head moved just the slightest in Rance's direction, where he was standing with his back to her, both hands gripping the mantelpiece. Young Susan Wilkins had been running after Rance for the last year or so; she made a nuisance of herself. He had taken her out once or twice to a dance, but then, as always, he had grown tired of her. He never kept his girls long but Susan waylaid him at every opportunity. She knew that he often left the car at the bottom of the street and came in the back way in order to avoid her. She was a silly girl was Susan.

She went through the door that Tishy was holding open for her, across the hall and into the dining-room. Mr Wilkins was standing to the side of the fireplace and he turned immediately towards her, and she saw that he was in a very agitated state. 'It's about Susan,' he began; 'she's gone, left home. She left a note. Her mother found it when she came in; she's nearly round the bend.'

'Oh, I'm sorry, Mr Wilkins, I am indeed. Have you no idea where she's gone?'

'No, none at all. We . . . we wondered if Rance might give us a lead.'

'Rance?'

'Yes, she thought a lot of your Rance.'

'Yes, I think she did, Mr Wilkins.'

'Well, he might have seen her the day.'

'But . . . but Rance has been in the garage all day and . . . well, you know he's never taken Susan out for months.'

'I . . . I know that, but . . . but I thought he might know who she was friendly with; she wouldn't tell us. And . . . and there is something else.' The man now bowed his head in shame as he said below his breath, 'She's started smoking.'

'Oh –' Annie gave a little laugh – 'that's no crime, Mr Wilkins; they all do it sooner or later.'

He lifted his sad bulbous eyes and looked at her as he said, 'No ordinary smoking, drugs.'

There was a long pause during which her heart seemed to miss a beat before she said, 'Oh no! Mr Wilkins,' and he replied, 'Aye, I'm afraid it's true. It was one night last week. She came in sort of dazed, and then she started to act daft. We've noticed she's been, well, not herself once or twice before, but it never dawned on us until we searched her room, and then . . . well, her mother nearly went mad. She shook it out of her. It apparently started at the party Rance took her to a few months back; somebody gave her a cigarette.'

'Not . . . not Rance?' Annie could scarcely hear her own voice.

'She didn't say who gave it to her, she just said somebody gave her a cigarette, but she didn't take to it all at once. I think she got miserable when Rance dropped her. She wouldn't face up to the fact that he didn't want her. Her mother told her; she was young and these things happened and she'd get over him, but . . . but she never seemed to, and lately she's been getting worse.' He rubbed his hand across his eyes, then round his chin as he muttered thickly, 'It's the shock. It's the shock, you see; her mother'll never get over it. I'm going to the police, I'll have to report it, but . . . but I thought if Rance could give us a lead.'

He stared at her for some time before she said, 'Yes, yes, all right, Mr Wilkins, I'll get him.'

Rance was no longer in the kitchen, and she had just reached the top of the stairs when she saw him coming out of his room dressed for outdoors. She stood in front of him and said without any preamble, 'Susan Wilkins has run away; her father wonders if you could give them any lead to where she might have gone.'

'What me! I haven't seen her for weeks, well –' he shook his head – 'days; it's over a week since I spoke to her.'

She stared at him as she repeated, 'Mr Wilkins wonders if you can give him a lead as to who her friends were, she's on drugs.' Her eyes looked straight into his, but his lids did not flicker nor did his expression alter as he repeated, 'Drugs?'

'That's what I said.'

'Well, I ask you, what lead could I give him on that? You don't think . . .?'

'I think nothing, I just want you to come down and tell him if you know any of her friends.'

'But I don't. How should I?'

'You took her out, you took her to a party.'

'Yes, but that was years ago.'

'It wasn't years ago.'

'I tell you, Mam –' his voice was low, harsh – 'I don't know who she's been going round with, an' I don't want anything to do with it.'

'Well, come down and tell him so.'

Pushing past her now, he growled, 'All right, if that's what you want I'll tell him so.'

Annie looked at Rance as he faced Mr Wilkins. There was that withdrawn look on his face, his cover-up look, as she termed it to herself. 'I wish I could help you,' he was saying, 'but I don't know who she's been going round with.'

'Can you remember who she met at the party? It was there all this started when this, this fellow gave her a cigarette. . . . Cigarette. My God! I wish I could lay my hands on him just for a minute, that would be enough.'

'The party was packed; there were people there I'd never set eyes on afore or since. Let me think.' He lowered his head. 'There was Arthur Devlin, Ronnie Mason . . . but Ronnie was married last week.'

'Arthur Devlin. That Arthur Devlin's no good. He was in the papers the other week.'

'Was he? I don't know anything about that. What had he done?'

'Robbed somebody, and was up for grievous bodily harm an' all. That's what worries me, her knowing that lot. You should have more care who you introduce young lasses to.'

'Look, Mr Wilkins, she plagued me to take her, I didn't bloody well press her.'

'No, perhaps you didn't.' Mr Wilkins's voice was flat and he sighed deeply.

'Hadn't she any girl friends?' Annie asked now, and he answered, 'Yes, she had one particular one, Connie Blackman, but they had a row.'

'Still, perhaps she'll be able to help you?'

'Aye.' Mr Wilkins now moved slowly towards the door, then added, 'There's only one real place we can go for help and that's the polis. But it's the scandal; it'll kill her mother.' He turned his head towards them and repeated, 'It'll kill her. Respectable we've been all our lives, respectable, and now this.'

Annie followed him into the hall and as she opened the front door for him he said, 'You know, it's funny, but at one time you were always afraid of some fellow taking your daughter down; the thought of a lass coming home and saying she was going to have a bairn hung like a nightmare over people; now if Susan was to walk in the door and say she was pregnant I wouldn't mind a damn. Anything but drugs.'

Annie nodded at him dumbly and he went out. When she closed the door Tishy was standing in the hall looking at her; then coming towards her she whispered, 'Susan on drugs?'

Annie gulped deeply in her throat. 'She's left home,' she said.

Tishy turned now and looked through the open dining-room door where she could see Rance standing at one side of the table. He was straightening his tie as he looked at his reflection in the mirror and Annie, following her gaze, hissed at her, 'No! girl, no, you're wrong this time. No.'

'Just as well then, isn't it?'

As Tishy was going up the stairs Rance came into the hall, shrugging his overcoat on to his shoulders, and he stood looking at Annie for a moment before he said, 'Satisfied?'

'He thought you might be able to help him; you can see he's desperate.'

'And you thought I was mixed up in it, didn't you?' His voice was low. 'What do you take me for?'

'I thought nothing of the sort.'

He pushed past her and went out, banging the door so hard that the house shook.

It was about fifteen minutes later when she excused herself to Kathy, Bill and Percy, saying, 'I'm going to have a bath while the going's good. Tomorrow night everybody will be lining up and there won't be enough hot water.' She smiled at Kathy.

'Are you going straight to bed, Mam?' asked Bill, and she answered, 'Straight to bed? Of course not. Who's going to cut sandwiches for the supper and . . .?'

'You go to bed if you want, Mam –' Kathy nodded towards her – 'we'll fend for ourselves.'

'Thank you, miss!' said Annie with mock humility, aiming to bring a little lightness into the sombre atmosphere.

'You're very welcome, Annie.'

'I'll Annie you if you're not careful.' She pursed her lips at her daughter, then went out smiling. But as she mounted the stairs there was no smile on her face as she said to herself, 'Now stop it. Don't be insane, woman; he can have nothing to do with this.'

In her bedroom, she collected her dressing gown and slippers from the wardrobe, and as she closed the door she stopped and looked towards the wall, then cocked her head to one side. There was somebody in Rance's room. Her hand went to her throat. Had he sneaked back to pick up something? Oh my God! No. No. The only other person upstairs was Tishy, and wild horses wouldn't have dragged Tishy into his room. Should she let it go? What would be his defence if she surprised him now? Couldn't he come back and pick something up without being accused of being in a drug racket? It was as if he were already answering her. He always had an answer.

She found herself rushing out of the room and on to the landing and thrusting his door open. Then she stood with her mouth agape. There, standing on a chair, her hands groping along the top of the high Scotch chest, was Tishy.

'What in the name of God, girl, are you doing?'

Tishy turned an unperturbed face towards her, saying, 'One of two things, Mam: trying either to prove your fears are right or to set your mind at rest, whichever way you like to take it.'

'You've got a bad mind, our Tishy; you'll never rest till you see him behind bars, will you?' She was standing close to the chair now looking up at her daughter. 'Come down out of that.'

'I will in a minute, Mam. It's some time since you cleaned the top of this, it's thick with dust.'

'I'm not a giraffe, I can't get up there every week; it gets done in spring-cleaning.'

'Give me something to force the lid up.' Tishy put her hand down and Annie barked at her, 'I'll do no such thing! That blanket box has never been opened for years.'

'That's all you know, Mam. Parts of it are clear of dust, but it was a piece of fluff hanging over the edge that led me up here in the first place. I've never seen lumps of dusty fluff hanging from anything in this house before.'

'*Z Cars* is missing out not having you in the gang.'

'There might be something in that an' all. Will you hand me that file off the dressing table or will I have to get it myself?'

Annie grabbed the file and thrust it into her daughter's hand. As she watched Tishy trying to prise up the lid of the top of the six-foot tall chest which she had picked up in a second-hand shop years ago, part of her mind was gabbling prayers.

She saw the edge of the lid move upwards. She watched Tishy peering downwards, then slowly turn her face to the side and look at her. And her expression was almost triumphant. Then putting her hand down into the blanket box she drew something out and said, 'Hold these.' And she handed down to her a flat packet of banknotes held together with an elastic band; then another and another and another and another.

When Tishy had stepped off the chair she twisted it round and said to Annie, 'Sit down,' and Annie sat down. Then she looked up at Tishy helplessly, and Tishy said, 'Well?'

'He –' she had to gather spittle into her mouth before she could go on – 'he could have won it gambling.'

'He's not supposed to be gambling, Mam; he was supposed to give it up.'

'How do we know what he does when he's out? Anyway, it could be ordinary gambling, not the tables; he could go to the betting shop any time of the day.'

'Do you think that amount of money came from gambling? Give it here.'

She took the bundles from Annie's unresisting hold and Annie watched her lay it on the bed, take the rubber bands from each bundle in turn and begin counting. Each time she spoke it was as if a knife were going through her. 'There's a hundred single pounds in that lot; and there's sixty five-pound notes in that one; a hundred in that one, and a hundred in that one; six hundred altogether.'

Tishy now sat down on the side of the bed and said quietly, 'He's either been cooking the garage books for a long time or he's in some racket.'

'He can't cook the books.' Annie shook her head slowly. 'I see to them; you know I do.'

'Some pay cash, don't they? You're only there about an hour in the day; he could have a job in and out every day for a week.'

'He wouldn't do that.'

'Well, it's better to think that's how he got this –' she flicked a bundle of notes aside – 'than from some other racket, say the one connected with Susan Wilkins.' Tishy's voice had taken on a harsh note and Annie's was equally harsh and low as she hissed back to her, 'Don't say that! Don't say it. Do you want to kill me, girl?'

Tishy now bowed her head and, putting her hands between her thin knees, she pressed them together before saying, 'There's only one thing I want. I want you to open your eyes and see what's before your nose in order that you won't get hurt; but I know that's an impossibility, for as long as he breathes he'll hurt you.'

'Tishy! Tishy! look at me.' There was a pleading note in Annie's voice, and when Tishy lifted her head, Annie said, 'If I open my eyes, as you put it, and say, all right he's getting this from some racket, am I going to be less hurt than if ... if I thought he had any dealings with ... with drugs? I'd die of shame in either case.'

Tishy got to her feet, saying quietly now, 'It takes a lot of shame to kill people, Mam.' And as Annie gazed at her she felt, as she had done last night while talking to Kathy, younger than either of her daughters. Neither of them closed their eyes to facts that were staring them in the face; but oh God! she could stand anything staring her in the face, except drugs. If this money was from that it meant he wasn't only taking drugs, he was profiting by the degradation he brought on others.

Of all the base creatures in the world the lowest, in her estimation, were those men who sold drugs to the young; slimy, stinking, putrid, were the adjectives she attached to them. She couldn't, she couldn't think that her son, her Rance, could be capable of such vileness. He was weak; oh yes, she admitted that; and he was a liar, he could look you in the face and swear black was white and you believed it in spite of yourself; but he wouldn't put youngsters on the road to hell, would he, just for money.

Tishy was searching through the dressing table drawers, but now she did not protest, she only stared at her, watching the swift movements of her hands, and waited. She watched her go to the wardrobe and take down his suits one by one and go through the pockets. When, out of one pocket, she brought a half burnt cigarette she took it to the light and examined it; then after a moment she put it back where she had found it. She watched her inserting two fingers into the watch pocket in the inside of a jacket. She watched her pull out a crumpled piece of paper, press it straight between her fingers, and read it; then, coming towards her, she held it out, saying quietly, 'This could be it after all.'

When Annie looked at the betting slip that registered a five-pound bet the wave of relief that passed through her made her feel faint. Pressing the slip between her hands as if holding something precious, she looked up at Tishy and said, 'Oh thank God! lass. Thank God! I don't mind about that; I don't mind if he gambles his shirt away.' With a bright eagerness, she now said, 'Put that money back, lass, and remember how it was placed. Leave everything as you found it. Oh, thank God! Thank God! She went towards the bed and herself folded up the betting slip and returned it to the inner pocket of the coat. Then she hung the suit back in the wardrobe.

A few minutes later she watched Tishy step down from the chair and lift it to the side of the bed, and she said to her, 'Come on now. Come on.'

On the landing, she stood looking at her daughter for a moment. Then with tears in her voice, she said, 'I couldn't be happier if I had won the pools.'

Simultaneously they turned away from each other and went into their rooms, Tishy to stand, as she often did, with her back to the door, her head well back on her shoulders looking upwards towards the ceiling. Her mother hadn't upbraided her for trying to expose him; she hadn't waved the ticket in her face and said, 'There! I knew my Rance wouldn't do such a thing as that'; she had just grasped at the flimsy evidence and literally held it to her as if it were an innocent child.

She moved from the door and sat on the dressing table stool and gazed at her reflection in the mirror and asked of it, 'Do I want him to be caught out on this?'

No; not that she didn't think he was capable of any trickery, or fiddle, but there was a special kind of disgrace about drugs that she wouldn't wish on him, not the taking of them so much but the selling of them.

What would have transpired if she had proved he was in this racket? Would it have benefited her in any way? Would her mother have suddenly stopped loving Rance and turned her affection wholly on to herself? No, of course she wouldn't. Her mother would never love her more than she did at this moment, and she knew that this love had for its main ingredients maternal duty threaded with pity.

Why did she hate Rance so? Was it that since she was a child she had been aware that he claimed her mother's whole attention? Or was it that since she was a child she knew that she herself had craved love? Her granda had been the only person who had really loved her. And then again his love had been born of pity; he had been sorry for the poor little lass because she looked so plain, for the ugly duckling that he had prophesied would turn into a swan.

'Why am I not pretty like Kathy, Granda?'

'Because you're a late starter, hinny. Just you wait; come sixteen or seventeen you'll turn into a swan. You've a swan inside you, it just has to come out.'

It didn't come out; the transformation didn't happen; but at odd times she still thought she was a swan inside. She only needed somebody to love her and she would turn into the swan.

Oh God! how she needed somebody to love her. She rested her face between the palms of her hands, her elbows on the dressing table, and moved her head slowly at herself, and her affection answered the movement. She was chock-a-block with love. If she didn't give vent to it in some way it would choke her. Would she end her days pouring it out on animals, a cat, a dog, a budgerigar, as so many women did?

Perhaps Stanley Stone might ask her to marry him. He was showing an interest, but then he would show an interest in anybody who would listen to him. He never stopped talking. God! fancy having to pass your days with a fellow like Stanley Stone. Why did parents give a child a christian name like Stanley when their surname was Stone? Stanley Stone, Barry Butcher, Clare Clark, May Minton. She knew all these people and the joint christian and surname names gave to them a silliness that seemed to seep into their characters. What about her own name, Tishy? Could you find a sillier name than that? There had been a horse called Tishy; the name now indicated a non-starter. And she was a non-starter, and how!

But she wasn't a non-starter in her mind; that was active enough. She knew she had never met a man as intelligent as herself, except one. When she allowed herself to think of him she didn't know if the pain that assailed her was created by love or by hate, for always when he came on to the screen of her mind she did not see him standing tall and shamefaced saying, 'I am going to be married,' but she saw him sitting on the couch, her mother lying across his knees and he with his arms about her, the look on his face like that of a man filled with deep, desire-filled love. No pain she would ever receive would come anywhere near to that which had rent her in that moment.

She had seen Alan twice in the past three years; the first time was eighteen months ago. She was shopping in Binns in Newcastle when she saw him walking slowly towards her. She had turned quickly about and gone up a side aisle, but while making a purchase she watched him and the young woman who was with him, and it was on her she focused her gaze, thinking the while with renewed bitterness, She's almost as plain as me. She was dowdy into the bargain. He must have picked her for her brains, she concluded. What a pity she hadn't got in first.

The second time she saw him was about three months ago, in Newcastle Central Station. She was making her way to the platform from where she would get the train to Shields when he came through the barrier from where the London train had just drawn in. For a moment she hadn't recognized him and she had stopped and stared. He looked so much older; there was no youth left in his face. Again her thoughts were cynical: he must be finding marriage hard work.

She stared into the mirror now with something of impatient surprise; it was as if she were looking at a different face, for the tears were running down the cheeks of her reflection. As her tongue came out and licked the salt drops she murmured aloud, 'Don't let me make a fool of myself at the wedding. Let me be happy for her.' Then dropping her face on to her crossed arms, she whimpered like a child, 'I wish me granda hadn't died. Me granda loved me, and there'll never be anybody else now, never.'

Part Six

THE COTTAGE

1

—

'Well if you don't put your name to it, Mam, I'll get it on me own.'

'A twelve thousand pound house ... on your own! Things must be looking up.' Annie closed the hamper into which she had packed foodstuff and, pushing it towards Rance, said, 'Put it in the boot for me.'

Rance went to lift the wickerwork hamper from the table but stopped in the act and, leaning heavily on it, looked to where Annie was picking up her handbag from the chair, and he said, 'Mam, I mean to have that house, with or without you.'

'Then you'll have it without me. Twelve thousand, huh!'

He lowered his head and looked down at his white knuckles gripping the handles of the hamper, and after a moment of silence he ground out, 'Mam, I'm twenty-seven; I've got to have a life of me own.'

Like lightning she rounded on him, crying now, 'Who's stopping you having a life of your own? I've told you for years to get yourself away. Take a flat. I've even gone and got you a flat. A life of your own! Don't you dare say to me I stopped you having a life of your own. Look, boy.' She leant across the table towards him now, her face only inches from his, and her voice came as a hiss as she went on, 'Get yourself away, do what you like, and leave me my life. I want a life of me own too, but I don't see it sharing a ten-roomed house, me in one part and Benny and you in the other, because he would be there wouldn't he?'

'He's a good pal.' His voice now was like that of an adolescent defending a friend.

'Pal!' Her lip curled.

'He's never done anything to you.'

'No, but I don't like him; he's too smooth, shifty. And his friends in London. Every time you come back from there you'd think you'd been on the razzle for a week. I've asked you this afore, and I'll ask you again, what's his real business? You can't tell me he can run that car of his and live like he does selling panties and girdles; reps don't make all that much. You can't tell me.'

'You've got no idea of what they make, Mam. It's a big business.'

'Big business, is it?' She nodded at him now. 'Well, you must be in it too if you can afford to take on a twelve thousand pound house.'

'I've got a bit put by.'

'A bit!' She stared at him hard.

'Benny will come in with me if you won't.'

'Well, Benny can go in with you because I'm not leaving here to live in half a house that's costing twelve thousand pounds. No, thank you. Now put that in the boot for me, will you?'

'You'll be sorry.'

'Sorry, what for? 'Cos I don't want to uproot my life? This house is good enough for me. It's too big for me as it is. Bill's gone now, that only leaves you and Tishy, and it wouldn't surprise me if she isn't off before the year's out. It won't be Stanley's fault if she isn't, so under ordinary circumstances that would leave the two of us. Surely there would be plenty of room here for you then.'

'You could never make this place into flats.'

Now Annie banged her fist on the table. 'Flats! flats! flats! For God's sake! go and take your house and make it into as many flats as you like, but without me.'

He stood now, his teeth gritted, shaking his head at her; then he muttered, 'Sometimes I could, I could . . .'

'You could what?'

'Mam –' he was a little boy again – 'it's too big to run as a house for the two of us, I mean Benny and me, and . . . and the main point is I want you, I want you about. You know that.'

Yes, she knew that, but it was a long time since the thought had brought her any happiness. Although she couldn't stand Benny Warlister she had wished more than once of late that Rance would go to London with him and stay there, yet at the same

182

time knowing that had Rance made this proposal she would have done all in her power to prevent him because there was something not right, to her mind, about Warlister. As she had said, he was too smooth, too polite. When he buttered her up, telling her that she was a fraud and couldn't possibly be the mother of four grown-ups, she wanted to push him on his back and say, 'Get out of my house and stay out.'

Suddenly she said, 'What about Tishy in your scheme of things? You don't plan for her to come to the new house, do you?'

'No, I don't.' His face and voice hardened. 'I've had enough of her to last me ten lifetimes. She could stay here with her Stanley, that's if she marries him, but I'd like to bet she'll never marry anybody.'

'She's like you then, isn't she?'

'I'll marry when I'm ready.'

'Well, so will she. But the trouble with you is you don't like anyone. What about Bill and his girl? You can't stand her either, can you, because she's coloured? And then there's Percy. One of these days that fellow is going to hit you in the mouth.'

'That'll be the day.'

'It will, and it'll come. But the point in question is, I can rely on all of them coming to see me here, but if I go into your house. . . .'

'It won't be my house, it'll be our house.'

'It'll be your house, my flat in your house. Tell me something, are you thinking of putting it in our joint names? It would have to be if I was standing half, wouldn't it?'

'That can be gone into.'

'It's been gone into.' She picked up her light coat and put it round her shoulders, saying, 'Tishy won't be back from abroad till Friday, but I'll be home by then. Bill and Alice, well, you never know with them, it could be any day. I've been round to Kathy's and told her. I think that takes care of everything.'

'And I can take care of meself, is that it?'

She stopped on her way to the door. 'Well, if you're going into flat life it'll be good practice, won't it?'

'Mam!' He had her by the shoulders now, his face crumpled almost as if he were going to cry. 'Look, don't go and leave me like this. When you go off in a tear I'm worked up for days.'

Again and again this side of him attempted to break her down.

She wanted to put up her hands and smooth his face straight, but she didn't; she remembered that only yesterday she had looked in the Scotch chest, as she did now from time to time, and found that there had been another three rolls of bank-notes added to the amount she had last seen. Sometimes she found no money in the box at all; then it would gradually grow. Besides the Scotch chest there was also a desk now, but she could never find out what it held. He had bought the desk himself, and it had arrived with a patent lock on it. She had tried to open it with several keys but without success. Her son, she knew, was in some racket; what it actually was she daren't let herself think.

One of the main reasons for her going to the cottage now was to get away from him, for she felt that if she didn't she would come into the open, not to ask questions, but to accuse him outright, accuse him of the thing that was keeping her awake at nights.

He was saying now, 'Will ... will you think about it because ... because you know how I feel about being separated from you?'

She lowered her eyes and as she turned from him, saying, 'Yes, all right, I'll think about it,' he put his arm around her shoulders and said, 'It'll work out, it'll work out fine.'

A few minutes later, as she drove down the street, she thought, Yes. Yes, I'll think about it, but that'll be as far as it'll go. ....

It would take her two hours to get to the cottage, so long as she wasn't held up in Newcastle. She had owned the cottage now for over two years, and she had come by it in a very simple way. Taking a cottage in the wilds of the Cheviots she would have said was not her idea of a holiday retreat. Now if it was a chalet on some quiet beach, that would be more like it.

She had been on the forecourt of the garage one day when a Mr Sampson, an old customer, had come up to her and said, 'I'm sorry to tell you, Mrs McCabe, I'll soon be coming for my last fill-up; we're leaving, going down south.'

'Oh, I'm sorry about that,' she had answered; 'you've been with us a long time, Mr Sampson.'

'Yes, ever since your husband started, and that's some time ago now. What is it, over twenty years? But these things happen. You've got to go where you're sent these days, that's if you want to get on. What's more, when you're getting on in years you don't say no, that's if you're wise.'

'You're right there, Mr Sampson,' she had said.

'I would have been off last week if it wasn't for this damn

cottage of mine. We've sold the house but I can't get rid of the cottage.'

'A cottage?' she had repeated.

'Aye, it's up in the Cheviot Hills and everybody wants it, until I state the price, and then they say, "What! fifteen hundred for a cottage. You must be mad, man." I paid seven hundred and fifty for that place ten years ago and I've spent over a thousand on it, having it gutted and completely rebuilt inside, that's not counting the week-ends of labour me and the wife put in and the lads an' all when they were younger. But now "Fifteen hundred!" they say. I took a bloke out there at the week-end and you know I got that mad at him I nearly did him in and buried him in a pot hole. He knew what I wanted for it afore we left, and he stood there having the neck to offer me eight hundred, and that was his last word he said because there was no piped water, and why wasn't there? I told him if he wanted piped water he should stay put in the town. But you see the way the brook is placed it would have cost me another mint to get it up to the cottage. Anyway, it's a good job he came in his own car else I'd have made him walk back.'

After they had both stopped laughing she said, 'Is it back of beyond?'

'Truthfully aye, it's back of beyond, and there's not many places left the day that's back of beyond. That, to my mind, was always the beauty of it. We could get away and forget all about everything. Many's the time I've gone up there by meself on a Saturday night feeling dead beat and come down on the Sunday night refreshed and armed for another start. Mind, I can't say I haven't had me money's worth out of it; we've had wonderful summers up there; but it hasn't been used much lately. The wife's got rheumatics you see, an' the lads are married and gone away. But I'm telling you, Mrs McCabe, I'd sooner burn it down, and believe me I mean it, I would, I'd sooner burn it down than take a penny less than I'm askin'.'

'Would you let me see it, Mr Sampson? Mind, I'm not promising anything. I don't know if I'd like the wilds, haven't seen much of them except passing through the country on my way to the Lake District in the car.'

'Be pleased to, Mrs McCabe. What about tomorrow?'

'Tomorrow'll do nicely, Mr Sampson.'

When the morrow had come she saw the cottage. They had

left the car in a copse at the end of a narrow track a mile from the main road, and after climbing over a broken stone wall, which took a hundred yards off the journey Mr Sampson informed her, she saw a grey stone house, standing on a rise. It wasn't her idea of a cottage and not pretty at all, and she made up her mind there and then that it wasn't for her. But she hadn't seen inside it then, nor the view from the window, nor had she sat on the top step and drunk a cup of tea while she looked over the wild and beautiful land enclosed by hills.

By the time she had taken the rough road down to the car again she had bought the cottage.

As she was passing through Gateshead she was tempted to stop and call in on Mollie, who had for some years now lived with her daughter Winnie, but she knew that once she got talking to Mollie she might be tempted to unburden herself, and so she went straight through, over a bridge into the maze of traffic, and fifteen minutes later she was passing through Gosforth on the road to Ponteland.

The farther she went the wider the country opened out, and when some thirty miles later she came to Otterburn she didn't stop at the Percy Arms as she usually did when she was alone and treat herself to a good lunch, but drove straight on until she passed Elishaw; then she turned into a road that was little more than a cart track and a few minutes later she drew the car to a halt within the shelter of the copse. Opening the boot she took out the hamper and small case and began the long trudge up to the cottage.

It was fifteen minutes later, after having to make stops to rest, that she arrived at the foot of the steps and looked upwards. She always paused here, as much from weariness as from her delight in seeing the place again, for no matter how often she came upon it after an absence of even a short time it brought to her a sense of peace.

When she unlocked the door she was assailed by a musty smell and she wrinkled her nose against it. Nobody had been here for the past month and it had rained almost incessantly up till a week ago, when the weather had changed, and now the second week in June the weather was giving them a tropical summer.

Before she brought the case and hamper up she went round opening the windows, telling herself as she did so she must make an effort to get out here once a fortnight during the summer, or at least get some of them to come out. It was odd, she thought, that during that first year the place had never been empty except for a couple of days at a time from May until late September. Kathy and Percy had spent weeks up here. Kathy was carrying the baby at the time and she always said it would grow up to be a wild man of the moors because she had roamed the hills so much during the early months of her pregnancy. It could well be right too, for young Percy, at two-and-a-half, was a rip, and you needed a lead on him like a dog to know where he was. Now she was carrying her second, the trip together with young Percy was too much for her.

Bill had used the cottage that first year as his headquarters, all through the summer vacation; he and his pals had kipped around in sleeping bags four to a room.

And Tishy, she had spent every week-end up here, and often of an evening when there was no one here she would ask for the loan of the car and set off straight after school and not get back until midnight. She liked to go places on her own. Tishy was still a loner, in spite of having Stanley.

And Rance. Rance was the only one who had never taken to the cottage. He considered she was mad in the first place for paying that price for it, and after his first visit he said the place would drive him starkers. Yet last year he and Benny had spent a week-end up here. She hadn't liked that.

As she unpacked the foodstuff into the cupboard she let out a long relaxing sigh. This, too, was strange but she felt more at home in this kitchen than she did in the one at home. It had neither running water nor electricity, every drop of water having to be carried either from the rain barrel at the back or from the burn three minutes' walk away. The lighting, like the cooking, was supplied by calor gas, and the canisters took some lugging up the hill. She paid nearly as much in tips as she did for the gas.

She made herself a pot of tea and, having set it on a tray, carried it into the main room. It was the sight of this room that had clinched the bargain immediately. The original three small front rooms of the cottages had been made into one, twenty-two feet by eighteen, and the sculleries at the back had been converted into a kitchen, on to the end of which had been built a glass porch to provide more light.

She had bought the place as it stood and she had altered nothing of the furnishing and little in the arrangement. The narrow floorboards were polished a light mahogany colour and the only floor covering was four large orange and green rugs. The front door opened into the middle of the room. The windows on each side were not large, but the old-fashioned frames had been taken out and replaced by modern ones which opened outwards. On the end wall to the left of the door was an open fireplace with a surround of natural stone.

The furniture was ordinary and comfortable; a well-worn three-piece suite which she had had re-covered in chintz, a dining table, the legs of which showed the imprints of numerous toe-caps and which she had been unable to erase even with regular polishing; the six chairs were plain and sturdy and the china cabinet that had once graced a drawing-room had two small glass panes missing – but still remained a valuable piece, so Percy said.

The stairs that led steeply up from the right-hand side of the room near the kitchen door were open and had no balustrade, merely a thick rope.

There were two bedrooms, three at a pinch, the latter being a seven by six storeroom. All the windows were on floor level, and Annie had not yet become used to lying in a bed which seemed at times to be floating in the sky, or resting on top of hills.

She sat now in the easy chair drawn up in front of the open door. She had taken her shoes and tights off and she was waggling her bare toes with the joy of a child. In a few minutes she'd change into slacks and get some water up from the burn, then fetch more wood in, for no matter how hot the day it always got chilly as soon as the twilight began.

Could she live here on her own? She shook her head uncertainly at the question. Perhaps; yes, she thought she might be able to.

If she had to pick one of them to live with, who would it be? Tishy?

Yes, Tishy. But why Tishy? Tishy didn't need her in the same way Rance did; Tishy was sufficient unto herself; she had an inner force, an inner strength. So why Tishy?

Because she needed Tishy. Was that it? Yes, yes, she supposed so. Anyway, she needed someone. Of late, she had felt very lonely; well, not so much lonely as alone. You couldn't be lonely with them all popping in and out and making demands on you, but you could be alone in the midst of them.

She thought of Georgie. Would he have liked it up here? No; like Rance he would have said it would have driven him crackers. You had to be a certain type of person to enjoy more than a passing glimpse of these fells and moors because they were secret places.

What did she mean by that?

Well, she supposed. . . . Oh, she didn't know what she meant, she was going off all poetic. This is what always happened when she sat here; she never thought like this at home. This place brought things out of you. If you just sat quiet something crept into you, stirred your thoughts, made you think as you had never done before – and made you pleased that you could think that way. Yes, yes, indeed.

When she awoke with a start she realized she had been dozing. Would you believe it! dropping off like that. But she had been tired when she arrived, and disturbed, and that was putting it mildly. She had told Rance she would think about it. Well, that's what she was going to do, but not in the way he expected. She had known for some time she wanted to make a break, get away, do something different with her life before it was too late. What exactly she didn't know, but what she knew in this relaxed moment was that before she left here on Friday everything would be clear in her mind.

She brought up two cans of water from the burn; she filled the straw skips at each side of the fireplace with wood; she set the fire all ready for lighting; she fried herself some bacon and eggs and had two cups of coffee; she washed herself down in soft rain water from the barrel, got back into her slacks and was pulling a red sweater over her head when she heard the knock on the door.

It wasn't unusual for someone to knock on the door; hikers often stopped and asked for hot water, some would ask if she had any eggs for sale, only to be informed that she didn't keep hens. There were even those slap-happy bare-faced picnickers who would come with such requests as: would she fry them a pound of bacon and half a dozen eggs? or had she any bread or cake she didn't want? They had gone through their own supply at dinner-time and had nothing left for the second meal. If they were youngsters she would meet their requests if she could, but if they were grown-ups she had learned to deal with them. Sometimes she got only a black look after delivering a homily on being prepared, but on other occasions she got a mouthful of abuse.

When she opened the door a young man stood there, definitely a climber by his clothes. 'Good afternoon,' he said. 'I'm sorry to trouble you but I wonder if you would be kind enough to put a drop of hot water on this tea?' He held out a can. 'Me friend has sprained his ankle and we're getting him down. We thought we might be stranded for the night but the other fellow –' he pointed behind him – 'he's a hiker, kindly offered to make a sling out of his sleeping bag. We've got a car down on the road. How far do you think it is to Horsley?'

'Oh, about two miles, but you want to go straight down now and cut over to the right.'

'Oh aye. Well, I'll tell him. It's only our second trip out.'

'Would you like to bring him up and rest here a while?'

He looked back down the trail where one figure was standing and the other lying on the ground, and he said, 'It's pretty steep and by the time we would get up here we could be well on our way. But thanks all the same.' He smiled apologetically.

'Yes, you're right. It'll be about five minutes.'

'Thanks. I'll be glad of a rest. May I sit down here for a minute?'

'Yes, you're very welcome.' She hurried into the kitchen, and after a moment his voice came to her, saying, 'By! it's a nice place this.'

'Yes,' she answered; 'I like it.'

'A bit lonely.'

'For some, I suppose.'

'You'd never dream there was a habitation here until you come round the hill.'

'No, you wouldn't . . . we're sheltered in a way. Where do you hail from?'

'Wallsend.'

'Oh, Wallsend. I'm from Shields.'

'Get away!'

'Yes, it's a small world.'

'Aye, it is. But it doesn't look small from up here. Eeh! you could lose yourself in these hills and never be found. Robby was getting the wind up; that's why I didn't leave him and go and get help on me own.'

After a few minutes she came back into the room carrying a tray with his steaming can on it; it also held three cups and saucers, a bowl of sugar, a jug of milk and a plate of buttered scones, the whole of which she had expected to last her during her stay, but then, she had told herself, she could always knock up some more.

'Don't bother to bring the tray back, I'll come down and get it.'

'It's very kind of you, missis. I'm very obliged to you.'

'That's all right. I hope you'll do the same for me some day when I break my ankle.'

They both laughed; then he went down the hill and she stood and watched him pouring out the tea and handing the scones round, and when after a while the three raised their hands to her, she walked down the steps, then on down the hill, to pick up the tray.

When she reached the track they were cutting at an angle over the slope below her, and the young man holding the back of the sling turned his head round and called 'Ta-rah! And thanks again.'

At this, the man in front also turned round and looked towards her, and as he did so the small cavalcade came to a jolting stop. The man stared up at her, and she stared down at him. She heard the young fellow at the back say, 'What is it?' She saw the man in front move his head, then walk on.

She stood watching them until they had gone over the hump and were out of sight. Then she stooped and picked up the tray and went slowly up and into the house. She did not take the tray into the kitchen but laid it beside her as she dropped on to the couch.

Him! after all this time. But it was him all right. She hadn't recognized him at first for he was so altered. But he had recognized her, and she had altered too. Oh yes, she knew she had altered in the last six years, and not just in one way, she was older looking, much older looking.

She must have sat for half an hour before she rose and took the tray of crockery into the kitchen. After she had washed up the cups she went upstairs, and the first thing she did was to look in the wardrobe. She had brought only one dress with her – she lived in slacks most of the time up here.

She took the dress from its hanger and laid it on the bed, then went to the mirror, and there she peered at her face. She hadn't many lines yet, a few under her eyes, one faint one starting at the right-hand side of her upper lip. There were one or two strands of grey in her hair, but they were at the back. She hadn't seen them herself, it was the hairdresser who had told her. She pulled the bedside chair round and sat down before the mirror; then taking a lipstick from the tray, she carefully made up her lips, applied a faint dusting of rouge to her cheeks, and was on the point of applying some eye liner when she banged the pencil down on to the table.

What was she up to? Well, he'd come back and she wanted to look decent.

All right, he'd come back, so what of it? What hadn't happened six years ago wasn't likely to happen now, was it? Be your age. She glared at herself in the mirror.

When he came in how should she greet him?

Well, how should she greet him? Politely, ordinary like, no fuss. She rose and, taking her dress from the bed, she hung it up in the wardrobe again, then went downstairs. The clock said ten to six. If it had taken him half an hour to get down to Horsley it would take him a little more to get back, then add the time for seeing those chaps off and he should be here any time now. She'd keep the door shut. When he knocked it would give her time to compose herself.

Why did she need to compose herself?

Oh, for God's sake shut up, woman!

By half past six he hadn't come. At quarter to seven she said to herself, 'There now, sure, weren't you, absolutely positive he'd come back. What about his wife? He's likely left her at some spot on the hills and is going to pick her up later. . . . You, you want your head looking, that's what you want. They say women in their forties go daft, and you're proving it. You must have started the change in your mind if nowhere else.'

For two pins she'd get in the car and go back home. If she started off now she could be home before dark. Well, she'd better make up her mind before she put a match to the fire. She stopped herself from going to the window yet once again by saying, 'Enough of that now. Enough of that. Go or stay. Decide now.'

It was as she stood in the middle of the room pondering that she heard the scraping of rough boots against the stone steps, and when the knock did come on the door she held her hand tight against her waist. She told herself not to rush, to take things easy, then went towards the door and opened it.

It was a full minute before either of them spoke, and then he said, 'I knew it was you; there couldn't be two of you. I ... I would have been back before now but those two chaps knew as much about cars as they did about climbing and that was very little. We couldn't get the thing to start; just the matter of an empty tank. We ... we had to go for petrol.'

He was explaining all this to her as if he had left her a short while before and been held up.

'Come in,' she said.

He came in, wiping his feet assiduously on the doormat before stepping on to the bare floorboards. He did not look round the room but at her and asked, 'How are you?'

'Oh, very well. And you?'

'Very well.' He inclined his head towards her, smiling slightly now. The action, and his voice made it sound as if he were amused as he would be at a child who was trying to be over polite. Then, the smile leaving his face, he said, 'I remember saying this to you before, and I have to again, you don't change.'

'Nor you; you still lie gallantly.' She turned from him and moved down the room, saying, 'Won't you sit down? I was just going to put a match to the fire.'

As she struck the match and set the paper alight he said, 'What an extraordinary room! You get no indication from outside. I've passed this place for years. Have you been long here?'

She took the bellows and worked them and the flame licked up between the wood before she said, 'Nearly three years.'

'How is the family?'

'Oh, very well. Kathy's married, has a little family of her own now.'

'How nice. And ... and the others?'

'Oh, just as they were, although Bill may be marrying soon I think. I lost my mother and father though.'

'Oh, I'm sorry. Your mother-in-law – Mollie, wasn't it? Is she still alive?'

'Oh very much so. They'll have to shoot Mollie, I think.'

She put down the bellows, dusted her hands, then coming towards him, she asked, 'Would you like a cup of tea, it's some time since you had the last one?'

'I would indeed. I haven't had a meal since twelve. . . .'

'I . . . I can make you something.'

'Oh no, please, I didn't mean that. I was going to say I've got some grub in my pack. Would . . . would you mind if I brought my pack in for a moment? I don't suppose anyone would steal it, not around here, but then again I'm not so sure. I was washing my feet in a burn once when somebody went off with my boots. It was only for a lark; I found them hanging on a tree about a mile farther on. And the foxes can get a bit nosy too, and they don't wait for the dark.'

'Yes, bring it in by all means.'

'Oh, not in here.' He looked round the room. 'Is there a shed at the back?'

'No, no,' she said hastily – the only shed at the back was the one that covered the Elsan pan – 'but there's an annexe to the kitchen where we store the deck chairs and things; it'll go in there.'

'Good.'

She watched him go quickly out of the door and down the steps; then she closed her eyes and bit on her lip. She had told herself she must act ordinary, but she could never act so ordinary as he was doing. It was unbelievable. Nobody coming in would believe that he had just dropped in out of the blue. He was so self-assured. That, she supposed, came from teaching, and not just schoolboys, but men. What was he now, thirty? Good gracious! he looked so much older. He had grown gaunt in a way, there was hardly any flesh on him. But that could be the hill climbing; the energy that took left men with only bone and muscle.

She sat down weakly on a chair, saying to herself the while that she couldn't believe it, she couldn't believe it. From the time she told him not to come back she hadn't been able to get him out of her mind for months. At night she would lie thinking about how she had lain in his arms and cried, and she would recapture the feel of his arms about her and hold on to the look in his eyes when he had said, 'If I had fallen in love with anybody it wouldn't have been Tishy.' And then she would think, Oh Georgie, I'm sorry. I'm sorry.

During those months too, the relationship between Tishy and her had been strained. Tishy would go for days, even a week at a time, and not open her mouth. She had wanted to say to her, 'He was only being kind, acting like our Bill or Rance would have done if they had been in.' But Bill or Rance would never have held her like that. She would never have lain across their knees and been cradled in their arms.

She recalled now that Tishy had never mentioned his name again; but she had got over him for she had taken up with Stanley Stone, and gradually her manner had thawed and returned to normal.

'I'm amazed. What a lovely kitchen. The whole place is delightful. How . . . how did you come across it?'

He had come in through the kitchen door, and now she rose and went past him and re-entered the kitchen, and as she put the kettle on the stove she told him briefly how she had come to own the cottage.

'What is it called?'

'Sheepcote Cottage. It was originally a shepherd's cottage; then they added on to it and made three farm cottages. I understand that the original end, where the fireplace is, is over three hundred and fifty years old.'

'I've no doubt about it. These . . . these places were built to last and to stand up against the weather. Do you use it often?'

She hesitated before saying, 'Yes, pretty often, but not so much as we used to. Everyone was newfangled with it the first year and the two hours' journey was nothing. You know, people's enthusiasms change.' She gave him a half smile as she spread a cloth over the formica-topped kitchen table, then said, 'You would prefer hot bacon and eggs to cold sandwiches if I'm not mistaken?' and he answered, 'You're not mistaken.'

As the bacon sizzled in the pan, and the eggs spluttered and he sat behind her at the table, talking all the while, she told herself that it was fantastic that she should be up here cooking him a meal after all this time. Of one thing she knew she was glad, and she emphasized this to herself, she didn't think she liked him now, in fact she was sure she didn't. He talked too much, too easily, too freely. But then, hadn't he always talked easily and freely? Still, he was different, and she was glad he was different. It had knocked all that nonsense on the head; funny, how you nursed a thing for years, blew it up out of all proportion, gave to a little incident a meaning that was ridiculous to say the least. Oh, women were fools. All of them were fools. From their early teens onwards they made fools of themselves in a thousand

and one ways. And she could cap them all. First, Georgie and then ... Oh, she shouldn't think that way about Georgie.

'There.' She put the plate of bacon and eggs on the table before him, and he smiled at her, saying, 'Thanks.' Then, as he picked up the knife and fork to begin eating, he paused and asked, 'Where's yours? Aren't you having any?'

'No, I had something just a little while ago. I'll have a cup of coffee though. I can drink coffee at any time.'

For the life of her she told herself she couldn't sit at that table and eat with him. There was something about him that was disturbing, but in a different way from that which she remembered. Yet he wasn't acting differently from what he had done seven years ago. His actions, his voice, his manner were still that of the young man of twenty-four. That was the point, he was no longer that young man, seven years divided him from that young man, and those years were written on his face. He appeared like an older man acting the boy. He startled her now by repeating her thoughts aloud. His voice grave, he said, 'I've been imagining that I had just come into your kitchen on that night, the second time we met. Do you remember?'

Did she remember! would she ever forget? There were periods when, night following night, Georgie hurled down the stairs towards her, sometimes knocking her over and tumbling with her down a further flight.

He said no more until he had finished eating, by which time she had brewed the coffee and carried it into the sitting-room. She placed a small table near the chair to the side of the fire and on it she put his cup, while she placed her own on a similar table but at the end of the couch farthest away from the chair.

When he asked from the kitchen door, 'Shall I wash up, I'm quite used to it?' she turned to him and said hastily, 'Of course not! Anyway, I've got to heat water. They can wait till the morning.'

As he came down the room she pointed to the coffee, saying, 'Do you take sugar?' She didn't add, I've forgotten, but ended, 'I'm sorry I didn't ask whether you like it black or white? I made it white.'

'That's how I like it, and without sugar, thank you.'

He sat down and when he picked his cup up and it rattled in the saucer she realized with surprise that he was as nervous as she, and it enabled her to speak to him calmly. 'Are you still teaching in Newcastle?' she asked.

'I was up till last term; I've left.'

'Oh!' She raised her eyebrows slightly.

'I may be going to America in August to teach at a university there; in fact, I'm sure I'm going.' He smiled now as he nodded, 'I have a research scholarship.'

'Oh! that's marvellous.'

'Well, that remains to be seen.' He was smiling again. 'I may get my head blown off on the campus.'

'Oh, don't say that. Yet there have been dreadful riots over there, haven't there? But then, why go to America for riots; we've got an assortment of them here, haven't we?'

'Yes, indeed.'

'I suppose your wife is looking forward to it; most women like the idea of going to America.'

He now sipped from his cup, then placed it on the table to his side, but he didn't look at her as he said, 'My wife won't be going with me, we were divorced two years ago.'

... 'Oh! Oh, I'm very sorry.'

'It would be very boorish of me to say I'm not, yet it would be true.'

She remained quiet, until the silence became embarrassing; then she asked as evenly as she could, 'Do you ever see your uncle now?'

'Uncle Arthur? Oh yes. I came from there yesterday. He doesn't live so very far away, just beyond Hawick. It's over the border in Roxburgh. Do you know it?'

'No, I haven't been that far. . . . How is he?'

'Very well. Very well indeed. Strange, but he was talking of you the other day.'

'Oh yes?'

He did not go on to say what Arthur Bailey had said but added evenly, 'And who do you think I saw last year?'

'I wouldn't know.'

'Mona.'

'Really!'

'And in Paris of all places.'

'Paris! . . . Mona?'

'Paris . . . Mona.'

'Was she on holiday?'

197

'Part that, and part honeymoon; she had just married again.'

'Really! Well, well.'

'And she looked marvellous, radiant.'

Annie moved her head slowly; she could never imagine Mona looking radiant.

'He's an Australian and a very warm Australian by the way he was spending money, and judging from the hotel they were staying in. But he was a nice fellow. I rather liked him, no swilling pints and slapping you on the back which, unfortunately, is the general picture of the Australian; quite an intelligent man.'

'You saw them a lot then?'

'Not a lot. I met them two or three times; we had a few meals together.'

Mona in Paris in a posh hotel with a rich Australian for a husband. Funny how things turned out. A girl with one eye and no looks to speak of could marry for a second time, and a rich man into the bargain. Oh now! down dog, she said to herself; cut out the bitchiness. Surely Mona was entitled to some compensation to make up for those sexless years with Arthur. She'd had her troubles with Georgie, but a starved body hadn't been one of them. Yet over these last few years she had known what it was to have a starved body, and more than once this had caused her to give a thought to Mona. . . . And now she was married again. Well, good luck to her.

She said now, 'How is your mother? She's in America, too, isn't she?'

'No, not now; she's gravitated to Switzerland.'

'Is she still . . .?' She stopped; it would be tactless to ask if she was still married. But he had guessed at the question and he laughed at her now as he said, 'Oh, she's still married, very much so. And very happy, I'm glad to say.'

'That's nice.'

Everybody he knew seemed to be happy. She felt herself receding farther and farther away from him. She wished he would go. She looked towards the window and said, 'The mist has cleared, thank goodness. It's very cold at nights when the mist settles. I should say it will be dark soon to-night; the sun went down early. It's funny how you get to know the weather up here; some nights the twilight seems endless, and at other times it seems to gallop towards the dark.'

He stared at her for a moment before bringing himself to the edge of the chair and rising to his feet, and she felt the colour rushing to her face as she, too, rose from the couch. She had been tactless, she might as well have told him openly to get himself away.

'I'll be off.'

'Are you making for the inn?'

'I'm not quite sure. If it's a fine night and the moon comes up, as it should, I'll go on walking. It's a wonderful feeling walking across the hills in the moonlight.'

'Yes, it must be. I must try it some time.' She laughed ironically, and he said, 'I wonder you haven't done it before, the tracks leading from here are all clear cut. . . . May I go through the kitchen to get my pack?'

'Yes, yes, of course.' She followed him down the room and through the kitchen, and after picking up his pack from the floor he put it outside the door; then standing on the square of flagstone he said, 'You're not afraid to stay here alone?'

'No; it's funny but I'm much more nervous in the town. I bolt and bar every door and window when I'm home.'

'You should lock up here, too. Remember –' he gave her a twisted smile – 'there are people who walk about in the moonlight.'

She ignored his joke and her face was straight as she said, 'I've never had any intruders so far.'

'It's been nice seeing you again, Annie.'

Her answer to this should have been, 'And you too'; but all she said was, 'Thank you.'

He held out his hand and she placed hers in it. He did not squeeze it with undue pressure, or hold it longer than was necessary. And then he was saying, 'Good-bye.'

And she answered, 'Good-bye.'

With a swing he brought the pack across his shoulders, then walked along the side of the house and round the corner and was gone.

She stepped back into the kitchen and slowly drew the bolt in the door. She went into the sitting-room and to the window and, standing to the side of it, she watched him going down the hill, not towards the inn but in the direction of the copse and the road that led to Otterburn. When she could no longer see him she walked towards the fire and, seating herself in the chair on which he had sat a few minutes earlier, she stared into the flames.

She could not in this moment describe how she felt. She had wanted him gone, and now he was gone she felt a loss, greater than that she had experienced seven years ago, oh much greater, because at that time the memory of Georgie was still clinging heavily to her.

There was stillness all around her, she was enveloped in it, and the aloneness that was in her flowed from her and filled the silence. The room was full of it, the house was full of it; all those miles of moors and hills were full of it; and he was walking away untouched by it.

For God's sake! don't cry.

Quickly she pulled herself up from the chair, placed a wire guard around the fire, locked the front door, then went upstairs, thinking as she did so, Thank God for one thing, Tishy isn't here.

2

The twilight hadn't been short, it had been long, and she had lain staring into the sky until there was nothing to see, not even the reflection from the window, for there was no moon, as he had foretold, and it was a starless night.

She didn't remember at what hour she fell asleep but she woke at first light and watched the dawn bring back the hills and clouds. She heard the birds in the copse start their dawn chorus. She heard some moor animal scream and an owl hoot, and she thought, Yesterday I was disturbed but I wasn't really unhappy, today I'm disturbed and I'm unhappy. But the unhappiness had clinched one matter in her mind: she was going to make a break, she was going to get right away, to some place where nobody could get at her; and not just for a week, or a fortnight, but a month, two months, three months.

Tishy could see to herself, Bill would get married, and Rance, well he could have his house, or his flat, but without her. She'd go on one of those cruises. She always despised the widows who went man-hunting on cruises; but she wouldn't be going man-hunting, she'd just be getting away, giving herself time to think, to find out what to do with the remainder of her life.

The sun was well up when she went to the window and looked towards Corby Pike. It was beautiful in the morning.

She walked across the room to the small window set in the side wall, it was the only one that wasn't on floor level, and from here she could see the continuation of the Pike where it met up with Highspoon. The sun was filling the craggy hollows with softness, it was giving a velvet sheen to the greenery that tightly cloaked the hills. It was beautiful. Why couldn't she stay here?

No! No! She swung around quickly, pulled her dressing gown from off the rail of the bed and put it on as she went out on to the tiny landing. She descended the stairs, went straight into the kitchen and put the kettle on. She opened the cupboard door and looked in. Should she leave all this tinned stuff here? Some of the others might want to come. Tishy would, most likely.

When the kettle boiled she brewed the tea and, having set the tray, she carried it into the sitting-room and, as she did every morning when it was fine, she went to open the door so that she could take in, as she drank her tea, the wonder of the moors. She had put the tray down on the table and had unlocked the door, but on pulling it open she sprang back, clutching at the front of her dressing gown as she made an unintelligible exclamatory sound.

He was sitting with his back against one stanchion and his feet against the other. He looked up at her and blinked before getting to his feet. His hair looked rumpled, as did his clothes. She looked at his sleeping bag draped for airing over the hand rail of the steps.

'I'm . . . I'm sorry I startled you.' His face was unsmiling, his voice flat, serious sounding, matching the sombreness of his looks.

When she could speak she said, 'You . . . you haven't been there all . . . all night?'

'No . . . no, just since dawn.'

'Where did you sleep?'

He pointed without speaking down towards the copse, then said, 'Your car makes good shelter.'

'You slept out?'

'Of course: yet I had no intention of doing so last night. But . . . but I found I had to.'

He was still standing outside the door, and now as if talking to an unruly child she said, 'Come in, come in; you must be stiff. Here.' She went quickly to the tray and poured him out a cup of tea; then after handing it to him she hurried up the room and, taking the bellows, blew on the fire, and he called to her, 'It's all right, I'm not really cold.'

When she returned to him he was standing just where she had left him, inside the door, and again she spoke to him as if to a boy. 'Go to the fire, I'll get you something to eat.'

He made no reply but obediently he walked up the room and, sitting in the chair, he put out his hands to the licking flame.

When she came back into the room she stood some way from him as she asked 'Do you like hard or soft boiled eggs?'

'Oh, medium, please. Can I help?'

'It doesn't need any assistance to boil an egg.'

Still acting the mother, she turned sharply away and went into the kitchen again, and a few minutes later she called from the doorway, 'Would you like to come and get it?'

When he entered the kitchen he did not sit down but, looking at her across the table, he said softly, 'Annie, I'd like to talk to you.'

She returned his look for a moment before she said, 'There'll ... there'll be plenty of time to talk later, after ... after you've eaten.' She pointed to the place that was set for him, with two eggs on the plate, but before he sat down he went to the other side of the small table where one egg reposed in an egg cup and drew the chair out for her.

The three slow steps she took towards her place could have given the impression that she was slightly drunk. She did not look up when he took the seat opposite to her and she did not speak until a smell of burning pervaded the room; then she sprang up, saying, 'Oh my goodness! the toast.'

When she retrieved two black squares from under the grill he smiled at her for the first time and said quietly, 'I'm glad you can make a mistake.'

She cut more bread, made more toast, poured out more tea and finished her egg, and all in silence. It was when she finally looked up and found his eyes on her that she said, 'Why on earth did you sleep out there all night?'

'What would you have said if I had suggested you offer me a bed?'

She moved her head slightly before she answered, 'I would have told you to go down to the inn. I thought that was where you were making for anyway.'

He said now, 'Did you sleep?'

'Of course I did.'

'You were lucky, I didn't.'

When he held her gaze she suddenly got up from the table and, pulling the belt of her dressing gown tightly about her, said, 'I must go and get dressed.'

'Why? You look beautiful as you are.'

She turned from him now and, resting her hands on each

corner of the stove, she bowed her head and said, 'That's enough of that, Alan. Don't start something that's going to bring embarrassment on us.'

'I'm not starting anything, Annie, I'm merely continuing something that began years ago. Come here.'

Before she could stop him he had gripped her hand and was pulling her out of the kitchen and through the room to the couch; and now sitting on it, he pulled her down beside him, saying, 'If nothing else I'm going to talk, and you're going to listen. Out there last night I was made to believe there's such a thing as destiny, that each one has it written for him from the day he is born. I could say it's even mapped out before that. Now this is how I see it. Look –' he took her by the shoulders and pressed her back into the couch – 'don't sit there like a ramrod, look at me, Annie, and listen to what I'm going to say. It begins with Uncle Arthur. Why was Uncle Arthur born a homosexual? Don't shrink like that, Annie; you might as well turn away from the mention of male or female; it's a quirk of nature, as we ourselves are. Well, Uncle being what he is, he meets Georgie. . . .'

She tugged her hands away from him, at the same time edging along the couch, and her voice was high and indignant as she cried, 'Georgie was never like that, I told you before.'

'I know he wasn't, I know he wasn't, Annie. Look, don't get upset. It was because Georgie wasn't like that, he was just the opposite and the kind of fellow, from what I gather, who would in the ordinary way make a big joke of it, but he didn't. There was something in Georgie below his roughness that understood Uncle Arthur's predicament. Uncle was going through one hell of a time mentally when he first met Georgie, not having the real guts to be a conscientious objector, knowing himself for what he was, pushed into a camp full of male specimens, their conversation enough to sicken a pig, and let me tell you the male in herds can become sick-making, no matter from what class they come.

'Are you listening to me?' He shook her two hands.

She didn't answer but stared at him now, and he went on, 'Well, now as I understand it, Georgie swore and cursed and was a bit of a rough neck, but there must have been in him a sensitivity that was hidden from most people. So we have the situation where, because he understands Uncle Arthur's plight and is sorry for him, Arthur's gratitude knows no bounds. He takes him home, and it's as if he were yelling, Look, I've got a friend, an ordinary

204

bloke. They were all well aware at home that class forms no barrier in cases like Uncle Arthur's, but from what mother said I think they all believed, that is with the exception of my father, of course, that here was an ordinary friendship. Anyway Uncle Arthur's gratitude, as I said, was boundless, so what must he do? Invite Georgie and his wife for Christmas.' He paused and gazed at her until her eyes dropped away from his, then he went on softly, 'And a little boy of five meets Georgie's wife and recognizes immediately that she is different from anyone else he has ever known, and they talk – of jigs.'

This did not bring a smile to her face, her eyes were still averted, and again he went on, 'I can still hear my father and mother quarrelling. At different times during my childhood I would look at my father and think, You're James Partridge, because on that memorable Christmas I witnessed their first open row. There had been many before that, but discreetly covered, I understand, for my sake; but it was on that day I heard mother say, "You're a swine, James Partridge. That's what you are, a swine, a pushed-up, cheap swine." I used to ponder on what a pushed-up cheap swine meant. Eventually I discovered, in my father's case, that it meant that he came from a very ordinary family, so ordinary that after marrying mother he disclaimed any connection with it.

'I didn't hear anything of Uncle Arthur for some time following that Christmas. Then after Father died I went to stay with them; I only went the once. It wasn't a happy time. Years later, during my first walking tour, I called on him and found him living alone, and from that time I felt for him as Georgie must have felt, a liking and a compassion for his situation. I said to him once, "Do you ever see the woman who came to the house for Christmas, that time there was the big row?" and he looked at me in surprise, saying, "You remember that time all those years ago? You were only five." And I said, "Of course I remember it. I particularly remember the woman, her name was Annie," and he said, "Yes, her name was Annie and she was a nice girl. Georgie's lucky".'

When she moved uneasily on the couch and went to draw her hands from his he held them firmly, saying quietly, 'I'm not finished yet. Grandmother had a friend, who had a granddaughter called Jane, she was three years younger than me. "Wouldn't it be nice," said the grandmothers, "if our grandchildren married."

They got their heads together very early on and they arranged that I was pushed at Jane, and Jane was pushed at me, every holiday. I had other girls; in fact there was one at college on whom I was very keen. I wanted to live with her, not marry her, I decided I wasn't going to marry for years, and this particular girl was quite willing to fall in with the suggestion, but at the last minute I withdrew. I had been home and there was Jane again; there were certain things expected of me, play up and play the game. Jane left school when she was eighteen. She didn't go on to college, it was considered that she wasn't very strong. Everyone protected Jane; I followed where the others led. Jane was sweet, she was good company and intelligent; she had nothing to speak of in the way of looks but she was attractive. Strangely, she was very like Tishy, I mean in that once you got to know her her looks didn't matter, in fact you saw a certain beauty in them. Anyway, Jane and I became engaged. It had to happen, my grandmother had arranged it, and any seed Grandmother planted bore fruit. Perhaps you remember my grandmother. I think of her as the eternal mini-skirt.'

Annie was looking at him now, waiting, and he leant his shoulder against the side of the couch for a full minute before he spoke again. 'When I showed no inclination to rush into marriage Grandma became annoyed. Since Mother had married again and gone off to the ends of the world, as she put it, it was her responsibility to see that I acted correctly. I used to think it was this attitude that drove me to take the position in Newcastle, but now I know that Grandma was merely part of the plan that had been mapped out for me, for I wasn't in Newcastle a day before I thought, I must look her up, that woman. Now why after all those years should I have thought that? In the ordinary way I shouldn't even have remembered what she looked like, let alone the conversation we'd had, but I did remember, and very clearly, for your face, Annie, was etched on my mind.'

She looked at him, her eyes unblinking; then she bit tightly on her lip and bowed her head.

'Well, you know what happened the first night I saw you. And the following month appeared to me as long as a year. I couldn't believe that I'd only been in your life four weeks, I felt I knew all about you, everything you thought; I anticipated your very actions, your very words. I would say to myself, Now she's going to do so-and-so; Now she's going to say so-and-so. I seemed to be living inside you. When I came and took Tishy out, it was merely to help you, to get her away from Rance. Also to give her the chance to expand, because she did expand in company, the right company. She was good to be with, and strangely I felt as if I were a psychiatrist effecting some kind of a cure on her, turning the introvert into an extrovert.'

He now let go of her hand and, taking a handkerchief from his pocket, wiped his face with it; but before he had finished he was talking again. 'Towards the end of that month there was a show-down. Jane's father wanted to know what I was up to. Jane's mother wanted to know what I was up to. Her grandmother was indignant, as was mine. Jane was twenty-two, I was twenty-three, what were we waiting for? everything was ready. Well, what was I waiting for? I named the date, told them I was going to look for a house this end and came back here to tell you, to tell you and Tishy, for I knew then that it was time I told Tishy. But believe me I never imagined that she would be so hurt; she was young but she was a girl very modern in her outlook; I had done nothing to make her think that I was being other than friendly. . . . Then you cried and I took you in my arms and I knew I had never known happiness before . . . but it froze when she came into the room and I saw her face.'

He now turned from her and, bending his body forward, he placed his elbows on his knees, joined his hands tightly between them and moved the pads of his thumbs against each other as he said, 'Two months later I married Jane and entered into a private hell. You know, there's a great deal to be said for promiscuity. I would advocate a trial run to every couple no matter what their morals, in fact I'd make it compulsory.' There was a deep bitterness in his voice now. 'Jane didn't like sex – it was nasty – our so-called honeymoon was a nightmare. At the end of it she wouldn't let me near her except to wipe away her tears, hold her hand or to stroke her hair. Even this she just tolerated. Why hadn't I become aware of this before we married? I soon understood she had put up with my surface love-making then because she wanted to marry me. What she wanted was a combination of father, brother and male nurse. I tried to get her to a doctor, but no. And so, after six months of it, I went to Grandma, and Grandma went to her grandma, and I was told to have patience. Her rejection of me, I was given to understand, was the result of a bad experience she'd had when she was twelve years old; a young uncle had raped her.'

The pads of his thumbs were still rubbing, and she brought her eyes from them to his face as he went on, 'I became very understanding, very gentle; I became her father, brother and male nurse. On the surface Alan and Jane were ever so happy. During the second year I realized that this could go on for ever, and I knew I couldn't stand it. Now it was me who wanted a male nurse. I went to my doctor. He said he would see her, but she wouldn't see him. I went to my solicitor. He said divorce would be quite easy. I went to Grandma, and her reactions were pure Victorian. No one would have guessed that she had been sleeping around for years. "Divorce!" she said. "No, you can't possibly. Jane's a nice girl." Yes, Jane was a nice girl; but I didn't want a nice girl, I wanted a wife. Anyway, two years ago I got a divorce, but it was too late to save me having a breakdown.'

'Oh, Alan.' It was the first time she had spoken his name since she had seen him yesterday, and he turned his head slowly towards her, saying, 'I once heard someone say that they wouldn't wish the devil in hell to have a breakdown and I can endorse that.'

'Oh, I'm sorry.'

He smiled now, saying, 'Well, since it's brought the first kind response from you, what I should say now is that I would go through it again just to get the same results, but I cannot be so gallant. What I can say though is that I know now it's all part of the plan. You see if it hadn't been for the breakdown and having to go away for treatment, I would have run from this country like a scalded cat; but during this bad period I seemed to lose all initiative, all I wanted was to get away from people, to be by myself. I took to walking again. This helped me back to normality. Anyway, this post came up in America and after long debate I took it. And I made up my mind that as soon as term ended I'd get my ticket and fly away. Yet what did I do? I plumped for one last holiday on these hills. I'm not due in the university until early September, so I told myself I'd stay with Uncle for a month and still have plenty of time left to see something of the country in which I was going to live.'

He hitched himself back on to the couch, turned towards her and took her hands again and, looking into her eyes, said, 'Yesterday morning I set off early, saying to Uncle, "Expect me when you see me," and I walked and I walked. Then rounding a butt

208

I come across those two idiots sitting like lost lambs and I devised a way of getting the injured one down to the road, and in the process we are all very dry and hot and longing for a cup of tea, so we stop at a cottage.' He pulled her hands towards him now. 'Do you see what I mean about it all being mapped out? Coming across those fellows yesterday, I would say on reflection, brought me to about the middle of the map; there's still the other half to be worked out. Do you get what I'm driving at, Annie?'

'Oh, Alan, don't, don't.' She went to withdraw from him again, but he held fast to her hands. 'Do you like me?'

She shook her head even as she said, 'Yes, yes, of course, I like you; no . . . no one could help liking you.'

'You're not answering my question: Do you like me?'

'Yes.' Her head was bowed deeply on her chest now.

'I love you, Annie.'

'No, Alan, no.' The movement of her head was wider now. 'You can't; you know nothing about me, except for that one month.'

'I've known you all my life; I was waiting for you when I was five. I recognized you. You know something? I follow no religion. I believe that religions are merely shelters for weak and frightened men, and God was created by man to assuage the inexplicable hunger in him. It is well known that all religions down the years have been but different forms of tyranny, the means of creating gods with which to provide men with power and, in turn, to subordinate nations. As for Christianity, it is but the modernization of heathen rituals. This can all be proved. Yet last night, lying out there, looking up into the blackness, I believed in God, or at least in a mind that can plan, and I couldn't discard yet again an idea that has been in my mind for a long time concerning you. When I first thought of reincarnation I laughed at it, yet last night I was forced to believe in it. How other did I recognize you at five years old? . . . We have met before, Annie.'

Her head had stopped shaking, she was looking at him now in utter bewilderment. She wasn't a very good Catholic but she was a Catholic. She believed in God. She had sometimes questioned the Virgin Birth but then, she had told herself, if God could do anything, then he could set a seed in a woman's womb. Really when you came to think of it there was nothing to the Virgin

Birth, He having in the first place created life. She had thought this out in her teens and she hadn't veered from it since. The Church was in a bad way now; there was the question of the pill, and priests were leaving to get married, which she thought was shocking. And this knowledge had made her a bit uncomfortable when going to confession. What if Father Campbell were sitting on the other side of the grille thinking of a woman while she was telling him her sins. These things could become disturbing if you gave your mind to them. But she hadn't given her mind to them, she had only kept praying to God to keep her family straight. And when her mind touched on the word straight, she thought of Rance. Now here was Alan wiping away the foundations of all religions and making reincarnation believable. Could they have met before? It sounded fantastic. Yet, as he had made out, it was strange how they had come together again after all these years. But he was still so young. Yet he didn't look young, he looked nearer forty than thirty-one; and she wasn't sorry for that, for it lessened the years between them.

What was she thinking about? This was madness. Yet deep within her she knew it was a madness that was welcome. She knew, even more than he did at this moment, that it was the beginning of something, a new existence filled with wonder and love, the kind of love she had dreamed of before she had lain on the bed with Georgie.

'Could you love me, Annie?'

Her head was swinging again. In spite of how she felt she couldn't say it. To put it into words would sound indecent somehow.

'You do love me, you must; it would be impossible for me to have felt like this about you for years, to have been waiting for you for years, because that's what I have been doing, and then you to say that you don't love me.'

With a movement that startled her he was holding her face between his hands. Then, his mouth dropping on hers, he pulled her still resisting body towards him and held her fiercely, until, as if a spring had snapped, she leant heavily against him.

Minutes passed and they still clung together. His mouth left her lips and moved over her face, and when she said, 'Oh, Alan! Alan,' he answered, 'Annie. Annie.'

Of one accord they rose from the couch. Their arms about each other, they went towards the stairs.

When she took off her dressing gown and got into bed she kept her face averted from him while he undressed.

When he lay facing her he did not immediately take her into his arms but lay looking at her as if in wonder; then his hand going gently to her breast he said, 'Oh, Annie. Annie, my love, this is the beginning of the other half.'

Part Seven

THE BREAKING OF THE CORD

1

Tishy came home to an empty house. Having obtained no answer to her ringing of the front door bell, she went round the back and found the door locked. After searching through her bag she found her front door key and, after letting herself in and bringing her cases from the pathway, she went straight into the kitchen. It had a deserted look, an unlived-in look; there were dirty dishes in the sink. That was unusual; her mother never went out and left dirty dishes in the sink. The solution came to her that Rance was here on his own and that her mother was away, likely at the cottage; she had said that she might go there for a day or two. Anyway, Kathy would know.

She took off her light coat, put the kettle on, because her first need was for a cup of tea, real tea, and she wanted something to steady her nerves. Not that tea would do much for her nerves, the state they were in at the present moment. But ten days of Stanley Stone had almost brought them to breaking point. How had she tolerated him all these years? Likely because she'd experienced him in small doses. But ten days of Stanley Stone putting over Stanley Stone had given her a terrifying insight into what it would be like to be Mrs Stanley Stone; not that she had ever really contemplated it.

She sat down in the chair by the table and ran her hands through her hair as her mind shouted at her, 'Oh, face up to it, you did contemplate it. It was either him or a dog, cat and budgerigar, remember?' She put her head back now and gave a short laugh. There had been quite a scene at the airport, subdued but nevertheless intense. What was it her granda used to sing? 'We parted on the shore, oh we parted on the shore; I said, Good-bye Love, I'm off to Baltimore.'

'Where you off to?' Stanley had said. 'Where do you think?' she had replied flippantly; 'Hong Kong? I'm going home and I don't want any more company.' As he had walked beside her out of the airport he had been speechless for the only time during their ten days together. When she said, 'I'm taking a taxi,' he had said, 'Why? there's the bus.'

'You take the bus, and I'll take the taxi, and I don't want company.' He had stared at her for some seconds before saying, 'I can't quite make you out, Tishy; you're a funny lass.'

'Yes, I know, both funny ha-ha and funny peculiar. Good-bye, Stanley.'

So that was the last of Stanley – until school started.

As she got up and mashed the tea she said to herself, 'What have I lost, anyway? I don't believe he had any intention of ever asking me to marry him, he never even tried to make it with me. I must be the only girl in this decade who has been with a fellow for ten days and remained intact. What if he had tried . . . would I?' She stared across the kitchen wanting to hear herself give an answer. What she said was, 'He doesn't want a wife, he wants an audience. I must have been a godsend to him.'

As she drank her tea she thought, I'll go to the cottage next week. There'll just be Mam, I'll like that.

Her tea finished, she was on the point of going into the hall to phone Kathy when she heard the key turning in the front door. A minute later Rance entered the kitchen. He stared at her blankly and she at him. They never spoke to each other unless it was absolutely necessary, but now, looking towards him, she said, 'What's happened?'

'Oh.' He looked down at his bandaged hand and his arm, which was in a sling, and said, 'I tried to slice my thumb off.'

'When did it happen?'

'Around dinner-time.'

'You went to the hospital?'

'Yes, of course. They put eight stitches in it. They say it'll save the pad, it was only hanging by a thread.'

She grimaced and said, 'I've just made some tea. Have you had anything to eat?'

'Not since this morning, I haven't wanted anything. But there's half a chicken in the fridge from yesterday.'

As she set about getting him a meal she asked 'Where's Mam?'

'At the cottage. I expected her back before this.'

'How are you managing with the car?' she asked now.

'I'm not; one of the fellows brought me home.'

There was no more conversation between them, and after she had buttered some bread and cut up the chicken for him she left the kitchen and, picking up her cases, went upstairs. After unpacking she went into the bathroom and felt the tank. There was plenty of hot water so she decided to have a bath.

Twenty minutes later she was leaving the bathroom when Rance opened his bedroom door and said, 'Will you help me change my coat? I can bend the arm but I can't get my hand through the sleeve, one side's all right but I'm stuck with the other.'

Even before she moved towards him she felt the revulsion rise in her, and when she eased his hand into his coat sleeve the feeling inside her was so strong that she admonished herself sternly, saying, 'He's your brother; you're taking animosity too far.'

'Will you knot my tie for me?' In the same breath he added, 'Mam should be back by now. What's keeping her?'

She kept her eyes away from his face and firmly on the tie as she thought, Yes, Mam would have dressed you. You would have liked that. Oh God! why was she so bitter against him?

'Will that do?'

He turned round and looked in the mirror, then said, 'Fine, thanks.'

They both turned now as the front door bell rang, and he smiled and nodded at her, saying, 'That's her; she's forgotten her key.'

Tishy ran down the stairs and opened the door to see Percy standing there.

'Oh, hello, Percy. I thought it was Mam and she had forgotten her key.'

'Hello, Tishy. You had a good time?'

'Oh . . . oh yes, Percy, I suppose I can say I had a good time. But give me England; at least if you get watery cabbage you know it's watery cabbage. But by the same token I hardly spoke to a foreigner, everybody seemed to be English.'

'Well, as I've always maintained, Tishy, if you want to meet people you want to get away from, go abroad.' Percy laughed his thin, piping laugh, and Tishy laughed with him, saying, 'That's Irish, but it's true.'

'It is indeed.'

Tishy now led the way into the front room. To her mind Percy and kitchens didn't seem to go together; he was the kind of person who only relaxed in formality, and as Kathy had confessed, she could get him to do almost anything but sit down to a meal in his shirt sleeves.

He turned to her now, saying, 'Kathy phoned several times this afternoon, she thought Mam would be back. Then she phoned me to say that my mother had called in to take them out to the beach and would I keep phoning in order to make a certain request. Well, I did up till five o'clock, but got no reply.'

'It was just about five when I got in.'

'Well, well.' He smiled widely at her now. 'I should have kept to the maxim of try, try, try and try again, shouldn't I?'

She made no reply to this but answered his smile, then he said, 'If Mam doesn't return in time I wonder – but really I feel it is a bit of an imposition when you haven't been in the house five minutes to ask you to baby sit for us. Mother would do it, but between you and me, Percy junior takes advantage of her and she gives in to him, and I'm afraid she pacifies him with sweeties, and you know –' he nodded at her now – 'how many children's teeth have been ruined by a grandmother's indulgence.'

'Yes, of course, I'd love to, Percy. What time?'

'Well, we'd like to be off at seven. Oh, I do feel it's an imposition. But the invitation came at short notice, I only received it this morning. It's to do with a very important client. Well, it isn't only the client that's involved, it's his father also, and his father has come up from Cornwall. Oh, it's a very involved story. It's got to do with a trusteeship about which we are acting, and my client said would we like to come to dinner at his hotel in Newcastle this evening at eight. But I do think it's an. ....'

'It's all right, perfectly all right, Percy, I'll just get into some clothes and be round by seven.'

'You're sure you're not too tired?'

'No, not at all.'

'Oh, Kathy will be grateful. You see she expected her mother to be home. And she's had no word from her; you know, she usually phones when she goes down to the road for milk.'

'She hasn't heard at all?'

'No, not at all. But she told Kathy before she left that she would be back today. Well, I must be going, but thank you again, Tishy.'

'That's all right, Percy.'

As Percy made towards the door, Rance entered the room.

There was still a feeling of enmity between the two men, but whereas the enmity that existed between Rance and Tishy could lead to open quarrels, Percy refused absolutely to quarrel with his brother-in-law and Rance's hatred against him had grown more deep if anything because of this. Percy's coolness and correctness infuriated him, yet now when he wanted to ask a favour of him he could be civil. 'Are you going back into the town?' he said.

'I wasn't, why? . . . You've hurt your hand?'

'Yes, tried to take my thumb off.'

'It must be painful.'

'It isn't that so much; they numbed it, but it's sticking out like a sore thumb,' he laughed. 'I'll get used to it in a little while but at the moment it's stiff.'

Percy said coolly, 'You want dropping somewhere?'

'Yes, back to the garage if you wouldn't mind; I've got an appointment there at seven.'

Percy looked at his watch. 'I could take you there now if that would be all right? It would mean you'd be early, but I must be in Newcastle by eight.'

'Yes, that'll be fine.'

Tishy, knowing that taking Rance to the garage would take another fifteen minutes of Percy's time, said, 'Why not phone for a taxi?'

'Oh no; if we go now it'll be all right. I myself should hate hiring a taxi if I had a number of cars at my disposal.' With his short quick steps Percy led the way to the front door, saying over his shoulder, 'And thanks for tonight. We should be leaving about quarter past seven, not later.'

'I'll be there, Percy.'

'Oh.' He turned towards her. 'Shall I come and pick you up?'

'No, you won't. I can use my feet. You'll be lucky if you get to Newcastle on time as it is.'

'Just as you say, Tishy. Good-bye.'

'Good-bye, Percy.'

Rance didn't speak, nor did he turn his head in her direction, and she closed the door before the car started up.

She was about to mount the stairs again when she heard the hard rapping on the back door. Now who could this be and her in her dressing gown.

She went through the kitchen and opened the door to see Mr Wilkins standing there, a strange dishevelled Mr Wilkins. But then Mr Wilkins had been going strange for a long time now, ever since Susan ran away, and he had got worse this last six months since he had been made redundant, for it had given him more time to go searching for Susan. He almost knocked her on to her back now as he pushed past her into the kitchen, crying, 'Where is he? Where is he?'

'Who, Mr Wilkins? Who do you want?'

'You know who I want. Shielding him you've been, you and your mother. Shielding him, the lot of you.'

Without again asking, 'Who do you mean?' she knew; but she still said, 'Who do you mean, Mr Wilkins?' and he cried at her, 'Your Rance!' He now went marching through into the hall yelling, 'Come down, you bugger you! come down, you bloody swine, out o' that!'

'Mr Wilkins! Mr Wilkins! Listen to me, please.' She caught hold of his arm. 'He isn't in.'

'Isn't in! Don't you tell me he isn't in. The missus said she saw him comin' in.'

'That was some time ago.'

'You can't hoodwink me.' He now swung round and burst into the sitting-room; from there he went to the dining-room, and he was about to go upstairs when she cried at him, 'He isn't in, I tell you, Mr Wilkins; he's gone to the garage.'

'The garage? the garage?' His head was bobbing as if it would come off his shoulders. 'I'll garage him when I get him. By God! I'll garage him.'

'Mr Wilkins, please, please.' She again caught hold of his arm. 'Try to calm down. Tell me, what is it?'

'What is it? Why ask the road you know? You've known all along what it is. It's my Susan. But I've got her back and she's told me everything. It was him that started her on it, an' not her alone. You know what I'm going to do? I'm going to the polis. You know what pushers get. My God Almighty! how many bairns has he ruined ...'

The truth was out at last. It had been staring them in the face for years. In her heart she had known all along what it was, but her mother had pulled a shield over her eyes with the betting slip.

As he now stormed back into the kitchen and towards the door she cried at him, 'Wait! wait till my mother comes in, Mr Wilkins, please ... Please!'

'Wait for your mother?' He turned on her. 'No, by God! an' let her shield him again? She'd shield him with her life. Yet when she sees what he's done to my poor Susan I ... I don't know. A wreck she is, a wreck. But she's home. In Doncaster I found her. Mrs Nesbitt who used to live in 42, they moved there, and she phoned John Pollock down below and told him she knew where Susan was. An' John run me through yesterday. We've just got back, just got back this minute, an' I'll not rest, I've sworn I'll not rest or eat, until that brother of yours gets his deserts.'

'Please! please, Mr Wilkins.' She was running down the yard after him now, but like someone demented he tore away from her.

From the back gate, with her hand pressed tightly against her mouth, she watched him. He did not go into his back yard but ran to where a car was parked at the end of the lane. It wasn't his car; he had sold his when he lost his job; it was Mr Pollock's old red banger.

Oh my God! She was back in the kitchen, her two hands covering her cheeks now. A pusher. Drug takers were victims, but pushers were creatures, vermin who, solely in order to make money, ruined thousands of young lives. They were the most ... She rocked from side to side and shook her head; she could find no words adequate enough to describe such people, and her brother was one of them.

Her mam. Oh! She dropped down on to a chair. This would break her. It would kill her. It wasn't so much the public disgrace that would affect her but the fact, as Mr Wilkins had said, that her son had ruined the lives of young girls. And how many? Yes, how many? All that money in the top of the Scotch chest; and that had been three years ago.

She got up now and began to pace the room. What should she do? Mr Wilkins would have likely gone straight to the garage. There would be a fight, and by the look of Mr Wilkins there could be murder. The garage was closed. There'd only be Rance in it and whoever he was going to meet. But she wasn't going to worry about Rance, let him take his chance. It was her mother she was worrying about. Mr Wilkins would be as good as his word; he'd go straight to the police and they moved quickly in such cases. If only her mother were here and she could break it to her.

She must get dressed. She ran upstairs and scrambled into her clothes; then, downstairs again, she stood undecided what to do. Her mother might turn up any minute and if she wasn't here and the police came. . . . She'd better phone Kathy. No. No, there was no need to tell Kathy or Percy tonight for they had this important dinner on, and if they were to go she must get round there. She looked at the clock. It was quarter to seven. She'd stay till seven. She could phone a taxi for then.

At five to seven Kathy rang. 'Oh hello, Tishy,' she said. 'You're back all right then? Did you have a good time? Is Percy there?'

'No; he was here, but he should be home by now. He was running our Rance to the garage. He's hurt his hand, Rance, I mean.'

'Oh Lord!' Kathy's tone expressed her impatience. 'He's cutting it fine. Is Mam back?'

'No. I'm wondering what's keeping her. I understand she was coming back this afternoon.'

'Yes, so she told me, at least she said some time on Friday. She'll turn up before dark; she hates driving in the dark. . . . Oh! wait till he comes in, I'll give him the length of my tongue. . . . By the way is anything the matter, you sound funny?'

'. . . No. No. Nothing the matter . . . and Kathy, don't go for Percy, it wasn't his fault. Our . . . our Rance should have taken a taxi. I said so.'

'The garage closes at six, why did he want to go back there?'

'He had to meet someone, I don't know who, I didn't ask, you know me. By the way, I've ordered a car to bring me around about seven; in fact, it should be here any minute now.'

'All right, Tishy. Thanks for sitting in at such short notice.'

'That's all right. Be seeing you.'

'Be seeing you.'

Tishy stood by the table for a moment and drew in a number of deep breaths before she went into the kitchen and wrote a note to Annie telling her she was baby-sitting at Kathy's, and to ring her up as soon as she came in. She ended by saying, 'It is important that you ring me immediately, Mam. There is something you should know.' She underlined the last words.

The taxi came at seven, and seven minutes later she was entering Kathy's house.

Kathy, dressed in a green velvet semi-evening dress and looking more beautiful than she had done in her single state, came to meet her, saying, 'I can't understand it. It's nearly ten past, and we should be leaving at quarter past.'

'Ring the garage,' said Tishy quietly.

Kathy rang the garage, but there was no reply.

'Ring the office,' said Tishy now. 'He may have gone back for some reason or other.'

Kathy rang the office, and there was no reply.

When a whimpering sound came from upstairs Kathy said, 'No, don't go up, he'll just keep you at it. He'll go off in a little while, he's dog-tired. He was in the water all afternoon.'

They were sitting looking at each other when the clock struck half-past seven, 'Something's happened,' Kathy exclaimed, jumping up, 'I know it has, he would have been back else. This is important; this dinner, it's very important.'

'Look, don't get all het up. But there's one thing certain, you won't get there by eight o'clock. Do you know where you were going?'

'To The Royal Station Hotel.'

'Well, phone them and leave a message. Say your husband's been delayed; he'll ring later as to what time he'll arrive.'

Kathy made the necessary call and she had just replaced the receiver when she said, 'I'm going to phone the police; there . . . there could have been an accident.'

'If there had been an accident you would have heard before now.' Tishy felt sick. If only her mother were here. 'Wait,' she said; 'I'll phone home again.'

When there was no reply to the ringing Kathy said, 'I'm not waiting any longer, Tishy, I'm going to phone the police.'

Kathy spoke to a policeman, who put her through to another policeman. He sounded very calm. No, he said; there hadn't been a report of an accident during the last three hours.

'I'll go to the garage,' said Tishy, 'but I'll have to go home first to get the keys.'

It was ten minutes before a taxi came to take her home. On the journey she prayed that her mother would be in, but the house was as she had left it. She picked up the keys, returned to the taxi, then later dismissed it in King Street. Whatever she was going to find in the garage she didn't want the taxi man in on it.

She was trembling as she opened the main door. She had to switch on the lights because it was dark inside. She walked slowly past the office, then round by the pit. There was a car above the pit, and she glanced underneath. Looking along to the end of the garage she saw that the doors were partly open. When she looked out into the lane, there was no car parked there. She closed the doors and bolted them, then as she returned up the garage she saw, in the far corner, Rance's own car. She went towards it and looked inside. Then she stood gazing about her. She couldn't understand it. Had he persuaded Percy to take him off somewhere? No, Percy wasn't the kind of man to be persuaded. Behind Percy's correct exterior and pedantic manner there was a will as strong as iron; his courtship of Kathy had been but small evidence of it.

She looked at Rance's car again. If she had the key she could drive it. There was no key in the ignition but she knew where the spare one was hidden. It was her mother who had insisted on putting a spare key under her car after she had locked herself out once, and she had suggested that Rance do the same.

She pulled the sticky tape off the key, then opened again the back doors that she had recently bolted. She backed the car into the lane, and left it there while she returned into the garage, re-bolted the doors, hurried out through the front gates, locking them after her, then ran into the back lane again. If there had been anyone about, her actions might have been questioned, but she saw no one.

Driving the car out of the lane, she turned it in the opposite direction to that by which she had approached the garage. This way she would avoid the main road. But she hadn't travelled more than fifty feet when she drew the car to an abrupt stop, for there, parked in a line of cars, was Mr Pollock's car, the one she had seen at the end of the lane, the one Mr Wilkins had taken. She couldn't mistake it, it was red and a botched-up affair with dabs of grey rust preventative here and there along the bottom of the doors.

She found that she was trembling. Mr Wilkins had got to the garage then. But where was he? If he had come out he would surely have taken the car back home to Mr Pollock. Their Rance, Percy, and Mr Wilkins, where were they? She put her foot down on the starter and the car leapt forward.

She was outside the house again, but as she stepped from the car she looked to the right of her and saw Mr Pollock standing in the Wilkins's front garden, and Mrs Wilkins was on her door-step and Mr Pollock's voice was loud and carried to anyone who had a mind to stop and listen, saying, 'It's bloody unfair, Jenny, that's all I can say. I went out of me way to take him there yesterday. I've lost two days, you know that, I've lost two days. And how does he repay me? Goes off with me bloody car, and not a by your leave or can I. I tell you, it's taking advantage, it's taking advantage.'

She heard Mrs Wilkins speak in a tear-filled voice, saying, 'Come in, Larry. Come in, and don't raise the street.'

As Tishy opened the front door Mr Pollock was repeating, 'Don't raise the street? It's enough to make anybody raise hell.'

'Mam!' She was standing with her back to the door. But there was no reply, and she closed her eyes and said, 'Oh dear God; bring her, bring her soon, because I don't want to have to do anything. If I do she'll blame me, she'll hold it against me for the rest of my life. She'll say I'd just been waiting for the chance.'

She went into the kitchen and added to the note: '8.30. Please, please, Mam, phone Kathy as soon as you come in. There is trouble.'

In the street, Mr Pollock was coming out of the Wilkinses' again. Should she go and say to him, 'I saw your car parked near our garage?' No, no, she must do nothing, nothing at all until her mother came on the scene. Yet she was fully aware that in the meantime something dreadful could be happening. Their Rance was vicious, he was bad, innately bad; she had known it since she was a child. He was sly and wily, and clever with it because he was one of those people who could look you in the face while swearing your life away. He had no moral sense. That was his trouble, he was utterly devoid of moral sense.

When she reached Kathy's it was to find her crying bitterly. 'Something's happened, Tishy, I know something's happened, I feel it, and it's to do with our Rance. He's been going round with funny people. That Benny Warlister. Percy saw him the other day and he said he looked like a prosperous gangster of the Al Capone type. Do you think I should phone the police again?'

'No, no; wait.'

'What's happened to Mam? Why isn't she home?'

'That's what I'd like to know. But it's likely the spell of good weather, and she wanted a break, she needed it. I tried to get her to come with me but she wouldn't.'

Jumping up suddenly, Kathy said, 'If I have to sit here and do nothing I'll go mad. There's no way of contacting Mam, is there?'

'You know there isn't, Kathy; the only way is to go there. I could do it but it would take me two hours, and two hours back, and then there's the chance I might pass her on the road.'

'If she's not here shortly she won't be coming. She won't drive in the dark.'

'No, that's certain.'

'What are we going to do?'

'Wait; that's all we can do.'

'Oh, Tishy, Tishy, I'm frightened.'

'Now, now –' Tishy put her arms about her sister – 'there'll be a simple explanation, you'll see.' . . . Oh dear God! if there only could be a simple explanation.

At quarter past nine the front door bell rang and they both rushed to the door together, then stared open-mouthed at the policeman and plain-clothes' man.

'Mrs Rinkton?' The plain-clothes man looked from one to the other.

'I'm . . . I'm Mrs Rinkton. Something's . . . something's happened, my husband?'

'May I come in?'

She stood aside, and they came into the hall but moved no further before the man said, 'Your husband's in hospital, Mrs Rinkton.'

'In hospital? So there has been an accident?' Kathy had her hands to her throat.

'I . . . I don't know about an accident, Mrs Rinkton, but –' the man seemed slightly uneasy – 'it is rather a complicated business. A short while ago a phone call was put through to the station to the effect that a car was parked on some waste land and that there were two men in it and one was bleeding. He had been stabbed.'

'Percy!'

'No; your husband was apparently unconscious, the man who was stabbed was a Mr Harry Wilkins. They are both in the General Hospital.'

'It's all right, it's all right. Sit down and put your head between your knees.' It wasn't Kathy to whom the policeman was speaking but Tishy.

'Right down,' said the policeman. 'That's it.'

After a while she muttered, 'I'm all right. I'm all right.'

'I . . . I must go. I can go, can't I, I mean to see my husband?'

'Yes, yes, of course. We'll take you now.'

'I . . . I must change this.' Kathy was patting the front of her dress. 'We . . . we were going to a dinner.'

The two officers looked at her, their glances seeming neutral, without either condemnation or sympathy.

She turned from them and ran up the stairs, and Tishy asked, 'Is . . . is the man badly wounded?'

'I can't rightly say, miss. I . . . I think they are going to operate.'

'What relation are you to –?' The plain-clothes man nodded towards the stairs, and she answered, 'My sister.'

'You knew her husband well?'

'Yes, oh yes.'

'Did you know anything about his personal life?'

'Personal life? What do you mean?'

'His habits or . . . or was he addicted to, say, drugs?'

'Percy?' She gulped deeply. 'No! No, not Percy; he's highly respectable; he's an accountant and Doctor Rinkton's son.'

'That doesn't mean much these days, miss. You could be the Queen's cousin and still fall for drugs.'

'But . . . but what makes you think that Percy, Mr Rinkton? . . .'

'Well, they were found on him and . . . and he's under the influence of them.'

Oh God no! She drooped her head on to her chest as she groaned inwardly, 'Oh, our Rance! our Rance!' But he'd not get off with it this time. In any case, when Mr Wilkins came round he would tell them . . . if he came round. What if he didn't? Percy would then have to fight his own way out. Oh no, no, she couldn't let that happen. Anyway, there was always Mrs Wilkins and Susan. . . . Where was her mother! *Where was her mother!*

Kathy came running down the stairs and said, 'You'll stay, won't you, Tishy?' Tishy nodded at her.

On the point of leaving, Kathy turned and said, 'His mother. His mother and father, they should know. . . . His father, he'll know what to do.'

'You go on, I'll phone them.'

'Tell . . . tell Dad to come to the hospital, will you?'

'I'll do that.'

When the door had closed on them Tishy went slowly into the dining-room and to a cabinet in the corner of the room. Taking from it a bottle, she poured out a good measure of brandy and drank it at one gulp, then sat choking and coughing.

Doctor Rinkton brought his wife and Kathy back to the house at half past ten. He had almost to support them through the front door. In the drawing-room, Kathy, looking up at Tishy through her tears, said, 'The world's gone mad. They say that Percy has been taking drugs.'

'My Percy taking drugs.'

Tishy now looked at Mrs Rinkton. She was in great distress. Then she turned her gaze on Doctor Rinkton, who was saying slowly, 'There's something very wrong here, very wrong. My son would no more take to drugs than he would run along the street naked.'

Tishy glanced from one to the other before she asked, 'What did he say? what did Percy say?'

'He hasn't come round yet, he's got concussion.' It was his father speaking. 'But he's also under the influence of drugs. They found two punctures in his arm and a packet in the car. I tell you, there's something very wrong here.'

On a high choked cry now Mrs Rinkton exclaimed, 'My Percy to stab anyone! It's fantastic even to contemplate. Someone's done this. They've done this. I've said to you someone's done this. They intended to kill that man, and Percy too, and make it look ... My Percy wouldn't hurt a fly.'

Doctor Rinkton came and stood directly in front of Tishy now and said quietly, 'Kathy tells me that Percy gave your brother a lift to the garage. Have you seen your brother since?'

She had to force the word out: 'No.'

'Is he likely to be home by now?'

'I ... I could ring.'

'I'll do that.'

She watched him go into the hall and she didn't move until he returned, saying, 'There's no reply,' then added, 'Why did he want a lift, your brother? He drives, doesn't he?'

'He had hurt his thumb.'

'Then he couldn't drive at all?'

'I ... I shouldn't say so.'

The doctor blinked and turned away, and now Kathy looking at Tishy asked pitifully, 'Mam, she's not back yet?'

'No. It doesn't look now as if she'll be back tonight.' Tishy paused a moment, then said, 'I ... I could go and get her.'

'Would you, Tishy?'

'Yes.'

They stared at each other, then nodded. Tishy, turning away, said, 'I'll call in home first and if . . . if she's there I'll phone you.'

She went out into the hall for her coat; then re-entering the room, she went hastily to the couch and hugged Kathy to her for a moment, saying, 'It'll be all right. Do you hear? it'll be all right.' Then straightening herself, she looked from Doctor Rinkton to his wife and she repeated, 'It will be all right. Believe me, it'll be all right.' Then she ran from the room and the house.

2

It had been raining when she left Shields, but by the time she was through Newcastle the thunder was frightening, with the lightning picking out the countryside all around her. Fortunately the traffic on the road was light, except for the heavy night lorries. At one point, when nearing Otterburn, it was as if a thunderbolt had dropped just behind the car for the pressure of it brought her crouching over the wheel. When she turned into the narrow road leading to the copse it was running with water like a mill stream.

Her headlights didn't pick out the Mini until she was nearly upon it, but she managed to bring the car to a sharp skidding stop; then sat back and closed her eyes for a moment, telling herself that she would never forget this night as long as she lived. Reaching over to the back seat she picked up her mac and the battery lantern. She struggled into the coat, pulled the hood over her head, then stepped out of the car and into ice cold water that came over her ankles. She could not hear her own exclamation above the fierceness of the wind. She had to fight her way up the first field, and when she reached the wall she clung to it, then lay against it, her back to the wind, in order to get her breath.

Twice as she went up towards the cottage she was almost lifted off her feet. Before mounting the steps she clung on to the iron post for a moment; then she was at the door knocking and calling, 'Mam! Mam!' She tried the latch, hoping that perhaps Annie had left the door open. She went down the steps again and fought her way to the back door. This, too, she found locked. She did not thump on this door, knowing it would be no use; if her mother hadn't heard her at the front, she wouldn't hear her at the back. But there was a way of getting in. She opened her bag and groped in the side pocket where, she knew, she would find a nail file, and this she inserted in the framework of the glass window in the kitchen annexe. With the first sharp lift the latch gave and the windows of their own accord burst outwards. Putting the lantern through she climbed in, then fell over the deck chairs. When she was on her feet again she forced the windows closed, and, picking up the lantern, went through the kitchen and into the sitting-room. Her mother was here all right, the embers of the fire were still glowing. She dropped her bag on to the couch so that she could take off her mac, which she threw down beside the bag; then, the lantern in her hand, she mounted the stairs.

'Mam! Mam!' She thought she'd better call so as not to frighten her.

When she pushed her bedroom door open and lifted the lantern high she stood staring at the sight before her. A short while before she had said she would never forget this night, but all that had happened so far paled now into insignificance. There in the bed was her mother lying on her back, her shoulders and breasts bare, and on his side, his arm across her, lay Alan Partridge.

'*Mother!*' She screamed the name at the highest pitch of her voice; it tore up out of her throat. Then again, '*Mother!*' Not Mam, but Mother. You couldn't get condemnation into the word Mam, not as you could into that of Mother.

'W . . . what! Who! O-oh God! God!' Annie was sitting up, clutching the bedclothes up around her chin now. 'Who . . . who is it?'

'Who do you think?' Her voice was still a scream. She looked down the beam of light and watched Alan pull himself up and blink and shade his eyes against the light. Now he was scrambling out of the bed and he didn't bother to cover himself up. She turned and ran from the room and down the stairs. After crashing the lantern on to the table, she went to the couch and, throwing herself on it, buried her face in a cushion and bit on her lip till the blood ran.

When she heard Annie beside her she didn't move. 'Oh my God! girl, you . . . you shouldn't have come. It . . . it isn't what you think. Look . . . look at me.'

When Tishy felt the hand on her shoulder she sprang away from it. But she looked at Annie, and now, dry-eyed but the tears breaking her voice, she cried, 'You're ... you're filthy! You're a filthy old woman!'

'I'm not. Don't you dare say that. Oh!' Annie groaned now and turned away, holding her head in her hands. Then as swiftly she turned to Tishy again, saying, 'It's all right, it's aboveboard, we're ... we're going to be married, I'm going to America. It doesn't matter about age.'

Tishy slowly drew herself up from the couch and, peering at Annie through the diffused light of the lantern, she said with slow bitterness, 'Well, I don't think you'll be going to America just yet. And when you do you might have to take long trips back to visit your son in prison.'

She watched her mother's lips tremble, she watched her fingers tapping her chin in small rapid movements, and it was a full minute before Annie said, 'What do you mean? What's brought you?'

'I'll tell you what's brought me. I've come to tell you that your son's a drug pusher. I tried to tell you three years ago, but you waved the betting slip at me. Well, now Susan Wilkins is back and she's spilled the beans, and her dad went after your dear Rance and Rance stabbed him. But what else did he do, eh? What else did he do? I'll tell you, he's got Percy in the hands of the police under suspicion. Percy gave him a lift to the garage because he had hurt his thumb. What happened after that is not yet clear to anybody, but this I do know, he stabbed Mr Wilkins, knocked Percy out, then he must have injected drugs into him and he left drugs on him. So if you're interested, that's why I'm here, that's what I've come to tell you, and if you hadn't been so busy whoring you would have been home now where you're needed.'

'If it wasn't for –' Annie gulped, then went on, 'If I knew you weren't a liar I ... I would slap your face for you this minute and for more reasons than one.'

'Why don't you?'

Now Annie, her hands again at her head, said, 'I can't ... I can't believe it.'

Alan walked into the rim of light and to her side. He now had his trousers on, but the rest of him was bare. He put his arm around her shoulders and looking at Tishy, he said, 'I'm ... I'm sorry, Tishy, it had to be broken to you like this but ... but it isn't what you think.'

'Oh! Oh!' She turned away, flapping her hand at him. 'I've

232

already heard that. And anyway it's no business of mine, but if you could spare my mother for a few hours there are matters she'll have to see to before she goes to America. And also –' she turned and looked to where they were standing beyond the rim of light close together, and she had to force her vituperation out while she still had a voice left, 'And you'll have to keep it dark, won't you, Mr Partridge? It wouldn't do if it became known in your high scholastic circles that you were stepfather to a murderer, because if Mr Wilkins dies that's what he'll be, that's if he doesn't manage skilfully, as usual, to put the blame on someone else, Percy this time.'

'*Stop it!* Your bitterness will burn you up one of these days, girl. . . . I –' Annie now turned to Alan – 'I must go. I must get dressed.' She pulled herself away from him and stumbled across the room towards the stairs, and Alan, looking towards the dark outline of Tishy, said, 'I'm deeply sorry about this trouble with Rance, but I'm more sorry that you have taken this attitude against your mother because of me, she's not to blame in any way. Nothing was planned. I was on a walking tour, I was helping an accident case over the fells, we stopped here for water. That was how it happened, nothing was planned. You mustn't hold anything against her.'

'Oh I don't, not really. I mean, what chance would she have against you. You tried your best seven years ago, didn't you?'

She waited for an answer but he remained silent, and she went on, 'Fourteen years younger than her. No woman could stand against that: flattery alone would get them down.'

'Tishy! Tishy! you're being cruel.'

'Oh my God! don't come that with me. Now let's get this straight, Mr Partridge. Your fine manners, your smooth tongue will never cut any ice with me, and don't, I'm warning you, come the old "we could be very good friends", for when you become my stepfather I'll be sick, nauseated, by the very unnaturalness of it.'

The wind howled around the house, a blast hit the windows, and for a moment the stout walls shuddered. She watched him turn slowly about and walk towards the kitchen.

When she was alone she went to the couch again and hung over the back of it for support while she told herself she mustn't be sick. She . . . must . . . not . . . be . . . sick.

As Annie descended the stairs, Alan came from the kitchen

with a lighted lamp, and after placing it on the table he went straight to her and, taking her hands, said, 'Shall I come with you?'

'No, no.' She shook her head. 'Stay here. I'll . . . I'll write.'

'Write? But I can't just wait for a letter, I'll come on tomorrow.'

'No, no. Please, Alan, please, just stay here, just wait.'

'I'll phone you.'

'Yes. Yes, do that. Sometime tomorrow, in the afternoon.'

'I'd rather you'd let me come with you.'

'No.' She was shaking her head widely. 'I've got to explain to them.' She turned from him and walked towards the closed door where Tishy was struggling into her mac again, but before she reached it Alan was by her side and as if they were entirely alone he pulled her round to him, saying, 'This makes no difference, you understand, about Rance? This makes no difference? No matter what's happened, promise me it'll make no difference.'

'I promise, Alan.'

'Sure?'

'Yes, yes, I'm sure.'

'Nothing's going to stop you coming away with me?'

'Nothing; I promise you, darling.'

They were in each other's arms.

She couldn't bear it. Her mother was shameless, utterly shameless. She pulled open the door and a blast of air filled the room. The wind checked her running down the steps; it drove her sideways towards the iron railings for a moment. Without waiting to share the light of the lantern she went tearing down the hill, but from the wavering light she knew that her mother was close behind, and when she paused at the broken wall Annie caught up with her. They did not speak but lay against it for a moment panting, before going on again.

Even when they reached the copse they still didn't speak, and Tishy got into the car and backed it harshly into a bank of mud, then drove it forward, sending the spray window high.

She did not wait at the end of the road to see whether the Mini were behind her; it wasn't until she was on the straight stretch going towards Otterburn that the headlights came up on her and remained at the same distance for most of the journey. . . .

From the moment they entered the house it was as if the incident in the cottage had never taken place, at least from the way Annie acted, for, almost pulling Tishy into the front room, she

234

demanded, 'Now without any heroics you tell me what's happened right from the beginning.'

'I've ... I've told you already.' Tishy's teeth were chattering with the cold.

'Well, tell me again.'

So, slowly and without venom now, more as if she were answering the inquiries of a stranger, she gave Annie the details, beginning from the time Rance had come in. When she had finished Annie sat down and stared straight before her. Why was it that nothing lasted? She had been in heaven for the past three days, and that was the right description; every minute she had spent with Alan had been nothing short of heaven. And now she had been thrust into hell. She believed every word that Tishy had said; Tishy was no liar, she didn't even exaggerate. She also knew that she was right when she had pointed out that she had used the betting slip as a cover up. She recalled the times of late when she had looked at Rance, and looked quickly away again, refusing to believe what her mind was telling her. She had, on these occasions, blinded herself by reasoning that if he were on drugs he would take them every day, wouldn't he? They all did; it got a hold of them. But Rance could go for days without coming with that odd look on his face, and her having to practically drag him out of bed the following morning to get him to work.

Then there was the fact that had kept niggling at her: she had never seen him with his shirt off for years. And again her twisted reasoning had turned on her and said, You know he's always been fastidious about his clothes, and his person. But what about in the garage? He never rolled his sleeves up like other men when doing a job, but always kept them buttoned. Yet it wasn't necessary for a boss to go around with his sleeves rolled up, was it? She had always given herself the answer she wanted to hear.

She looked down at her feet, wet and covered with mud, then at Tishy's, and as if to prove she had left her other self completely back there in the cottage she said to her, 'You'd better get those wet things off.'

As she walked slowly to the door, Tishy said, 'What are you going to do?'

She turned to her. 'I don't know, I'll have to talk to him first. I should say if all you tell me is true, that there's nothing I can do, is there?'

As she entered the kitchen Tishy was behind her, saying, 'But

235

you would if you could, wouldn't you? You would still help him to get out of it.'

Annie had reached the stove. She looked from the kettle to the cup and saucer and teapot that were on the table; then she put her hand on the kettle and turned and gazed at Tishy, and her look said, 'He must be in.' The next minute she was rushing out of the kitchen, across the hall and up the stairs.

She did not tap on her son's bedroom door but thrust it open and switched on the light. He was in bed, his head almost buried under the clothes. She went to him. She did not touch him, but said loudly, 'Rance!' Then again, 'Rance!'

'What . . . what is it? Oh!' He turned over and looked at her. 'Hello, you're back?' He was blinking the sleep from his eyes.

'Yes, I'm back. And you're back apparently. Get up!'

'What!'

'I said get up! you heard me.'

'Now look! it's the middle of the night.'

'Get up!' It was a bellow and before the sound had faded away she had gripped the bedclothes and pulled them from him, then stood staring down at him where he lay fully dressed, even to his light overcoat. After gazing at him for a moment she backed from him, then went to the wardrobe and pulled the door open. There were no suits hanging on the rails but his suitcase was there. When she lifted it out she found it was heavy.

Looking towards the bed, her eyes lowered to the floor, she saw the outline of his other case. She went slowly towards him again where he was sitting on the edge of the bed now and she asked grimly, 'Going some place?'

He didn't answer, but after staring at her for a moment his head drooped.

She now whipped the chair from the side of the bed and, climbing on it, thrust open the top of the Scotch chest. It was empty. When she stepped down he was staring at her, his eyes wide and his mouth open, and she nodded at him. 'Oh yes, I know about it; and I knew there was some fiddle you were up to, but God in heaven!' Her head now moved in a slow sweep from one shoulder to the other. 'I wouldn't have it that you were making it from drugs.'

'People need them, Mam.'

'What?' She had not made out his muttering, and he said again, 'People need them, it's . . . it's sort of medical. . . .'

'Medical! My God! you can sit there and delude yourself that it's, it's ... sort of medical.' Her voice had been low, but now it rose to a shout. 'Is it medical to stab a man? Is it medical to arrange it so as your brother-in-law takes the blame? Though how, in the name of God! you expected that to pass I'll never know. You must have been hard up for an escape route to pin this on Percy. But the dirtiest trick you've ever done in your life was to pump him full of your filth.' Her lips curled back from her teeth. 'You've always hated him because he was streets above you, not only in class but in every other way, but to ...'

He thrust his head towards her now and for the first time he showed fight by saying, 'You've never liked him, so what are you on about?'

'No, it's true I never cared much for him, but at this moment I love him, and if it lies with me he'll not bear this suspicion a minute longer.'

He now rose to his feet and stood staring at her while his whole face, his whole body, quivered and he reverted back to the pleading little boy as he said, 'Mam, look; give me a chance. I ... I could have been away, miles away out of the country but ... but I wanted to see you again. I waited ... I waited hours in the rain. I ... I couldn't come in because –' he dipped his head, shook it, then lifted it again and looked at her where she was standing as if she had died, so colourless, so immobile was she, and, his voice almost a whimper, he said, 'I ... I couldn't go without seeing you. Then when you didn't come I knew I'd have to because, because I've got to be there –' he stopped, swallowed deeply then ended, 'I've got to be there before five.'

Her voice came stiffly through her pale lips. 'Where?'

'Oh, it ... it doesn't matter.'

'Where?'

'You ... you wouldn't know the place, it's outside of New-castle. Anyway, what does it matter?'

'You're hopping off by plane then? I suppose Benny has arranged it all.'

He was gazing at her with that little-boy-lost look in his eyes, but he made no answer until she said, sharply, 'Take your coat off!'

'Now, Mam, Mam, I don't want to argue.'

She had advanced on him. 'Take your coat off. If you don't I'll tear it off.'

'Look, Mam –' he moved a step back from her, 'Look, I've hurt my hand.' He held out his bandaged hand towards her then added quickly, 'Stop it, you'll get hurt. I'm telling you, you'll get hurt.'

'Don't you worry about me. Take your coat off.'

When the back of his legs touched the bed he took his coat off and, flinging it behind him, said, 'There now! Are you satisfied?'

'No. Take the other off.'

'Look, Mam. . . .'

Her hand shot out and with a blow to the side of the face she knocked him backwards on to the bed. When he went to right himself she thrust her hand towards the dressing table, and after a second of groping clutched at a metal statue. It was about a foot high and represented a running boy. He had bought it a few years previously, and no matter where she put it in his room he would always move it back on to the dressing table. Now she held it above his head as she cried, 'Take that coat off else I'll brain you!' and then, 'I'll take it off for you.'

'Ma-am!' He drew out her name as if he were singing it, and she barked at him, 'Don't mam me any more. Take your coat off!'

And he took his coat off.

'Now your shirt.'

'No, Mam, no . . . Aw no, Mam.'

'Get your shirt off.' Her voice was low and almost toneless now.

'Mam, I'll tell you anything, anything you want to . . .'

'All I want at this moment is for you to take your shirt off. *Now! Now!*' Her voice rose as her free hand shot out and grabbed the front of his shirt. The next minute they were struggling together.

Neither of them was aware that the door had burst open until Tishy cried, 'Mam! Mam! stop it!' With a fierce tug she managed to pull Annie away and with her came the sleeve of Rance's shirt, and the sound of it tearing was like a knife being drawn against glass.

Annie was now leaning back against the dressing table, the top of the sleeve gripped against her waist. The other end of it, still attached to Rance's wrist, was in this moment symbolical of the cord that had ever been between them. As she stared at the

pock-marked flesh her lips slowly moved away from her teeth;
then as if it were a reptile she threw the shirt sleeve back at him.
'You filthy! filthy –' she swallowed deeply now, gulped at some
spittle and began to cough.

'Come away. Come away.' Tishy was leading her from the
room as if she were an old woman, and she seemed to have turned
into an old woman for she allowed herself to be led. She made no
resistance until she had reached the hall, but when Tishy guided
her towards the sitting-room door she slowly pushed her aside
and walked towards the front door.

'Where you going? They . . . they won't let you in the hospital
at this time of night.'

'Hospital?' Annie turned slowly and looked at Tishy. 'I'm
not going to any hospital, lass, I'm going to do what I should
have done years ago.' Even her voice sounded old.

'Mam! Mam!' Tishy's voice was low and agitated. 'Hadn't . . .
hadn't you better wait? Don't go out in this state.'

'Huh! it's funny.' Annie was shaking her head now. 'You tell
me to wait; you've been pitching the truth at me for years,
urging me to do something, and now you're telling me to wait.
Well, the time's come, lass; the waiting's past.'

As she picked up her coat casually from the hall chair Tishy
muttered, 'Wait. Wait a minute; I'll get mine, I'll come with
you.'

'No!' Annie's voice was firm now. 'No, you keep out of this.
He's going to have no one to blame but me.'

'But Mam!'

'No, I've said no, girl.' And on that she opened the door and
went out.

Tishy stood in the porch watching her fight her way against
the wind and rain towards the car. At one point the wind billowed
her coat over her head and she turned her back and lifted her hands
up in order to pull it down, and the lamplight shone on her face,
picking out each white feature and setting it in a cameo to be
forever remembered.

Not until the car had moved off did Tishy close the door;
then characteristically she stood with her back to it and looked
towards the stairs, and all she could say was, 'Dear God! Dear
God!' In this moment her own pain was utterly blotted out; she
could think only of those two, and she didn't know whom she
was most sorry for, her mother or Rance. That she should feel

the slightest pity for him amazed her. He was filthy, unclean, he was as good as a murderer, and at bottom he was a snivelling coward; yet a moment ago, when from the doorway she had watched them struggling, she had known that one good blow from him could have knocked her mother flying, and he hadn't lifted his hand. She had seen her mother gripping his bandaged thumb and the pain of that alone must have been excruciating; still he hadn't hit her.

She stumbled into the sitting-room and, her arms folded about her thin body, she began pacing the floor. Soon the police would be here. They would take him; he would go to prison. For life, if Mr Wilkins died. She'd always hated him, she still did, yet in spite of herself there was rising in her a pity for him, and strangely, she knew, it was not because he might have to spend the rest of his life in prison but because he had already lost his mother. If he had ever loved anyone as much as himself he had loved her. All her life she herself had been jealous of the love between them; more so, because she knew that her mother had returned his love twofold; but during the last hour she had seen that love turn into cold hate.

Her teeth began to chatter, her whole body to tremble. She must have something hot to drink. She mustn't land up with one of her colds, not at this time.

She went into the kitchen and put the kettle on the stove. A few minutes later she had mashed the tea, and a few minutes later still she had drunk two cupfuls so scalding that it burned her mouth.

There was no sound in the house except the wind tearing down the chimneys. What was he doing up there? Scheming for some way finally to get round Mam? But surely he would see that was impossible now.

It was about half an hour later when the kitchen door opened and he came in. He was fully dressed again but without a tie. After one glance at him she turned her head away; but he came slowly towards the table, and in a voice that he had never used to her before in his life, he said, 'I'm sorry, Tishy.'

When she looked up at him she felt for a moment that her heart would break, for she was seeing him as her mother had seen him all these years, the vulnerable, weak boy, needing something that no one could give.

'Where is she?' He moved his head back towards the wall,

indicating the sitting-room, and she shook her head, she couldn't speak. Hadn't he any idea of where she was? He must know where she was. Yet she herself hadn't known what her mother's intentions were until she had voiced them.

Apparently taking her silence for an affirmative answer, he turned from the table and made towards the door, but there he paused and, looking back at her, he said, 'Good-bye, Tishy. I doubt if we'll ever see each other again. I'm . . . I'm sorry.'

She now spoke his name as she had never spoken it before. 'Rance,' she said softly, 'Mam . . . Mam's gone out.'

He turned fully towards her but stood still. She saw the expression on his face change. She saw fear like a mask drop over it.

'Where? Where's she gone?'

When she didn't answer, he simply stared back at her. Then she saw him change into the Rance that she knew, the one she had been acquainted with all her life. His face going stiff, his jaws locking, his anger set the blood in his head pulsing until his face looked almost purple.

'She wouldn't, she wouldn't do that. She wouldn't!' He was bawling at her now, and, her pity of the previous moment vanishing, she cried at him, 'Well, she has.'

'Aw no! No!'

As she watched the expression on his face changing again, she became afraid and rose from the chair and moved to the end of the table. He looked like someone gone mad and when he screamed at her, 'The polis station! She's gone there?' she thought it better to remain quiet. She saw him dash into the hall: but before she could move he was back, saying, 'How long? how long?' He looked at his watch.

She was going to say, 'Long enough for her to have told them everything,' but what she muttered was, 'Not . . . not long.'

He ran from her now and not until she heard the wind rushing into the hall did she move. The front door was open, his two cases were standing at the bottom of the stairs. As she went slowly forwards to close the door she heard the car being revved up, then on a screech tear down the street.

She closed the door once again, but this time she didn't stand with her back to it but ran into the kitchen and, laying her head on her arms on the table, began to cry. She cried for her mother; she cried for Rance; and then she cried for herself and the deep inner loneliness inside her. She cried for how she looked, how she appeared to other people; she cried for the course her life would take from now on.

Meanwhile Rance was speeding erratically down Fowler Street which was fortunately bare of traffic. He did not turn the car into King Street but took a side road into Keppel Street where the police station was, and his headlights immediately picked out Annie's car parked on the opposite side to the station and about thirty feet along the kerb from the main door.

He drew the car to a screeching halt in the centre of the road as his eyes took in a small group of people outside the station door. There were three officers and a woman. When the group broke up, two of the officers went along the pavement towards a parked car. The third man spoke to the woman and, as she turned away, he remained standing watching her crossing the road to her car.

She had her head deep down on her chest when his headlights fell on her, then her head jerking she lifted her arm to shield her eyes, but not before he saw the look in them and it told him what she had done. . . . His Mam had given him away. But no, she couldn't. She wouldn't, not her, she loved him. She had always loved him. He'd had her love as her husband never had. In fact he knew he was her husband, her lover, everything to her. All he'd had to do was to touch her and her eyes told him what he needed to know, that she was his. That he had a power over her none of the others knew anything about, and because of it she was the one person who would always stand by him. Even a short while ago when they had struggled together he had known her fury would pass as it always had done. He had even been making plans in his mind to send for her once he got settled abroad, for he'd really be in the money then. . . . But here she was, backing away from him, her face full of terror.

He wasn't aware of starting the car, but he was aware of plunging his foot down on the accelerator and of the hard bump as the front wheels mounted the pavement.

She hadn't her arm over her eyes when he hit her, her hands were outstretched towards him. When she fell forward over the bonnet he reversed just the slightest then rammed the gears forward again. She had slipped down now and on the second impact he could not see her.

He was attempting to repeat the operation when they got the door open and dragged him out on to the road.

Tishy hadn't moved until she heard the door bell ring and she didn't get up until it had rung for the second time. Then, like someone dazed, she went through the hall and opened the door, and there stood a policeman and behind him on the pavement near a car was another.

'Miss McCabe?'

'Yes.'

'I've . . . I've some sad news for you.'

She stared at him, then from him to the other officer, then back to him again.

'Your . . . your mother has met with an accident.'

'My . . . my mother?' Her voice was high in her head, then she repeated, 'My mother?'

When she gripped the door with both hands the policeman said, 'Can I come in a moment?' Then he looked back towards his companion before stepping over the threshold.

'Sit down,' he said.

It was the second time a policeman had said that to her within the last few hours, but she didn't sit down. 'Where . . . where's my mother?' she said.

His gaze flicked from her for a moment and he repeated, 'You'd better sit down.'

'My mother, what's happened to her? What's happened to my mother?'

'She . . . she had an accident.'

'You've said that.'

'She . . . she was run down by a car.'

'My mother was run down by a car in the middle of the night? She was going to you, she was going to the police station.'

'She had been to the station, she was coming out. I mean she had come out, she was walking across the road to her car, when this car comes at her . . . full tilt.'

There was something final about the words, full tilt; it was as if he had no need to explain any further. There was a deep blackness coming towards her. It was thick, shrouding the police-man and dimming his voice as he went on, 'It . . . it was your brother's car. I'm very sorry to have to tell you this but . . . but it wasn't really an accident, he . . . he rammed her. There were

243

witnesses. The Inspector had come to the door with her and . . . and . . . a . . . patrol . . . car . . . was . . . coming . . . in . . . from . . . the . . . other . . . end . . . of . . . the . . . street . . . It . . . is . . . a . . . dreadful . . . thing . . . not . . . really . . . understandable.'

Not really understandable. Not really understandable, *Not really understandable. Not really understandable.*

3

They came into the house one after the other, Tishy first, then Kathy, then Bill. They walked like people in a dream and they all wore similar expressions on their faces, it was like a family resemblance. But once the door was closed on them they began, as it were, to unfreeze. Kathy started to cry slowly and painfully. Her head buried in her arms and her arms against the wing of a chair, she gave herself ease. Bill, too, began to cry. Hiding his tears, he went straight upstairs.

Only Tishy didn't cry now. When she came out of the faint last night – or was it this morning? Anyway, it was some time long ago – a strange thought persisted in her mind saying, She cannot be dead that way; she was going to be married and go to America. She knew that if her mother had married Alan she would have died to her, but now she had died in a different way. She had told herself she would have preferred that she had died in the first way and not like the policeman had said. She hadn't really believed the policeman until she had entered the mortuary. Even then she couldn't associate that bandaged face and broken body with her mam. They had said he hadn't been satisfied with crushing her against the wall, but when she fell he had backed and did it again before they had overpowered him.

She had moaned, 'Oh Mam! Mam!' while at the same time feeling that her mother had knowingly brought this terrible end on herself. She should have known that Rance wouldn't stand for it. Anybody else could have given him away but not her, not the one who had shielded him since he could breathe, not the one he had been capable of convincing, hoodwinking, and bamboozling; not the woman he had loved – the only woman he had loved, for she hadn't just been a mother to him, she had

245

been everything, if only in his mind she had been everything, and she must have been aware of this. She herself had been aware of it, and this had been the cause of her deep jealousy.

She couldn't analyse her feelings against Rance at this moment, nor measure the depths of sorrow for her mother, but what was to the forefront of her mind was a rising feeling of resentment against Alan Partridge. If it hadn't been for him her mother would have been here on Friday, and although that wouldn't have stopped Mr Wilkins coming and exposing Rance, things would never have reached this pass, for her mother would have done something, managed something – she always had – but instead of being here he'd had her in bed.

She made tea automatically and called Bill downstairs and the three of them sat round the kitchen table drinking it; nobody wanted to eat, individually they felt they never wanted to eat again. They sat in silence for almost five minutes before Kathy said, 'What'll happen to him?'

A space of time passed again before Bill answered, 'He'll likely get life for one or the other, although Mr Wilkins might pull through. But then there's the other thing.' Bill couldn't bring himself to voice the word, drugs. It was too dirty, much viler than murder; murder was often the outcome of passion, but drug-running was something else.

He now ran his hands through his hair and, looking at Tishy, said, 'What's going to happen to the business?'

'The business?' She spoke as if coming out of sleep. 'I . . . I haven't thought.'

'That Jimmy Lake seems a good fellow.'

'Yes, yes.' She nodded. Jimmy Lake was a good fellow. She had thought often that if it wasn't for Jimmy Lake there would have been very little business done in the garage. But what did it matter about the garage, or Jimmy Lake, or anything else? Why was Bill talking about the garage? He had just come back from the mortuary. She looked at his face. It was pale; he looked sick. She looked at Kathy's face. Kathy wasn't the same person she had seen last night in the green velvet dress; the years had mounted on Kathy since last night.

After a while Kathy said, 'I'd better get home,' and when Bill, rising from the table, said, 'I'll run you back,' Kathy looked at Tishy. 'Come back and stay with us,' she said, 'both of you.'

'No, no, thanks all the same. I'd rather stay put.'

246

'We've got to get used to it,' said Bill.

'Just for the time being. Percy's mother seeing to things, she would. . . .'

'We'll be all right.' Bill took her arm. 'Don't worry.'

'Gran McCabe'll have to be told.'

They turned and looked at Tishy and Bill said, 'I'll slip over later. I won't be long. Go and lie down.'

She didn't answer, but turned her head away and stared at the kitchen cabinet on the wall opposite.

The day passed somehow. There were tentative knocks on the door by a few neighbours offering their sympathy. Mrs Wilkins wasn't among them; she had her own set of visitors. The phone rang innumerable times. After Bill had banged the door in the face of three separate reporters he phoned the police, and shortly a patrol car came to a stop a little way down the road, and stayed there.

Tishy was passing through the hall when the phone rang yet again. Wearily she picked it up. It was someone phoning from a call box. She heard the coins drop, then as the voice spoke she took the phone away from her ear and looked at it as if confronting the speaker.

The voice came again. 'Hello. Who's there?'

Still she didn't answer.

'Hello. Who's there? . . . This is Alan Partridge. I . . . I want to speak with Mrs . . . Mrs McCabe. Hello. Hello.'

Slowly she brought the mouthpiece nearer and, her voice low and harsh, she spoke into it. 'You can't speak to Mrs McCabe. Mrs McCabe is dead.' And with that she banged the receiver down.

She shouldn't have done it, not like that. How other should she have broken it to him then? Gently, easing his hurt? when he was to blame for most of what had happened!

Don't. Don't. She bent her body forward and gripped her head with her hands. Recriminations, blame. Where did they get you? She was gone, dead. Nothing could bring her back. She had been a lovely mother, a lovely woman, young looking, like a girl. But she had called her old, and filthy. Recriminations. She should be heaping them on her own head. She was. She was. She would never forget the things she had said to her mother in the cottage. After a moment she mounted the stairs and as she reached the top the phone rang again, and Bill, coming from the bathroom, said, 'I'll take it.'

A few minutes later he knocked on her door and when she said, 'Come in,' he stood within the opening. 'It was Alan Partridge,' he said; 'he ... he seemed shocked. He wanted to know if he had heard aright, what you had said. He must have met mother lately. He talked oddly. He seemed very shocked.'

She did not say as she might have, 'He would be, seeing that the last time she slept was with him.' No, that was something only she knew, and it wouldn't go any further, they wouldn't understand, Kathy less than Bill. Yet she understood. Oh yes, she understood how her mother had fallen for him. He was the easiest person in the world to fall for; he had everything going for him, had Mr Alan Partridge.

When she turned her head away Bill went out and closed the door, a vague memory stirring in his mind. He recalled that after his dad had died their Tishy had taken up with Alan Partridge, and then it had come to an abrupt end. He never knew why.

During the evening she went to the hospital with Kathy to visit Percy. Percy was conscious now, but still dazed, not able to take in what had happened to him. She left Kathy with him and his father, and returned home to find Alice, Bill's controversial choice of a future wife, in the house together with her mother and father.

The grizzled-haired, ebony-skinned big Negro, whose colour made that of his daughter appear as merely a deep sunburn showed his sympathy in a most genuine fashion, as did his wife, a faded and much painted blonde about half his size.

It was Tishy's first meeting with Alice's parents, and some part of her was touched that these people should openly show that they were connected in any way with such a family as the McCabes had now become, having in it a man who was not only a drug-pusher but a murderer.

When the visitors were leaving, Bill, taking Tishy aside, whispered, 'Do you mind if I walk Alice home? I won't be half an hour.'

'Go on,' she said. 'I'm all right. Don't worry about me.'

'Nobody will trouble you; there's still somebody on the watch, though the car went a short while ago.'

So she was in the house alone when the doorbell rang, and she paused before she opened the door. Then she heard someone

248

say, 'What is your business?' and when she opened the door the policeman and Alan turned together towards her.

'Do you know this man, miss?'

She looked through the gathering dusk at the white face. Did she know this man? Oh yes, she knew this man. In a way she had been expecting him, but not so soon; she thought he would arrive tomorrow morning.

'Yes, constable, thank you.' She stood back, and Alan went past her into the hall, and she purposely took a long time in closing the door, for she didn't want to look at him again. His face looked bleached, and there was a look in his eyes that as yet she couldn't put a name to. Her head down, she moved past him into the sitting-room, and he followed. As she pointed to a chair she didn't speak, nor did he, not even after he had sat down.

From the apparently small fact that she was standing and he was sitting she gauged the extent of his distress. He had almost been as meticulous about this point of etiquette as Percy, only his manner of doing it was more easy, more relaxed. She put her hand on to the mantelpiece to support herself while she looked at him; and now he said, 'I can't take it in. No matter how often I tell myself, I can't take it in.' He now put his hand into his macintosh pocket and pulled out a newspaper and, unfolding it until it was half its width showing big black headlines, he said, 'Why? Why should he do it when he loved her? She . . . she had told me about him, the tie that was between them, how . . . how difficult it was going to be to break. It was the only real tie, she said; but she would break it.'

When she slowly lowered her head, he put in on a slightly higher note, 'Oh . . . oh, I'm not inferring that she meant it would be easy to leave you, or the others, but she reckoned on your understanding. It was only him she thought might not understand, and he didn't, did he?'

She looked into his eyes now and recognized the look that was deep in them as remorse and guilt. He imagined that in some way he was responsible for this crime.

It would be rough justice to let him stew in his own juice, but she couldn't do that. She said flatly, 'He knew nothing about you.'

He got to his feet now but didn't come towards her, just stared at her, one hand held in front of him opening and closing as if trying to grasp at something that evaded him.

'You mean she ... she hadn't told him?'

'No.'

'Then I in no way contributed to ...?'

'No.' Her voice was high now. 'You can go away with a clear conscience on that point anyway. What he did wasn't because he thought she was leaving him for you. But I'm going to tell you this: if it hadn't been for you she'd have been home on Friday, and in her usual way she would have tackled this business and straightened it out. And she would have been alive now.'

A moment ago she had eased his personal agony, now she had added to it tenfold. When his lips began to tremble and he hunched his shoulders and his head drooped she cried at herself, 'Why had you to say that?' Now he turned from her, one hand covering his face, and he began to cry audibly, like a woman might.

Bill had cried, but it had been a silent crying. She had never heard a man cry like this before. It didn't seem right that a big man like him should give way to grief in such a fashion.

When he continued to cry she stood behind him and said, 'Sit down. I'll get you a cup of tea. I'm ... I'm sorry. I'm sorry I went at you like that, I shouldn't have.

Obeying her, he groped at the head of the couch. His elbows on his knees, his face buried in his hands, he continued to cry, and it was impossible to bear the sight and not to touch him.

She went into the kitchen, the kettle was already spluttering on the low ring. Hastily she mashed the tea, and when she took the tray into the room a few minutes later he was lying back on the couch, his hands hanging limply at his sides.

He was still crying, but silently now; his eyes were blurred with his tears and his face awash with them.

'Drink this,' she said.

It seemed an effort for him to pull himself forward. He took the cup from her, then put it down on the table again and, taking a handkerchief from his pocket, he wiped his face a number of times before getting abruptly to his feet, turned the collar of his raincoat high up around his ears and without looking at her he walked towards the door.

She felt completely at a loss. She didn't know what to say now. He hadn't spoken since she had thrown the accusation at him. It seemed as if he were going without uttering a word when, at the front door, he asked under his breath, while still not looking at her, 'When ... when is the funeral?'

'Wednesday,' she murmured; 'two o'clock.'

He said no more, but opened the door and went out, his head down, his face half-buried in his coat collar.

She did not wait to see which way he went, or if he had come by car. Quickly she closed the door and leaning her face against it in the crook of her arm she moaned aloud.

4

They stood in a small group in a side street where they had parked their cars some distance from the court-house. The trial was over and they were not talking about it any longer. What Kathy and Percy, Bill and Alice, were all trying to do now was to persuade Tishy to come back with them.

For the third time Bill said, 'But what will you do up there on your own? You'll go mad.'

'Well, if I'm to go mad I'd much rather be on my own. . . . I'll be all right, I tell you, I'll be all right.' She looked around them. 'I . . . I just want to get away for a time.'

'Don't we all!' Kathy hung her head; then looking at Tishy, she said, 'I didn't mean that nasty, Tishy.'

'I know. I know.'

'I think we should go home and discuss the business, go into it further, now we are all together,' said Bill now.

'What more is there to discuss? I've told you I'd like the cottage as my share, and if it doesn't run to the price that we agreed on, then I'll take out a mortgage.'

'Don't be silly,' said Bill and Kathy almost simultaneously.

'Anyway the garage is carrying on,' said Bill, 'and Jimmy'll make a good job of it. We should talk about what he suggested last week, expanding.'

When Tishy closed her eyes Bill said on an impatient note, 'Well, somebody's got to do the talking. And there's another thing.' He stopped and looked away from them and down the narrow street before he said, 'There's the fourth share. He . . . he may want it some day, you never know. Life doesn't mean life any longer and . . . and he may recover. . . .'

His voice trailed away as Tishy turned towards her car. Unlocking the door she got into the driving seat, then looked at them where they were standing on the pavement now gazing down at her. Kathy, bending forward, said, 'We'll come over on Sunday no matter what the weather.'

'All right.'

'How long do you intend to stay?' asked Bill.

'I don't know.'

'You'll have to send a note to school next Tuesday if you don't turn up.'

'I'll see. I'll see.'

Speaking for the first time, Percy said, 'If you want us, phone me any time at the office, Tishy – any time.'

'I'll do that, Percy. Good-bye.' She looked from one to the other, and they said, 'Good-bye, Tishy.'

She started the car, brought it out of its parking space, then drove off down the hill and out of Durham, and as she left the city behind she said, 'I'll never come here again as long as I live.'

She stopped in Newcastle and bought some food, just the necessities, milk, bread, tea, sugar, butter, some fruit and steak. She was caught up in the five o'clock rush of traffic which put another half an hour on to her journey, but it didn't matter. She wasn't impatient, she had all the time in the world before her; even wedged in between cars, lorries and buses, with their combined noise pressing in on her, made no impression on the void that she was living in and which stretched before her ad infinitum. The concern of her family, the fact that she was but twenty-five, and that even plain women had been known to marry when they were thirty or over, afforded her not the slightest consolation. In fact, she didn't see any compensations for herself. What she saw was a life of teaching and the thousand and one irritations that accompanied the word, which was recognized even by those who considered it a vocation, and she wasn't one of them. She saw the sameness stretching down the years until she retired – retired to the cottage.

Why did she want to return there? Why? It should be the last place she should want to go to. Somewhere at the back of her mind she had the faint idea that she would be nearer her mother there, yet the picture of her mother, as she had last seen her in that room, should be no inducement for her to return, just the opposite if she were using her reason.

But she could find no reason in the urge to return to the cottage, only the fact that it was the only place in which she could be alone with her misery. . . .

The long twilight was beginning when she parked the car in the copse. From the boot she took out a suitcase and the bag of groceries, and slowly made her way up the field. When she reached the broken wall she rested for a moment and, leaning her arms on the top of it, she looked about her. The strange white light that cloaked the moors on a fine day was being diffused now into grey. There were pink patches on the hills, and inky black hollows, and sloping stretches of green rolling like carpets to the valleys.

She took in a deep breath. This is what she needed, the ever changing picture, the unpeopled picture, the lonely desolate picture. Here she would find some sort of peace, but more important still here she could hide herself and her feelings and no one would say, 'Now you must forget about the past and pull yourself together; we've all got to live.'

Gran McCabe had said that to her yesterday. She had meant well. 'No one will miss Annie more than I will. Lass and woman, I liked her. Salt of the earth was Annie. She could tackle mountains. She tackled my Georgie when she was but a girl, and made a man out of him. God rest his soul, an' hers an' all. She made one mistake in her life an' it was a natural one. It wasn't that she fell with Rance afore she married but that she broke his neck from the day he was born. . . . Well, it's over, lass. God makes the back to bear the burden, that's what I've learned from life, so come on now, your back might be narrow but it's tough. You've got your mother in you, and you've got your dad in you, and perhaps a little bit of me an' all, eh?'

Strange, how people like Gran McCabe could face life. When she had asked her if she should pick her up on the way to the trial, she had answered, 'I'm hard up at this minute, lass, but I wouldn't take a thousand pounds an' look on him again, for God knows what I might be driven to say, or do, meself. No, lass,' she had said; 'do you know what I am going to do the day? I'm goin' to bingo, that's all he's worth to me, I'm goin' to bingo, 'cos I'm goin' to tell you somethin' that I've never mentioned afore, an' it's this, I've always thought there was somethin' fishy about the way my Georgie died. I'd seen him just a while afore in the pub. He'd had a drop, but he wasn't drunk enough to fall downstairs.

When he was home along of me, he'd come in paralytic night after night, mortallious, stinking, but he always made those back stairs, an' they were as steep as a cliff. No, lass, from me first sight of Annie I knew there was something there I'd better not probe into. . . . Can you throw any light on it for me, lass?'

And because it would make no difference now she had said, 'He kicked me dad downstairs.'

Mollie had nodded as she said quietly, 'I knew it, I knew it was somethin' like that . . . aye, I'll go to bingo.'

She picked up the bag and case again and walked slowly up the hill. The evening light was shining on the windows of the cottage, softening its hard exterior. As she neared the steps she thought, I've got to make this my home. When she reached the verandah she put down the case and took her key from her handbag, but when she went to insert it in the door she found that it was open. Pushing it forward she tentatively entered the room; then her face stretched and her mouth fell into a gape.

The place was filthy. What had happened? Had tramps been in, or hikers? She looked at the floor, mud stains all over it. There was unwashed crockery on the table to the side of the couch; the couch itself was pushed up close to the fire. Her gape widened; the fire was on. She went slowly up the room and rounded the couch but keeping her distance from it. Then she stared wide-eyed at the figure lying there asleep under huddled-up blankets. If it hadn't been for the colour of his hair she would have taken the man for a stranger. The face was unrecognizable with its ragged beard and a thick growth on the cheeks. The couch was not long enough to take his length and he was lying on his side with his knees bent. He was breathing deeply like a man in drink. She looked round for evidence of bottles, but as far as she could see there weren't any.

The hearth had a pile of ash on it which meant it hadn't been cleared for days. There were burnt pieces of wood lying near the edge, almost touching the rug. The place could have been burned down.

As she went to turn away the soles of her shoes brought a squeak from the floor boards, and he moved. He turned on to his back, and she watched his tongue come out and lick around the thick stubble on his lips. Then he groaned and went to turn on to his other side but stopped and, slowly opening his eyes, peered at her through his flickering lids. Closing them again, he kept them shut for some seconds. When he again looked at her he slowly pulled himself up into a sitting position and was about to speak when he began to cough.

After the spasm had passed he said in a voice, thick and croaking, 'I ... I can go any time. I ... I had the key and ... and looked in a while ago. ...' He closed his eyes again, and now his body slid down until his head was resting on the arm of the couch.

If he wasn't drunk or getting over a drinking bout then he was ill. She forced herself to say, 'Aren't you well?'

'What?'

'I said, aren't you well?'

'Off colour, that's all. I ... I can go any time, kit's outside ... sleeping bag ... I can go any time.' He said no more but slid farther down the couch.

After a moment she went slowly down the room, picked up the bag of groceries and the case from the verandah, then went into the kitchen.

It looked as if he had used every dish in the place. The washing-up bowl was full of plates, cups and saucers. There were three dirty pans on the stove, there was the remains of a loaf on the table and a tin of corned beef with the lid half opened.

She looked in the pans. One held congealed porridge that had shrunk away from the sides of the pan, which meant it had been there some days; another had held milk and was burnt; the third pan had three potatoes stuck to the bottom.

What was she to do? Go back home, leave him? ... She couldn't just walk out and leave the place like this; nor him for that matter. She picked up the half opened tin of corned beef. He must be ill.

She went to the kitchen door and looked towards the far end of the room. He was still lying down. In ordinary circumstances he would have been up and talking ... and walking away.

Why had this to happen to her? Why? Talk about turning the screws. The last person on God's earth she wanted to be confronted by at this time was him. She had stood enough, it wasn't fair. Oh! She turned about on an inward groan; then going into the room again, she lifted her case and went upstairs.

On the landing she hesitated and looked at the door through which she had rushed on that far off night. She went to pass it. It would likely be in the same state as down below. With a jerk she thrust it open.

It was just as if her mother had left it at the end of a visit, everything neat and tidy awaiting her return. Even the odd things on the dressing table were arranged carefully, not as her mother might have arranged them, but in a straight line in front of the mirror. Why had he done this, straightened everything up?

Slowly she closed the door. He must have stayed downstairs all this time. But surely he hadn't been here since she had last seen him? She wouldn't know until he told her and by the look of him he wouldn't be able to tell her much for some time. Hurriedly now she went into her room and changed.

Downstairs again, she went to the couch. His eyes were closed as if he were sleeping. She touched his shoulder. 'How ... how long have you been like this?'

He lifted his lids and blinked at her, then shook his head.

'When did you last eat?'

Again he shook his head, and at this she left him and went into the kitchen.

The first thing she did was to clean a pan and heat some milk. When it was ready she spooned two heaped spoonfuls of glucose into it, then took it to him.

'Sit up,' she said abruptly, 'and drink this.'

Obediently but slowly, he pulled himself upwards; then leaning his shoulder against the back of the couch for support he took the cup from her and drank the milk. When he had finished he handed her the cup back, saying, 'Thanks ... thanks,' then slid down the couch again.

Standing looking down at him, she said, 'You should see a doctor.'

He shook his head, and after a moment of silence he muttered, 'It's over. I'm better now; I'll be on my feet tomorrow.' Then turning his head and looking at her, he added, 'I'm sorry. I ... I meant to be away.'

'How long have you been here?'

He made a small movement with his head, then drooped it forward as if thinking. 'Two weeks ... three. I don't know.'

Her own head was shaking as she went from him. Halfway down the room she stopped and looked about her. 'What a mess!' In the kitchen she repeated the words, then added, 'Well, it won't clean itself, will it? You'd better get on with it.'

She was getting on with it; she was in the act of washing some of the glar from the floor when with a startled exclamation she turned and looked towards the kitchen door, and there he was, like some wild man of the hills, supporting himself with hands outstretched against the stanchions. When he shambled forward and steadied himself by gripping the table she did not say, ' Where do you think you're going?' but watched him making his way through the annexe and out of the back door. The Elsan pan was at the bottom of the garden forty feet away. He had a temperature; he must have had it for days and he'd been going out there.

She went on scrubbing the floor. She didn't even look up when a few minutes later he passed her on his way back into the room; nor did he speak to her. . . .

By ten o'clock she had order restored in the kitchen. Also she had made him a meal of sorts, mashed potatoes and corned beef and boiled rice, but he had hardly touched it. She had brought in wood and made the fire up, then fastened the guard round it. Now she had to force herself to do something else, something distasteful. She went upstairs and into the boxroom and, lifting up the chair commode that Annie had thought it necessary to install to save passages down the garden on wet and stormy nights, she carried it down the stairs by easing it from one tread to the next. Having placed it in the alcove to the side of the fireplace, she found the most difficult part of the proceedings was yet to be accomplished.

She stood at the bottom of the couch. 'I'm . . . I'm going to bed,' she said.

His eyes were closed; he seemed to be in a continuous doze.

'Oh yes.' He moved his head once; then turning on his elbow, he raised himself slightly and said, 'Thanks. Thanks, Tishy.'

She blinked; her face tightened. She turned half from him, saying, 'In the corner there.' She thrust her arm backwards. 'I brought the commode down.'

He made no answer and she went to the table, turned down the lamp to a flicker, hurried into the kitchen and extinguished the lamp there, then back in the room, she glanced towards the glowing fire before mounting the stairs.

When she entered her room she closed the door and, going to the bed, she slowly lowered herself down on to it and, gripping the pillow, asked herself why in the name of God had she to be let in for this an' all.

5

On the Friday afternoon she went down the hill, took the car and drove to a call box. When she spoke, Percy said immediately, 'Oh hello, Tishy. How are you?'

'I'm . . . I'm all right, Percy,' she said; then went on hurriedly, 'Look . . . look, would you mind not coming up on Sunday, Percy?'

'Are you all right?'

'Yes, yes, I'm quite all right, but I would rather you didn't come up on Sunday.'

'Kathy will be worried.'

'Tell her not to worry, I'm perfectly all right.'

'Are you coming down for school on Tuesday?'

She didn't answer for a moment but turned her head and looked down the long bare road. Then her glance swept over the moors before she said, 'I . . . I'm not quite sure yet; very likely I'll be back on Monday night, but I'm not quite sure yet. I'll phone you again Monday morning.'

'Is . . . is anything wrong? I mean are you not feeling . . .? Look, Tishy, Kathy's worried about you. If we could just pop over for . . .'

'No, Percy, no, please. I'm asking you particularly, Percy, not to bring Kathy. There's . . . there's a reason, and I'll explain it later.'

There was a moment of silence before he said, 'Very well, as you wish, Tishy. But . . . but we just thought you'd be lonely.'

'I'm not lonely, Percy.'

'I'm glad of that, Tishy.'

'Good-bye, Percy.'

'Good-bye, Tishy . . . I'll expect you to phone on Monday.'

'I'll do that. Good-bye.'

Once she had replaced the receiver she did not delay, but hurried out to the car, then drove away.

She stopped at the first general shop she came to, and so many were her purchases that the grocer himself carried out the two cardboard boxes and placed them on the back seat of the car. He told her he had been very pleased to meet her and would be equally pleased to serve her at any time. Her cynical thoughts suggested that it mustn't be every day a passing motorist left four pounds seventeen pence with him.

She had to make two journeys from the car to the wall, and again two journeys from the wall to the house.

When she entered the room with the first box and dropped it on the table Alan looked at her over the head of the couch but didn't speak, and she in turn gazed at him and only just prevented herself from saying, 'Why! you've had a shave.'

He looked different, but worse than when he had his beard on, for his cheeks were hollow and his eyes deep bedded in their sockets, while his skin had a muddy tinge. Looking at him now it was hard to believe that he was good looking, handsome, or at least that he had been at one time.

When she brought the second box in she said to him, 'The old fellow nearly salaamed, he carried the stuff out for me.'

'It looks heavy.' His voice was thin and flat.

'It's the milk, there's four pints. And there's a frozen chicken; it says roaster, but I bet it's an old boiler. It's so big it must have been the mother of them all; it was the only one he had.'

In the kitchen she did not unpack the groceries straight away but put some milk on to boil; then having made two cups of coffee, she took them into the room, set the tray on the table near him and lifting one of the cups went and sat on the chair near the fire.

'It seems lovely out,' he said.

'Yes, it is.'

'If it's like this to morrow I'll make a move.'

She made no reply but sipped at her coffee. It was the first time he had made any reference to leaving, and she didn't know if this remark referred to him finding his legs again or going away.

The conversation for the most part over the last three days had been monosyllabic. A few minutes ago she had spoken at more length than she had done since she had first seen him lying there; she surprised herself when she said, tartly, 'You'll get on your feet, but that's as far as you'll get I should imagine, for the next day or so.'

'I've . . . I've been a nuisance.'

She didn't contradict him.

'I . . . I meant to ask you before you left if you would phone my uncle. There's . . . there's a phone box along the road. About a mile I think.'

'Yes, I know it.'

'He . . . he thinks I'm abroad.'

'Abroad?'

'Yes, when I last saw him I said I would likely go abroad.'

'Won't he be wondering at not hearing from you?'

'He's used to not hearing from me, then my turning up suddenly.'

'What would you want me to say to him?'

He took in a deep breath before he answered, 'You . . . you could tell him he could bring the car and pick me up. You could direct him how to get here.'

'Yes, I can do that. But you've got to get down to the copse, and you won't make that for a few days unless you're carried. Shall I tell him to bring a stretcher?'

He turned his head and looked fully at her; then after a moment of staring into her face he said, 'I can always tell when you're vexed, Tishy. I only suggested this because I don't want to impose on you any further. It . . . it was different when I was here on my own.'

'I should say it was.'

He turned his gaze from her, his head drooping. 'Yes, yes, the place was in a shambles. I'm sorry about that. Annie . . . Annie kept it so lovely.'

It was the first time he had mentioned her name and her teeth dug into her lip. She lifted up the cup and drank from it as he began again, his voice a little above a mutter now, 'I . . . I meant to come to the funeral but once back here I knew that I couldn't go, because then I would have to admit that she was dead and my mind rebelled against accepting the fact. I . . . I stayed on here until I knew it was over. Then I went to my uncle's, but I couldn't stay there. Then I went to my flat in Newcastle, but . . . but I couldn't rest. I took my kit and came up here again. I slept out a few nights and got wet, and didn't eat, and every day I looked for one of you coming. I don't know why.' He shook his head. 'I don't know why. And then when I knew I was ill I came inside. I thought at first some hot grub would soon put me right; then the old trouble hit me.'

He turned his head slowly and stated simply, 'I had a breakdown. The main ingredient of it was fear, of what I don't know. Well –' he shook his head – 'that's about it. I don't know what would have happened if you hadn't come on the scene. I knew I was near the end of my tether; another few days and you'd likely have found me dead I suppose.'

'Very likely.'

'When do you go back?'

'I don't know, I haven't made up my mind, not fully. I'm due back at school on Tuesday but I'm of two minds whether to go or not.'

'Oh . . . oh you mustn't let me stop you.'

'You won't stop me.' Why did she say it like that? Why had she to spit everything at him? Couldn't she call a truce?

It was as if he were thinking along the same lines for he said now, sadly, 'I know I won't stop you, Tishy. I . . . I was just meaning . . . well, I didn't want to put you to further inconvenience. . . .'

She closed her eyes and bowed her head and said, 'I'm . . . I'm sorry.'

'You know, Tishy,' he said, 'we should talk,' and at this she got up and went hastily down the room.

On Monday she went down to the phone box. She told Percy she wouldn't be coming home that night and would he send a note to the school to say that she wasn't well and that she'd be sending a letter or a doctor's certificate.

Percy's concern touched her. Wasn't she well? Wouldn't she let one of them come over? Bill was very worried about her being there on her own.

'Percy,' she said quietly, 'I am not on my own, I have someone with me, and . . . and I don't want to be disturbed for a few days. Don't let any of them come, Percy. Please, do this for me.'

'Yes, yes, of course, Tishy. As long as you're all right, that's all we need to know.'

'I'm all right, Percy,' she had said; 'perfectly all right.'

But as she walked back to the car she knew that she was far

from all right. She could go and get that doctor's certificate and send it to the school because she felt that there was something about to snap inside her. There was a constant feeling of sickness in her chest; her temples felt as if they were being drawn into the middle of her head; there were emotions building up inside her that she was becoming afraid of.

When she arrived back at the cottage and entered the room she walked straight to where he was sitting by the side of the fire, and she looked at him and said, 'I couldn't get through to your uncle; I tried three times.'

'Oh, he's likely away on one of his jaunts. Well, perhaps ... perhaps tomorrow; or do you think you could run me over? I'd be very obliged if it wouldn't be putting you out too much.'

She turned from him as she said, 'Yes, yes, I could do that. But ... but if there's no one there, how are you going to manage?'

'Oh, I'll manage. You've got me on my feet, I'll manage.'

She didn't turn to look at his face as he spoke but continued on down the room, saying, 'I'll make a cup of tea.'

As she waited for the kettle to boil she sat down on the edge of the kitchen chair and leant her elbow on the table and dropped her head on to the palm of her hand. She felt tired, utterly exhausted. She had been here six days and she had been on the go from morning till night. It wasn't only looking after him, and the cooking, and getting the place put straight; there was also the water to be brought up from the burn, and the wood to be chopped. That reminded her; they were getting low on wood. She'd have to go down to the copse shortly and bring up a few more branches. ... But if he was going tomorrow would it matter? There was enough to last till then.

The kettle whistled and she made the tea, then took the tray into the room. And now it was she who sat on the couch.

She made no attempt to open the conversation, nor did he speak until he had finished his first cup of tea. Then, leaning over and putting it on the tray, he said, 'What happened to Rance, you never said? Has the trial come off yet?'

There was a pause before she answered, 'It was last Tuesday. I came straight here from the court.'

'Oh! ... what did he get?'

'Her Majesty's pleasure'.

'Oh my God!'

'Are you sorry for him?'

'No, no. Yet I don't know. Her Majesty's pleasure. But in some cases it just means a set number of years.'

'In his case I think it will be life.'

'Why?'

'They brought him in insane; he was sent to Broadmoor.'

'Well, that's about the only thing they could do, because he must have been insane. Did it ... did it come out about your father?'

'No. ... Well, it couldn't, could it? There was only me ... and you left who knew about that.'

'Yes, that's true.'

As she poured out more tea she spilled it over the edge of the cup and she shivered as she remembered back to the court-room. A moment before they brought him into the dock she had thought, If they let him off I'll tell them about Dad. She had wanted him to be confined for life because he was bad, evil. He was a danger to anybody he came in contact with, he mustn't be allowed to go free, yet the moment she saw him she knew he would never be free. It wasn't that he'd be aware of being imprisoned in a cell, or within walls, he was already deeply imprisoned within himself. She hardly recognized him. His eyes were fear-filled yet vacant. He had looked towards them where they were all sitting together, but seemingly without recognition, except that his gaze strangely enough lingered on Alice, and she had wondered why he should be looking at her. Perhaps it was because he had always objected to her and now found, in the colour of her skin, something left for him to hate.

When the sentence was passed on him he had shown no emotion whatever. Bill was the only one who saw him in private before he was finally taken away, and the meeting seemed to have unnerved him. It was Alice who asked, 'Did he say anything?' and Bill, after a moment of evident distress, muttered, 'It was awful, awful. All he said was, "It won't be long before I see Mam, will it, Bill?" He spoke like a child.'

Alan said now softly, 'I ... I would have made her very happy you know, Tishy. It wasn't a matter of years; there was an affinity between us. I ... I must have recognized it when I was a small child. You know ... you know I told her that because of this feeling I believed in transubstantiation; I felt we must have been together in some other existence. It may sound silly but ...

but I still firmly believe it. Perhaps in that existence too we were torn apart; in the next one we might be more lucky.'

She was on the point of springing up when he said, 'Don't think badly of me, Tishy. And ... and you must never think badly of her, for she was full of concern for you.'

He had closed his eyes, and there was silence between them until she forced herself to ask, 'What are you going to do? I mean when you're quite well?'

He lifted his head now and looked at her. 'Oh, I've an appointment at an American university. But this time last week I thought that was that. I had managed to cable them before I went down. I said I might be delayed ... Delayed!' He gave a small laugh. 'And if it hadn't been for you, Tishy, I would have been ... finally. I'm sure of that now.'

'When do you intend to go then?' Her tone was abrupt.

'Oh, it's more than three weeks before term starts; I can give myself a fortnight. I'll be pulled round sufficiently by then.'

'Do you want to go?'

He didn't answer her for a moment but turned his head and looked down the room, then towards the stairs, before bringing his eyes back to her. 'Yes, yes, I want to go, Tishy,' he said. 'I'll never be healed if I stay here, either in mind or body. It'll be a new life. You see ... well, you're not to know, but ... but Annie knew all about it. My marriage went wrong; there was a divorce; it was a very bad time.'

It was odd but even when her mother had said to her, 'Everything's aboveboard, we're going to be married and go to America,' she hadn't said in reply, 'What about his wife?' She remembered seeing him with the girl that once, and feeling still more cheated when she realized that he had chosen someone almost as plain as herself.

'It's strange,' he said now, 'but prior to the first time I came to your home that night seven years ago I would have said that my life had been easy going; there had been small frustrations, annoyances, disappointments; but when I look back now it would appear that on that particular night I experienced an earthquake and my world has rocked ever since, and I don't think it will steady until I get away from this country into another atmosphere, another way of life.'

She rose now and picked up the tray, and he said apologetically, 'I'm sorry, I've kept talking.'

'It does one good to talk sometimes.'

He watched her moving down the room. She walked well, straight; she had a good figure in the modern sense. But she was a strange girl, Tishy. She had a strength about her that frightened him. Nothing, he felt, could break through her armour; she was one of those people who were sufficient unto themselves. How had she been born of Annie, Annie who was soft and loving and giving? Oh! Annie ... Annie ... will the pain of you ever leave me? He rose from the chair and, walking to the door, he opened it. Then turning his head in the direction of the kitchen, he called, 'I'll go out and stretch my legs, Tishy, practice for tomorrow.'

She came into the room almost at a run, then stopped abruptly some feet from him, saying, 'Be careful. Don't go far; you haven't got your strength back yet.'

He smiled gently at her. He was touched by her concern, she wasn't all bristles.

She waited until he had gone down the steps, then she moved to the window and watched him and she had to check herself, from running to the door and shouting, 'Don't go down the hill, you'll only have to walk up again.' She watched him until he came to the wall, then go beyond it down towards the copse, and when he was out of sight she sat down on a wooden hall chair standing to the right of the door and leant her head against the wall....

When, almost half an hour later, he hadn't returned she was on the point of going down the steps, but she saw him coming from the shelter of the trees, and so she went into the kitchen and put the kettle on, thinking as she did so of the countless times she had put the kettle on and heated milk for coffee during the last week. The making of tea or coffee had in a way become therapeutic for her; when her mind dashed along forbidden channels she would go to the stove and put the kettle on.

She heard him panting as he came in at the door, and when he entered the kitchen she turned her head towards him, saying, 'You're out of puff.'

'Yes, yes I am a bit, but I walked as far as the road. Bit too long, but just as well I did. I saw a taxi passing. He had been taking some people to the inn. I ... I asked him to come back for me around five; I thought it would save you tomorrow, and you can get away early.

'What is it?' He came towards her. 'Don't you feel well?'

She put one hand out quickly towards him as if thrusting him away, the other went to her mouth and she said through her fingers, 'Go on, leave me alone, I'm ... I'm going to be sick.'

'No. No, why should I? What is it?'

She was leaning over the washing-up dish now, and when she retched he put his hand out and held her brow. As the sweat from it stuck to his fingers he said, 'What's ... what's upset you like this? The tinned meat?'

She retched again; then turning away from the dish and him, she wiped her face on the roller towel that was hanging on the back of the door, and he watched her helplessly for a moment before saying, 'Come and have a cup of tea.' He lifted the tray and went into the room, and after a moment she followed him. He had put the tray down on the table that was standing on the hearth-rug to the side of the big chair and waited for her to sit down. But she didn't. Instead, she stood at the back of the couch and placing her hands on it she gripped the upholstery while gazing at him in silence.

'What is it, Tishy?'

'Alan.'

He seemed slightly startled by the use of his name; she had never called him Alan during all the days they had been together. 'Yes, Tishy?'

'Don't ... don't leave me, Alan. Don't go. Please, please, Alan, don't leave me.'

His face became thinner in its stretching. When he brought his mouth closed, he gulped but said nothing, just stared at her, and her next words brought his head bowing to his chest for it was like seeing her ripping her body apart and exposing her innermost depths, 'I've ... I've got to say it, because it's the only time in my life I'll say it to anybody. ... I love you. I've always loved you. You're the only one I'll ever love, or can love. Without you there's nothing. From that first night I knew that I would love you and nobody else, and I thought a miracle had happened when you took me out. I thought you loved me, me who had nothing to offer, in looks anyway, because I knew I was irrevocably plain, which no amount of titivating could improve. And ... and when I found it was the last thing in your mind I wanted to die, doubly, because you wanted Mam.'

'Oh! Tishy. Tishy. Don't, don't.' There was agony in his voice as he lifted his head and looked at her.

The tears were streaming down her face but she went on, 'I hated Mam. For a long time I hated Mam. I'd fought for her love for years, but she gave it to Rance; everything she had she gave to Rance; and then it seemed she had taken you. But, of course, that was wrong. She wasn't to blame there, but ... but try as I might I couldn't hate you, I never hated you until –' now she lowered her head as she murmured – 'I ... I saw you in bed with her. But I only thought I hated you, for now I know I didn't. I could never hate you, Alan, I love you too much. Please, please, take me with you. I ... I know you don't love me, but ... but I've so much to give you, and ... and you need looking after. And I promise you I won't be possessive; I ... I just want to be near you. I'm not asking you to marry me; you can have me on the side, or anyway. ...'

'Tishy! Tishy!' He was grinding the words out through his teeth. 'Don't! What can I say? Your mother and I were. ...'

'I know, I know.' She flung her head from side to side. 'And I don't care. Do you hear? I don't care.' She was shouting now. 'I care about nothing only being with you. I thought yesterday I would do anything, try to get my face altered – they can re-make noses, look at Cilla Black. I'd scorned such ideas before, but I'll do it now.'

'Tishy! be quiet! Please, please, be quiet.' He had swung away from her and as he walked towards the window she bent her body over the couch. She was gabbling as if talking to herself. 'I've been quiet for too long, for too many years; I've hidden all I've felt; I've built up a cast-iron case around my feelings. Plain people like me are not supposed to have any feelings; feelings are just the attributes of good-looking girls. Any good-looking girl attracts a man's sympathy, but not people like me, no, not people like me. I've been quiet too long. I may never talk like this again; in fact, I know I won't. I'll never beg like this again in my life, but I'm doing it now.' She straightened up and turned to him, the tears spurting from her eyes now. 'I need you, Alan, and no one's ever needed you before, not even Mam. She didn't need you as I do. She'd had a husband and four children; in a way she'd had a full life; I've had nothing to call my own. You know the future I saw for myself? I saw myself here, ending my days in this cottage; that was, after I had spent years teaching other people's children, and for recreation joining literary groups, or poetry circles, or pottery classes or some such bloody nonsense.' She now tossed her head wildly. 'A life in doing voluntary service, a life of good works; and the reward? a dog, a cat and a budgerigar, and, of course –' her head was bouncing up and down now – 'there's always the television.'

She didn't know that he had moved from the window and was by her side. When he spoke her name she started and blinked up at him through her streaming eyes.

Her tears weren't enhancing her, but it was the very look of her that dragged pity from him. Yet pity wasn't enough. He told himself that he could no more take her than he could commit incest. He liked her; strangely, he liked her a lot. He remembered he'd enjoyed those trips to Newcastle with her. She had sparkled then. But as for marrying her; it had never crossed his mind even then. And now Annie lay like an insurmountable obstacle between him and his pity.

He knew that women who looked like Tishy, and of such intelligence, often made a great success of marriage, and also that, as she had said, he needed someone, he needed someone to care for him, more so than he should have to care for them. The balance of love was never equal; there was always one partner who loved, and the other who was willing to be loved, and this, too, seemed to work well. He could do a lot worse than take her at her word, and she needed him. As she had said, no one would ever need him as she needed him. . . . But . . . but let him remember. A few short weeks ago he had spent three blissful days and nights with her mother in this very cottage. The whole thing would be indecent, definitely indecent. It wasn't the fact of what people would say, because unless she had told the family no one except herself knew about his association with her mother, but he knew . . . he knew.

She was drying her eyes now while still looking at him, and after a long moment during which they were both silent she said in a small whisper, 'No?' and he answered, 'I'm . . . I'm sorry, Tishy. If it was at all possible I . . . I would, but –' he shook his head.

She drew in a long shuddering breath; then turning from him, she went down the room and mounted the stairs; and he took his chin in his fist and gripped it until the pain from his nails digging into his flesh became unbearable.

. . . .

She remained upstairs a full hour, and he sat staring into the fire and feeling as he had never done, not even in the depths of his matrimonial trouble, for his emotions now were a mixture of shame and regret, and the regret made him apologetic to the memory of Annie, for he knew that if it wasn't for Annie he would, in his present state, have clutched at the straw being offered him. Yet Tishy was no straw, more like a sturdy life raft that one could cling to in order to sustain life.

The feeling of guilt was emphasized further when he asked himself if his association with Annie would prevent him from ever taking another woman. Time was the great healer, it was said. A more appropriate version would be, a blotter-out of events both good and bad. But the question of whether he would ever take another woman wasn't relevant to this situation, for Tishy was just not another woman, she was Annie's daughter. . . . Yes, Annie's daughter, who during the last hour had proved herself to be Annie's daughter, for she had stood there pouring out her feelings for him. It was as if Annie had come back.

Yesterday he had wondered why there was no evidence of Annie in Tishy. Now he realized he had been blind, for beneath that hard, cynical veneer Annie was very much alive, honest, vulnerable, loving. But it was the very fact of her being part of Annie that was the obstacle. And there was no way round it that he could see. The quicker he got away the better.

When she came downstairs she did not turn left and go into the kitchen as he expected her to do, but she came towards him. She had changed her clothes and was wearing brown slacks and a green sweater. She had washed her face and her hair had been freshly combed and looked damp. She appeared very young.

She said to him, 'I'm . . . I'm sorry for embarrassing you'; and when he waved his hand before his face she said, 'Let me speak just this once more. I did embarrass you, I know I did, but what I said had to be said. If I'd let you go without telling you I would have imagined for the rest of my life that things would have been different if only I had spoken out. Well, I . . . I don't want you to feel bad about this, I don't want you to go away now and worry and think that I'll do something silly, like . . . like committing suicide, or anything like that. I can't stand moral blackmailers, so I'll ask you just . . . just to forget the last hour or so if you can.' The muscles of her throat worked, and then she ended, 'I'll ... I'll get you some tea before you go.'

He couldn't speak, not a word. All he could do was to gnaw on his lip and move his head in a despairing fashion. Then he turned and leant his arms on the stone mantelshelf. Don't worry, she had said; I won't commit suicide; I can't stand moral black-mailers. At least once a week for a year Jane had threatened him with just that. 'If you dare mention divorce again I'll commit suicide. If you dare go to your grandmother I'll commit suicide. If you dare go to the solicitor I'll commit suicide. If you leave me, Alan, I swear to you I'll commit suicide,' until at last he had said, 'Right! do it. Do just that.' But Tishy had said, 'Don't go away and worry that I'll do anything silly, like committing suicide. I'll live with you on the side,' she had said. 'You can live your own life, as long as you let me stay with you; she had said. 'I just want to be with you,' she had said, 'just to be with you. I love you, Alan,' she had said. That was odd, wasn't it? That was odd. She was the only one who had ever said, 'I love you, Alan.' Jane had never said it. 'You're sweet,' she had said; 'You're a dear,' she had said, but never, 'I love you, Alan.' And when he came to think of it, Annie had never actually said, 'I love you, Alan.' She had said beautiful things, beautiful because they were ordinary and simple and meaningful, but she had never said, 'I love you, Alan.'

When he heard her coming into the room he turned about, then went towards her to take the heavy tray from her, but she made a movement with her shoulder and continued to carry it down the room and set it on the table.

After she had poured the tea she handed him a plate of but-tered scones, and he shook his head and muttered, 'No'; and the scones remained untouched while they both sat in silence drink-ing the tea.

When she went to refill his cup he rose abruptly from the chair, saying, 'I'll ... I'll get my pack together,' and she looked up at him and said, 'It's all right; I've brought it into the kitchen. I dried off the things the other day. It's all ready.'

'Tishy.' He screwed up his face as if in agony, then went down the room, his head bent.

He brought his pack from the kitchen and went outside and put it on the verandah; then buttoning his coat he stood in the open doorway looking across the fells. He must have been standing like this for five minutes when he heard the car hooter; three times it hooted before he turned round and looked at her. She had risen from the couch and was standing at the corner of it. Her hands were behind her hiding their trembling. He came quickly towards her.

'Good-bye, Tishy.'

'Good-bye.'

'Thank you. Thank you for all you've done for me, for your care and everything.'

'That's ... that's all right.'

'Good-bye.'

'Good-bye, Alan, don't worry.'

Concern again. Her concern was that he shouldn't worry.

'Oh! Tishy, Tishy, I –' his whole body writhed as if in pain – 'I ... I can't leave you like this, I can't.'

'It's all right, it's all right. Go on, Alan, go on. Please. Look.' Her face was quivering. 'I'm telling you, I'm all right, just go ... now. Do this for me, go *now*.'

'No, Tishy.' The words came quiet and flat; and then he said again, 'No, Tishy; I'm not going now. And ... and I'm not going by myself. I can't; I've ... I've got a feeling Annie wouldn't want me to. But ... but I must tell you, Tishy, there's, there's nothing left in me; I've ... I've got nothing to offer. You deserve something better, I'm, I'm like an empty husk.'

'Look, don't. Don't. I'm sorry I put you on a spot. I am. Look, just ...'

Her hand had gone to her mouth and the tears were spurting once more from her eyes, and when her body swayed he put his arms about her, saying, 'There now. There now. It'll be all right.'

Moments passed, then slowly she raised her head and looking up into his face, she said, 'Yes, yes, it'll be all right. I'll ... I'll make it all right. Oh, Alan, I promise you I'll make it all right. You'll see, you'll see.'

The hooting of the car horn came stridently at them, and they turned and looked at the open door and he said, 'I ... I must go down and tell him.'

'No, no, let me, I can run ... I can run.' She began to dash about, first to the door then back again, saying, 'Money! my purse.'

'Here!' He put his hand in his pocket. 'Give him that.' He

pushed a couple of notes at her, and she smiled at him while rubbing her hand over her wet face.

He stood at the door and watched her running like a young gazelle over the field, through the gap in the wall down to the copse, and when she was gone from his sight he closed his eyes tightly as if shutting from his gaze some gigantic obstacle with which he knew he must grapple if he ever hoped to find himself and live.

About the Author

CATHERINE COOKSON has written more than thirty popular books; her reputation is now world-wide, with translations into eight languages and two films to her credit. She lives in Hastings, England, where she has been acclaimed both as a regional writer and as the author of taut, accurate, warmly-felt historical fiction.